EAST EN

By Kim Hunter

Kim Hunter

Copyright © 2013 By Kim Hunter

The right of Kim Hunter to be identified as author of this work has been asserted in accordance with sections 77 and 78 of the Copyright, Designs and Patents Act 1988.

All rights Reserved

No reproduction, copy or transmission of this publication
may be made without written permission.
No paragraph of this publication may be reproduced,
Copied or transmitted save with the written permission of the author, or in accordance with the provisions of the Copyright Act 1956 (as amended)

This is a work of fiction.
Names, places, characters and incidents originate from the writers imagination.
Any resemblance to actual places or persons, living or dead is purely coincidental.

OTHER WORKS BY KIM HUNTER

EAST END HONOUR
WHATEVER IT TAKES
TRAFFICKED
BELL LANE LONDON E1
EAST END A FAMILY OF STEEL
PHILLIMORE PLACE LONDON

Web site www.kimhunterauthor.com

PROLOGUE

BACK FROM THE NURSERY SCHOOL RUN.

"What's the matter baby?"
The small child slowly took a sip of his milk before he spoke. Every single thing he did was a mirror image of her and she loved the little man with all her heart.
"Mummy, why are all the other kids so nasty to me?"
"What do you mean?"
"Well they say that you will come and beat them up!"
His mother laughed. As she removed a carton of fresh orange juice from the fridge she rubbed the top of her sons head.
"Baby people will always be nasty it's in their nature."
He started to cry and the sight tore at her heart but more than that it made her angry.
"But I want them to be nice to me!"
Kneeling down to face him, she placed her hands on his small shoulders and stared deep into his big brown eyes.
"One day sweetheart, in the not so distant future, people will be falling over themselves to be nice to you. Remember the mean ones, remember them all!"

CHAPTER ONE

Charlie Edwards sat up in bed and twisted his legs over the side. The bed clothes hadn't seen a wash in months and his string vest even longer. Scratching his head, he let out a large yawn as he stood up. Ever since the news had arrived he'd been dreading today. It was always bad when a man from one of the firms had delivered his instructions. It had been the same time and again over the years but somehow this lot seemed worse. Charlie had been the landlord of the Flying Pig for more than twenty five years and in that time it had become tradition for all the major firms to hold their funeral wakes at his pub. For the East Enders it was local and firms from further afield enjoyed its privacy. His ageing barmaid and chief glass washer Daphne always laid on a good spread and Charlie hoped she wasn't about to let him down now. He couldn't face breakfast and decided to get washed and ready early in case anything unforeseen cropped up. Dressing in the only good black suit he owned, he realised that he was sweating already and it had only just turned nine. The party wasn't due to arrive until one and at this rate he would be stinking like a pig if he didn't calm himself down. Making his way along the landing and down the rickety staircase, he was pleasantly surprised at how for a change the bar smelled sweet. Daphne had kicked everyone out early last night so she could make a start and a fine job she'd done too. The Flying Pig was known as one of the oldest pubs in the whole of the east end. Except for its mock Tudor façade that had been applied to the front of building in the nineteen twenties, for some strange reason the brewery had never bothered to upgrade the inside. All of the original brown stained woodwork still remained and along with the ancient tables and chairs, made you feel as if you were in a weird time warp. The sand blasted glass panels which let the only natural light into the inner rooms via window lights above the doors, still spelled out the words 'SNUG' and 'LOUNGE.' Everything in the place was from a bygone era and in some reclaim yard would fetch a pretty penny from the new money that now filled the city. Of course no such renovations were on the cards and were ever likely to be, more was the pity as far as Charlie was concerned. Glancing round the place he remembered some of the old times, well times when he didn't spend his life in fear. Back then this pub had been a real money earner, always full of regulars who every Saturday would bring out their wives for their weekly airing. Wedding do's had been held here, even the odd christening but that was back when Betty had been alive. He felt a tear in the corner of his eye and silently chastised himself for being a silly old fool. Betty Edwards had been dead for fifteen years but he still got emotional when he thought of her and Charlie had always believed that Betty's death had been the beginning of everything bad that now happened.

It had been less than a month after his loss that the regulars had started to dwindle in numbers. Only a few at first and he didn't really take much notice until he sat down with the books. His wife always took care of that side of the business and it was difficult at first but after four or five hours he'd gathered the gist of things. He added the columns up again and again but every time the total was the same, something was happening and he didn't know what to do about it.

Shaking himself back to the here and now, Charlie poured a large brandy and walked over to the juke box. About to play their favourite song, he nearly jumped out of his skin at the loud thud on the front doors.

"We're not open so fuck off!"

"Charlie it's me, Daphne.'"

Charlie Edwards breathed a sigh of relief and pulled the heavy bolt down above the door.

"Sorry Daph love. As usual I'm a bundle of nerves, I fuckin' hate these do's."

Daphne Short sniggered as she walked passed

her boss and headed for the room that she'd named 'The dungeon' but was really the back kitchen.

"I don't suppose fuckin' Marty likes it much either but then he can't moan, can he poor bastard?"

They both laughed which lightened the mood but Charlie couldn't help but glance over his shoulder. If any of the firm had heard him joking about their late boss, Marty McCann wouldn't be the only one they would be burying today.

Following her into the kitchen, Charlie saw Daphne placing a freshly filled kettle onto the old stove.

"Nice cuppa, that's what you need."

"What I need is for this fuckin' day to be over, better still for me to be out of this dump."

The woman smiled as she busied herself with the enormous task of making over two hundred sandwiches. Those beefy men really could eat and she wanted to do Marty proud if nothing else.

"You don't mean that Charlie, this place is your life."

"Yeh and it'll be the fuckin' death of me as well!"

Continuing to butter the bread she didn't answer. When Charlie Edwards got out of bed in this mood it was best to stay silent, that or spend the next hour trying to comfort him while he cried his eyes out like a baby. Daphne Short knew she had far too much to do today for any of that malarkey, no today Charlie would just have to sort himself out.

At eleven on the dot the front doors once again emitted a loud banging but the landlord stayed seated in the warm kitchen.

"Charlie! Aren't you going to answer that, I can't do everything. Lord knows today of all days I need a little help."

As he slowly stood and made his way towards the public area, Daphne noticed how old he looked. Far far older than his sixty five years and it was a sad fact but she had to agree with her boss, this place probably would be the death of him. It was a silent thought and one she wasn't about to share with him.

Reaching up to once again unbolt the heavy door, Charlie could definitely smell himself and knew a strip wash would be in order before any of the known faces arrived. Big Bernie's massive frame filled the doorway and blocked out most of the light.

"Hi Bern mate, how's it going?"

Bernie Preston was a little simple and had the mental age of a child but everyone loved him. He'd been given the job as gofer for the firm as soon as he'd left school. Running errands was about as much as he could handle but he did carry large amounts of cash on occasions to help out. His size would be enough to frighten the best of men but they were not aware of the fact, that if they'd shouted at him, Bernie would have burst into tears.

"Hello Mr Edwards, the new boss sent me round to see if you needed any help?"

"That's nice Bern and by the way who is the new boss?"

Charlie could immediately see fear in the eyes of the big man and wished he hadn't asked the question. Big Bernie started to stutter and it took several 'Calm down mate's' before the words Charlie had been dreading, escaped from this giant of a man's mouth.

"Johnny Vale Mr Edwards. It's Johnny Vale!"

Charlie felt the colour drain from his cheeks, of all the men who could have possibly taken over, Johnny Vale had to be the worst choice. True the bloke had been Marty McCann's right hand man and by all accounts adored his boss or that's how it appeared but it seemed Marty had been the only one who had returned the likeness. Johnny was a charmer and at fifty five was thirteen years older than his boss. He carried himself well, dressing in fine suits and drowning himself in expensive aftershave. He was what the old school would have called 'A bit of a dandy' but looks were deceiving when it came to this man. His nasty streak knew no bounds and less than a month ago Charlie had witnessed with his own eyes and in this very bar, a terrible sickening act of violence.

A young lad, who had looked the wrong way for a few seconds to many, received a smile that stretched from ear to ear and would never again leave his face. Johnny Vale hadn't cared that the event had been in full view of a packed pub; he was more concerned that a tiny speck of blood had dared to touch his new Versace tie.

By twelve thirty Charlie and his helper had put out the extra chairs and polished the tables again, even though Daphne had done an excellent job on them last night. The floral tributes which had been sent over by taxi, now adorned the bar and Daphne had filled the trestle tables with a fine buffet complete with jellied eels. All three now stood silently having a nerve calming drink before the funeral party arrived.

"Skin of our teeth Daphne love, hey?"

Daphne Short smiled but felt a little peeved at her boss's comments, after all without her he'd still be clearing up all the shit from last night.

As the first guests arrived Bernie began to move from one foot to the other, a trait he'd had for years and which only came out when he was nervous.

"Do you want a piss or what Bernie?"

"Sorry Mr Edwards, I'm getting a bit scared that's all."

Charlie didn't reply he knew only too well what the boy meant and once again turned his head to check his armpits weren't omitting the disgusting odour of earlier. Thankfully Daphne's deodorant was holding up, at least for the time being.

At ten to one the doors opened and Johnny Vale along with two of Marty's runners walked into the Flying Pig. Heading over to Charlie and Bernie he nodded to the food and congratulated the landlord on his spread.

"You've done Marty proud Charlie and it's not gone unnoticed. For fucks sake cheer up man, you look like you'll be next!"

Charlie Edwards smiled and prayed that his shaking legs weren't visible to the man standing in front of him. Johnny Vale commanded respect but it was born from fear and nothing else, not one person who would fill the place today could stand him.

Seconds later and once more the doors swung open and a small woman with the whitest of hair entered. Although in her early seventies it was obvious to all that today she had made a real effort with her appearance and for the first time in anyone's memory, her old cream Mac had been replaced by a smart navy two piece and camel coat.

"Hello Flo love, how you bearing up?"

The woman gave a hollow smile as she replied

'not too bad Daphne.'
Flo McCann had raised her only child alone and was as proud as punch regarding what he'd achieved. Today was the saddest day of her life, she missed him terribly and bitterly regretted the fact that he'd never married and gave her the grandchildren she would have loved so much. Flo was real east end and with or without her sons reputation, she would have been adored by everyone.
Before anyone else had time to offer their condolences, Johnny Vale interrupted.
"I think it's about time we headed off, the hearse has just arrived and we don't want to keep poor old Marty waitin' now do we?"
Leading a reluctant Flo outside, Johnny nodded and the other mourners filled their arms with the tributes and headed out of the door. The Flying Pig and its users had a reputation that spread much wider than its Bethnal Green location. True most members of the firm were east ender's born and bred but the majority of business was now carried out up west. The McCann crew, which after today would probably be renamed, were one of the most revered crime firms in the area. Marty McCann, Herbie Spires, Jimmy Forbes and Johnny Vale made up the main body of the firm. Each had a small posse of two or three men but they were never included when it came to the finer details of business. Mostly

these men fetched and carried, ran errands and at odd times were used for their brute force but that was about it. Johnny Vale was Marty's right hand man but was loathed by the others and at times Johnny had complained bitterly about how he was treated.

The firm dealt in anything you cared to imagine and until now had all jelled along nicely, although in more recent months Marty had been trying to veer away from most things that were dodgy. Everyone knew that the clubs brought in a healthy living and Marty McCann had always carried a dream of being legitimate. The remaining firm members attended the funeral and for today only and out of respect for Marty, had put any grievances they had towards Johnny Vale to one side. Tomorrow was another day and Johnny would soon find himself with only a few employees left. It wasn't something that would bother the man, as far as he was concerned hired help were ten a penny and they could easily be replaced. For Herbie Spires and Jimmy Forbes it was a different situation. The men were getting on in years and if the runners refused to work for Vale and wanted out, there would be little or no firm left.

The only person to remain at the pub was Daphne, over the years she had always volunteered to stay behind and this too was now a custom. It was a pointless exercise as no one would dare touch anything, even if the front doors had been left wide open. Still it was the quiet before the storm and she knew that once everyone came back she wouldn't have a minute to herself for the next four or five hours. Daphne Short poured herself a shot of whisky while she waited.

After a basic service at the local church the mourners headed off to Highgate cemetery. Flo McCann's parents were interned there and even though many years of neglect had left the place looking overgrown and desolate, it had been the only cemetery she would consider. With his original show of concern now wearing thin, Johnny Vale left the white haired woman to stand at the graveside alone. The only people to offer any comfort came in the form of Herbie and Jimmy. Standing either side of the Tiny woman and looming over her like two inner city tower blocks, they gently tried to persuade her to go to the waiting car.

"Come on Flo; let's get you back to the pig and the large brandy that's waiting with your name on it."

"That's right Mrs M; it's too cold out here for you."

Flo McCann looked from Herbie to Jimmy then back to Herbie again as she spoke.

"You two are the nicest boys anyone could wish to meet, my Marty always said that."

Stopping dead in her tracks she frowned as she craned her neck up towards their faces.

"A word of warning to you both, don't trust that bastard Vale an inch. I always told Marty that but he would just laugh and kiss me on the cheek, look where that got him."

Glancing back over her shoulder, she blew a kiss in the direction of the grave then slowly walked on. Neither of the men continued the conversation but Herbie Spires's brow wore a frown all the way back to the pub. He'd heard what Flo had said but he didn't really know how to take it, was she saying that Johnny had something to do with Marty's demise? He decided that whatever she'd meant, he didn't want to know, at least not today.

The Flying Pig was in full swing when the unlikely looking three arrived back. The drink flowed freely and Johnny Vale sat in a corner holding court.

Flo McCann downed the brandy in one and several more followed in hot pursuit. The alcohol soon took effect and her bad feeling towards the new big shot was temporarily forgotten. With the assistance of big Bernie, Flo stood up and gently began to sing Danny boy. The whole place immediately fell silent until she had finished her rendition, then a voice from the crowd called out.

"I didn't know Marty was Irish Flo?"

"You silly sod! I know there's a lot of Del Boys in here today but you must be fuckin' Trigger! Anyway I aint sure he was either love but I'm hedging me bets, if I'd known the words to fuckin' Ave Maria you'd have got that as well 'cause I was also well acquainted with a little Italian at the time."

With the alcohol running through her aging veins, Flo McCann began to laugh. The revelations much to the disgust of Johnny Vale had the whole place in fits of laughter and a true east end knees up began in earnest. As Daphne had presumed it was early evening before the last of the mourners left. Flo McCann had stayed almost to the end but the long day, her mourning and the large amount of alcohol had taken its toll. Becoming maudlin, she had begun to talk of Marty and his fear of water.

"I don't know what happened but something ain't fuckin' right. My boy wouldn't look at water let alone go near it. I don't care what that coroner said, it ain't fuckin' right."

Johnny Vale beckoned Bernie over to the table and whispered in the man's ear.

"Get her fuckin' out of here now!"

Bernie fetched her coat from the stand and gently took hold of Flo's arm.

"Come on Mrs M, time we got you home."

She insisted on kissing everyone in spitting distance as she was led outside to a waiting taxi.

Bernie travelled with her and made sure she was seated in her fireside chair before he left. Even with his simple mind, Bernie felt like crying as he saw how frail and alone Marty's old mum now looked.

Back at the Pig, Daphne Short began to tidy up ready for the evening punters. It had been a long day and she would be glad when it was finally over. Careful not to disturb the far corner where Johnny was deep in conversation with two men she had never seen before, Daphne dusted the bar like the invisible woman. When a banging began on the front doors, her usual shouts of 'Piss off we ain't open' went unspoken and she silently went to answer. Walking back over to the corner table with two men following close behind, she coughed loudly.

"Excuse Mr Vale but the police would like a word."

Johnny dismissed her with a wave and grinned at the men who now stood directly in front of him.

"Hello! If it aint the Plod twins, what can I do for you?"

The CID officers were used to the abuse that London's entire underworld regularly dished out. Knowing that they had no real justification for being here, they both trod carefully in their reply.

"Afternoon Johnny! Just like to ask you a few

questions regarding the death of Marty McCann, if you don't mind."

'Well I fuckin' do mind. How many more times do you have to hear it, I was out of the country and beside it was recorded as accidental death. Now if that's all, I was in the middle of a meeting before you two so rudely interrupted it. Go catch a bag snatcher and get out of my fuckin' face Plod!"

Steve Myers and Tom Walton had together accumulated over forty years in the force, with the latter part of their careers having been spent in the serious crime squad. Without any further confrontation the officers turned and walked out of the pub but they weren't too disappointed. Every dog has its day and theirs would come soon enough. With Johnny Vale it was only a matter of time before he felt their bite.

CHAPTER TWO

Second to Johnny Vale, Marty's other two major men working for him were located in Bow and Stepney. Any business in Bow was run by Herbie Spires from a second hand shop just off Morgan Street. The front window displayed stock that was old and sun bleached. Everyone living in the manor was aware of the premises true use and no one tried to purchase anything. Well that wasn't strictly true, they didn't want to buy anything from the window but the stock Herbie carried inside was a totally different story. Fencing stolen goods on a large scale was one thing Herbie Spires excelled in. Nothing was ever turned down and in his time he had dealt in everything from small items of jewellery to old masters. Herbie was so well informed and had so many contacts that a person could pop in and leave a shopping list, sure in the knowledge that a day or two later the order would be ready for collection. Even the Old Bill was aware of what went on but as long as things were kept discreet and they received a monthly payoff, then they left well alone. Herbie, a man in his mid sixties and whose reputation was legendary had adored his late boss. He had earned the nick name of 'The Dentist' back in his early twenties. At the time Herbie was working for a loan shark over in White chapel and on several occasions had tied bad payers to a chair and pulled out their teeth with a set of pliers. If his victim's teeth happened to be false, then he would just snip off the odd digit. It didn't really matter what body part it was as long as something came off that could be shown to any other debtors who were thinking of taking liberties by not paying. His vicious streak had mellowed somewhat over the years and Herbie now hated being referred to as 'The Dentist'. It had been several years since anyone had dared call him it to his face. His build was stocky and with a head of silver grey hair he stood at almost six feet tall. Sharp suits and an air of authority that had taken years to perfect, now gave Herbie the confidence that he'd lacked in his younger years. East End born and bred, Herbie had moved over the water to Bermondsey once he married. Marjorie Spires loved the life her husband provided but never openly disclosed their beginnings to her new friends at the golf club. Unable to conceive a child, she replaced her desperate yearning with a love for Chihuahua dogs. Every weekend would be spent traipsing up and down the country to one show or another. Herbie never accompanied her; he hated the little creatures and saw them as nothing more than pampered rats. It wasn't an opinion he would ever voice to Marge though, if she was happy then he was too. Herbie Spires wouldn't have minded being a dad but unlike his wife it wasn't something that gnawed away at him. Poor Marge had spent the first ten years of her married life desperately trying to get pregnant but there were always tears each month when her period had arrived. Now after so many years of disappointment the subject much to Herbie's pleasure was rarely mentioned. In some ways Herbie had looked upon Marty as a surrogate son and his death had hit the man harder than he had ever thought possible. Since the day he'd received the news, snouts had been sent out and told to keep their ears to the ground but as yet nothing had turned up. Herbie wasn't a man to give up easily and had decided to let things settle back down to some kind of normality, before once again resuming his search for the truth.

Stepney was led by Jimmy Forbes. Jimmy had arrived in the smoke from Liverpool when he was a boy but his accent still carried the mild twang of a Scouser and he became known by this name in his inner circle. Closer to Herbie Spires than to Marty McCann, Jimmy still had a soft spot for the man. Marty was forty two when he died but to the two others he was still just a youngster, albeit one with a fantastic brain for business.

Jimmy Forbes lived in a small old style terrace

on Smithy Street. The new Clichy Estate had been built to the rear of the property but for some reason the old terrace had remained. Having many of the local constabulary on his payroll gave Jimmy the feeling of invincibility, so much so that all his affairs were carried out in his own front room. Known behind his back as a long streak of piss, Jimmy Forbes was tall by anyone's standards. Family genes had blessed him with a marvellous head of hair that still retained all the colour of its youth, much to Herbie Spires's annoyance. Of the three areas, Stepney dealt in the seedier line of things and anything that brought in readies was ok by Jimmy. Drugs weren't a major part of his day to day business but he didn't say no if the right deal came along, which it often did. The main bulk of his cash came from prostitution and it wasn't high class either. Jimmy Forbes's girls had been round the block more times than the average Ford Sierra. As he never paid, it didn't worry him and he would often sample the merchandise to make sure the girls were still giving a good service. Many times when the others had ribbed him about the state of his Toms he'd quickly shoot back with 'you don't look at the mantelpiece when you're stoking the fire' and Herbie had always responded with 'Yeh but you do like a fuckin' clock on it'.
The three, Marty being the main man had been

friends and business colleagues for the best part of twenty five years with not so much as a bad word. Everything ran smoothly and that was the way they liked it, working side by side with no one stepping on the others toes. If any other firm from the smoke carried out business in one of Marty's manors, permission would be sought and then a generous donation would always be passed over. It was polite and it was tradition but since Marty's demise everyone had been in a nervous frame of mind. From the day he was brought into the firm neither Herbie or Jimmy had liked Johnny Vale. They knew he was a loose cannon but hadn't said anything to Marty. It wasn't something you did, if the boss liked him then it was normal to just accept the situation and not rock the boat. Since Marty's death Johnny Vale had crowned himself the new king and was acting as deputy boss. Everyone thought or at least hoped that this was only a temporary measure but until things were sorted properly they all had to go along with it. The trouble was no one knew what was going to happen next. Unbeknown to Johnny Vale, Herbie and Jimmy had been meeting on a daily basis. Their imaginations were working in over drive regarding the future, not just for them but for the sake of the whole east end.

Two days after Marty's funeral saw Herbie Spires drive over to Jimmy's little house. Jimmy

Forbes's right hand man Melly announced the visitor and Herbie was led into the small but well furnished front room. Marlene Truman, the latest in a long list of girls Jimmy had been grooming for the street, offered their guest refreshments.

"No thanks sweetheart, I've not long had breakfast."

After a quick glance at her boss, the love of her life or so she thought, the young girl of Caribbean decent left the room.

"Nice bit of skirt for a change Jimmy. What's the matter, standards fuckin' slippin'?"

Jimmy Forbes ignored the comment and walked over to the fireplace.

"So Herbie what brings you here at this early hour or was it just to get away from Marge's fuckin' yappy rats for a bit."

The men laughed but the laughter was hollow, they were both aware of the real reason Herbie was here at nine thirty in the morning.

"Jimbo I don't like what's goin' on, I don't like it one fuckin' bit!"

Jimmy Forbes rested his elbow on the mantle as he turned to face his pal and long time associate.

"Me neither old mate but I don't see there's much we can do at the moment. As hard as it is, we have to sit tight, at least for the time being. I contacted Marty's solicitor yesterday but got no joy. Apparently Marty McCann's will was done

in a good and proper way but that was as much as he would say until all parties had been informed. What that meant fuck knows but you know these legal cunts, they have to justify their over inflated charges. For now we have no choice but to sit back and wait."
Herbie Spires wasn't happy but he knew the Scouser had done his best.
"Understood Jimmy, but I've got a fuckin' bad feeling about this. That cunt Vale's goin' to upset the apple cart in a big way, you mark my words."
Jimmy Forbes laughed as Herbie spoke but inside he had to agree. One thing was for sure, they had to stick together on this if they wanted to prevent a takeover war and stop the Old Bill coming down on them all like a ton of bricks.
"Herb, you had anyone leave your crew lately?"
"Have I! Like fuckin' rats fleeing a sinking ship. Why?"
"Melly's just told me he's packing it all in and going out to Kent. looks like no one wants to be connected to Vale."
"Can't say I blame 'em, I've been thinking the same myself since Marty; well you know what I mean?"
"Say no more mate, I understand."
Herbie accepted the second offer of refreshment and after politely drinking their tea; the two men said goodbye and Herbie Spires left.

Climbing into the soft leather seats of his gleaming new Jag, he didn't go to his so called office; instead Herbie drove himself to Cleveland Way over in Bethnal Green. Knocking gently on the door, he felt like a school boy who was about to face the headmistress. Flo McCann took several minutes to answer the door but was delighted to see a friend of her sons and warmly invited him into her spotlessly clean council flat. The building was a purpose built block of six which had been constructed in the later part of the fifties. Although updated regularly over the years it hadn't stopped Marty wanting to set her up in her own place. It was something they argued over constantly but Flo wouldn't hear of it, Townsend Court was her home and more than that it was where she'd raised her boy. No fancy private house could ever have the memories that number twenty two held.
"Hello my darlin'! how lovely to see you."
The sight of Herbie made Flo want to cry. Previously the only time she ever saw the man now standing in her doorway, was when he'd been with her boy. The realisation that sight would never again be seen, felt like a fresh blow to her and silently Flo McCann wondered how many more knocks she could take.
"Mornin' Mrs M, just thought I'd call in and see how you was doin'?"
Flo hadn't survived for as long as she had

without being able to spot a lie when she saw one but decided to give him a little longer before she said anything.
"Well that's grand of you Herbie I must say. You take a seat in the front room and I'll make us a nice pot of tea."
Herbie Spires did as he was told and with every second he felt more and more like a little boy. His own mother had been dead for years so he wasn't used to being in the company of elderly women. His host called through from time to time as she busied herself in the kitchen.
"It's nice to see a fresh face; I haven't seen a soul since we buried my Marty. Well that aint strictly true, Edna from next door is good but even she hasn't called round much. I expect people don't know what to say, funny thing is I don't want them to say anythin'. A little bit of company goes a long way when you get to my age, anyhow here we are."
Herbie almost jumped out of his skin. Silently and like a ghost the old woman appeared by his side with a tea tray complete with china cups and small fairy cakes, just like the ones he'd always had on Sundays when he'd been small. Half an hour of small talk passed and when she realised her guest must have lost his nerve, Flo finally broached the subject of why she had a surprise visitor.
"So then Herbie, what really brought you to my

neck of the woods?"

"Like I said Mrs M, I just wanted to check you were ok."

The woman smiled and moved her head from side to side.

"You must be at least twenty years older than my boy but in some ways you're no different. My Marty used to get a sneaky look in his eyes when he lied to me and you've got the same look now. Are you goin' to tell me what's up or just sit there and drink tea for the rest of the fuckin' day?"

Herbie knew the old woman had rumbled him and he smiled. Like Marty she was blunt and straight to the point and he liked that quality in her.

"Me and Jimmy's been worrying Mrs M. Seems Johnny's took over the runnin' of things and we didn't know if that's what Marty would have wanted?"

Flo was not only like her son regarding getting straight to the point, she also had his temper. The ferocity of her tone took even a man like Herbie Spires by surprise.

"Not on your fuckin' Nelly was it! That cunt couldn't run a piss up in a brewery and my boy knew it. Marty had everythin' taken care of and it will all be sorted in a few days. I don't know why the hold up, only that we will all be gettin' letters and things will be explained then. Why

the fuckin' cloak and dagger stuff I don't know but Marty must have had his reasons. Now don't worry yourself about Johnny Vale, I'm sure his reign will be short lived."
Herbie smiled as he finished the last of his tea. "I hope you're right Mrs M, for all our sakes I hope you're right."
The next thing Herbie knew he was standing outside the flat with the door firmly closed behind him. He had been dismissed without even realising it but now felt a little more reassured about the situation than he had a couple of hours earlier. Silently he chastised himself for feeling the need to seek solace from an old woman. Jimmy would have laughed at his friend's lack of strength but then things had changed so much lately and the Scouser hadn't had the love for Marty that Herbie had felt.
The traffic back to Bow was thick and slow moving, fifteen minutes passed and Herbie's car was still in almost the same position. While he waited his mind wandered back to the early days. Days when he and the Scouser were just starting out and when the likes of Johnny Vale wouldn't have lasted five minutes. Back then if Johnny had come on the scene Herbie would have ended the man's reign, if he hadn't then the Scouser definitely would and Johnny would have been in the ground years before Marty. The only difference being that there wouldn't

have been a service or mourners to weep over him. He found himself remembering the first time he'd met Marty McCann and how he had known straight away that the boy would someday be a serious player. The Scouser had been of the same opinion and the two had discussed the matter on many late night drinking sessions. The reminiscing made Herbie miss the man terribly. Stuck in the now non moving traffic the enormity of what had happened suddenly hit Herbie Spires. Wiping away a lone tear he began to laugh at the mental image that popped into his mind. It was a picture of Marty looking down on him and the Scouser earlier that day, when they had shared a pot of tea. The pair had resembled two old women more than the hard men that they were renowned for being. If Marty was up there now, then Herbie Spires knew he was having a good laugh at them both.

Herbie and the Scouser along with their respective, although now fast dwindling teams could have taken Johnny Vale out at any opportunity. Only the deep respect held by both of them for Marty was stopping a war. Curiosity was also a big factor as they were in agreement that they wanted to wait and see what their late boss had planned.

At last Morgan Street and the second hand shop came into sight and Herbie breathed a sigh of relief. Opening up and seeing that no one had arrived for work yet, he closed the door and turned the key. Leaning against the cold pane he seriously wondered why he was still living this life. Recently Marge had been on his back to retire and for the first time he was really considering the prospect. As things stood at the moment even spending all day with the wife and yapping dogs seemed more appealing than what he knew deep down was sitting on the side lines waiting to rear its ugly head. Herbie admitted to himself that if Marty had still been alive retirement wouldn't have even entered his mind. The idea that without the man being around, he was so easily contemplating giving it all up frightened him more than anything. Was he getting to old for this game, had his nerve finally gone or had he simply lost the plot? Herbie Spires didn't have an answer but one thing was for sure, he didn't like the feeling one little bit.

CHAPTER THREE

Marty McCann had been loved by all who knew him. The man could be vicious when it was necessary but he was also well known for being fair. Just because he'd made a name for himself in the city, didn't mean he had turned his back on his own manor. Anyone in the east end young or old could rely on Marty in times of need and unless they were a nonce or hurt old people he would help them. Payment was never asked for but it was an unwritten rule that if the day came and you were asked to help out, then you did so willingly.
Johnny Vale had kept a book on all of Marty's good deeds and now that he had taken over he would be calling in the favours. Marty's business portfolio ranged from a chain of small bookmakers to two west end clubs. Herbie Spires took care of robberies, payroll deals and occasionally helped out up west. Jimmy Forbes sorted out the brasses, something which he loved and which Marty preferred not to bother with. Johnny Vale was never far from Marty McCann's side and he also, when given the choice, liked to be up west rather than have to get his hands dirty dealing with the less glamorous side of business.
Marty's workforce was a mixed bunch and those who carried out the dirty or violent work were

never allowed to meet or mix with the west end bodies. The only exceptions to the rule were Herbie and Johnny. The Scouser had complained on many occasions but his grievances were always ignored. It was nothing to do with snob value but purely down to the fact that the less people knew, then the less chance they had of dropping you in it from a great height. The day to day running of business was from the back room of his Bethnal Green bookmakers. Situated in the middle of a row of seventies style purpose built single storey shops, it didn't stand out in any way and on first appearance the premises resembled those in the rest of the row. On closer inspection several surveillance cameras could be seen, more than was needed but they made Marty feel safe. Steel doors and automatic shutters that could come down with the touch of a button were Marty's security. In seconds the place could become almost fortress like and with this all in place a variety of deals were carried out daily. The day after the funeral Johnny Vale couldn't wait and had gone into work early. He sat behind the large modern desk where only a few days ago Marty had himself been seated. Spreading his hands out onto the ash veneer Johnny smiled. His old mum always told him 'everything comes to those who wait'. Well he'd waited, waited ten long years and now he was right where he belonged. His only regret being that he hadn't acted sooner, he'd been a fool to let things carry on for as long as they had. Finally it had all been so easy and he felt like kicking himself to think he'd toed the line for so long. In the beginning he'd liked Marty, looked up to him even but over the past couple of years he'd come to see the man as weak. Johnny would never have turned away business and it had made his blood boil when Marty had said 'no' to deals that could have made them rich beyond their wildest dreams. It had always been known that Marty shied away from anything connected to drugs. He was aware that the Scouser did the odd deal here and there but he didn't want to know about it. So long as it was only the odd time and wasn't pushed in his face, then he would turn a blind eye regarding what the Stepney boys got up to. Over the years he'd seen too much of the damage drugs did and it was a personal choice not to trade in them. The day after Marty McCann's death, Johnny Vale changed the rules and decided pretty soon he would have a major shakeup. The business agenda would increase and was definitely going to include a huge share of the opium market.

Jimmy Forbes and Herbie were both aware of Johnny's plans and neither was prepared to hand over such a lucrative little earner. Herbie only dabbled when he needed some readies and it was easy money but mostly he left that side of things to the Scouser. Still it was comforting to know he could lay his hands on large amounts of cash if he needed to. Now if Johnny took over properly, all of their incomes would suffer and it would be a crying shame after so many years of everything running so smoothly. The rumours of change had everyone on edge and it definitely didn't make for good business.

Johnny Vale was still stroking the soft wooden top of the desk when the first knock of the day came at his door. Sitting back in the large leather swivel chair, he puffed up his chest as he called out 'Enter'. Bernie Preston's huge frame came through the door and Johnny rolled his eyes. His tone was curt and cruel as he spoke.
"What the fuck do you want?"
"Sorry to bother you mister Vale, I just wondered what you wanted me to do."
With Marty out of the picture, Johnny knew he no longer had to put up with the simpleton standing before him. Reason or not Bernie always seemed to piss him off big time but he'd never been able to do anything about it, till now.
"To tell the truth Bern I don't want you to do fuck all! In fact I want you to take that oversized fuckin' head and body of yours and get out of my face."
Bernie Preston's bottom lip began to quiver. He didn't know what he'd done wrong and wished

with all his heart that Mr McCann was still here.
"Shall I call in again tomorrow Mr Vale?"
"I know you're a bit simple but are you so fuckin' thick that you can't get the message, you daft cunt. I don't want you here today, tomorrow or any other day. Now fuck off!"
Bernie shuffled out into the open area of the bookmakers with tears streaming down his large plump cheeks. Kathy who ran the day to day business at the bookies stood behind the counter as the big man emerged with his shoulders slumped. She had always had a soft spot when it came to poor old Bernie and the look on his face broke her heart.
"Bern whatever's the matter? Are you all right love?"
"Mr Vale don't want me no more Kath. I don't know what me old mums goin' to say."
Kathy Jones stood on her tip toes and with her best endeavour tried to give the big man a cuddle.
"He's a spiteful bastard Bern and you're better off out of it believe me?"
"But Kath, me and mums got to eat!"
"I know darlin' and you will. I'm sure one of the other boys will hire you straight away so why don't you go and see Herbie or the Scouser?"
Big Bernie sniffed loudly and wiped his nose on the back of his hand. A trail of green snot continued to hang from his nose and the sight

made Kathy Jones want to heave. She tried to avert her eyes as she handed him a tissue. "Everyone loves you Bernie and just you remember that."
"I will Kath and thanks, see you later?"
"Definitely babe, now get yourself over to Stepney."
The giant of a man walked out of the front door but for once Kathy Jones thought he looked a little smaller. It would be a sad place to work in without Bernie's cheery smile and comical childlike outlook on life. Kathy hadn't taken kindly to the orders Johnny Vale had started to dish out but knew better than to argue. Her dear sweet Marty wasn't cold in his grave and the leeches had already moved in. Kathy had always thought of Johnny that way and she didn't see her opinion changing in the near future. After serving her first customer of the day and watching him walk from the door, the buzzer on the internal intercom went off and Kathy Jones tutted. She knew that the newly acquired power had instantly gone to Johnny's head and his finger would be permanently glued to the little red button for the foreseeable future.
"Yeh?"
"A little more respect please Kath if you don't mind, now get me a coffee."
Kathy Jones knew she'd overstepped the mark and made a mental note to try and not ruffle

Johnny's feathers again, at least for the next few days. After making his drink she sheepishly knocked on the office door and walked in. Johnny still sat at the desk as if the woodwork had hypnotised him and he didn't look up for several seconds. Placing his drink onto the highly polished surface, she turned to leave.
"Don't put that hot fuckin' mug on my desk, get a coaster. Fuck me girl! If they put your brain in a bird it'd fly fuckin' backwards."
Kathy did as she was told and was about to leave when her new boss spoke again.
"Have any of the boys been in today?"
Aware of the unrest felt by the others she didn't want to get involved and decided that pleading ignorant was her best chance of not having to answer too many questions.
"And who would they be Mr Vale?"
"Who would they be? Fuckin' Herbie, Jimmy and the cunts that hang on their coat tails, that's who. Have you got any fuckin' brains between those ears? Oh piss off I ain't in the mood."
Kathy shot out of the office like a bullet and retreated back to the sanctuary of her counter. She didn't know how much longer she could put up with this man and prayed Herbie or Jimmy would get here soon. Marty had never spoken to her like that in all the years she'd known him and they were too many to count. Growing up together in Globe road, Kathy had been heart

broken when her sweetheart was whisked away to a new home by his mother. Still situated in Bethnal Green it had seemed like he'd gone to the end of the earth and not just to the other end of the manor. It hadn't stopped the two seeing each other at any opportunity and even though Marty had never looked upon her in that way, Kathy had never given up hope. After Marty was sent to Borstal at such an early age, she'd felt as if her life was over. Several years later when the job at the bookies came up she had jumped at the chance to at least be able to see him on a daily basis. Kathy wasn't deluded and hadn't waited for Marty, she wasn't that foolish. Marrying Barry Jones eight years later had produced two children and when the relationship broke down five years into supposedly wedded bliss, it hadn't torn her apart. Life revolved around her kids and the pay from her job along with the small amount of maintenance she received, meant the little family of three somehow managed to survive. Katie was a small, pretty little girl but very cheeky, whereas Spider, a nickname given to him when he'd first began to crawl, was a serious child and saw himself as the man of their little unit. The kids always came to the shop after school, Marty had let them do their homework in his office while they waited for their mother to finish work but today Kath was dreading three thirty.

She knew that with Johnny Vale being boss there would now be a problem with the arrangement. Deciding to raise the issue early instead of waiting for the kids to arrive she knocked on the office door.
"Enter."
Poking her head round the door frame, Kathy asked in her politest tone if he could spare her a minute.
"As long as it is only a minute I am busy you know."
Walking in, she now felt she was making a mistake but with the kids due in a few hours she didn't have a lot of choice in the matter.
"It's about Katie and Spider Mr Vale."
Johnny Vale looked annoyed and Kath realised he didn't have a clue who she was talking about.
"Katie and Simon my children!"
"Oh yeh! What about them?"
"Well Marty, I mean Mr McCann always let them come here after school. There's a two hour overlap from them finishing and me leaving off work and I was wondering if it's ok to carry on with the arrangement?"
"Sorry Kath but things have got to change round here. I can't have a couple of kids on the premises but look I'm not an unreasonable man. How about you change your working hours and finish at three thirty from now on?"
Kathy was just about to voice her thanks when

her new boss continued.
"Of course I'll have to dock your wages; I'm not a fuckin' charity."
Kathy Jones couldn't believe what she was hearing and wanted to walk over to the desk and slap the man straight across the face, of course she didn't but the feeling was there all the same.
"But I need that money; I'm a single parent Mr Vale."
Johnny Vale started to get annoyed; he'd seen enough hangers on when Marty was running things and here was yet another."
"You should have thought about that before you dropped your fuckin' knickers now take it or leave it. Quite Frankly I don't give a fuck what you do, there's plenty of birds out there who'd be only too happy to step into your shoes, just make your mind up and let me know."
Kathy knew she had no choice but to accept and after informing her boss that she'd be staying, she walked back to the counter with her head down and her shoulders slumped. The kids for once would be happy at the thought of going straight home from school but she knew their little faces would be full of disappointment when she told them their long planned holiday this year would have to be shelved. Knowing it was out of her hands brought her little comfort but at the end of the day, food on the table was the main priority. As much as she loved her

little angles, they would just have to accept the fact that money didn't grow on trees. Three forty arrived and the two small children walked into the bookies. Kathy felt guilty as soon as she saw their little faces and decided to hold off breaking the news until after dinner that night. Acting in a light hearted mood when she saw them had them both immediately on their guard. "Hello my babies and how was your day?" Spider didn't answer; he wanted to be treated as an adult and cringed when his mum spoke to him in a babyish way. Katie on the other hand, though weary, revelled in the warmth that her mother emitted and recounted her whole day's events. After patiently listening to her child, Kath told them both not to take off their coats as they wouldn't be stopping today. The kind Mr Vale had let her off early and they were going home to a nice family dinner. The three left the premises and made their way home, all the while Kath dreaded telling them what had really gone on today but one thing was for sure she wouldn't lie to them. Their tiny family unit had always been based on truth and she knew though disappointed, they'd get through this together. The kids were her life and she was theirs, it would take more than the disappointment of losing a holiday to affect them. Kathy Jones smiled to herself, Johnny Vale may have Marty's business but he'd never know the warmth and love that she had. He'd never feel the total at oneness that the three of them would share curled up on the sofa after their meal, just happy to be together. Her council flat though clean, wasn't much compared to the splendour that she could only imagine he lived in but Kathy wouldn't have swapped places with the man for all the tea in china and in a funny way she felt sorry for him. What was the point of having all that money when you hadn't got love?

CHAPTER FOUR

Flo McCann received her letter exactly twenty four hours after Angel Canning Brown received hers.
The knock on the door was forceful and after staring through the spy hole for several seconds Flo decided to find out who was calling. The smart suited man looked more like a debt collector than a solicitor and it had taken him several minutes of heavy persuasion once the door had been opened, to get inside the small council flat. Steve Thompson's job would take considerably longer this time but he wasn't complaining. The firm of solicitors had been paid handsomely in advance by Marty regarding this matter and dealing with probate would see the firm reap further costs, so this visit could take as long as was necessary as far as he was concerned. Standing inside the tiny but neat hallway he handed her a crisp white envelope.
"So what's this then Mr? What did you say your name was again?"
"Thompson Mrs McCann, Steve Thompson. I'm from Bendish and Backham Solicitors and we are acting on behalf of your late son."
Flo was now totally confused. How could she be receiving a letter from Marty two weeks after he'd died.

"Listen Mr whatever your name is? If this is some kind of sick joke you can fuck off right here and now."

Steve Thompson wasn't shocked by the old woman's outburst. In fact, hearing such words from a woman of her age made him want to smile. In all honesty he was beginning to find it increasingly difficult to hold back the laughter that he could feel starting to simmer in the pit of his stomach.

"Calm down Mrs McCann! This isn't a joke, far from it. My firm have been working for your son for the last twenty five years. Although Mr McCann wanted us to deliver the letter, he also wanted us to go through it with you to make sure you understood everything."

Flo looked at her now unwanted guest as if he was about to mug her.

"Make sure I understand! What do you think I'm fuckin' thick or somethin'?"

"No not at all but I think once you've read the contents, then it will come as a great shock to say the least."

Making her way into the sitting room, Flo sat down heavily in her fireside chair and carefully opened the envelope. Suddenly she became frightened at the possibility of what was inside. Glancing over her shoulder to make sure the man had followed her and not gone into the bedroom to rob her, she held up her hand.

"Here sonny you do it. My hands are shaking; all this has shaken me up good and proper."
Steve Thompson removed the faded paper from its wrapper and began to read. By the time he'd finished, the old woman's face was as white as a ghost not to mention two shades lighter than her hair.
"You mean to tell me that all these years I've had a granddaughter and no one saw fit to tell me?"
"Well put like that I suppose so but things are never as clean cut as they seem. Mr McCann had no contact with the child himself."
"Well that was up to him but I didn't have any fuckin' choice in the matter did I?"
Steve Thompson again felt like laughing but he was also aware of the seriousness not to mention the hurt his revelations were causing the woman.
"I'm not privy to all the facts Mrs McCann. As for what I do know, I can tell you that I don't think your son had any choice in the matter either."
Flo's eyes narrowed and her lips became pursed as she gave her visitor a look that said 'I don't know whether to believe you or not'.
"Well Mrs McCann I think I've covered everything. If you will excuse me, I have a busy schedule back at the office."
As quick as a flash Flo stood up from her chair and blocked the doorway.

"Not so fast sonny. What happens now, when am I going to meet the girl?"

"I'm sorry Mrs McCann but that has nothing to do with me or my company. If you read your sons letter again you will see that he doesn't want you to contact Miss Canning Brown. If the young lady does wish to make contact herself, I'm sure she will."

"If she wishes to make contact? Oh fuck off you jumped up little twat, what the fuck do you know about family?"

Letting out a sigh the man shook his head in exasperation.

"Not much I'm afraid but I really cannot help you any further. I have carried out my instructions to the letter and if you are not satisfied then it's your prerogative to make a complaint to my seniors."

Flo stood speechless as Steve Thompson left the small flat as quickly as he could. Seated in the warmth of his company car he thought how much he hated this aspect of a job he normally loved. Three hours later, Flo McCann was still seated in the fireside chair staring at the wall. She had read and re read Marty's letter a dozen times and still it didn't make any sense. He knew she had always longed for grandchildren, so why had he kept the fact that she had one a secret for all these years. The urge to phone directory inquiries and seek out anyone named

Canning Brown was overwhelming but something inside stopped Flo from betraying her only child. No, she knew she had to do what her boy wanted and wait it out but the idea that perhaps the girl didn't want to know, invaded her mind every few minutes. As fast as the thoughts entered her head she dismissed them. That was one scenario she couldn't bear to entertain.

Marty McCann was the proverbial bachelor and married to the job. Apart from a few one night stands over the years, he was never seen with a woman. Early on rumours had circulated that he was gay but when he was never seen with anyone of the same sex either, excepting his crew, that piece of gossip quickly died a death. Only Herbie and the Scouser were aware of the real reason. Several times over the years Herbie had almost let the cat out of the bag but always at the last minute his nerve had faltered and the secret had remained just that, a private and very personal secret. As with all human beings hearing a juicy bit of gossip would have gone down a storm with the other members of the firm but both Herbie and Jimmy stayed true to their pal. Marty trusted them completely and realised soon after their first meeting that they were friends, true friends and that fact alone made them loyal to the man and not pry into his private life. Still in his formative years, Marty had been just sixteen when he first got mixed up with a group of car ringers. After six months of a very good standard of living, the gang had been caught red handed in the middle of the night preparing a shipment bound for Asia. Marty was sent to a young offenders institute for a year. Not a long sentence by any standards but at the time it had seemed like an eternity. His incarceration would be spent at Borstal. Still bearing the name of the horrendous sixties institute, it had long since been a semi open prison. Life inside for one so young was hard but Marty soon learnt how to play the system and it wasn't long before he'd worked out a way of escaping for a few hours here and there. The distance was never great, travelling only to the nearest village but it was far enough away to give him a taste of freedom. In all the time he was incarcerated he hadn't allowed Flo to visit. Mostly because he couldn't bear to see the pain he had caused his old mum and partly because he didn't want the other lads to see how close he was to her. Marty McCann had little trouble in the place he came to loath, he never had to vie for the title of 'Daddy' but the Daddy left him alone all the same. Even at an early age Marty had an air about him and knew how to carry himself. The regime was hard and at the end he had learnt, if nothing else, how to polish his shoes until he could see his face in them.

Marty's outings were always alone and he was never asked by the others where he went to. Joanna Canning Brown was a beautiful young society girl and full term border at the exclusive nearby St Agnes School for young ladies, which was situated in the small village of Wouldham. It hadn't taken Marty long to spot her through the high gates and fall head over heels in love. Joanna had been as much of a tearaway as Marty and that was the main reason her parents had sent her to Wouldham, or to the end of the earth was how she'd seen it. Being a circuit judge meant her father couldn't risk having a delinquent child and her mother's charity work took up so much time that she really didn't have any spare for her only child. Julian and Elizabeth Canning Brown enjoyed a full and happy life together and neither had ever understood why they had ventured into parenthood. A drunken night of unadulterated sex was the real reason but neither would ever admit to being so out of control. When their only child showed the first signs of a strong will they had shipped her off to St Agnes's without a second thought, content in the knowledge that she couldn't cause them any trouble. Now so far away from Bekesbourne in Canterbury, Joanna felt as though she'd been abandoned and now decided to give her parents and also the establishment a run for their money.

The attraction towards Marty was as strong on Joanna's part as it was on his and soon the two were meeting in secret whenever Marty was able to get away for a few hours. The young lovers planned a future and dreamed of running away together when Marty was released but deep down Joanna knew that it was all just a dream. Her father would rather have died than allow her to end up with someone like Marty McCann but it didn't stop her having the time of her life. Any time that Marty could escape, even if it was only for a short while, would be spent in the nearby bluebell wood, where soon after their first meeting they made love. Both of the youngsters were naive and inexperienced but they soon made up for lost time and making love became their all consuming passion. As with most young loves, the dream finally ended one month before Marty's release. On finding out that she was pregnant, Joanna had no choice but to tell the Dean, who immediately summoned her parents. The Canning Browns were mortified and drove straight down to the school, hell bent on suing whoever was to blame in the neglect of their child. On finding out that it was Joanna herself who had left the grounds and taken up with a convict they were devastated. Abortion was mentioned but only briefly after Joanna made it clear it wasn't an option she would even consider. After serious thought, Julian Canning Brown decided his daughter would be allowed to keep the child and raise it at the family home on one condition, that she never saw the father again. Aware of the life changing experience that was only a few months away, she agreed but Joanna had a condition too. She insisted on being allowed to see Marty one last time to say goodbye. Firsthand experience of how head strong she could be, gave her father little choice but to agree to her demand. On Marty's next few hours away the couple met as normal. Blissfully unaware of the revelations that were about to unfold, Marty couldn't understand why his princess was so moody. Joanna was quiet and it took much cajoling and hugging by Marty to get her to open up. When she finally told him about the child, he wrapped his arms firmly around her in a tender and loving way.

"Jo I really do love you and I'm goin' to make the best dad ever."

Scared that what she was about to say would break his heart she took in a deep breath.

"Marty I love you too but we're from different worlds. I don't think that after the luxury I've been given all my life, well I know I couldn't live in your world."

Marty stepped back from the beautiful girl who stood before him, the girl he would willingly have died for.

"What! You mean you're putting fuckin' cash before us? You're prepared to leave me, all for the sake of a few quid?"
"Marty it's not like that!"
Marty McCann didn't wait to hear anymore. He ran as fast as he could from bluebell wood, a wood that would always be special to them alone. After he'd calmed down he put pen to paper several times over the following weeks but none of his letters were answered, not until the day before his release. The envelope contained a single page with just a few scrawled words in which she begged him to forget her and to let her raise the child alone. Marty McCann had no choice but to agree. Acceptance that he would never see his child or be a dad to it changed him forever.

Back in the smoke and turning eighteen, Marty threw himself into business and making a name for himself. If he couldn't give his child anything in life then he'd make damn sure it was well provided for after his death. Mostly small time, his income was generated by petty theft and the odd con when he could get away with it. Marty McCann didn't really care where the money came from as long as he reached his target which didn't take too long. As soon as he had enough cash he instructed Jack Lister & Son, a small firm of private investigators who were located right in the heart of the city. Happy to take on Marty's business and money, he was soon informed that he'd become the father to a beautiful baby girl. On the day he'd received the news it had felt as if he'd been stabbed through the heart. It took all the will power he could muster to stop himself driving straight to Canterbury to be with Joanna and his baby. Distraught, Marty spent the next forty eight hours on a bender, drinking himself into a stupor in every late opening pub or club he could find. It should have been a time of celebration but all he wanted to do was drown his sorrows and try to forget. Well into the night and more than a little the worse for wear, he bumped into Herbie and the Scouser. The three men's paths had vaguely crossed a few months earlier so he accepted their offer of another drink. Marty laid his feelings bear as most of the sorry tale spilled out. When he'd finished his story, although he'd been somewhat economical with the truth, both the men's hearts went out to this poor young lad who felt his life had fallen apart. The Scouser found Marty a warm and funny character and he didn't like to see anyone in pain. Herbie was in agreement as he could see all of Marge's suffering reflected in the young boys face. The only difference being that they couldn't have a child and this youngster was being stopped from seeing his. When the boy went to the toilet, the two men put their heads together and decided to offer this bright young man a job in their firm. Things had started to become stale recently and on more than one occasion the two men had spoken about bringing new blood into the set up, now seemed the perfect opportunity. Marty McCann had readily accepted the proposition offered to him by the two middle aged men. Steadily over the next fifteen years, he laid more and more deals on the firms table. Realising that they were on to a good thing, Herbie Spires and Jimmy Forbes gradually allowed him a free hand. If they'd been told on that sorrowful night all those years ago that little Marty McCann would eventually become head of the firm and take them all from small time villains to serious players, they would have fallen about laughing at the idea.

CHAPTER FIVE

The morning after her twenty fifth birthday, Angela Canning Brown woke late. The birds were singing and the room was bathed in a glorious golden sunshine. None of this made her feel any better; in fact she would have felt much happier if it had been over cast and pouring with rain. Lying in her snug bed staring up at the ceiling and trying not to think of anything was proving difficult, so difficult that she was glad of the interruption when the knock came at her bedroom door.

"Whoever you are, come in."

Angela was expecting to see her mother, so was somewhat taken aback when her grandfather entered the room.

"Good morning my darling and how are you feeling this beautiful day?"

"Do you mean after that fiasco of a party Pops, or the life changing revelations about my father?"

Her sharp words hurt Julian Canning Brown, he found it heart breaking to see his granddaughter so angry and in so much pain. Whatever had happened twenty five years ago was all behind them now and he wished that Angela could move on with her life. From the second Angela was born all the hurt her mother had caused him had been instantly forgotten. Julian had never seen anything so beautiful or felt such a strong bond, not even when his own child had come into the world.

"Please! Angela just listen to what I have to say. Even when you've heard the whole story you still won't know or understand the feelings a parent has for its child and how they only want the best for them."

"What like mother wanted for me?"

Again her words cut like a knife but he wasn't about to let the situation fester and simmer until it erupted beyond repair. Julian was determined to try and make his granddaughter understand one way or another. Sitting on the edge of the bed, he turned to face Angela with his stern courtroom look. A look, which as a child Angela had known meant she'd gone too far this time.

"Now you listen to me young lady. Your mother may not have always been the easiest person to live with and if anyone should know it's me but she loves you one hundred percent. It was her not us who was adamant on keeping you. When you were born it was still a stigma to have a child out of wedlock not to mention our social status."

"Social status!"

"Don't interrupt Angela my dear, I haven't finished yet. As I was saying, it was still a stigma but your mother wouldn't hear of abortion and adoption was thrown out of the window seconds after it was mentioned. She loves you Angela with all her heart, you must believe me!"

"I'm not questioning that but do you know what makes me so angry Pops? The fact that for all those years, I had a father I could have known but that decision was taken out of my hands by others. All those lost years and now I can never get them back. You know something else Pop's, for my whole life whenever I asked mother about my dad she told me he was dead. Can you believe that?"

Angela could feel the tears that were starting to build and placed her palm up, she didn't want to discuss or hear anymore about it. Right now she couldn't deal with this or any other situation. Her head was swimming with her grandfather's words and her own angry outburst. Angela buried her mop of dark unruly hair under the duvet.

"Please Pops can we drop it for now. Until I've spoken to mother about this I don't think I can take much more."

He gently patted her hand, just as he'd done when she was a small child and then silently left the room. A few minutes later she peeked a look over the bed clothes but the room was empty. Finally deciding that if she didn't get up and face the music now, then she may as well stay

put forever, Angela threw off the duvet and energetically jumped out of bed. Dressing in the same sweat pants and top that had so annoyed her mother yesterday, she reluctantly made her way down the stairs. Anticipating that the whole of her family would show a united front and be seated together in the kitchen, she was dreading going into the room. Surprisingly her mother was alone and glanced up from the problem page of her daily newspaper as her daughter entered. Angela looked into her mother's eyes and could see that she must have been crying. Even though it pained her to see her mother's sadness, the stubbornness she'd inherited from Marty wouldn't allow her to speak first. Joanna patted the side of the long wooden bench seat and silently invited her daughter to join her.
"I know you feel like this is all too much for you and believe me if there had been any other way then I would....."
"You would never have told me about my father?"
"That's not what I was going to say and I can see this is going to be far more difficult than I had imagined it would. Perhaps you are the one who is going to make it difficult!"
At her mother's words, Angela's feelings now turned from pity to anger.
"Don't you dare turn this around on me mother.

I'm not to blame for any of this and I won't allow you to say anything to the contrary." Silently Joanna stood up and taking her daughters hand, led her out to the front of the house.

"Don't ask any questions just get in the car." To Joanna's amazement not to mention relief and for the second time in less than twenty four hours, her daughter actually did as she was told. They drove to a nearby wood and began to walk. Soon old memories began to flood Joanna's mind, true this place wasn't Bluebell wood and Marty wasn't here but the sights and smells came a very close second. Sitting down on the stump of a fallen tree Joanna Canning Brown again patted the space at her side silently asking for her daughter to join her. When they were both as comfortable as was possible given the surroundings, she began. Starting slowly she told Angela all about her father. Never once daring to glance in her daughter's direction, she described his looks, their love for each other and the sheer desolate heart break she had felt for the last twenty five years. Joanna guessed that Marty had felt the same pain right up until the day he'd died but her mind didn't want to venture down that road, at least not today. Expecting an outburst of temper, Joanna was taken back when she looked at Angela and noticed the tears that slid slowly down onto her cheeks.

"So I wasn't an unwanted bastard then?"

"What? God no darling, no other child on this earth could have been conceived with as much love as you were. When suggestions were made about adoption and, well never mind what else. What I'm trying to say is, not having Marty's child in my life and caring for her never came into question."

The two women hugged, stood up and slowly they walked back to the car with an arm around each other's shoulder. Joanna Canning Brown knew that after this conversation their relationship had definitely turned a corner and one she felt was for the better. Still the nagging thought invaded her mind that this wasn't over yet, not by a long way. Making their way home the two women didn't speak. Joanna was thinking of Marty and what might have been and Angela was trying with all her imagination to picture her father. Angela's grandparents had been apprehensively waiting back at the house and when Joanna's car came into view, Julian breathed out a sigh of relief. The family walked silently inside, Angela beside her grandfather and Joanna with her arm wrapped around her mother. Quietly she bent down and whispered into Elizabeth's ear.

"I think it's going to be alright mum, I really think Angela and me are going to be fine."

"Angela and I dear, Angela and I."
Joanna Canning Brown gave a hearty laugh, things would never really change.
Many miles away in Bethnal Green, Flo McCann paced the small area that made up her front room. After Steve Thompson had left she'd phoned Herbie Spires in a blind panic. Now that he was due any minute Flo wondered if she'd made a mistake involving an outsider. The thought automatically made her feel guilty as Marty had looked on both Herbie and Jimmy as not so much father figures but more elderly brothers. In times of need they would have been the only two he would have turned to; she just wished he'd hurry up. As if by will, the doorbell burst into life and Flo almost ran to answer it. By the time she'd made the few steps she was well and truly out of breath and took a moment to remind herself that she was no spring chicken anymore. Making sure to check through the spy hole as Marty had always told her, she opened the door.
"Hello Flo darlin', now whatever's the matter girl?"
As the words tumbled from her mouth at thirty miles an hour, Herbie didn't understand a thing she was saying.
"Flo! Slow down love, I can't make head nor tale of what you're on about. Now why don't you make us both a nice cup of rosie and we'll start

from the beginning?"
Doing as she'd been asked, Flo McCann appeared in the small sitting room a few minutes later with her customary tea tray. Glad of her guest's suggestion, it had given her time to calm down and compose herself.
"Feel better girl?"
'Yes I do Herbie and thanks for comin' over.'
"Anytime sweetheart you know that. Now what's got you so worked up?"
Starting from the moment Steve Thompson rang the flat bell, Flo relayed everything that had been said. When she'd finished she stared in Herbie's direction and expecting to see a flabbergasted look, was disappointed.
"Oh no! Don't tell me you already knew about this?"
"I'm sorry Flo love but it wasn't my place to say anything and anyway Marty had sworn us both to secrecy."
"Us both! What you telling me that the whole of fuckin' London knew somethin' I should have known over twenty fuckin' years ago?"
"No no! It wasn't like that and I don't really know that much. I felt at the time Marty was being economical with the truth. You probably know more than we do."
"Who's fuckin' we?"
Suddenly Herbie felt like a traitor, not to the old woman standing in front of him but to Marty,

the best friend he had ever known.
"The Scouser knows as well but that's as much as I'm saying Flo, now I think I'd better be off before we fall out good and proper."
Flo McCann began to plead with Herbie, something she would never normally do but as her old mum used to say 'If needs must.'
"Please Herb, I have to know everythin'. Lord knows I've lost the only thing I cherished in life. Now that I have a granddaughter, well that's some consolation if only a small one. Don't you see, you have to help me. Please!!!"
Herbie Spires started to feel embarrassed. Normally nothing much fazed him but now to see his late boss's mum almost begging, well it really hurt him. Grabbing the old woman gently but firmly by the hands, Herbie stared straight into Flo's eyes.
"Please don't Flo. I can't betray Marty and even if I could, I don't know any more than you do. Love you've got to believe that."
"Would the Scouser be able to shed any more light on things?"
Herbie shook his head.
"I can honestly say hand on heart that he wouldn't and even if he could, then he'd be of the same mind as me. Now I've got to get off but if you need anythin'?"
Flo didn't answer; she stood in the small front room with tears streaming down her face.

Herbie Spires walked out of the flat with a terrible feeling of guilt. Throughout his life he'd seen many horrendous things, done many horrendous things, things to grisly to talk about. Things which would cause most of the normal Joe Blogg's of London town never to sleep again but what he'd just witnessed in that small council flat cut him more than any of the other. A woman of Flo McCann's age shouldn't be reduced to begging. Looking up to the skies Herbie hoped Marty had just witnessed what had occurred and if he had, then Herbie hoped he felt bad. Slowly he made his way back to the office, today was turning into a nightmare of a day and he knew that it wasn't over yet. Entering his base he saw the green light on the answer machine was flashing, signalling a message. Herbie Spires pressed the button half expecting to hear Marge's voice but when Johnny Vale's dulcet tones burst into life; he wearily sat down and lay back in his leather swivel chair.

"Herb its Johnny, I need everyone over at the bookies A S A P. I haven't been able to get hold of Jimmy so if you could stop over at Stepney on the way it'll be appreciated."

Herbie could feel his heckles begin to rise, if it hadn't been for his encounter with Flo less than an hour ago he probably wouldn't have taken offence. Now being summoned by the new big

shot, who was throwing his weight about, somehow didn't seem right. Once again he locked up the shop and got into his car. The traffic was as thick as ever and Herbie knew he was never going to get over to Stepney, pick up Jimmy and get back to Bethnal Green in what Johnny would see as an acceptable time. Finally reaching his destination, he rang the shiny brass bell on the front door of the little terrace house. The Scouser's new girl answered and invited him in. Usually no one got over the threshold without it first being checked with the boss but as far as this visitor was concerned, she knew there was no question of having to ask first. Entering the front room Herbie saw his friend napping in the chair and felt a little bad about disturbing him. As he reached Jimmy Forbes's feet, the man woke up.
"Fuck me mate second visit in nearly as many days. Ain't you got no work to do?"
"I wish that was all it was but we've been summoned."
Jimmy sat upright in his chair.
"Who's summoned us?"
"The new boss wants us over at the bookies straight away! Come on get a move on!"
Standing up Jimmy wore a mask of stone and Herbie knew he was mad.
"What the fucks wrong with you man? You get a call from that jumped up little cunt Vale and

you're pissing in your boots. I can remember a time when you'd have snipped off his fuckin' fingers before he'd had chance to pick up the phone! Now out of politeness, we will attend this so called fuckin' meetin' and I might add it's goin' to be on our terms and not that cunt Vale's. Understood?"

A feeling of shame came over Herbie; he knew his old mate was right. Since Marty had died he hadn't been himself, maybe he'd lost his bottle or maybe it was just the grieving process, either way he didn't like the feeling.

CHAPTER SIX

Opening the car door Herbie Spires glanced at his watch and knew that over an hour had passed since he'd received Johnny's call. Inwardly he started to panic but seconds later the panic was replaced with an all consuming anger. Knowing that Marty would have been gutted to see his friend in fear of another firm member, somehow gave him strength. As Jimmy Forbes closed the car door, he didn't take his eyes off his companion. Instinct told him what his pal was thinking and when he saw Herbie's expression change to that of the old days, he smiled. Together as if showing a united front, the two men walked into the betting shop. Kathy Jones sat behind the counter of the bookies but didn't wear her usual cheery smile, in fact both men thought in unison how sad and drawn she seemed. Everyone had know about her feelings for the boss so they accepted her look for one of grieving.
"Hi Kath babe, is he in?"
Instead of the constant chatter and babbling that they usually received on visits, all she did was nod. Herbie walked through to the back office thinking Jimmy was following behind. Tapping on the door he heard the words 'enter' and his blood again started to boil. Turning to look for

the Scouser he was stunned to see he was alone. With no alternative Herbie Spires walked in and the sight of Johnny Vale perched like a king behind the boss's desk made him want to rush over and slam the cocky bastards face into the polished veneer of the desk.
"You took your fuckin' time. Where's Jimmy?"
"Not sure he was with me a minute ago; maybe he's having a quick word with Kath."
With the racing screens blaring out the day's forthcoming events and most of the regulars more interested in studying form, no one was listening to the Scouser's words.
"Alright girl? Only I noticed you weren't your normal chatty self. I expect you're missin' the boss like we all are?"
Tears welled up in Kathy's eyes and a pleading expression covered her face.
"Oh Jimmy I wish that was all it was."
Just as she was about to explain her reduction in working hours and the effect it was going to have on her family, the internal intercom started to flash. Kathy Jones sighed heavily as she pressed the button.
"Yeh boss?"
"Is that fuckin' Scouser with you? Well tell him to get his arse in here fuckin' pronto!"
Kathy looked up and witnessed pure unadulterated rage in the face of the man before her. Maybe it was a blessing the kids wouldn't

be coming round here after school anymore because Kathy Jones could actually sense the trouble that was brewing. Over the years she had come to know and love most of the crew members but she had always been weary of Herbie and Jimmy. Their violent reputations preceded the two wherever they went and no one took liberties with either. Still the man's show of caring seemed genuine and made a big impact on her. Jimmy Forbes didn't utter another word; instead he walked towards the office. After what he'd heard Johnny Vale call Jimmy, Herbie knew there could be trouble. Only two people had ever been able to call the man 'Scouser', himself being one and Marty the other. Suddenly the door flew open and Jimmy shot across the room and a second later had Johnny Vale pinned by the throat to the back of his leather recliner.

"Listen cunt! No one calls me that. You might think you're fuckin' king of the hill now but tread very carefully, do you hear?"

Jay Jay Porter, a man in his early thirties and who'd been on the firm's payroll since his teens, lightly placed a hand on Jimmy's shoulder. Johnny Vale's eyes bulged and the minute Jimmy released his grip the man fell forward coughing and spluttering. This time Johnny knew he'd overstepped the mark and realised he had to mend fences and fast. He was aware that

if it hadn't been for Jay Jay then he would probably have been finished off there and then. It took several seconds to compose himself and when he spoke the words came out in husky tones.
"Sorry Jimmy, no offence meant. I though everyone called you by your nickname."
Jimmy Forbes was about to stand and give the man another taste of his anger, when Herbie placed his hand out as if to say 'not here.'
"You know that only my friends call me that and you cunt aren't counted among them. Now we may be willin' to go along with Marty's wishes out of loyalty but that's as far as it goes. Never and I repeat never, presume we are your fuckin' servants!"
For the first time in longer than he cared to remember, Johnny Vale felt threatened and it wasn't a feeling he liked. He was boss now and things weren't supposed to be like this. He decided that for his own safety he would have to bring in some outside muscle.
"Understood Jimmy. Now for the sake of peace and business, can we start this meeting again?"
The men standing on the other side of the desk both nodded but Herbie and Johnny Vale could clearly see that Jimmy wasn't happy with the situation. As Johnny began to speak he was stopped mid sentence by Jimmy's palm.
"One more thing before we get started. What

makes you think you're in charge now anyway?" Tiny beads of sweat began to form on Johnny Vale's immaculate brow. He wasn't used to being questioned but knew that if he didn't give a good answer things could suddenly get out of hand again.

"Marty always told me that if anything ever happened to him, then everything would be left to me. Got a problem with that?"

The Scouser thought for a moment before answering and gave the reply that the man in front of him wanted to hear, rather than the way he actually felt. Shrugging his shoulders he looked directly into Johnny face.

"If and I do mean if that's what the boss wanted."

"It was, now can we get on?"

Neither visitor answered so it was taken that the meeting had finally started but it wouldn't be long before anger reared its ugly head again.

"Now boys we all know Marty had very strong views on the drugs trade. In fact he lost the firm a lot of fuckin' wonga by not getting in on the scene. Jimmy I would like all the names of your contacts, I feel it's about time we branched out."

Instead of the agreement he was expecting, Johnny was stunned by the tirade that followed. Both Jimmy and Herbie suddenly stood up but it was the Scouser who spoke, slamming his fist onto the highly polished desk as he did so.

"No fuckin' way Jose!"
"What do you mean, no way?"
It was now Johnny Vale's turn to get annoyed, true the others had violent pasts but so did he and his violence had never known any ground rules.
"Listen cunt, I may have taken your reprimand over the name calling but when it comes down to business that's my fuckin' domain. As part of this firm you will toe the line just as you did when Marty was alive!"
Herbie and Jimmy once again took their seats. No matter how hard you were, it was tradition that you didn't front up to the boss, not once his status had been agreed. As it hadn't been discussed prior to their arrival, Jimmy Forbes for the moment held his tongue. Fifteen minutes later and the meeting was concluded. Leaving the premises neither of the men acknowledged Kath and once again she felt lost and alone. The silence remained as they made their way from the bookies to the car but once inside and they were on their way it was a different story.
"Fuckin' hell Jimmy, we can't let that wanker get away with this can we?"
"Give us a minute to think Herb. I hadn't planned on the bastard havin' that much front."
The duo had almost reached Stepney and the small terraced house before they resumed anything that resembled a conversation. Pulling

the car in to the curb, Herbie Spires switched off the engine and turned to face his friend.
"Well?"
"Well What?"
Herbie shook his head as the words of disappointment left his mouth.
"Are you just goin' to sit back and take whatever that slimy fucker dishes out? I never thought I'd see the day when Jimmy Forbes let someone shit on him from a great height and took it lying down."
"It's not about that Herb! A few years ago that meet wouldn't have even taken place but a turf war? Not at my age."
"You mean you're not up for any action nowadays?"
Suddenly Jimmy's face took on the same expression it had back at the bookies but not so much from anger as a feeling of being insulted.
"Fuck me Herb; you should know me better than that. I'm as much up for trouble now as I was twenty years ago but if we do this and I do mean if, what happens after?"
"Well that cunt will be out of our hair for a start."
"Yeh but who's goin' to run things 'cause I don't want the job, do you?"
Herbie Spires finally understood what his mate was trying to get at; at his age he didn't want or need that kind of responsibility either. Not wanting to voice his thoughts he sat quietly and

it was the Scouser who this time broke the silence.
"I think we just need to bide our time."
Suddenly Herbie Spires was on his feet.
"Bide our fuckin' time!"
Jimmy Forbes was quickly becoming pissed off with his dearest friend but there was nothing in the world that could make him fall out with the man. After all, they only had each other now.
"There's no way on this earth that Marty would have left Johnny Vale in charge. It was you who told me what the solicitor had said to Flo remember?"
"That we would all be receivin' letters?"
"Yeh! Now I think it's in both our best interests to sit it out and wait, if only for the time being. Let Vale think he's in charge, give him a little of what he wants to keep him happy and when the times right!"
"We'll crucify the bastard!"
"Too fuckin' right we will Herbie my son, too fuckin' right!"
The men parted in high spirits and agreed to see each other again the following day to discuss a plan of action, regarding what information they would and wouldn't give Johnny Vale.
Three days later, Herbie Spires and Jimmy Forbes once more walked into the high street bookmakers for a meeting with the new boss. As they entered Kathy wore the same sad

expression as before and Herbie knew it would have upset Marty to see her looking so miserable. Nodding in her direction neither man stopped to speak, which unbeknown to them caused her even more misery. Instead they headed straight for the office. Jimmy knocked on the door and walked in to see Johnny Vale seated at the desk and flanked on either side by two burly bodyguards. Jay Jay Porter was nowhere to be seen but he didn't inquire after the man. Jimmy hadn't been that well acquainted with him and besides in this game, faces came and went and you didn't ask questions.
"Didn't scare you did I Johnny?"
His words were spoken comically but all in the room knew he was deadly serious. Johnny Vale gave a sly grin and gestured for the two men to take a seat.
"So boys what have you brought me?"
Jimmy passed over a small rather worn looking black book, which had in fact been empty until yesterday. It had taken all morning to sift through his list of contacts and write in the book all that were now either dead, or only purchased in small quantities. Anyone of any value had been left in his genuine ledger for future trade. For a moment Johnny Vale browsed the list of names and then looked in the direction of his visitors.

"Is this it?"
Jimmy stifled back the urge to laugh and Herbie stared straight at the floor as his friend spoke.
"Yeh! As you know the boss turned a blind eye to my little bit of dealin' but that's all it ever was, a little bit. Anyway what's with the heavies?"
Johnny looked at the man standing to his right then the one to his left, proud and now feeling safe, his chest swelled.
"This is the future my friends. From now on I go nowhere without Al and Seth. Call it security, in fact call it what you like but just in case either of you was plannin' a little take over, you can fuckin' think again!"
Before the Scouser had time to lose his rag, Herbie spoke.
"Whatever makes you think we'd even contemplate a turf war boss? In case it's passed your notice neither of us are spring chickens. I don't know about Jimmy here but as far as I'm concerned, it won't be long before I retire."
Suddenly Johnny Vale felt stupid for giving time to the idea that two old farts like the pair sitting in front of him, would even dream of doing anything. Maybe since Marty's demise he was getting paranoid but all the same it made him feel good to have a little protection.
"Of course not boys, I don't know what I was thinking of. Now I need you both to organise your crews. We've got a big job goin' down and

one that will put me safely at the top of the pile as far as the big crews in the smoke are concerned."

Jimmy, finding it hard to maintain his agreeable composure couldn't hold back from asking. "And what job might that be?"

Johnny Vale loved the fact that he had them both on the edge of their seats and everything he'd done had been worth it, if only for this moment. "Patience Jimmy, patience. Two weeks from now and you'll know as much as I do. Now unless you have any other business, I suggest we call this meeting to an end."

Jimmy was as angry about being dismissed as he was for being summoned and couldn't resist one last dig.

"Fine but as far as the crews go, there ain't many left. Seems Johnny me old son, that people ain't that keen on workin' for you."

Johnny made no attempt at replying, he didn't care about the workforce. As far as he was concerned, they were ten a penny and easily replaced. The two men stood up and walked towards the door as the new boss informed them that he would be in touch shortly to discuss details. Again leaving the building without even speaking to Kathy, they solemnly got into the car and began the journey home. Herbie dropped the Scouser at his house and was about to pull away when Jimmy lent back into the car.

"Herb I don't want your thinkin' I've given in 'cause nothing could be further from the truth. I'm just praying that those letters and whatever they contain will be here before we have to actually do any business with that scum bag. Oh! and by the way, no fuckin' spring chicken, you cheeky cunt!"
With that he closed the car door laughing and Herbie drove off.
Going straight home as he couldn't face the office, Herbie Spires knew there was definitely agro in store. In what form he wasn't sure but he was aware that it wouldn't be long before he found out.

CHAPTER SEVEN

Walking past her local church on the outskirts of Canterbury, just as the bells burst into life made Angela stop dead in her tracks at the ancient arched gates. The peel told her that a marriage had just taken place and she felt compelled to watch the wedding party emerge. The bride appeared magnificent in her ivory gown and she wore the look of a girl totally and utterly in love. The handsome groom beamed with pride as he stared at the young woman beside him. Standing alone Angela wondered if she would ever look so happy and then she laughed out loud as the proud parents jostled with one another for a prime photo position. Perhaps it was the event taking place right in front of her or maybe it was something else entirely but either way there and then Angela accepted that she would never be happy or content with Edward. Going along with all the hopes and dreams her mother had wanted now seemed so wrong. Tonight Edward Dellingwood was due at the house for his twice weekly visit and Angela resigned herself to the fact that they had some serious talking to do. Remaining at the wrought iron railings until the final photograph had been taken and the last of the guests had departed for the reception, she now had an overwhelming sense of loneliness. Canterbury really was a beautiful city but one in which she had never truly felt at home. Until recently Angela hadn't been able to fathom out why but slowly and with each passing day, things were becoming clearer. After the disaster and embarrassment that private school had caused her mother and grandparents, Angel had been sent to the local comprehensive. Julian Canning Brown had chosen the best school available locally but he had never boasted of his granddaughter to the other judge's on the circuit. He had seen it as a social disgrace and a total failure on his part, not to mention the stigma that his only child's daughter should end up with a state education. For Angela on the other hand, school had been relatively normal. Being an average student she was never bullied or picked on in any way. All the same her circle of friends had been limited to three girls who all came from the local council estate. Frightened that their opinions of her would change once they witnessed the opulence in which she lived, they were never invited back to the house and neither her mother nor grandparents ever encouraged such activities. Summer holidays were spent alone strolling the grounds of the house, with not one member of her family bothering to find out if she was lonely or happy or needed just to talk. In fact it wasn't until she was about to leave school that anyone showed the least bit of interest in her. When it came to work they had all discouraged her, saying it wasn't the place of a judge's granddaughter to find menial employment. Julian was more than happy to support Angela if she wanted to carry out any charitable duties but that was as far as it went. For Julian the idea of his granddaughter actually being paid to work for someone was totally out of the question. Two years after finishing her education, Angela obtained unpaid employment at the local library two afternoons a week. The post was helping disabled children from the surrounding areas learn to read. Although rewarding it wasn't what she wanted from life but then she didn't have the slightest idea of what she really did want. Accepting that she had little choice in the matter she welcomed any chance to get away from the vast house that had become her personal prison. Finally after the church grounds man had begun to sweep away the confetti and given her more than a fair share of odd glances she headed for home and the impending visit by her oh so boring fiancé. With each step she began to experience a feeling that was totally alien to her. Almost like a vacuum, Angela felt as though she was beginning to disappear. So strong was this weird feeling, that she thought at any moment she would become invisible. Vigorously shaking her head, brought

her back to reality and she realised it was her mind psychologically telling her that she was no longer in control of her life. Angela now readily accepted the fact that whatever her future held, it didn't include Edward Dellingwood or anything else her mother wanted for her.
After unburdening the emotional weight that had almost drowned Joanna Canning Brown over the last twenty five years, she now had a better relationship with her daughter. They no longer spent every waking hour at each other's throats and had actually begun to have grown up conversations, although Angela still never allowed herself to truly express her feelings to her mother. At this moment in time she didn't actually know herself what she felt, so many ideas and images flashed through her mind that some days she actually thought she was going insane. Joanna didn't possess a photograph of Marty, so Angela had to invent her own mental image of what her father looked like. Since she'd received Steve Thompson's letter and all the revelations of her mother's past had come to light it was as if she was incomplete, as if not knowing about her father made her only half a person.
Walking up the long sweeping drive that formed the grand entrance to the house, Angela looked up towards the sky and enjoyed the warmth of the late afternoon sun on her skin. The massive

white building that had partially come into view was known to every local as 'Journeys End Defiant'. A name Elizabeth Canning Brown had given the place after constantly moving home to enable her husband's career to progress. On her first viewing of the property, it was love at first sight. Elizabeth had longed for a home like this and was determined to spend the rest of her days here. As if from nowhere, the name had popped into her head. No amount of persuasion by Julian to call it something 'manor' or something 'lodge' could change her mind. A black granite slab had been inserted in the high front wall, with the name she was so proud of emblazed in gold letters. Opening the heavy oak front door, Angela slipped of her coat and hung it on one of the antique pegs in the inner hall. Emerging from the sitting room with a rolled up newspaper under her arm, Joanna embraced her daughter in an awkward fashion which made Angela feel uncomfortable.
"Nice walk darling?"
"Not bad. I stopped at the church to watch a wedding."
"Did you dear, that was nice. I expect it won't be long before we'll be planning your big day. Maybe I should have a quiet word with Edward this evening."
A look of sheer horror took over Angela's face as she grabbed her mother by both arms.

"Don't you dare?"
Joanna Canning Brown roared with laughter at the sight of her only child.
"Darling I'm only teasing. I think this is one time that neither I nor your grandmother will be interfering."
Angela quietly muttered 'thank god' as she made her way upstairs to the sanctity of her room. Not bothering to undress, she lay fully clothed on the bed and drifted off to sleep, once more trying to picture her father. After what seemed like only five minutes but was in fact over two hours, Angela heard a knock at the door. As usual her mother didn't wait to be invited in and appeared shocked when she saw her daughter in the same clothes she'd been wearing all day.
"What are we going to do with you? Edwards here and you haven't even changed!"
Rubbing her eyes sleepily with the back of her hands, Angela slowly sat up on the bed.
"Don't make a fuss mother. Edward's seen me like this before."
Joanna made her way over to the large wardrobe that spanned the whole length of the room and began to rifle through her daughter's clothes. Settling on a delicate black cocktail dress, she pulled it out from the bulging mass of designer labels and walked back over to the bed.
"Maybe he has but just don't make a habit of it,

well at least not until you've got him to the altar. If he continually sees you at your worst, you'll frighten him off before we've sent out the invitations. I'll tell Edward you'll be down in five minutes."
Without waiting for a reply Joanna Canning Brown swept out of the room to entertain her future son in law. Just as she'd been asked, Angela appeared from behind the drawing room door five minutes later. Joanna's face was set like stone when she saw that her daughter wasn't wearing the little black number she had selected for her. Good breeding made her too polite to comment in Edwards's company and Angela could feel that the forced silence was almost killing her. Julian and Elizabeth Canning Brown were dressed up as if they were ready for a night out on the town. Seated in their matching armchairs they appeared mesmerized by Edwards's conversation but Angela knew that nothing could be further from the truth. Pops had never actually come right out and said he didn't like the boy but there had been one too many snide remarks which had convinced her. The sight of her relatives and fiancé behaving in a way that epitomised the traditional British upper class family, suddenly made her want to laugh and for once she gave in to her emotions. As if from out of nowhere, a side splitting high pitched giggle emerged from her mouth. Joanna

Canning Brown stood up, her face a picture of suppressed rage.

"Angela whatever is the matter? Do take control dear we have a guest.'

Her mother's words did nothing to calm the situation in fact they only fuelled the fire of Angela's laughter. Grabbing Edward by the hands she pulled him up from the chair and began to drag him towards the door.

"Eddie we need to talk!"

"But I was just telling......."

"For pity's sake do as I ask for once."

Silently like a lamb to the slaughter he followed and as she closed the front door another onset of giggles erupted. The mental picture she had of the flabbergasted faces of her family was too much to hold inside. Leading Edward away from the main house, they walked to the secret garden and all the time she continued to snicker. Taking a seat on the bench where she and Pops had often spent time and where until now she had never invited Edward, she turned to him.

"Guess what?"

"What Angela? What's all this about?"

"I'm a bastard. Did you hear what I said I'm a bastard?"

The disgusted reaction she had hoped for didn't materialize, instead he embraced her in a tight hold and Angela knew she would have to lay everything on the line if she was to be rid of him.

"I don't care; nothing in this whole world could put me off wanting you. I knew from the first moment I saw you that I loved you."
Neither one of them had ever been given the opportunity to voice their honest opinions or feelings about each other. Old man Dellingwood had thought it a good idea to have a judge on side even if it was a retired one and the Canning Browns had wanted to marry off their only heir to moneyed stock. Again Edward held her in an almost vice like grip and planted slobbering kisses on her neck. Managing to push him away she let everything out, all she knew of Marty and her mother and the fact that her grandparents had wanted to have her aborted. Nothing she said was enough to dampen his love for her and as his hand slipped underneath her top she thought back to a month ago and the one and only time they had attempted to have sex. The Canning Browns had gone to a concert at the Cathedral and Angela had given Edward a door key and told him to come in through the back. Edward had been on tender hooks all day and his nerves were in tatters. Oh he loved her but his sexual experiences in the past had been limited to say the least and he was frightened of disappointing her. Entering the house he made his way upstairs and knocked on her bedroom door.
"Come in Edward."

The sight before him was mind blowing.
"Angela, oh my word!"
"Do you like what you see Edward?"
Seated in reverse on a bentwood chair her arms were placed on the curved wood of the chair back. Seductively she rested her chin on her delicate manicures hands. Angela had taken time to get the pose exactly right, she had placed her flowing hair in such a way that it laid sexually on her shoulders and with her long ivory legs spread wide on each side of the chair, it was an invitation no man could refuse. Her delicate sleek body had been enhanced with a see through pink baby doll nightdress with the tiniest shoe string straps and matching panties. Standing up she sauntered over to the bed in six inch coral pink Louboutin's.
"Come here Edward."
As he advanced she positioned herself on the plush double bed. Edward did as he was asked and now stood in front of her fully clothed in a tweed jacket and checked trousers. Angela released his belt and as she unzipped his flies Edward's trousers dropped to the floor revealing the most horrendous pair of greying Y fronts she'd ever seen. The sight was an instant turn off for Angela and she tried hard not to let her disappointment be noted. The large bulge showed just how excited Edward had become and he desperately wrestled trying to remove

the rest of his clothing. Angela grabbed his wrists and pulled him on top of her. The feeling of skin on skin and the sight of her pink erect nipples through the nightdress was all too much for him. Just as she opened her legs ready for him to enter he let out a groan.
"Oh Edward! This was new on."
The whole experience had been a disaster and once again Edward Dellingwood was devastatingly embarrassed. Now out in the garden as he once more tried to make love to her she pulled away.
"I'm sorry but I just can't."
Angela now knew that if he was the last man on earth she couldn't marry him. The realisation that Edward Dellingwood was probably one of the kindest men alive didn't help matters but it didn't change anything either.
"Edward you do know I can't marry you, don't you?"
Turning away from her, Angela guessed that he had tears in his eyes and it hurt her deeply. In all the time they had known each other, not once had they had a meaningful conversation like they were at this moment. Raising her voice Angela hoped to shock him into hearing her once and for all.
"Edward you deserve better than me, someone you can really love and I don't mean a girl your father chooses. Go out and see the world, find

out what you want and for once stop living your life for other people."
Expecting more tears, his words caught her off guard. As if seeing him for the first time Angela realised that he really was ok and that he could have a future all of his own, if only he'd fight for it.
"Don't flatter yourself! My father didn't pick you if that's what you're thinking; I choose you all by myself. I actually had to convince the old man that you were good enough for me; well he's going to make a meal out of this one. God! I've been a fool"
Angela knew his words were lies and only said to protect him but she didn't have the heart to tell him she was aware of his parents and her grandparent's little agreement.
"Eddie it's not like that, can't you try to see things from my side. A week ago I believed my father had died before I was born, only to find out that he was alive all along. Now that he is dead, I have to find out who I am and where I come from."
"Where you come from? You come from here Angela!"
She shook her head in dismay; he really couldn't grasp what she had been trying to tell him.
"Half of me belongs here but there's another side that I need, no have to, find out about. It might all end in tears but unless I try I'll never know."

"And you expect me to be here waiting when you come back I suppose?"

Angela Canning Brown looked him in the eye and he knew that she was deadly serious, so serious that it scared him.

"That's exactly what I don't want. I'm going to find my family and I don't think you're part of the plan Edward. I'm so sorry and I never meant to hurt you but better its now than after we're married."

Their courtship, at the Judges request had been a lengthy one. In that time he had come to know how stubborn she was and accepted that it was futile to protest further. He felt as though his heart was about to break but private schooling had taught him not to show his emotions and keep a stiff upper lip. The slip of a tear earlier, now made him feel embarrassed and he wanted to get as far away from Angela and the rest of the Canning Browns as quickly as possible. Walking her back to the front door he gently kissed her cheek.

"I hope you find what you're looking for my darling and I truly hope it makes you happy, although somehow I doubt that."

Angela didn't say goodbye she was too upset to talk and after letting herself inside, tried to slip unnoticed up to her room. Her foot had barely touched the second stair when she heard her mother's voice.

"And what young lady, was all that about?"
Not turning to face Joanna she spoke as if talking to the invisible woman.

"Mother, if you value our relationship in the slightest, you won't quiz me tonight. I'm nearly at the end of my tether and if you persist, you just might send me over the edge."

Continuing to climb the stairs Angela was amazed, that for once her mother remained silent and not another word was heard. It wasn't long before the rest of the family were safely tucked up in bed and when Angela could vaguely hear Pops begin to snore, she knew the coast was clear. Throwing a cocktail dress for emergencies only, followed by a pair of jeans and a couple of jumpers into a holdall and at the last minute remembering her toothbrush, she slipped on a warm jacket. Gently placing her feet on the stair treads she took things slowly, her mind alert to the fact that nearly every other step had a squeaky section. Old houses were always full of invisible places that would give you away when you were trying to be as quiet as a church mouse but at last she made it to the foot of the stairs. Waiting until she reached the end of the drive, Angela called a taxi from her mobile. Fifteen minutes later and Angela Canning Brown found herself booked into one of Canterbury's finest hotels under the name of a Miss McCann. The following morning and as soon as his office opened she contacted Steve Thompson. It only took a few minutes for her to gain all the information she needed at this stage and any other papers were quickly faxed through to the hotel.

Joanna Canning Brown woke late that day and entered her daughter's room eager to find out just what had gone on between her and Edward the previous evening. On seeing the bed had not been slept in, a feeling of sheer terror surged through her body. Noticing the envelope that had been placed on the mantelpiece she tore it open and began to read. Angela had only left a few brief details about how she needed some time to think and would be in touch later. Running around the house in a blind panic Joanna screamed to her mother and father that it had all gone horribly wrong. Her daughter had run away and it was all their fault. Unaware of the commotion happening back at the house and with a feeling of excitement slowly but steadily building up inside, Angela boarded the eleven twenty five train to London. The carriage was all but deserted and a few minutes after boarding, Angela removed from her handbag, the bound pack of letters that Steve Thompson had given her. On his visit to the house he was at first reluctant to hand over the old letters. Past experience had shown him that they could contain untold pain. Steve had taken a shine to

Angela and didn't want to hurt her but he was professional through and through and the wishes of his client had to come first.
Tentatively she opened the first and although it was relatively short, it had her in tears before the last word. As the train pulled into Kings cross station, Angela opened up number twenty five and remained seated until she had read her father's final words. Placing the envelopes back into her bag, she at last had a feeling of closeness to the man. Her wild imagination of what Marty McCann had been like wasn't so very far removed from the truth she'd just read. The cold hard facts didn't scare her, in fact more than ever it made Angela want to claim what was rightfully hers.

CHAPTER EIGHT

Business in the east end had been slow since Marty's funeral and it was starting to annoy Johnny Vale in a big way. True he had the armed robbery to look forward to in the next few days and was expecting the boys over soon for a briefing but somehow he'd thought that being in charge would be more of a buzz. He had envisaged money coming in from all over the place but the true reason for his unhappiness was the fact that there was no aggravation. Johnny wanted to live on the edge and being in charge was turning out to be dull, as dull as dish water. When the only cash he'd seen came from either the bookies or a small slice from Jimmy's girls, he was more than a little disappointed. He pressed the intercom, to what Kathy, felt like the umpteenth time that morning and she bit down on her lip before answering.
"Yeh boss?"
"A coffee and make it quick before the others get here."
There was never any please or thank you and she was so fed up with his constant orders. Since he had changed her hours, things hadn't been working out so well. It had only been a week but the drop in money had made it a real struggle.

Nadia Grantly was sixteen and lived in the opposite flat to Kathy with her obese and overbearing mother. The slave like treatment she received from old woman Grantly and the fact there had never been a man on the scene, probably accounted for the reason Nadia had got herself pregnant six months ago. Happy to help out while of course earning a few extra quid, she'd offered to look after the kids each day so that Kath could resume her normal hours. Kathy Jones was reluctant to leave her precious angels with a girl so young and Spider had gone into the mother of all sulks, adamant that he didn't need a baby sitter. Laying awake for most of the night worrying about how they were going to manage helped make up Kathy's mind. Mentally doing the sums in her head she worked out that after giving Nadia a few pounds to look after the kids she was still better off than she was by losing time from the bookies. The holiday fund wouldn't be up and running again for a good few months but at least they would be able to manage. After a stern lecture to both her children about behaving themselves, she resumed her full day at work and tried to carry on as normal but with Johnny Vale in charge that was proving difficult. After resisting the urge to hawk up a large mouthful of phlegm and add it to the boss's drink, she knocked on the door and waited to be invited inside.

"Enter."
Without being told, Kathy picked up a coaster from the shelf as she passed by. Placing the circular cork disk onto the highly polished surface of his desk, she put down the steaming hot coffee in his favourite china mug. Silently she turned and left the room without a word and Johnny Vale smiled to himself. Since he'd laid the law down after taking over, Kathy Jones had been the model employee. She now knew exactly how he liked things done and had lost the back chat attitude that he had always hated when Marty was around. Now that she was back to full time he never had to make another drink for himself and as his old mum used to say 'what's the point in having a dog and barking yourself'.

The shop was quiet as things didn't liven up until after eleven, so Kathy sat behind the counter flicking through one of the old teen magazines that Nadia had passed on to her. No wonder girls got into trouble nowadays, the problem pages talked of sexual positions that she hadn't even heard of let alone tried. Tutting as she read on Kathy didn't see the postman until he placed the bundle of letters on the counter.

"Oh! Thanks mate."

He didn't reply. Getting out of that place was his main priority and striking up a conversation

with someone employed by the firm, no matter how menial their position, was not on his to do list.
"Please yourself you miserable old bastard." Kathy picked up the mail and after swiftly scanning the envelopes she removed the junk ones. Johnny hated it if she missed any, so just to be safe she glanced through them a second time. Again she waited outside the office and when she heard the commanding word, walked in and placed the bundle neatly in front of her boss. For some strange reason Kathy had noticed the top letter, she never normally took any interest but this one was different. The envelope was thick and expensive looking not like the usual brown type they received. On further inspection she had seen the name of Bendish and Backham and wondered what a solicitor was doing writing to the likes of her boss. Johnny Vale sipped his coffee and a few seconds later picked up the brass letter opener that he thought looked classy and had been a gift to himself after his recent promotion. Ignoring the front wording, he slipped the blade along the back flap and removed the sheet of paper complete with water mark. After reading the contents over and over again he slammed his fist onto the desk. Grabbing the imitation chrome handset of his trendy new telephone, Johnny Vale proceeded to dial the number of Bendish

and Backham and in a very unfriendly voice, asked to speak to Steve Thompson.

"Good morning, Steve Thompson speaking, how may I help?"

"Thompson, its Johnny Vale."

"Glad to hear from you Mr Vale, I've been expecting your call."

"Expecting my fuckin' call, you cunt!"

"Please Mr Vale I'm only the messenger. If you are not happy with the contents of the letter I can only inform you that it was written by your late employer and only placed with our company for safe keeping."

The line went silent and Steve Thompson was about to ask if his caller was still there when Johnny spoke.

"I don't give a flying fuck what's in this letter, 'cause it don't make a shits worth of difference. Marty McCann's dead and gone and if anyone thinks they are goin' to muscle in and take over then they can fuckin' think again!"'

"Mr Vale as I said, we are only carrying out our clients wishes and passing on letters that he left in our care. What the beneficiary decides to do with Mr McCann's estate is entirely up to them."

Johnny didn't continue the conversation, instead he threw the new phone across the office, where it slammed against the door and landed on the floor smashing into several pieces. His eyes narrowed as he once again picked up the white paper and slowly began to take in the enormity of its words. After scanning the lines again Johnny began to get agitated as he felt the anxiety start to build up inside. He couldn't think straight and looked down at the letter one more time, only to find the words fuzzy and running into each other. Rubbing his eyes hard he tried to concentrate, tried to find something within the short note that would give him a clue, there was nothing.

Hi Johnny! If you're reading this then I'm obviously dead. Not to worry I suppose there's not a lot I can do about it. Herbie and the Scouser will probably be receiving their letters about now and I reckon you'll all have a lot to talk about. My daughter has been informed about my death and also the state of my affairs. She may or may not decide to claim her birthright but that will be her decision. I hope that if she does, you and the boys will help her out as much as possible and make things easy for her. Angela has led a sheltered life and stepping into the old man's shoes will be a big challenge. I assume you've been acting boss and I appreciate that fact, someone has to keep the wheels oiled and Herb and Jimmy are getting a bit long in the tooth to start taking charge. Well my friend there's not much more to say, there'll be plenty of time to reminisce when we meet up again, and that's if you don't end up going south. Take care and please look out for my girl. Best regards Marty.'

Anger enveloped Johnny Vale and he suddenly felt like he was going to explode. Everything had been a complete waste of time, now that some jumped up little tart was going to take over and probably push him out. Hearing Al and Seth in the front of the shop Johnny called out to them before proceeding to pour himself a large scotch. Herbie Spires swigged back the last of his coffee, picked up the mail from the hall table and after kissing Marge on the cheek walked outside to the car. He was due to collect Jimmy on the way over to the bookies and as usual was running late. Placing the letters onto the passenger's seat he eased the seat belt over his shoulder and turned the key in the ignition. About to pull away, for some reason he glanced down at the bundle of mail and the top letter now caught his attention. Remembering what Flo had said days earlier about them all getting solicitors letter, he switched off the engine. Taking a deep breath, Herbie swiftly tore open the envelope and began to read. By the time he'd finished a huge grin stretched across his face, he knew there'd been more to this than anyone had let on. Marty had wanted his girl to claim what was rightfully hers and Herbie said a silent prayer, hoping that somehow it would come true. In a happier frame of mind he set off

for Stepney and couldn't wait to see the
Scouser's face when he showed him the letter.
Much to his pleasure the traffic was relatively
light and it only took fifteen minutes to reach his
destination. Piping the horn outside the small
terrace he impatiently waited for Jimmy to
emerge. Before the Scouser had closed the car
door, Herbie began to spill out all the contents of
his letter. Jimmy stopped him mid flow and
held up an identical copy and the two men burst
out laughing.
"Fuck me Herb, if we've got these then Johnny's
bound to have a similar one!"
They both sat in silence not relishing this
morning's meet. Once more firing the Jag into
life, Herbie Spires sighed.
"I suppose we'd best get it over with then."
Jimmy nodded in agreement and they set off for
Bethnal Green and the bookmakers. Kath Jones
sat quietly behind the counter as the two men
walked in. Three punters, all of different ethnic
backgrounds stood along the far wall studying
form from the day's papers that Kath had earlier
pinned up.
"Hi babe, is he in?"
Studying her lined face with dark circles under
both eyes, Herbie knew there was more to her
sadness than grief. Everyone had loved Marty
and no one more than her but this girl had the
appearance of someone who'd had the stuffing

totally knocked out of her. Kathy nodded her head towards the office, she hadn't planned on making conversation with the two but suddenly a thought crossed her mind.
"Mr Spires has big Bernie been to see you?"
Already having taken several steps towards Johnny Vales office, Herbie stopped in his tracks and made his way back to the counter.
"No love. Why, should he have?"
Kathy Jones inhaled a large breath. She knew that what she was about to say could land her in deep trouble but she was a caring sort and felt big Bernie had really had the dirty done to him.
"It's just that he."
She moved her head again in the direction of the office.
"He sacked Bernie the day after Marty's funeral and I've been so worried. I told Bernie to come and see you or Mr Forbes and he said he would. Poor sod is the only bread winner in that house and I don't know how they'll be able to manage."
The news made Herbie's blood boil, he along with Marty had always had a soft spot for Bernie and Johnny was out of order getting rid of him.
"Don't worry Kath love, as soon as we've done here I'll go and find the big lump."
Kathy felt a little easier about speaking out of turn and she smiled to herself as the men headed towards the back room. Jimmy Forbes didn't

knock or wait to be invited into the office he just barged straight through the door. Herbie followed close behind and noticed that Johnny was agitated as soon as they stepped into the room. Flanked on either side by the two goons he'd hired a few days ago, the boss didn't appear at first glance to be in a good mood.
"About fuckin' time! I was expecting you two over half an hour ago."
The Scouser wore a smirk on his face and Herbie, not wanting any trouble, didn't give him chance to answer.
"Sorry about that Johnny but we both received a bit of unexpected news this morning."
Johnny Vale gripped the edge of the desk so tightly that his knuckles began to turn white.
"Same fuckin' news that I got no doubt. Well I'll let you both into a little fuckin' secret, no bastard kid of Marty's is goin' to come in here giving it the big I am and think at the last hour they can upset the fuckin' proverbial apple cart."
Herbie looked at Jimmy and they both smiled but it was Herbie Spires that again continued.
"I thought you was only standing in until things were sorted? I expected, no we expected you to hand over the reins now that the wills all kosher!"
Slamming his fist onto the desk Johnny's face was as white as his knuckles and Herbie knew that his words had got to the man. About to

continue putting the pieces of the jigsaw into place he was stopped before he got started. Johnny Vales hair which was always so well groomed and slicked back from his forehead, now flopped forward onto his face and both of the men on the opposite side of the desk could see he was as mad as hell.

"How many more times! Now you pair of slag's listen and listen good. No jumped up little whore that Marty decided to keep a secret for over twenty years is goin' to come in and take over what's rightfully mine, have you both fuckin' got that?"

Herbie and the Scouser nodded but Jimmy never let the grin slip from his face. The men were in agreement that if Marty's offspring decided to show up then there would be a fight and strangely enough it would be one they would both look forward to.

"Right let's get down to business then."

Johnny continued to inform them about a payroll heist he was planning. Details were explained and he told them that for a change they were both expected to take a participating role. So proud was he of the plan that he couldn't contain himself and shared every bit of information. The location, other crew members, the parts they would both play and the fact that the money over five hundred grand at least, would only be on site for three days. The job

would be carried out on the last day when he had arranged for security to be a little slacker than it would be on the previous two.
"So what do you think? Have you lost your fuckin' bottle or are you up for it?"
Reluctantly they both nodded.
"Right the clock is ticking to blast off so make sure you're ready and if either of you hear anything more about that bastard brat; make sure you tell me straight away."
Herbie had one last thing to say before they got up to leave.
"Johnny is it right what I've just heard? You've gone and sacked our Bernie?"
Being questioned about his judgement was something Johnny Vale didn't like and he took offence at Herbie's words.
"Listen cunt! I'm in charge now and I couldn't stand having that gormless lump hanging around, he made my fuckin' skin crawl. Marty might have been a soft touch but I ain't. Have you got a problem with that?"
Herbie Spires looked up at the two men who flanked his boss on either side and thought better than to argue, for the moment at least. Whatever he felt would keep and besides he was happy to wait, happy to sit it out and have a ringside seat at Johnny Vales Armageddon party.
"No just wondered that was all."

As the men left the bookies, Johnny instructed his henchmen to go and find big Bernie. He was sick of not being taken seriously and decided to show them all, that he was not to be messed with. He didn't care who he hurt and hopefully this would put them all in their place. Arriving back in Stepney and with the Jag parked outside Jimmy's house, the two sat in the car discussing what had gone on at the meet.

"What a fuckin' prick Herb! Marty would never have revealed specific details until the day it was going down. The cocky bastard was tryin' to be the big man; well I tell you I can't wait to bring him down to fuckin' earth."

"You'll have to get in the queue my friend 'cause I'm first in line."

The Scouser was glad to see his old mukka was back on form and squeezed Herbie's shoulder as he got out of the car. Driving away Herbie suddenly remembered Kath's question and decided to go and find Bernie Preston. He was sure he could use Bernie for something and thinking of Marty, he felt it was his duty to look out for the lad. Pulling up at the block of flats Herbie Spires rang the plastic bell on the Preston family's door. He could hear someone huffing and puffing as they made their way along the hall and slowly undid what sounded like a dozen dead bolts. Iris Preston was as wide as her son was tall and years of chain smoking had

left her lungs barely able to cope. She carried a portable oxygen tank that was permanently strapped to her shoulder. Iris's voice was deep and raspy and with the cigarette still hanging from her mouth, dropped ash as her large red cheeks wobbled in recognition of Herbie.
"Hello Mr Spires and what do I owe this pleasure?"
"Hello Iris. I was wondering if Bernie was at home?"
"Oh you've just missed him. Two men called about fifteen minutes ago and he went off with them, you know my boy always in demand."
Herbie wanted to laugh. The poor old cow actually thought her boy was a big shot and not the simpleton he actually was.
"Never mind Iris, I expect I'll see him sooner or later. Nice to see you again and you take care of yourself, do you hear?"
"I will love and thanks for comin' bye."
As soon as the door was closed, the noise of the bolts being slid into position could be heard all along the outer landing. Walking back to the car Herbie tried to think who the two men could be. Something wasn't right here but he couldn't put his finger on exactly what it was. He hoped for big Bernie's sake that it wasn't anything to do with Johnny Vale but his gut instinct told him different. The east end was a big place and he hadn't a clue where to begin searching. With

nothing to go on he decided to wait and see if anything turned up. If it was anything unsavoury then he would know pretty quickly. Bad news always travelled fast, especially in the east end.

CHAPTER NINE

The numerous streets and alley ways passed by in a blur but riding in the back of the Mercedes still made Bernie Preston feel like a big man. He couldn't believe that Al and Seth, on the boss's orders had called at his house to collect him. Actually drove to his house, he couldn't take the grin of off his face and more than that, he couldn't wait to get home and tell mum all about it.
"So boys where are we goin' to?"
Neither the driver or front passenger spoke, and Bernie shrugged his shoulders as he looked out of the window at the passers-by. He wondered if any of them thought he was famous, maybe one of those big actors or a pop star even. One thing was for sure; he'd known how proud mum had been when she'd leaned over the balcony and watched him get into this posh car. Her face had beamed as he'd waved up at her like royalty. Bernie could feel the juices begin to accumulate in his mouth as he thought of the something special that would be waiting back at the flat tonight for his tea and he licked his lips in anticipation. As the car drove on he didn't recognize any of the streets, the viaduct they passed resembled so many that were part and parcel of London town. Again he asked what

the boss wanted and where they were going and again the two men in front didn't answer his question. From time to time Al would glance at his partner in crime and they would both grin in a sickly manner. Ten minutes later and after turning down a narrow alley the Mercedes stopped outside a lock up. Al got out of the driver's side and undid the padlock then climbed back into the car and drove inside. The building was in darkness but from the echo anyone would be able to tell the place was big. The two men left Bernie alone in the car for a couple of minutes and the next thing he knew was a feeling of almost blindness as a massive torch shone into his face, illuminating it like a full moon. Bernie squinted and tried to see what was happening but the glare was too strong.
"Come on mate lets have you out of there!"
In a child like manner Bernie Preston shook his head from side to side, he knew something was wrong. Seth Larkman started to get annoyed and leaning into the car, grabbed the huge figure of a man by the shoulders. His attempts to pull Bernie from the car were futile and his massive frame remained rigid in the seat. Starting to cry like a baby Bernie asked if he could go home now. His bottom lip quivered as he explained his mum would be worried if he stayed out for very long.
"Please I need to pee and I've got me best suit

on."
The two heavies realised that a touch of child psychology was needed just to get the idiot out of the car. Of the two, Al had a calmer voice so it was decided he would be the one to do the talking.

"Come on mate the boss will be here soon and if he sees you still sat in the car he won't be best pleased. Anyway there's a lav just over there, we don't want you pissin' yourself now do we?"

Suddenly Bernie stopped crying and wiped his tears with the back of his hand.

"Mr Vale's coming here? To see me?"

Al Kingston rolled his eyes in frustration. He felt a fool talking to a grown man in such babyish terms but there was no alternative, not if they wanted to get home tonight.

"'Course he is! We had special orders to collect you; it's an important job you've got now."

Still seated in the car, Bernie tried to straighten the wrinkles from his nylon suit with the palms of his hands.

"Are you getting out or what?"

Looking at the two men, Bernie still felt uneasy and again shook his head.

"I've fuckin' had enough of this!"

Walking round to the rear of the car, Seth Larkman was now seriously pissed off. Opening up the boot he leaned inside and Bernie could hear him rooting around.

"Ah! Found it!"
Bernie Preston was all ears, trying to listen to what was going on outside. Looking out of the window into almost darkness, he didn't see Seth on the other side. Once again leaning into the car, Seth swung a large meat hook in the direction of Bernie's left thigh.
"Arrrgh!"
As the hook went deep into his muscle it curled round and came out of the other side. Screams echoed round the buildings walls but there was no one to hear.
"Come here you stupid cunt!"
As Seth pulled the hook Bernie had no choice but to move in the man's direction, anything to try and ease the searing pain. Seth used all his strength and giving one last pull saw the two men land in a heap on the floor. Bernie was now on top of Seth and his weight pushed down on his assailant. Al, who had been retrieving something from the cars boot, returned with a long length of rope and on seeing the two men struggling quickly placed it around Bernie's neck and pulled him off of Seth. With Al in control of Bernie's head he was completely at their mercy. Seth regained his composure and now in a rage he once more grabbed hold of the hook. Bernie screamed out as pain like he'd never felt before seared through his leg.
"Arrrgh!"

"Seth get the tape from the boot I've got him now."
Bernie sat upright on the floor but couldn't move. Al still had the rope around his neck and was pressing his knee hard into Bernie's back. He was close to being strangled as the rope tightened and burned into his skin. Within seconds Seth was back with two rolls of duct tape and swiftly bound Bernie's legs together.
"Roll him onto his front; I want his arms behind him."
Al yanked the rope and Bernie fell onto his front smashing his face into the cold concrete.
"Please mister don't hurt me, please I'll do anything you want pleeeeeeease!"
Bernie Preston's heartbreaking pleas fell on deaf ears.
"Right! Take the rope off his neck and put it over his feet so we can hook him up to the block and tackle."
Before collecting Bernie the two men had paid a visit to the lock up and prepared everything in advance. It took both of them all the strength they could muster to lift Bernie's large frame from the floor, the last thing being his head which once again smashed onto the concrete. Again he pleaded for mercy.
"Please don't hurt me, mummy I want my mummy, don't hurt me pleeeeeease!"
"Tape his fuckin' mouth up the blah arse cunt's

gettin' on me nerves!"
Bernie Preston's body hung down like the carcass of a bull at the slaughter house, the only difference being, that Bernie was still alive. The meat hook was still deeply embed in his leg and blood dripped constantly onto the concrete floor. He felt dizzy at being upside down and from the blows to his head. When he saw the puddle of red sticky liquid, his eyes were as wide as saucers. Desperately trying to lift his head drained any strength he had left and when he saw Al Kingston staring back at him, Bernie knew he was in real trouble. Seth Larkman was busy trying to rid his trousers of the stains that Bernie's blood had caused and the more he rubbed the worse they looked. With every stroke he was becoming more and more frustrated, until he gave up and turned to his partner.
"Ready?"
"Let's do it!"
They walked over to Bernie who instantly let go of the contents of his bladder, much to the amusement of the two men. Seth was the first to begin, with a kick to Bernie Preston's head and the two men heartily laughed. Seth kicked and punched Bernie like the poor soul was his own personal punch bag and Al decided to administer several flying kicks to Bernie's ribs, kidneys and groin. The screams were horrific

even through the gag but soon subsided to a gurgle and Seth patted his partner on the back.
"Fuckin' blindin' man, where'd you learn all that shit?"
"Just natural talent Sethy old boy!"
The assault only lasted for a couple of minutes but to the men it seemed as if their vicious acts had been carried out in slow motion. Their adrenalin had been pumping the whole time but now they were exhausted and sweating profusely.
"Seconds out! round two."
Once again he kicked and punched Bernie over and over again. The only sound Bernie Preston now emitted was a few slight groans. He was almost to the point of unconsciousness and only the dull thuds of his attacker's punches could be heard. Seth now held back and grabbing Al's arm told him they'd done enough but Al was enjoying himself and shrugged off the man's grip. Bernie Preston's face was virtually unrecognisable, his rib cage was smashed and they had broken his back. When Al was finally exhausted he stood back to admire his work, it was a job well done and they had beaten the poor halfwit to a pulp. Lowering him to the floor they placed the equipment back into the car and changed into spare clothes that were stored in the cars boot. It took only a matter of minutes before the men were ready to make a quick exit.

Reversing the Mercedes out of the lock up, they didn't bother to hide the crime and left the doors to the lock up wide open. Confident that the big lump inside was dead; they assumed that sooner or later someone would find him and call the police. Luckily for big Bernie, it was only a further fifteen minutes before he was found. A group of youths looking for a place to sniff their newly purchased lighter fuel came across the crippled body that was now unrecognisable as Bernie Preston. Not yet high they had the intelligence to call for help. They were also street wise enough not to stay around and get caught up in all the agro that giving a statement would bring. Knowing how slow the city's wheels were and that help wouldn't arrive for quite some time anything of any value was removed from the now unconscious Bernie's body. The leader felt it was the least they were owed for the inconvenience of losing a place to sniff their gas. Finding somewhere else that was suitable would take a while and in any case it didn't look like the poor sucker on the floor was ever going to need money again. By the time the ambulance and police arrived there was no one else around and after going over his pockets several times the paramedic's could find no credible identification, apart from a scrap of paper with a phone number scribbled on it. Johnny Vale had instructed the men to leave the paper somewhere on Bernie so that it could easily be found. Once inside the hospital's emergency department all hell broke loose. A crash trolley was summoned and no less than three doctors were in attendance. The ward sister wasn't able to process her admission properly, due to the fact that he was unknown and studying the state of the man she did wonder to herself if it was a futile even trying to find out. The poor man didn't look like he would survive long enough for anyone to get to the hospital.

Kathy Jones had just served the kids their evening meal and was sitting at the kitchen table reading another of Nadia's magazines when a knock came at the door. Spider as usual ran to answer and when Kath heard him say 'who wants to know' she made her way into the hall to see who it was. Pushing the youngster back inside, Kathy stood on the step with the door almost closed behind her.

"Hello officer, sorry about that, Kids hey? Anyway how can I help?"

The constable explained that a man had been brought into casualty with no identification, only a phone number written on a piece of paper. They had been able to trace the number to her address and were now in the process of making inquiries. Kathy racked her brains trying to think who it could be. It wasn't her ex

husband as he'd brought the kids back only half an hour ago. A wicked smile crossed her lips when she thought that maybe it was Johnny. "Give me a few minutes and I'll be right with you. Do you mind waiting downstairs, only I don't want to upset the kids?"
Closing the door she grabbed her coat and ran across the hall to the Grantly's front door. Banging as hard as she could brought Nadia rushing to answer and as soon as she saw Kath's face knew that something bad had occurred.
"Nadia somethin's happened. I don't know what yet but can you watch the kids?"
"Whatever it is Kath just go, they'll be fine with me."
Not bothering to say bye to Katie and Spider, she ran into the central courtyard and the waiting patrol car. Twenty minutes later Kathy Jones burst through the accident and emergency doors escorted by the officers and hoping above hope that the person laying hurt was Johnny Vale. The ward sister led her into intensive care and the bed that was almost covered by the colossus of a man. Immediately Kathy saw it was Bernie but his swollen bloodied face didn't resemble the Bernie she knew. The crisp white bedding was dotted in places with spots of crimson blood and a tube ran from his side into a large bottle that stood on the floor. It continually drained away the liquid that had

filled his lungs and would have, if it wasn't for the paramedic's swift action, drowned him. Reaching for his bruised oversized hand she began to cry.

"Oh you poor poor love, whoever could do such a terrible thing?"

Bernie Preston didn't reply, he couldn't as he'd been sedated up to his eyeballs. A tall distinguished looking doctor in a white coat walked over to her side.

"He can't hear you thank god. If it was anyone else I'd say they wouldn't survive the night but he's as strong as an ox and has a fighting chance."

Nodding, she quietly said 'thanks.' Kathy gave them Bernie's first name and tactfully explained about his mental state. The one thing she wouldn't divulge was his address, knowing that if Iris had a visit from the Old Bill it would probably finish her off. The two constables who had called for her at the flat, patiently waited outside intensive care to ask a barrage of questions but that was the last thing Kathy felt like doing. Walking into the corridor she approached the young officers.

"I know there are things you need to speak to me about and I will be only too glad to help in any way that I can, but please not tonight. I know the man's first name but that's as far as it goes, he's someone I met through work. I haven't got the first inkling as to who would do this to him or why he would have my number, so there's not much I can really help you with. I expect the doctors have told you that they haven't got a clue when Bernie will be up to speaking to you, so if you don't mind I'd like to be left alone. It's not like I'm going to do a runner or anything, you know where I live so for now boys please just let me go home."

Realising that no matter how long they waited, they weren't going to get any fresh information tonight, the constable left the hospital agreeing with Kath to call back the following day. Glad that she'd remembered to pick up her handbag on the rush out, Kathy flicked through her diary. After asking for directions to the public phone box she dialled Jimmy Forbes's number. Jimmy was just about to sit down to a dinner which had been lovingly cooked by his recently acquired Caribbean girlfriend, when the phone rang. Nodding for her to answer, he told her to inform whoever it was he was out for the night. Marlene picked up the handset but as Jimmy watched her from the corner of his eye he could see she didn't understand a word that was being said on the other end. Impatiently and irate at having been disturbed, he slammed his fork down onto the plate. Walking across the room he snatched the phone from her hand. By now Kathy Jones was in a real state and Jimmy didn't have clue who he was talking to. Slowly he calmed the caller down and was taken aback when he realised who was on the other end. Without saying a word he fled the house and drove like a maniac over to Bermondsey and a stunned Herbie Spires.

Herbie and his wife were also about to sit down to dinner when Marge heard a car pull up on the gravel drive.

"Oh Herb you're not going out tonight? I've spent ages making this!"

"And lovely it looks too but let me see who it is first."

Planting a tender kiss on her forehead he got up from the table while assuring her that nothing could tear him away from the beautiful spread she'd prepared. On parting the curtains and seeing the Scouser, Herbie knew he was about to go back on his word. He was also aware there was trouble with a capital T. Jimmy had only ever been to the house once in all the years Herbie had lived there. He wouldn't turn up on the doorstep uninvited unless it was absolutely necessary. Closing the dining room doors behind him, he made his way to the front only to be greeted by a stony faced Jimmy. As soon as he heard Bernie's name mentioned, Herbie grabbed his jacket and the two men set off for the hospital. Feeling guilty about Marge he called her from his mobile and made up a cock

and bull story about the shop being burgled. He didn't know if she believed him but right at this minute Herbie Spires couldn't care less. The only thing on his mind was Bernie and the bastards who had hurt him. As they entered intensive care, Kathy Jones ran sobbing into Herbie's arms. Jimmy walked over to the bed and stood nipping his forehead between his thumb and forefinger as he stared down at the terrible sight that was Bernie Preston.
"Fuck Herb, look at the poor cunt!"
Herbie released Kathy and walked over to the bed.
"We both know which bastards done this Jim, what say we go and take him out right now?"
Grabbing his friend by both shoulders, Jimmy Forbes looked directly into the man's eyes.
"Get a grip mate! This was done for a reason and I can guarantee that if we turn up at the bookies, Johnny Vale will be mob handed and it won't be just those two goons by his side. As hard as it is, we don't want to end up here with poor fuckin' Bernie. We have to wait, It'll get sorted my friend, but at the right time OK?"
Herbie nodded his agreement and gently stroked Bernie's hand.
"We'll get the bastard Bernie old son; you mark my words we'll get him for you."
As if to remind the men that she was still there, Kathy Jones walked over to join them.

"Excuse me Mr Spires Mr Forbes but I need to get off. As much as I want to stay, I've had to leave the kids with a neighbour."
Herbie placed a hand on her shoulder.
"That's ok Kath. You've been a fuckin' brick tonight, if it wasn't for you Bernie would be here all alone and it won't go unrewarded."
"Not necessary Mr Spires. I love the big lump and I'd do anything for him. I just wish it could have been something nice instead of this."
She smiled and began to turn away but the thought of Bernie's old mum emerged and she made her way back over to the bed.
"Oh! I nearly forgot to tell you, I gave them his name but I wouldn't say where he lived. I thought it better that you two broke the news to Iris. If the Old Bill turned up on her doorstep I think the poor old cow would have a coronary."
"Thanks Kath you're a good girl. One more thing, be careful what you say tomorrow love. Johnny obviously meant to include you in all of this because of your phone number and I wouldn't put anything past him."
Once more she smiled.
"I will Mr Spires but it'll take a lot more than the likes of Johnny Vale to finish me. Marty taught me well and one of those lessons was never show your hand."
Kathy Jones made her way from the unit and hailed a cab to take her home. The hopeful

holiday fund would take a real pounding after this but she didn't care. Getting back to her little flat and holding her babies close was the only thing on her mind. If anyone had hurt a child of hers, she'd have wanted to commit murder and lord knows that was how poor Iris Preston was going to feel before she saw another nightfall. Herbie and Jimmy sat by the bedside for the remainder of the night. Agreeing that it wasn't fair to wake Iris in the early hours, they hadn't wanted to leave Bernie alone. The hospital chairs were hard and it was a restless and uncomfortable night but by three am both were snoring softly.

Waking at six they were each suffering from aching backs and stiff necks. A quick splash of water in the public toilets saw them on their way to the Preston house. Neither had eaten for over twelve hours but somehow seeing Bernie laying helpless and connected to all those tubes had killed any desire for food. Climbing the concrete stairwells and walking along the open air landing of the old pre war flats Jimmy breathed in the clean air. It was the only time of day that London smelled sweet and was still relatively quiet.

"Who's goin' to tell the old girl then?"

"I think it had better come from me Jim, I was only here yesterday looking for Bernie."

After tapping gently on the front door, the

familiar sound of the deadbolts being pulled back rang out. Herbie could remember years ago living in these kind of cramped conditions, where everyone knows everyone else's business. The constant noise, smells and bitching from neighbours was something he'd hate to have to live with now. He supposed the sound of the bolts was nothing compared to some of the things you heard on an estate. Iris, still wearing her flannelette nightdress was a sight for sore eyes. Her more than ample bosom swayed under the material as she held either side of the hall walls for support.

"Mr Spires! This is an early visit? I'm afraid he's still in bed, must have come in late 'cause I didn't hear him. Mind you it's like trying to wake the dead once I go off. Bernie! Bernie love get up now, we've got visitors. Bernie! Did you hear me?"

As he took a step closer to the door Herbie knew he wasn't going to enjoy this one bit.

"Iris we need to talk, I'm afraid Bernie had a bit of an accident."

As the words 'Bernie and accident' escaped his mouth, both he and the Scouser saw the old woman's knees buckle as she fell to the ground.

"Fuck me Herb now what we goin' to do? She's out cold and by the looks of her; she must weigh all of twenty stone."

For some reason only known to him, Herbie

Spires started to laugh and it wasn't long before Jimmy joined in as well. Every time they attempted to lift the old girl, they both got an attack of the giggles and ended up back where they started. Several minutes later and after the Scouser had put the kettle on and placed a blanket round Iris Preston's lower half to protect her modesty, she began to come round.
Grabbing Jimmy's arm she dug her nails so hard into his skin that she drew blood.
"Is he dead?"
"Of course not Iris but you went and passed out on us before we had time to tell you."
Holding her hand to her chest Iris repeated 'Oh thank god, Oh thank god' over and over again.
"Now drink this tea and when you feel able, we'll get you up and dressed. We've got the car downstairs waiting to take you to the hospital."
Tears welled up in the old woman's eyes as she began to thank the two men.
"My baby's all I have in the world; it would kill me if anything happened to him. Mr Spires what did happen to my Bernie?"
Herbie had to be careful how he answered this one and as much as Iris loved her boy she was also one of the biggest gossips you could ever wish to meet.
"To be honest Iris I don't know any details yet but you can bet your life on it I'll make it my business to find out."

CHAPTER TEN

Flo McCann drank the last of her morning coffee and staring at her guest, wished with all her heart for the hundredth time that Edna would go home. Nearly every day since Marty's death, her neighbour had popped round and it was always uninvited. She expected coffee and gossip no matter how bad Flo was feeling. Edna Burrows was the type of woman who wouldn't take no for an answer and aired her opinion whether it was asked for or not. Being Flo's neighbour for as long as the McCann's had lived in Townsend Court, made it difficult for Flo. Many times over the years she had wanted to tell Edna in no uncertain terms to go away but friends were hard to find, if indeed that's what Edna was, sometimes she wasn't so sure. It crossed Flo's mind that maybe she only came round for the gossip and Marty's death had given her enough to survive on for the next six months at least. Clearing her throat Flo got up from the small formica table and placed her cup and saucer in the sink.
"Well Edna, I really need to be getting on now. I promised Kitty and Arnold I'd meet them this mornin' and I hate to let people down."
Edna Burrows immediately took offence at Flo's words and wasn't backwards in coming forward

when it came to voicing her complaint.
"You mean you want me to piss off now don't you? Don't worry I get the message!"
For all of Flo McCann's bravado she hated to hurt people's feelings and that included Edna.
"No not at all but you know Kitty she can get real arsy if you're late."
"Oh I know fuckin' Kitty McManus alright. There's not much anyone can tell me about her, moaning old cow! Anyway I'm going down the market myself today so you're not the only one who's got things to do Flo McCann!"
Leaving her cup on the table Edna stomped out of the flat, slamming the front door as she went. Flo knew she'd now be punished, at least for the next couple of days. The stupid woman was too wrapped up in herself to realise that if she stayed away it wasn't punishment to her neighbour; it would be pure pleasure. The thought of not having to talk to or even see the woman for a while made her feel light hearted. Edna was more than a little overpowering and it had taken all of Flo's willpower not to confide in her about her granddaughter. Now she was alone again Flo felt proud of herself, for once her personal business wouldn't be spread all over the estate by Edna Burrows. Rinsing the cups and after taking a pork chop out of the freezer for her dinner, Flo put on her trademark old Mac, grabbed the shopping bag that stood in the

corner and closed the front door behind her. Kitty McManus had lived in the smoke all of her life and had known Flo McCann almost as long. A goodtime girl, she'd never married nor had children. Many jobs had passed her way over the years and even a short stint on the game hadn't been unknown if Kitty needed cash but she was a kind sort and that in itself had caused her more than a little grief over her lifetime.
As Flo McCann left her flat, Kitty McManus did the same less than a mile away but where Flo's place shone like a palace; Kitty's was a complete dump. The second floor bedsit hadn't seen a duster in years, cobwebs hung in every corner and piles of magazines and newspapers overflowed from the furniture and onto the floor. She seldom had visitors and anyone who could stand the smell, couldn't find a place to sit but Kitty didn't care in the least. Her love of life and human company, Arnold in particular made her look upon housework as a waste of precious time. No if the weather was half decent you wouldn't find her in doors for any reason, she'd much rather be out socialising somewhere.
Kitty's hair was bleached a very unflattering shade of blond and set in tight ringlets. Money was too tight to spend it on fancy salons and if she couldn't get her locks coloured cheap at the local day centre, she had been known to apply household bleach to her hair instead. The bright

electric blue eye shadow and crimson lipstick she wore did nothing for her seventy plus years. Since she had been able to walk Kitty McManus hadn't bothered what other people thought. If she liked something then that was fine by her and everyone else could go fuck themselves. Her skin was as wrinkled as a walnut and even though the pan stick she coated her face in, filled most of the cracks, she still resembled an extra from the hammer house of horrors. Kitty McManus didn't see herself as others did, looking in the bathroom mirror each morning, she still saw a pretty twenty year old who had the world at her feet. Walking the few hundred paces to the high street, she was excited at the prospect of seeing Arnold Newman. Friends for over a year they met up twice weekly in the pie and mash shop. Even at her age Kitty still fantasised about the opposite sex and relished her daydreams. Never one to shy away from what she was thinking, she thought nothing of relaying the lurid details, much to Flo's disgust. With visions of Arnold filling her mind Kitty walked slowly on. She didn't see the estate gang slowly begin to surround her until it was too late. Their filthy voices filled the air before she realised what was happening but it didn't faze her, nothing had ever seemed to bother Kitty. The gang leader was the first to speak and at all of fifteen he thought he knew the lot.

"You leery old cow, whatever do you think you look like?"
Several others joined in as they followed her along the pavement, uncaring as to an old woman's feelings or the fact that people stopped to watch the bullying.
"Yeh! You old pro goin' to try and get laid are you?"
Kitty smiled in a grandmotherly fashion before inhaling as much air as possible and screaming at the top of her lungs.
"Fuck off you little cunts!"
Kitty swung her bag in their direction and just missed one of their heads. Her bravado and guts had the teenagers stumped for words and realising that they weren't bothering their mark, they walked away.
"Gutless bastards!"
Kitty smiled to herself, the youth of today were all mouth and no trousers. Continuing on, she soon reached her destination and after checking her reflection in the shop window, Kitty McManus walked in. Arnold Newman had already taken up residency in their designated booth and Kitty's heart fluttered at the mere sight of him. As dapper as ever Arnold wore a fawn suit, pale blue shirt and a pink tie. The outfit was crowned off with a brown felt fedora hat, which he raised with his hand as she approached.

"Hello there my beauty and don't you look gorgeous today!"'

Kitty blushed slightly but none the less revelled in the attention. Even if she did see herself as he did, vanity was not something she had ever suffered from.

'Whatever are you talking about you silly old fool?'

Grabbing her hand Arnold looked deep into her blue eyes and the even deeper shade of her eyelids.

"You listen here Kitty McManus. I may be old, but foolish I'm not and I think you're wonderful. To be given a chance of love at our age is somethin' not to be sniffed at. Lord knows it comes along seldom enough when you're young."

For once she was lost for words but nodding heartily took on board all that he said.

"Shall we call it a truce for now? Flo McCann's coming down and I think the conversation is goin' to be a little bit more serious than our love lives."

"Point taken my love, shall we order?"

Kitty as usual was starving and always looked forward to her twice weekly treat but thought it would be bad manners not to wait for their luncheon guest.

"No I think we'd better hold off till she gets here, you don't mind do you?"'

Arnold Newman didn't care if he never ate again and felt that just to be in Kitty's company was enough to keep him alive forever.

"Whatever you want is fine by me sweetheart."

Neither had to wait long as ten minutes later Flo entered the pie and mash shop. The place, had been such a big part of her life for more years than she cared to remember.

"Sorry to keep you both waiting, only I had a visit from Edna this morning."

Kitty McManus held her hand up as if saying 'enough said'.

"Don't explain Flo, I know enough about that one to last me a life time. Nosy old cow is Edna Burrows. You don't want to be tellin' her anything Flo or it'll be round the estate quicker than you can spit."

"I'm well aware of that Kitty but what I really want to know is what's so important that we had to meet today. Don't think I'm being nasty because nothing could be further from the truth. I enjoy the company of you both but your voice sounded so urgent on the phone, that I didn't sleep a wink all night."

Kitty didn't want to miss her much looked forward to lunch and once the proverbial shit had hit the fan, knew that food would be out of the window.

"I know you do love but can't we eat first, I'm bloody starvin'."

Although desperate to hear what the woman had to say, Flo once again didn't want to appear rude, so nodded in agreement. All three ordered the house special with extra toppings of green liquor and even if she didn't admit it, Flo McCann enjoyed the food more than she had any meal since losing Marty. Half an hour later and with their plates cleared away and three steaming cups of tea placed on the freshly wiped table, Flo McCann turned to her host.
"Right Kitty I've waited long enough. Lord knows if you don't explain yourself I'm goin' to burst right here at this table."
Arnold who'd been quiet throughout the meal took Kitty's hand in his.
"Mrs McCann, we're both terribly sad by the news about your boy."
"Thank you both but that's not what I'm here for. Kitty said she had something to say about the day my Marty died and I need to hear it now. I've had a lovely lunch but as you can both guess I'm now more than a little anxious."
Arnold Newman looked deep into the eyes of the woman he adored and nodded with a meaningful look, as if to say 'go ahead'. Kitty took a deep breath before she started to relay the fateful day two weeks earlier.
"God Flo! This has really been playing on my mind. I've been in fuckin' turmoil over it, should I tell her, shouldn't I tell her?"

Placing her cup noisily on the table, Flo's tone was now stern and Kitty knew she'd pushed the woman to her limits.
"For fucks sake Kit, just spit it out please!!!"
"Ok! Ok! Well me and Arnold had met up as normal, well not really as normal 'cause we'd decided instead of lunch we would have our evening meal here. Our usual booth, well this one where we're all sitting actually, was taken and the only other free one was by the window." Pointing to the large glass shop front she was trying to remember which of the seats it had been.
"Does it really matter Kit?"
"Flo if we'd had our special place we wouldn't have seen what we did. Where was I, oh yeh I remember? We sat by the window just chatting as you do, when your Marty's flash car stopped at the traffic lights just over there. He wasn't alone, that Johnny what's his name?"
"Vale!"
"Yeh Johnny Vale was with him. I noticed because he was the one driving and not your boy. Anyway they were going at it hammer and tongs; your boy was waving his hands in the air and everything."
Flo McCann sighed deeply.
"Kitty it couldn't have been the day my Marty died because Johnny Vale was in Spain. He didn't get back until the day after."

Flo's words had ruffled Kitty McManus's feathers good and proper. She knew what she saw and wasn't happy about being told she'd got it wrong.
"Listen to me Flo McCann, I may be getting old but senile I'm not. It was still light and that Vale bloke was as brown as a nigger, so he must have come back early and that's all I'm goin' to say on the matter."
Flo picked up her tea cup and took a large gulp, right at this moment she could have done with something much stronger. Everything Kitty had said swam round in her head. She'd known something hadn't been right when the news of Marty's death had broke but she'd hadn't been able to work out what it was. So if Johnny Vale was with him only hours before he died, did that make him his killer? Flo felt weak at the thought.
"Kitty I need to get out of here. Thanks for the lunch but this has all shook me up a bit."
"'Course it has love, do you want Arnold here to walk you back?"
Pulling on her trusty old Mac, she slowly did up the buttons and picked up her shopping bag.
"No I'll be fine. The walk will do me good and to tell you the truth, I'd rather be on me own."
They both stood up as she left and Kitty was heartfelt sorry for her old chum. It had been a relief to get what she'd seen off her chest but she

now wondered at what cost or more to the point whose?

Heading home, everything passed Flo McCann in a blur. Acquaintances of hers and Marty's called out but she didn't see any of them. Her head was pounding and all she could picture was her beautiful boy lying dead on that mortuary slab. That bastard Vale had been so kind to her, he'd even helped her plan the funeral and all along it was him who'd murdered her boy. It couldn't have been him could it? She was so mixed up she didn't know what to think. Finally she made it Townsend Court and after turning the key in the lock, went through to the kitchen and made a cup of tea. Things always seemed clearer after a nice hot cuppa or that's what she was hoping for. Three hours later and after consuming as much of India's finest that Flo could stomach, no answer had come to mind. Walking into the neat but tiny front room she picked up the receiver and dialled Herbie Spires' number. Asleep on the overstuffed sofa, he didn't answer straight away and Flo started to panic that he wasn't home. When she at last heard his voice relief washed over her.

"Oh Herbie thank god you're in."

"Whatever's the matter Mrs M?"

Flo took a deep breath then continued to repeat all that Kitty had told her.

"Is this Kitty absolutely sure about when she saw Marty?"
"Hundred percent, got a bit stroppy when I said she must be mistaken. That bastard couldn't have murdered my boy, could he?"
Herbie Spires had felt a shiver run down his spine as he'd listened to the revelations passed on to Flo by Kitty McManus.
"Sweetheart I don't know. I need to see the Scouser and find out what he thinks, give me a few hours and I promise I'll get back to you."
"Promise you aint just sayin' that to keep me calm?"
'Not in the least my old darlin'."
"Alright Herbie and thanks love."
"Don't thank me Mrs M; I swore on Marty's grave that I'd get to the bottom of things and one way or another that's exactly what I'm goin' to do. This is the break I've been waiting for, albeit a little sooner than I'd thought. Just sit tight until I've had a chance to speak to Jimmy."
Again Herbie Spires found himself in the Jag driving over to Stepney and Jimmy Forbes's house. For once breaking every speed limit on route didn't worry him, he needed to see the Scouser and he needed to see him now!

CHAPTER ELEVEN

By now Angela had been in London for two days. She'd checked into a small boutique hotel situated in one of Chelsea's exclusive side streets. It was expensive but nothing more than the Canning Browns would have expected and besides her father's money had made her a woman of means. The journey down by train had given her time to mull over a plan of action and where she had at first thought of going straight round to her grandmothers, she then decided to wait. Now after two days of just walking round the city with no one to talk to and nothing to do, followed by two nights of being in bed by ten o'clock, left her feeling agitated and with a need to get things moving. Wanting to gain a feel of the place and check out the clubs that Steve Thompson had said her father owned and which by rights were now hers, she decided to get dressed up and head for the west end. Her first port of call was The Chamber, a small but very up market members only establishment, situated in the heart of club land. Even Angela's polished voice and designer dress couldn't, much to her annoyance, gain her access. On arrival she had elegantly climbed the steps but was halted by one of the large burly doorman.

"I would like to go in please, now if you don't mind I would appreciate it if you removed your arm."

"Sorry love, members only. The place across the street ain't so fussy, try your luck there!"

Her father's daughter in every way saw a darker side emerge and the two doormen found the sideshow of her temper highly amusing.

"You don't have a clue who I am do you?"

The larger of the two men shrugged his shoulders as if to say 'Should I?

"Haven't got a clue sweetheart but it wouldn't make a shits worth of difference. No one gets in here unless they're a member or they are with the boss. Now piss off before I get angry."

Angela had never been spoken to like that in her life, if anything being the granddaughter of a judge had made people bow and scrap to her.

"Listen to me you pair of ignorant gorillas, I am Marty McCann's daughter and this club is now my property, so in fact I am the boss!"

The two men, both of African descent and with teeth as bright as any star, began to laugh.

"Yeh and I'm the queen of fuckin' Sheba now piss off!"

Angela Canning Brown realised that she wasn't going to get in no matter what she said. Turning to walk away, she took one long last stare at the two men.

"Take a good look at my face gentlemen, because

when I return you will know you've made a big mistake."

She continued on her way with her shoulders straight and her head held high. Joanna had always told her how deportment was vital to a woman, now she understood why. The two doormen just gawped open mouthed at the young woman, who even if they didn't like to admit it, had a lot of balls. Seconds later and Angela Canning Brown had disappeared into the mass of Saturday night revellers who crowded the busy street. Deciding to walk the short distance to her next destination, she began to enjoy all the noise and commotion that over spilled from the pubs and bars. The warm evening saw people standing out on the pavement swigging bottles of bud and laughing out loud. Everything felt so much more alive than anything she had ever been part of and Angela was enjoying every minute of it. Reaching Exeter Street on the outskirts of Covent Garden she soon found Morgan's night club and this time had no difficulty gaining entry, although she found the thirty pounds fee a little steep to say the least. The music was loud and over powering and not what Angela was used to. Making her way to the bar area where the deafening decibels were slightly lower, she ordered a mineral water. The place was packed to capacity and Angela realised it must be a gold mine, though not the sort of establishment Pops would be happy to see her frequent. Trying hard not to be noticed, she slowly walked round the outer walls taking in all that was happening in her club. Sheltered from anything bad life had to offer, even she recognised the dealers as they made their way out of the gent's toilets. Although something she had no experience of, the sight of the youngsters emerging several seconds later with their eyes wide open or the remnants of white powder still dusted around their nostrils, made her feel sick. She made a mental note that when everything was hers; a massive cleanup would be in order. Over the years Pops had tried to protect her from anything that wasn't sugar coated but even he wasn't aware of the videos she often hired and would watch until the small hours while tucked away in the safety of her room. Her favourite and undoubtedly the most violent had to be Goodfellas. Walking around the room and surveying everything, Angela knew she wanted to turn herself into a mob boss.. Stopping at the staircase that led up to the main doors she hid in the shadows as Johnny Vale and two others walked down. Unaware of who he was but at the same time hearing everyone call him boss, soon led her to the conclusion that he was the man in charge. Intrigued she wanted to walk over and introduce herself but something deep down held her back. The novelty of the club soon wore off and the loud music had given her a headache. Calling it a night she hailed a cab back to Chelsea and the hotel.

The next day Angela Canning Brown finally decided it was time to pay her long lost grandmother a visit. Not knowing what to expect but still living in a fantasy world, she pictured someone like Ma Baker would come to the door. Dressing casually in jeans she went down to breakfast and after ordering tea and toast took out Steve Thompson's papers. The information given to her on Flo McCann was limited apart from an address, Angela realised that if she wanted to find out more, then she would have to meet the woman in person. There was no axe to grind and she didn't hold any grudge towards Flo, if anything her grandmother was as innocent in all of this as she was. That fact still didn't stop the butterflies that began to flutter in her stomach. Luckily her recently acquired trust fund from her father was so large that the money she was spending on accommodation and the numerous taxis that she had been using to travel around the capital didn't even make a dent. The fund was actually large enough to live on for the rest of her life but that wasn't something Angela was remotely interested in. If that had been the kind of life she'd wanted, then she could have stayed with

the rest of the Canning Browns in Canterbury. Within the last couple of days life had suddenly become exciting for Angela and she liked it, she liked it a lot.
Bethnal Green was nothing like she had imagined, it was dirty, grimy and bore none of the refinements of the West end or come to that even Canterbury. The buildings were old and tired looking and she thought it must be awfully depressing having to wake up to these views every day. Deep in thought Angela was jolted back to reality as the taxi pulled up outside the block of flats. Looking up at the grey skyline, a felling of foreboding washed over her and the cabbie, glancing in his rear view mirror noticed this.
"You alright love?"
I'm fine thank you, how much?"
She passed a twenty pound note through the gap in the glass partition and told him to keep the change. Standing on the pavement, Angela stared up at the building for several seconds and when she heard the cab pull away, pushed open the door to the stairwell. Taking her time to climb the stairs, her nerves started to get the better of her and for a second she contemplated turning round but something, she didn't know what, urged her on.
Flo McCann sat at the kitchen table having a quiet five minutes after finally getting rid of

Edna Burrows. The woman was becoming a nightmare and every day was a trial just making it to lunch time. The second knock of the day saw her roll her eyes thinking the nosy woman had forgotten something. Wearily she trudged down the hall way and unusually for Flo; she forgot to look through the spy hole and began to speak before the door was fully open.
"Edna you'd forget your...."
The words came to an abrupt halt as she gazed at the young woman standing in the door way. Putting her arms out and embracing Angela, Flo McCann clung on for dear life as she sobbed her heart out. Seeing that her relative didn't resemble Ma Baker in the least, Angela's nerves instantly disappeared. When the tiny old lady had begun to cry, she thought her own heart would break at the sight. The hugging and crying lasted for several seconds before Flo tightly took hold of her guests hand and led her through to the kitchen. With no words spoken, Angela was a little afraid that her paternal grandmother may possibly be senile.
"How do you know who I am?"
Flo smiled and it seemed as though the whole of her face lit up. Her beautiful snow white hair shone and the dark circles under her eyes, which had only appeared since losing Marty suddenly seemed to disappear.
"Darlin' I'd know you anywhere. You're the

spitting image of your dad when he was young and I've got to say you're a fuckin' tonic to me as well."
Angela started to giggle at the way her grandmother spoke and wondered if her dad would have been the same. She decided to refrain from asking, at least for the time being. Flo filled the kettle, placed it on her sparkling cooker and taking a seat opposite Angel she once again grasped the young woman's hands in hers.
"I want to know everything about you and not just the recent stuff. How much did you weigh? Were you a good baby? Did you ever wonder about me?"
Angela laughed at the barrage of questions but she could see how much this all meant to the woman and did her best to answer. An hour later, she finally felt that most of the things she'd been asked had been covered. Smiling at the woman sitting opposite Angela tried to shake free her hand which was becoming numb as she spoke.
"I don't know what to call you?"
Flo smiled.
"Nan will be fine unless that's not posh enough for you? Or grandmamma like the queen sounds nice."
Now it was Angela's turn to smile and even though there was nothing refined about this

woman and she bore no similarities to Elizabeth Canning Brown, Angela really liked her.
"Nan will be fine but I suppose I'd better be making tracks back to the hotel."
Flo stood up and seeing her face, Angela caught her first glimpse of how strong this frail looking lady could be.
"Not on your fuckin' Nelly. No granddaughter of mine is goin' to sleep in a hotel, not when there's a perfectly good bed in the spare room."
It was agreed that while Flo prepared a meal for them both Angela would return to her hotel and collect the few belongings she had brought with her to London. For once she didn't mind being told what to do. It would be nice to feel at home somewhere and have a chance to learn all about her father at the same time. By five that evening the two women once again sat round the formica table, only this time they were tucking into roast beef with all the trimmings and Angela had to admit, Nana McCann could certainly cook. After the dishes had been cleared and the washing up shared, they sat together on the small sofa and Flo got out her old photo albums. As soon as she saw a picture of her father Angela wanted to cry. He was handsome, his eyes seemed so warm and she suddenly felt robbed of his life, a life where they should have known each other but had been kept apart.
"Tell me about him Nan?"

Flo had been dreading this question and dreading her answer even more. Did she make up a fairytale or tell this beautiful girl what her father had really been like. Deciding that honesty was the best policy and now that Marty was no longer here and couldn't complain, she began.

"Darlin' your dad wasn't always the nicest of people you know?"

Angela smiled as she guessed Flo was trying to be protective by cushioning her from the truth. "I'm twenty five not fifteen and I've seen the clubs, well one of them anyway. I may have had a sheltered upbringing but not so much that I don't know what goes on in the world."

Flo McCann took a deep breath.

"Point taken but some of what I tell you and believe me I don't know it all, will shock you. Marty was my boy and I loved every hair on his precious head but he could also be a spiteful, cruel bastard. Never to me mind, he always treated me like the queen."

Continuing Flo explained about the kind of life they led and the things Marty did to earn money. When she'd finished she looked into Angela's eyes and tried to gauge her feelings. The girls face remained a total blank and Flo thought how much like her father she really was.

"Nothing you've said has shocked me, in fact it was pretty much as I expected. Please don't

think for one minute that I'm looking down my nose at him or you but as I said earlier I'm not that naive."
"I didn't think you was love but this is all new to you and I'm worried."
Angela lent forward and hugged her new found relative.
"Well don't be! Right Nan where do we go from here?"
Flo McCann was confused, she really didn't have a clue what the girl was on about.
"Go where?"'
Angela sighed.
"How do I start to get back my father's little empire?"'
Flo held her hand to her breast as if she'd been stabbed; the words she'd just heard had come out of the blue.
"After all I've just told you about your dad and how he earned his money and you still think you've got a chance in his world?"
"Nan don't be so pedantic!"
"Fuckin' peda what?"
"Talking about insignificant details."
"Now you listen to me sweetheart, there's nothin' insignificant about having to torture people, kill them even!"
Angel knew she had said all the wrong things and wished she could take them back.
"Nan I'm not talking about killing anyone, I'm

talking about taking back what's rightfully mine."

"Yeh! And you don't think that certain people ain't goin' to be too happy about that. People who wouldn't give a second thought about ordering your disappearance."

"Surely my dad had trusty men working for him, men I could call on?"

"I dare say he did but whether they'd want to get involved is a different story."

Angela yawned and raising both arms above her head, stretched out.

"Well tomorrow we'll just have to find out, wont we? Now I think I'll turn in I'm absolutely exhausted, you coming through?"

Sleep was the last thing Flo McCann could think of, her mind was racing in all directions.

"No not for a bit love but you go ahead, no one stands on ceremony in this house."

Bending down Angela kissed her grandmothers forehead before heading for the inner hallway and the inviting divan. Flo sat on the couch for over an hour trying to think of some way to get the girl to change her mind. When no idea was forthcoming she hoped with all her being that by the morning Angela would be thinking differently. Switching the sitting room light off, she wearily made her way to the bedroom and the sleeplessness night that was to follow.

CHAPTER TWELVE

After dropping Iris Preston off at the hospital and doing a quick check to make sure big Bernie hadn't deteriorated, Herbie and Jimmy Forbes set off in search of Johnny Vale. They hadn't got far when Jimmy spoke.
"I don't know about you old pal but I'm fuckin' famished. Let's grab a bite to eat before we get down to business."
In agreement that the first port of call should be Stan's cafe on Globe road they were soon pulling up outside the greasy spoon that they loved to eat in whenever they were passing. Now with full stomachs they pulled out into the traffic in the direction of the bookies. When the car came to a standstill because a cyclist had been knocked from his bike by a delivery van, Jimmy Spires let out a loud groan and farted.
"Did you just draw one off?"
"For fuck's sake Herb, I'm strugglin' here!"
"Why, what's the matter?"
"What's the matter? I'll tell you what's the bleedin' matter! I've been nursing a shit for the last ten minutes and its now touchin' cloth!"
"Well you shouldn't be such a greedy cunt!"
Herbie Spires started to laugh which made Jimmy grimace even more.
"Oh don't make me laugh Herbie or I swear I'll

fuckin' follow through."
At last the traffic started to move and as they passed a public toilet Herbie screeched the car to a halt and Jimmy flew out much to his friend's amusement. Luckily he made it in time and they were soon able to continue on their way.
Kathy had only opened the shop five minutes earlier and was still out in the kitchen making coffee. She didn't hear the two men come in and head towards the back office. Disappointed the room was empty, they decided to wait. This thing had to be sorted out now while anger still cursed through their veins. Donning rubber gloves and overalls to protect their clothes not a single word passed between them. They heard Kathy Jones walk back to the shop front and switch on the screens ready for the morning punters. A few minutes later Seth Larkman made his entrance.
"Hi darlin', up for a bit of slap and tickle later?"
Kathy ignored the man but her cheeks still reddened slightly. His crude remark, loud enough for all to hear and aimed directly at Kath made them both want to rush out and punch his lights out. Marty always had a great respect for the opposite sex and to hear that wide boy mouthing off at one of his special friends, saw their rage build to a crescendo.
"I bet you shag like a fuckin' rabbit?"

Now he had gone too far and Kathy didn't care who he was, she wouldn't take any shit and told the gorilla in no uncertain terms.
"I don't have much time for little pricks and if what I've heard is true that's exactly what you've got. Now if you don't mind I've got work to do, so just piss off!"
Hearing her verbally slam into the idiot made Herbie Spires chest swell, she'd done herself and Marty proud. Everything went silent for a few seconds and then much to their surprise the office door handle began to turn. Instantly they pressed their backs to the wall and stood either side of the doorframe. Seth Larkman was inside before he saw them and with his hands on his hips, felt the hairs stand up on the back of his neck. The room appeared empty but he didn't feel alone, taking a further step forward he looked from side to side. Jimmy turning sideways on swiftly stamped at the back of Seth's knees, reducing him to a pile on the floor. The Scouser looked over to his mate and Herbie shrugged his shoulders, as if to say 'He'll have to do if the other ones not around.' Closing the door so that as much sound as possible would be cut out and with the man still stunned from the surprise attack, Jimmy Forbes let the full weight of his body fall onto his victim. His knees hit the man's buttocks with force and Seth's genitals were rammed into the floor. Letting out an

almighty scream, nothing was great enough to muffle the noise and even the sound of the pundits forecasting the day's events, couldn't drown out the terrible high pitched wail.
"Help me get this bag of shit up will you Jim?" Jimmy Forbes stood up and joined by Herbie, hauled Seth Larkman to his feet. Each grabbed a wrist in one hand and pulled back hard while pressing firmly on the man's shoulder blades with the other. Now in a double arm lock, the man was powerless to fight back.
"Right cunt! We've got a few questions that need answering and you're just the person to help us."
Their hold may have been enough to halt Seth's movements and cause great pain but it didn't stop him mouthing off at the top of his voice.
"Fuck off you wanker's! When the boss hears about this you're both fuckin' dead men."
If Seth was under the illusion that Kathy would hear everything and go and get help, he couldn't have been more wrong. Kathy Jones did hear the commotion alright but knew better than to investigate. As if stuck like glue, she remained behind the counter. Realising that it was Seth who was shouting she turned the sound up on the screens, whatever was going on, it wasn't any of her business. It was however, as far as Kath was concerned, a shame that it wasn't Johnny Vale receiving the punishment.

Frog marching Seth over to the desk, he was pushed face down onto it and Jimmy removed a length of rope from the bag he'd brought with him. With Herbie still holding him in an arm lock, there was no way Seth could fight back. The rope was securely tied several times around their victim's legs just like Seth had done to Bernie and when the job was done, he stood up and grabbed a handful of Seth's hair before slamming the man's face into the shiny surface of the desk. On impact, Seth's slightly protruding teeth made contact with the wood. As Jimmy again pulled his head back by his hair Seth's front teeth were left lying on the desk. Blood now flowed freely, filling his mouth and dripping from the bottom of his chin. Surprisingly, though stunned from the assault, he wasn't in fear for his life. Lifting Seth Larkman's head, Jimmy slammed it down for a second time. It was virtually a knock out and Herbie let go of the arm he'd been holding, as its owner had now been rendered helpless. The two men stood on either side and Herbie resumed the questioning.
"Where's Vale?"
No answer. Herbie slapped the man hard around the face.
"Are you deaf cunt, or what?"
Again pushing his victims head onto the desk Jimmy Forbes forced Seth's hands up.

Instructing Herbie to do as he did, Jimmy took hold of Seth Larkman's index finger and bent it backwards until it snapped. Like a game of Simple Simon, Herbie copied his mate to the letter, only he used greater force. The bone at the base of Seth's finger burst through the skin and even Herbie grimaced at the sight. The pain was unimaginable and so severe that as he screamed, vomit erupted from Seth's mouth. Without giving him time to reply to the questions, the act was repeated on his second fingers. The image was surreal; fingers on both hands seemed to dance with the pain and pointed straight up and at right angles, all at the same time. In the shop, Kathy Jones's whole body shook from head to toe. Apart from in the odd horror film, she'd never heard such agonising screams. Kathy wanted to run, to get as far away from this place as possible but she was paralysed with fear. By now Seth knew he wouldn't be leaving the room alive and gasping for air looked in Jimmy's direction.
"You fuckin' cunts, go fuck yourselves!"
With no pity felt for the scumbag writhing in pain right in front of their eyes, they were aware that time was running out for getting any answers. Herbie Spires yanked Seth's head up, so that he had little choice but to look Herbie straight in the eyes.
"Listen wanker! You know it's over, I know it's

over, now we can do this the hard way or the easy way. Personally I couldn't give a flyin' fuck if we slice you up bit by bit and I expect Jimmy here would rather fuckin' enjoy it but no doubt you'd prefer the easy option."
Seth Larkman grimaced in pain as he spoke. "Why do you want the boss?"'
At last they were getting somewhere and Jimmy sighed with relief.
"The cunt hurt big Bernie and we're goin' to make sure he fuckin' has a taste of his own medicine."
For all his pain, Seth was still able to snigger. Resolved to the fact that he was a dead man and much to the boys shock, he revealed the truth. Gaining strength from somewhere, his voice was pure venom as he spoke. Aware that he was now close to death, he still wore the sick look of enjoyment.
"It wasn't Johnny it was me and Al. Do you want to know somethin' else, that fuckin' big lump cried like a baby with every kick we gave him. He cried for his mummy the soppy twat."
Jimmy saw a baseball bat leaning up against the wall in the corner of the room. Marching over and without clearing his action with his pal, he picked it up and swung round with as much strength as he could muster. As the bat made contact with Seth's skull, a loud crack was heard and it sounded like a champagne cork had been

released. The top half of his torso twitched and his throat made a gurgling noise that for a moment had Jimmy Forbes mesmerised. Swiftly he swung the bat four more times in quick succession. It was psychotic and brutal and as Seth Larkman's head slumped forward Herbie was faced with a bloody hole the size of a saucer. Jimmy brought the end of the bat up towards his eyes for inspection. He pulled his face back in distaste when he saw the jelly like, grey matter which coated the wood. Removing their overalls and gloves and not wanting to leave any evidence, they along with the bat were placed inside Jimmy's bag.

Walking through to the front they saw Kathy sitting behind the counter and shaking like a leaf. Although half scared to death she'd had the sense to lock the front door and luckily for them all, no one had tried to get in. In fear of her own life she stared pleadingly at the two men. The sight filled Herbie with guilt but not a guilt regarding Seth Larkman, that was business pure and simple. No this was different, he felt guilty that little Kathy Jones could be frightened of either of them.

"What you looking at us like that for girl? Don't tell me you're scared of us?"'

Kathy shook her head but her fear was apparent for them both to see. Herbie walked over to the counter and as he placed a hand on top, Kathy

nervously pushed her chair back.
"Oh come on Kath! That piece of shit back there had it comin' to him. He was the one along with that other streak of piss, who hurt Bernie."
The colour slowly began to return to her face as she realised that Marty's men had only dished out punishment that had been rightly deserved. Kathy had never been in danger and if she'd seen the men arrive and had given the matter any serious thought, she would have known that.
"For a minute Mr Spires I thought I'd had me lot."
"Don't be silly girl, you're one of us. Now listen, what I'm goin' to ask you to do will take guts and I don't know if you're up to pullin' it off? Stay behind the counter and when that slag Vale gets here act normal. Don't go out the back and when he finds the little present we've left him, say it must have happened before you opened up. Do you think you can manage that?"
Kathy Jones wore a smile so weak, it was hard to tell if she was sneering or happy but she thought that for a few minutes anyway she'd be able to carry it off.
"Don't worry Mr Spires I won't let you down, besides I owe big Bernie this one."
The two men left the building and Kathy Jones turned the volume on the monitors slightly lower. The hands on her watch moved slowly as

she waited for her boss to arrive and when he eventually walked in accompanied by Al Kingston, she nearly jumped out of her skin. Luckily there were already four or five punters in the shop and Johnny Vale didn't notice her emotional state. As he walked through to the office Kathy mentally began to count and had only reached three when she heard him shout out.
"Fuckin' hell! Some cunts goin' to pay for this, Kathy get your scrawny fuckin' arse in here now!"
Swallowing hard she thought that any second her breakfast would be reappearing and did her best to think happy thoughts. As she entered the room and saw the bloody mess that had a short while earlier been giving her verbal grief, she had no choice but to let go of the contents of her stomach.
"For fucks sake you dirty bitch, do you know how much this Wilton cost? Now I've not only got this cunts claret all over it but your fuckin' puke as well."
Kathy Jones couldn't take her eyes off of the grisly sight and had to tightly hold her hand over her mouth to stop more vomit escaping.
"Sorry Mr Vale but look at the state of him?"
"I'm fuckin' well aware of the state the poor cunt's in. Did you see anything?"
Taking a deep breath and with an Oscar winning

performance she turned to face her boss.
"I swear I didn't. I came in like normal, made a cuppa, switched on the screens and went behind the counter to wait for the first customers. I didn't venture in here, had no reason to."
He studied her face to what Kathy seemed like forever but finally he nodded giving her the ok to leave the room. Making her way to the ladies, she wretched until she felt the only thing left to come up was the lining of her stomach. Eventually she composed herself and staring into the mirror she grinned. Licking one finger she slowly drew it down the cold surface, it was one up to the boys. Once more behind the counter, Kathy started to shake again when the intercom began to flash. Knowing she had no choice but to answer, she pressed the red button.
"Yes boss?"
"I want you to shut the shop and get off home; I'll be in contact when we're reopening. Until then, treat it as a little unpaid holiday."
The shop was now empty of punters so after switching the screens and computers off, Kathy fetched her bag and coat, locked the front door behind her and began to make her way home. On first sight of the grisly mess in the office, she'd known this was coming but had thought at least he'd pay her. Not in a position or daring to argue, she shrugged her shoulders and continued walking.

Back in the office, Johnny Vale picked up the telephone and dialled. After several rings it was finally answered and Johnny informed the man on the other end, that a consignment of meat was ready for collection. Over the years Harry Cunningham had been employed on a regular basis by most of the firms in London. A pig farmer, he was the perfect disposal man for anyone who had been rendered surplus to requirements. A portly man who resided in Norfolk, Harry was the soul of discretion. His dress was eccentric to say the least and brought smirks from all who came into contact with him. A checked shirt was always open to the waist no matter what the weather. Long shorts were held up with garish brasses and Wellington boots and a deer stalker hat completed the outfit. Harry was always accompanied by his son and daughter in-law. Henry and Martha eerily bore more than a striking resemblance to each other and it was widely accepted the pair were brother and sister as well as lovers. The idea sickened most bosses but it hadn't stopped them calling on the man when needed. Now it was Johnny's turn and within two hours the odd looking people pulled their wagon into the rear yard. As Kathy Jones had been sent home for the day, it was Al Kingston who had let them in via the back door. Entering the office, Harry walked straight over to Seth's remains.

"Nice big lump a meat Mr Vale."
Al Kingston was disgusted. If it had been anyone but Seth he wouldn't have minded but knowing his partner was going to end up as pig fodder or worse, well it just wasn't right. Harry Cunningham noticed the sickened look.
"Got na stomach for it boooooy?"
"It's fuckin' disgustin' what you're doin'."
"Ain't never had long pork boooooy? Best meat yell ever taste! Booooootiful yow mark my wurds."
Al suddenly felt sick and strode past the bloody scene to get some air. Harry held out his hand and Johnny Vale placed a large brown envelope into it.
"Henry, Martha do yow busness."
The grossly overweight couple hauled Seth's carcass up and after a few heaves; Henry had it over his shoulder in a fireman's lift. Seconds later and they passed Al who followed them outside to the back yard and watched as they dumped the body of his pal into the back of the van. Returning to join his boss, the only evidence that his partner had ever existed was a few blood stains and a splattering of brain tissue on the desk.
On the drive back to Stepney, Herbie and Jimmy Forbes hadn't mentioned what had gone down. Not until they were safely in Jimmy's terraced house did the discussion continue.

With Marlene sent out on a shopping spree and the coast now clear they began to talk.
"Now what Jim?"
Jimmy Forbes stood beside the fireplace and nervously pushed his fingers through his hair.
"Fuckin' hell Herb! Why is it me who always has to come up with the answers?"
Suddenly Herbie felt more than a little small, not to mention embarrassed at his friends choice of words.
"I didn't mean anything mate, it's just that you always seem to know what to do."
"Well I need time to think!"
Sipping tea like two old women the time seemed to drag until the front door latch was heard and Marlene much to Jimmy's annoyance reappeared.
"Sorry babe, ran out of reddies?"
"Fuck me Mar, I gave you three hundred nicker! You can't have spent it fuckin' already?"
Rolling her eyes in Herbie's direction she tutted.
"This one's still living in the sixties. He thinks I can get a new dress for a fiver! Well I suppose I could if he wants me to dress in that tat from the market."
Jimmy didn't say another word and after fishing deep in his pocket pulled out a wedge of cash and peeled off several fifties. The dark skinned beauty didn't say anything, not even a thank you as she snatched the notes from Jimmy's

hand and flounced out of the room. Several seconds later after they heard the front door slam, Herbie inwardly thought to himself how much his old mukka had mellowed. There was a time when the cheeky mare would have got nothing more than a back hander. Even Marge had more manners than this leery cow and she could be a right gold digger if the fancy took her. As if sensing his guest's silent disapproval, Jimmy Forbes began to make excuses but even he knew that there really weren't any worth mentioning.
"She's a bitch Herb but she does something to me and I can't deny her anything. Maybe it's me age or maybe I've finally fallen in love I don't know."
Herbie Spires gave a polite smile but he really wanted to tell his mate not to be so soppy and give the bitch a slap. That would surely put her in her place and stop the Scouser looking a complete idiot.
"It's your life mate and not for me to tell you what to do. As long as she makes you happy?"
"Oh she does that. She cooks like a bleedin' chef and she's the best fuck I've ever had. I'm even in two minds whether to put her on the streets or keep her to myself."
"That serious hey? Are we talking weddin' bells here?"
Jimmy Forbes gave his pal a look of complete

contempt as the words reached his ears.
"Fuckin' weddin'! What sort of a daft cunt do you take me for?"
The two men couldn't stop laughing and it was only the telephone bursting into life that lessened the merriment. Jimmy picked up the handset.
"Yeh?"
Suddenly his face took on a solemn mask and Herbie's own laughter stopped dead in its tracks.
"What did you say, someone's done what?"
As soon as Herbie Spires heard the words, another onslaught of laughter began and he had to place a hand tightly over his mouth. Even this wasn't enough to dampen his euphoria and he ended up walking out of the room. After what seemed like a life time Jimmy finally opened the front room door and beckoned for his friend to enter.
"Sorry about that Jim, I couldn't fuckin' contain myself."
"Glad to hear it you bastard! I'm the prick who had to act all shocked, not you."
"Point taken Pal, now what did he want? I'm guessing it was Vale on the other end?"
"'Course it was. He wants us both down at Bethnal later today, can you handle that?"
"Don't be daft but did he mention Kath?"
"He did as it happens. She must have played a

blinder 'cause he took what she said hook line and sinker. Daft cunt ain't got a clue who done it and even if that wanker weren't our original target, it worked like magic."

The friends enjoyed another pot of tea before Herbie left the house. On his way out he passed Marlene laden down with designer carrier bags and he grinned. She took offence at his expression but knew better than to voice an opinion. If only she realised that her days as number one babe were fast running out and that pretty soon she'd be just another hooker with fond memories of high living to look back on. Jimmy Forbes was always falling in love and falling out even quicker. Marty McCann had over the years found Jimmy's love life highly amusing and now Herbie was doing the same.

CHAPTER THIRTEEN

Flo McCann had been awake since first light and after lying in bed for over an hour and with no sign of Angela stirring, she decided to get up. Quietly making her way to the kitchen she pushed the button on the electric kettle. Her usual preference was the whistling one Marty had given her years ago but she didn't want to risk the noise waking her granddaughter. The sun shone brightly through the kitchen window and Flo thought how this should have been one of the happiest times of her life. It wasn't, the pain of losing her son was still too raw and learning of her granddaughter's existence had been a shock to say the least. Instead of what should have been a happy family reunion, she couldn't help but worry over what the future had in store for Angela and herself come to that. After the third pot of tea had been drunk dry she decided to go and get dressed. Edna Burrows normally called round but Flo hoped today would be the day she had something else on and wouldn't come. About to enter the bathroom Flo let out an annoying sigh at the sound of someone knocking on the front door. Edna wasn't the type of person to be kept waiting and not wanting another round of tat tat tatting that would surely wake Angela, Flo Mitchell almost

ran to answer the door. Opening it just wide enough to see who was calling but already knowing without looking that it was her so called friend, Flo sighed. Edna pushed hard on the woodwork with her shoulder.
"Come on Flo get the door open, it's bloody freezing out here on this landing."
"I'm sorry Edna but I can't have any visitors today, my granddaughters still a kip and I don't want to wake her."
Edna Burrows wasn't used to being refused anything least of all from the likes of Flo McCann. Standing in the cold corridor made her think how much the silly little woman was starting to get up her nose.
"What you on about you daft old mare? You ain't got any grand kids!"
It was now Flo's turn to take the high and mighty stance and it was something she was going to enjoy, even if it was only for a short while.
"Edna just because I've never told you about her doesn't mean she don't exist. Now if you will excuse me."
Closing the door, Flo leaned against the white paint work and chuckled to herself as she imagined the woman's flabbergasted expression on the other side. Staying put until she heard her walk away, Flo giggled as Edna muttered under her breath 'I don't fuckin' believe it, well if

she thinks I'm coming round here again she's fuckin' mistaken'. The words were like music to Flo's ears, she'd finally gotten rid of the old busy body. Friends were hard to come by and several years ago that would have been the term Flo used to describe the woman. Always aware that Edna Burrows was a medal winning gossip, she had still warmed to her but just lately Edna had developed a nasty envious streak and Flo didn't like it. Months of making allowances and putting it down to her age was now wearing thin and Flo McCann was glad to finally be rid of the woman, if only for a few days. Feeling as light as a feather, she floated down the hallway and into the bathroom, humming an old dance tune as she went. Angela Canning Brown slept well and finally woke around ten. Walking into the kitchen still half asleep she made her way over to the table where Flo was sitting. The image made her think of home and how similar her two families were. Oh the Canning Brown household was much grander and their kitchen table was antique scrubbed pine not cheap seventies formica like this one but it was still the same. In both families everyone congregated in the kitchen to talk and somehow the vision in this kitchen made her feel as though she belonged. Bending down she kissed her grandmothers forehead.

"Morning Nan, sleep well?"

"No not really, you?"
"Like a log, any tea going?"
Flo poured the girl a large mug of the steaming hot liquid, then made her way over to the cooker. Removing a large pan from the top of the eye level grill she started to fry up a breakfast of eggs and bacon.
"God that smells good, I'm absolutely famished."
Flo McCann laughed out loud and Angela's inquisitive look made her reply to a question that hadn't even been asked.
"Your old dad was just the same. He'd come round here three or four times a week for breakfast, only his words weren't so posh. Instead of famished he was fuckin' starving."
Angela smiled but it was quickly replaced with sadness, every single time her grandmother mentioned her father she felt more and more robbed of a life that she'd never been given the chance to know. Flo McCann could eat along with the best and after finishing off two eggs, four rashers and two rounds of bread and butter she stared at Angela.
"Well?"
"Well what Nan?"
"Have you given it anymore thought, you know what you was on about last night?"
Pushing her plate towards the centre of the table, Angela knew what was coming and she really didn't feel like an argument so soon after getting

up.
"I haven't changed my mind if that's what you mean but it's too early to talk about such things. Can we just leave it until later, when I'm fully awake and ready for this?"
Accepting she'd lost this round but not the fight, Flo McCann got up and leaving her granddaughter sitting at the table walked out of the kitchen. Alone in the small front room she dialled Herbie's number.
Running late Marge Spires was about to set out for one of her many dog shows. After laying awake most of the night she'd finally managed to convince herself that she'd win this time. Closing the front door she vaguely heard the ivory candlestick telephone burst into life and glancing at her designer watch decided to ignore the interruption. Seconds later she'd thought better of it, after all maybe it was Herbie and it wouldn't due to ignore him. She raced back inside and snatched up the receiver.
"Hello."
"Is that Mrs Spires?"
"Yes but I'm in a dreadful hurry so if you don't mind, whatever you're selling I'm not interested."
Flo took more than a little offence at the woman's tone.
"Listen you jumped up trollop! I'm Marty McCann's mum so you can just show a bit of

fuckin' respect, do you hear?"
Marjorie Spires face turned red with embarrassment, not to mention the fact she was worried. As far as Herbie was concerned the McCann's were gods and if he found out about this, well he'd skin her alive. Normally the house was run by her rules, unless it interfered with her husband's work. Herbie could be hard even with her, if she ever attempted to get in the way of his precious other family.
"I'm so sorry Mrs McCann you know how it is when you're rushing about. How can I help you?"
Flo now felt like top dog and took on the tone of being in charge.
"You can't, it's the organ grinder I want not the fuckin' monkey. Do you know where he is?"
"Herbie's out with the Scouser, I mean Jimmy Forbes."
With that Flo slammed the receiver down and searched through her imitation leather directory for Jimmy's number. Knowing that any minute Angela would come in to find out where she'd got to, Flo dialled as quickly as she could. Luckily the telephone only rang twice before it was answered.
"Hello."
"Is that Jimmy?"
"Yeh, who wants to know?"
"Its Marty's mum and I need to speak to Herbie

as soon as possible."
"Hello Mrs McCann how you keepin'?"
"Jimmy I don't mean to be rude love but I have to speak to Herbie now!"
Sensing the urgency in her voice, he lay down the receiver and ran into the hall. Flinging open the front door he knocked Marlene and her designer bags onto the floor.
"Sorry babe!"
Marlene's hair was a dishevelled mess and he helped her up from the floor then raced out into the street. He was just in the nick of time to catch his pal as he pulled away. Jimmy Forbes banged loudly onto the passenger side glass with such force that Herbie nearly jumped out of his skin. Unclipping his seat belt and with the engine still running, Herbie got out and slammed his hand on the cars roof.
"You daft cunt whatever's the matter? You nearly gave me a fuckin' heart attack!"
"Marty's mums on the blower and she sounds kind of upset."
Without another word, Herbie ran back into the house and again Marlene's bags were shot all over the floor just as she'd finished picking them up but this time there were no apologies. Rushing into the front room he lifted the handset to his ear.
"Mrs M?"
"Thank god Herb. I need to see you and the

Scouser as soon as possible."
Flo could have told this to Jimmy but for some reason she had always been closer to Herbie, maybe deep down she trusted him more.
"Sure darlin'. When and where?"
"Not at mine that's for sure. Shall we say the Flyin' Pig in half an hour?"
"Fine by me. See you there Mrs M."
With that Herbie hung up the phone and was still wearing a troubled look on his face as the Scouser walked in. Relaying the conversation still didn't make things any clearer and for the life of him Herbie couldn't think what could be so urgent and not possible to talk about at the woman's flat. Pulling on her faithful old Mac, Flo told Angela she was just popping out for a few bits and pieces and she'd be back within the hour.
"If you wait for me to get dressed Nan, I'll come with you."
Immediately Flo panicked but she quickly got out of the sticky situation.
"Sweetheart you stay indoors and rest. Why not go back to bed for a while, it'll do you more good than traipsing round the shops with me."
"Maybe you're right, I am still awfully tired."
As Angela walked into the bedroom, Flo McCann slipped outside and began the fifteen minute walk over to the Flying Pig.
With the traffic now subsiding, Herbie and the

Scouser made it to their destination before Flo. Charlie Edwards sat alone in the back kitchen reminiscing, a practice which had now become a daily part of his life. So much so, that he often slipped off into his own private dream world while serving. Ringing the doorbell several times brought no answer and Jimmy Forbes slammed his fist onto the peeling paintwork. Not used to being kept waiting, the men started to get agitated and none more so than the Scouser.
"Alright alright I'm coming!"
Charlie slowly made his way through to the bar area and began to unbolt the heavy doors. On seeing who his early visitors were, he began to shake.
"Sorry lads didn't know who it was. What can I do for you?"
The two men didn't wait to be invited in and barged passed Charlie Edwards almost knocking him over in the process.
"We need to hold a little meetin' here this lunchtime, is that goin' to cause you any agro."
"No not at all Mr Spires. What times Mr Vale arriving only he….."
Without allowing the landlord to finish his words, Jimmy pushed him up against the jukebox.
"He's not goin' to be here and you're not goin' to fuckin' let on that we were here either!"

"No of course not, if you're havin' a private meet that's none of my business. I'll be out the back if you need anythin', otherwise I ain't seen nothin' and this place will stay closed till I'm told any different."

"Before you go Charlie do us a favour, get us two pints and a cuppa oh and you'd better add a brandy to that list."

Charlie Edwards gave a nervous wink as he turned towards the bar. He poured the drinks and boiled the kettle as asked but once he'd served the men he did a hasty retreat to the back kitchen. Whatever was happening, you could guarantee it wasn't good and he didn't want any part of it. Herbie and Jimmy took a seat in the booth next to the main doors and began the wait for Flo McCann. Five minutes later and like a whirling dervish she made her entrance. Herbie Spires immediately stood up and went to embrace the small woman but Flo pushed his arm away. The topic to be discussed was too important to waste precious time on pleasantries. Waving her hand in a frustrated fashion she beckoned for them to sit down.

"By the time I've finished you'll both need one of these."

Tilting her head back she downed the brandy in one and enjoyed the warm feeling it gave to the back of her throat.

"I've got a surprise house guest, any guesses as

to who I'm talkin' about?"
Jimmy stared at her blankly but deep down Herbie knew what she was talking about and was the first to speak.
"Marty's girls turned up ain't she?"
Flo looked surprised but only nodded, that was until Jimmy clapped his hands together and Herbie smiled from ear to ear. The sight of the two, who appeared so happy while Flo herself was worried sick, made her react in a hostile manner and their euphoria was short lived.
"Listen you pair of tosser's there's nothing good about this. The daft little mare only wants to step in where her dad left off."
The old woman's words were like music to their ears and Flo couldn't believe the look of sheer happiness on both of their faces.
"I know you both hate Vale almost as much as I do but that's no reason to sacrifice my only granddaughter and believe me that's what you would be doing. Johnny Vale would eat her up and spit her out for breakfast but do you think I can get that through her posh little head."
Jimmy could see Flo's point but he also knew that without the girl, Johnny would probably stay in power for years to come. That was unless he or Herbie wanted the job and that was a definite no no. Slipping off her coat, Flo went behind the bar and filled a glass with a couple more shots of brandy before joining the men

back at the table.
"So what have you come to us for Mrs M?"
"Angela thinks that with the help of her dads trusted crew, she can somehow topple Vale and be queen of the east end. She had a life of living like a princess and I honestly think she sees herself as some kind of female gangster. Well she ain't livin' in the fuckin' real world I can tell you. I thought if you took her up west to Marty's clubs and showed her how it really is, then maybe she'd change her mind."
Herbie was about to protest when Jimmy stopped him.
"If that's what you want Mrs M then that's what we'll do. Tell the girlie we'll pick her up about eight, alright?"
"That's fine Jimmy but don't call her a girlie. Her names Angela and she's got the temper of her father and no mistake."
After draining the dregs of her brandy and pushing the cup of tea to one side, Flo McCann put on her old Mac and kissed each man in turn before walking out of the flying Pig. No sooner had the door closed when Herbie turned on Jimmy. The aggressive manner in which he spoke was seldom used towards his friend and for a moment Jimmy was taken aback.
"What the fuck did you tell her that for? We owe it to Marty to make sure his girl is safe not put her in danger even if it is to get rid of that fuckin'

slag Vale."

Jimmy Forbes sucked in a large mouthful of air and shook his head in annoyance.

"Twat! For once why don't you just trust me? You're always on at me to make the decisions and when I do you fuckin' moan at me you cunt! Of course I want Marty's sprogg to take over and be safe into the bargain but that ain't what Mrs M wanted to hear. We'll take the girl out and try and talk her out of it but if she's anything like her old man we ain't got a prayer. We'll be able to see if she's got what it's goin' to take and at least we can tell the old lady we tried. Hey presto, everyone's happy."

Herbie knew that his pal was right and as much as it pained him he had to agree that the only way to topple Vale was to use Marty's daughter.

"Sorry Jim I know you're right but I can't help thinkin' about Marty."

"Apology accepted and me and you are goin' to do our best to keep the little girl out of harm's way."

After shouting to Charlie Edwards that they were now off and receiving no reply, the two left the pub and went their separate ways. Charlie Edwards never did tell a soul that the pair had been at his place that day; in fact he never even heard them leave. After spending so many of his days lost in the world of yesteryear, he'd finally gotten to live the dream. Sitting alone in

the dank sad kitchen, a massive heart attack had at last reunited him with his beloved Betty. Outside Herbie got into the Jag and drove to Bow, while Jimmy Forbes wanted to walk and clear his head ready for tonight. It had just begun to drizzle with rain and Jimmy always loved being out side when the weather was wet. Somehow it reminded him of being back home and the vague memories he still held onto of Liverpool. He hadn't gone more than two hundred yards when his mobile began to vibrate in his pocket. Annoyed at having his relaxation disturbed, he snapped open the flip and shouted into the small receiver.
"Yeh?"
"Jimmy its Myrtle. Lanky Lorraine and small Susan have been at it again, it's been like fuckin' world war three down here."
Jimmy was really pissed off, he'd had more stress in the last few days than he'd had in years and now his whores were kicking off.
"Fuck me don't I ever get any peace from those bitches! Tell 'em to get off the street now and I'll be down to sort it out later tonight."
"Jimmy I don't think it can wait till then, they're really fuckin' gunning for each other."
"Well that's fuckin' tough; I've got too much other stuff to deal with right now."
Without a goodbye he snapped the phone shut and resumed his walk but it was too late, he was

no longer in the mood and instead of enjoying the rain he now felt wet and cold. Hailing the first black cab he saw, Jimmy Forbes told the driver to take him to Stepney and not to take the piss by going the long route.

CHAPTER FOURTEEN

Joanna Canning Brown had waited patiently for her daughter to get in contact with her or anyone else at the house. After four days her patience with Angela was quickly running out, not to mention the fact that all sorts of worse case scenarios were beginning to run through her mind. Sleep had been in short supply and as she entered the kitchen her father's worried expression told her all she needed to know about her appearance. Pouring a coffee from the percolator, Joanna sat next to him and laid her head on his shoulder.
"Oh daddy whatever are we going to do? I haven't got a clue where she is or even where to start looking."
"Darling have you contacted her friends?"'
Elizabeth Canning Browns words were a red rag to a bull and Joanna couldn't help but raise her voice.
"Don't ask such stupid questions mother, of course I have."
Biting her lip, she knew the terse manner in which she'd just spoken to her mother had hurt the woman deeply and now she felt as guilty as sin. Walking round to the other side of the table she sat down beside Elizabeth and placed her arms around the woman.

"I'm sorry mother I didn't mean to snap, it's just that I'm so terribly worried."

Julian Canning Brown with all his power and friends in high places was as lost as the two women sitting with him at the table. On the second day of Angela's disappearance he'd contacted the local chief of police to ask for help. Over a lengthy game of golf he was told that there really wasn't much they could do. Angela was of age and if she didn't want to be found or come home no one could make her. Knowing this already hadn't helped but he'd thought that his standing in society could have pulled a few strings. It now seemed that retired judges didn't have the clout they once had. After a demoralising loss on the golf course, Julian made his way over to the Dellingwood's to see if Edward could shed any light on the situation. It had been past two in the afternoon but Edward was still in bed and had to be forced to get up by his mother. Alone in the sitting room, the two men sat opposite each other in silence. Julian studied the young man and for the life of him couldn't see what they'd all got so excited about. Standing over six feet tall and as thin as a rake, Edward Dellingwood had somewhat of a gormless look about him. Edward himself couldn't stand old man Canning Brown but had never voiced an opinion for Angela's sake. Now that they were no longer an item he didn't fell like being so generous.

"So Mr Canning Brown to what do I owe this little visit?"

The question came out sarcastically just as it had been intended and it shocked Julian. It wasn't the boy's rudeness but the fact that he had some balls after all.

"I'm aware you and my granddaughter had a falling out and....."

"Falling out! That's an understatement. Angela dumped me once and for all and if you've come here to try and smooth things over, you can forget it!"

"On the contrary Edward. I never thought the two of you were suited in the first place but I wanted it to be Angela's decision to end it and not her mother or grandparents."

Edward was shocked at the man's frankness but it wasn't an earth shattering revelation or something he didn't already know.

"Fair enough! So why are you here then?"

"Angela went missing two days ago and before you start panicking, it's nothing sinister. No doubt she needed to get away to think. It's just that no one knows where she is and I wondered if you had any ideas."

"And if I have, what makes you think I'd tell you after the way I've been treated?"

"Because her mother is at her wits end, because she has always treated you with the utmost

respect and at the end of the day doesn't deserve to be hurt in such a way."
Edward Dellingwood mulled over the man's words for a few seconds and came to the conclusion that what little he did know shouldn't be kept secret.
"I haven't a clue where she is but she did speak about finding her other family. I can only assume she's headed to London, if that's any help."
Julian left the Dellingwood's home shortly after. On the morning Joanna discovered her daughter was missing the notion that Angela may seek out her other grandmother had fleetingly entered his mind but had been dismissed just as quickly. Now he knew he shouldn't have been so hasty but what on earth could she want with those people. After all they were common and not the sort she was used to mixing with. It didn't enter his head that she didn't care about their background, only the fact that they were her family. Now as his wife and daughter sat cuddling on the kitchen seat, the conversation he'd had with Edward resurfaced in his mind and Julian knew he would have to reveal all.
"Darling I've something to tell you and I don't think it will make you happy in the slightest."
Both women looked up but it was Joanna's eyes that her father looked into.
"Whatever is it Daddy? Please I beg you, don't

Keep anything from me. Is she alright? Has she been hurt?"
"It's nothing like that. I went to see Edward a couple of days ago."
Julian continued to reveal all that his now defunct future grandson in law had said. After he'd finished, he waited for the anger to erupt from his daughter but nothing came. Joanna had tears in her eyes but that was the only response she gave. Sliding off the bench she left the kitchen and made her way upstairs. Waiting for their daughter to reappear, neither Julian nor his wife had anything to say to each other. Julian knew that for all these years it had been Joanna and Angela who had kept the family alive and without them this huge house would be like a mausoleum. Elizabeth realised how far she'd drifted away from her daughter, although if Joanna herself had been asked she would have said they were never close. After Angela's birth she had promised the tiny infant that theirs would be a different sort of relationship and one that was full of love if nothing else. Like so many human beings before her, as time passed the idea of a life seen through rose tinted glasses soon began to fade. Joanna behaved the same towards her daughter as Elizabeth had to her and by the time the child had started school their mother daughter bond had reached an all time low. As a child Angela had disobeyed anything

Joanna asked her to do and the only person who had ever been able to get her to toe the line, was her grandfather. For the first time ever he wasn't able to resolve the situation and Joanna decided it was time to take charge herself. Doing what she should have done years ago, Joanna packed a small bag, grabbed her Burberry raincoat and swiftly descended the staircase. Her thundering footsteps brought both her parents rushing out of the kitchen. As soon as he saw the bag, realisation hit Julian that he could now possibly lose his daughter as well as his granddaughter.

"Joanna! It's no good chasing after her. For a start you haven't got a clue where to begin looking."

"Yes I have daddy. I still have Marty's address and I remember him saying that east end families never moved far away from the nest. Not so different to us really are they?"

Her father wore a hurt and confused look but it did nothing to quell the flames of his daughter's already roaring fire. Nothing and no one would stop her finding Angela and after bending down to kiss her mother; Joanna fled the house and drove like a maniac to Canterbury east station. The next train to London was due to leave in just under the hour so she took a seat in the cold waiting room and ran through everything again in her mind. At certain times through her

mental journey she would smile and then frown, which brought stares from the other passengers but for once Joanna didn't care what anyone else thought of her. For once the only thing she was interested in was finding her beautiful girl. At last and with a numb backside, she got up from the hard wooden bench and boarded the one thirty seven train to the capital. Opting for a seat as far away from the other passengers as possible, Joanna was lost in thought for the whole of the journey. It wasn't until the train had pulled into Victoria and had been standing in the station for several seconds with most of her fellow passengers disembarked, that Joanna Canning Brown was jolted back to reality. Unlikely as it may seem, her journey down memory lane had been a pleasant experience. If only for a shot while she was back in Bluebell wood in Marty's arms and as much as she needed to get back on track for the task in hand, a small part of her wished it didn't have to end. The taxi rank was full and Joanna walked to the far end and opened the door of the last black hackney.
"Where to love?"
"Bethnal Green."
"That's my manor darlin', what part you goin' to?"'
"Cleveland Way."
"Lovely day for it!"

Joanna didn't feel like small talk, she just wanted this all to be over.

"Do you mind if we don't chat, only I have a dreadful headache?"

"Not at all sweetheart. You just sit back and enjoy the ride, with the traffic like it is I figure we've got a half hour ride ahead of us."

True to his word the journey took thirty minutes. Joanna didn't know if it was down to the many cars that filled the never ending streets or just that he was trying to make a few extra pounds and had taken the long route. Either way she didn't care. Pulling up outside the small block of flats, the cabbie turned and stared at her through the partially open glass panel.

"Here we are princes, that'll be twenty five nicker."

Unbeknown to him, Joanna could have closed her eyes and listened to the man talk all day. Every word he spoke sounded just like Marty had in the days when nothing more mattered than just being together. Paying her fare she stepped from the taxi and after slamming the door, gazed up at the building in front of her. Like her daughter before her Joanna was now a bundle of nerves but unlike her daughter, the idea of turning round and going home never entered her head. Climbing the stairs she knocked on the door and prayed that someone from the McCann family still lived there or at

least the occupier would know where the family now resided. Twenty four hours had passed since Flo first set eyes on Angela. Enough time for them to start to get acquainted and for her to prepare and share a couple of meals with her only grandchild. Angela had decided to go out for a walk and get to know the area, while Flo took her usual afternoon nap in the fireside chair. The knock at the door didn't alarm the old woman, she thought Angela had forgotten her key and slowly made her way down the hallway. For the second time she forgot to look through the spy hole and just opened the door. Seeing Joanna and not having the faintest idea who she was, Flo McCann mentally reprimanded herself for not being more careful and putting on the chain.
"Mrs McCann?"
Flo eyed the woman suspiciously, noting immediately that her fine clothes meant she wasn't from this manor.
'Who wants to know?'
Joanna smiled, the woman was just as Marty had described her all those years ago and she suddenly felt a warm feeling inside. Not knowing if it was because she now stood face to face with Angela's grandmother or maybe it was because this frail little woman could have, should have been her mother in law. Either way she laughed out loud which took Flo by surprise.

"What's so fuckin' funny?"
Joanna suddenly became embarrassed and composed herself as quickly as she could manage.
"I'm so sorry; please do forgive my bad manners. I'm trying to find my daughter Angela and I wondered if you may be able to help me?"
For a minute Flo thought about telling the stuck up bitch to piss off and never darken her doorstep again but being a mother herself or at least she was once, she had empathy for the pain that she could only imagine the woman was in, even if it was well hidden.
"I suppose you'd better come in then."
Joanna did as she was asked and on entering the tiny flat noticed how clean and house proud the woman was. The sight before her brought back the last conversation she'd had with Marty.
"Marty I love you too but we're from different worlds. I don't think that after the luxury I've been given all my life, well I know, I couldn't live in your world."
"You mean you're putting cash before us? You're prepared to leave me all for the sake of a few quid?"
God she now felt so angry with herself to think that she'd put money and possessions before the love of her life and the father of her child. This place wasn't Buckingham palace but it wouldn't have been destitution either. What a stupid fool

she was, never to have taken the opportunity to find out, never to have given herself the chance of happiness. Flo McCann's words brought Joanna back down to earth with a bump.
"So what's made you turn up here after all these fuckin' years?"
Joanna hadn't ever been spoken to in this way and for a minute didn't know what to say. As soon as the shock passed, she was firing on both cylinders and she retaliated with all that she had.
"There's no need to take that tone with me Mrs McCann! No matter what you think of me I am still Angela's mother and I love her with all my heart, contrary to what she may have told you!"
"Don't fuckin' flatter yourself; the girl ain't even mentioned you. I don't know if that's a good thing or not. Do you want a cuppa?"
Joanna nodded and followed this lion of a woman through to the small kitchen. Sitting at opposite ends of the table and with each of the women trying to weigh up the other, the atmosphere could have been cut with a knife. It was Flo who broke the ice and spoke first.
"Tell me about my boy back then, did you love him?"
Joanna started to talk and as she did so the years rolled back. By the time she had finished Flo McCann had tears in her eyes.
"So it wasn't just a quick fumble, you really did

love each other?"

"He was the love of my life Mrs McCann. Since Angela came along I have never looked at another man. If we had been older who knows but at that age we were both easily lead, maybe me more than him."

Flo was about to add her five penneth when Angela could be heard calling from the front hall.

"Nan I'm home!"

The happy go lucky manner in which her daughter called out cut Joanna to the bone and the fact that she referred to this place as home, was more than she could bear. Angela's expression on seeing Joanna was a mixture of anger and happiness jumbled together. In the short time she'd been away she had missed the old dragon as she often referred to her mother. Making her way over to the table, Angela stood behind her grandmother and rested her hands on the old woman's shoulders.

"I'm not coming home. If that's the reason you're here then I'm afraid you've had a wasted journey mother!"

"Angela the only reason I'm here is to make sure you are alright. Your grandmother and Pops are at their wits end; didn't you think all this would upset them?"

"For goodness sake mother I'm not a baby; I'm twenty five years old!"

"I'm well aware of how old you are, don't forget it was me who gave birth to you."
Suddenly Flo halted the cat fight and asked both her guests if they'd like a cup of tea. It always broke the ice and gave everyone something else to think about for a second. Turning to face her granddaughter, Flo asked if she'd had a good walk then proceeded to inform the girl that she was going out that evening.
"You remember what we talked about last night and you said about your dads best friends?"
"Yes."
"Well they're collectin' you at eight so you'd better start getting ready. I'm sure me and your mums got lots to talk about and you can catch up with her tomorrow."
With a swift turn of her neck, she addressed Joanna in a snappy tone.
"That's if you're staying?"
Flo's expression was cold and hard as she stared directly into the woman's eyes, forcing Joanna to turn away. Flo knew there and then that she could win any battle she came up against with this one.
"That would be most hospitable Mrs McCann, thank you very much."
"Don't go gettin' excited as it'll only be a blanket and pillow on the couch."
Inwardly Angela smiled; her Nan really was a sly old character. Excusing herself she ran a bath

and after picking out the little black cocktail number that she'd thankfully thought to pack, she reappeared in the small front room. Joanna was concentrating on writing a letter of explanation to her parents and Flo, glasses perched on the tip of her nose, was studying the racing post. In unison they glanced up together as Angela entered the room and Flo couldn't believe her eyes. The young hippie like thing that had turned up on her doorstep a little more than twenty four hours ago, was now a vision of sheer loveliness. Joanna was in agreement, thinking her daughter appeared more beautiful tonight than ever before.
"So Angela what's the occasion?"
Angela Canning Brown didn't know how to reply to the question. Not wanting her mother to go ballistic when she found out what she'd got planned, Angela's eyes pleaded with Flo for help. The old woman instantly recognised the request and turned to Joanna.
"She's having dinner with a couple of her dad's old mates but I'll fill you in on all the details later when we're on our own."
Normally this wouldn't have been enough to satisfy Joanna but being in someone else's home, she didn't want to cause a scene. Flo was aware that her reply had halted a family argument occurring but for how long she didn't know. Hoping that Herbie Spires wouldn't be much

longer she decided to concentrate on keeping the atmosphere light.

"If only your dad could see you now, he'd be so proud."

"Oh don't Nan, you'll make me cry and then my mascara will run. Too late I can feel it's already happened; now I'll have to start all over again and believe me this look wasn't easy to achieve." All three women laughed and Flo silently wished that Marty was here. Closing her eyes she prayed he was looking down on them. Right at this moment Flo McCann would have willingly given her life to trade places with her boy.

CHAPTER FIFTEEN

Herbie came down the stairs dressed to the nines. He hadn't worn his Saville row suit since Marty's funeral and the memory didn't go unnoticed. His designer shirt and tie was topped off with a diamond encrusted tie pin baring the initials HS. It had been a Christmas present from Marty two years ago and was now his most treasured possession. Making his way into the elegant drawing room, Herbie found Marge seated on the fine antique sofa, surrounded by her three babies. Nuzzling the youngest to her neck, she eyed Herbie up and down as she spoke in a babyish manner.
"Aw look bwabeeees, dwaddy's all dwessed up."
Whenever Marge talked like this it pissed Herbie off big time and what with everything else going on, his patience was fast running out.
"For fucks sake Marjorie! They ain't got a fuckin' clue what you're on about and I ain't their dwaddy!"
Just as she'd known it would, the hurt expression she wore made him feel guilty and ashamed of himself for being so sharp with her.
"Now don't go getting' all upset."
Placing a tiny puppy on the silk cushion beside her, Marge Spires held out her arms for a hug. It was a closeness that her husband constantly

craved and she knew he couldn't refuse.
"Don't be late Herbie; I get lonely here all by myself."
"I'll try sweets but its business and you know how it can sometimes run on. I wouldn't go but this one's important and......."
Tenderly kissing his cheek Marge whispered in his ear and he smiled. The thought of returning to a warm bed and a willing wife almost made him cancel tonight. Sex was always on Herbie Spires mind but seldom on his wife's. He realised she was angling for something and prayed it wasn't a fourth puppy. With sleep still filling his eyes, standing in puddles of piss first thing in the morning was something he hated. He was sure the little bastards did it on purpose just to annoy him. Straightening his tie and smoothing the wrinkles from his jacket, Herbie waved goodbye and walked from the house checking his watch. As usual it would be him who had to collect the Scouser, before making their way to Mrs M's flat and the meet with Marty's offspring.
Over in Stepney Jimmy was also decked out in his finest, including a diamond encrusted tie pin bearing the initials JF. Marty McCann always tended to buy in bulk but with each setting him back over three grand, his two old mates hadn't minded receiving similar gifts. Pouring himself a stiff scotch, Jimmy glanced at his watch and

knew Herbie wouldn't be here for at least another half hour. He was about to switch on the telly and listen to the day's news when Marlene made an entrance. Dressed in a sexy little number that Jimmy had paid for that very day, she draped her slender dark skinned arms around his neck.
"Take me out tonight Jim!"
"Sorry babe I can't."
"Please!!!! Baby."
His refusal of her request was unusual and something she wasn't used to hearing. Jimmy Forbes only had to look at her face as her normally wide eyes narrowed and he could tell she had the nark. Pushing her away from him, his gaze didn't leave the screen.
"Marlene its business! I'll take you out tomorrow."
Unfamiliar with not getting her own way, his explanation didn't console her and she sat heavily in the opposite chair and sulked.
"If that's what you want, I'll fuckin' go out on me own and if I don't come back tonight, well that's your fault."
As quick as a flash he darted across the room and for the first time since she'd been with Jimmy Forbes, Marlene felt the back of his hand as it lashed against her cheek.
"Don't fuckin' start with me bitch! I give you everythin' you ask for and this is how you repay

me. Keep it up and you can get out on that bastard street and earn for me like the rest of them dirty bitches."

Marlene Dawson knew there and then that she'd overstepped the mark. Her face stung from his slap but she still jumped out of the chair and was on her feet once more draping herself round Jimmy's neck.

"I'm sorry honey but when you go out without me I get jealous. Sometimes I think I'm not enough for you and you'll find another girl. I couldn't bare it if you left me Jimmy."

Slowly she fell to her knees and before he knew what was happening she'd unbuckled his belt and opened up the front of his trousers. Releasing his erect penis, she went down on him as if her life depended on it. Jimmy Forbes wasn't about to replace the best thing that had happened to him in a long time but at this present moment he wasn't about to tell her that either. Three minutes later he felt more alive than he had in a long time and as Marlene wiped the evidence from her mouth with the back of her hand she swallowed and licked her lips. From the corner of his eye Jimmy saw the headlights of the Jag shine through the net curtains and quickly began to straighten himself out. After tucking in his shirt and zipping up his trousers he hauled Marlene to her feet and pulled her to him.

"Listen I'm not interested in anyone else but you know the nature of my work and nothing will ever come before that."

Kissing her gently on her full luscious mouth he left the room and headed out to meet his friend. Herbie had caught the couple's refection as he'd pulled up and decided to wait in the car. He wore a broad smile as the Scouser got in beside him.

"Ready?"

Jimmy Forbes smiled back.

"As I'll ever be."

The car slowly pulled away but neither man mentioned the incident. Jimmy because he didn't think Herb had seen and Herbie because he didn't want to embarrass his old pal. Secretly he wished that Marge would occasionally indulge him but with her it was strictly the missionary position.

Over in Bethnal Green, Angela paced the floor with excitement which didn't go down well with Flo.

"For gawd's sake sit down girl you'll wear me fuckin' carpet out."

The crude language again shocked Joanna. Her face now wore a complete look of horror which made Angela burst into a fit of giggles.

"Mum if that shocked you then perhaps you shouldn't stay around."

Realising her distaste had been overly evident,

Joanna's face turned scarlet.

"No, no! It's just, well I'm not........"

Flo McCann finished the woman's sentence much to the delight of Angela.

"You're not used to a foul mouth. Well I'm afraid it's the only one I've got so if you're stayin' in my house you'll have to fuckin' get used to it."

Once again Angela started to giggle and only stopped when the knock came at the door. Nimbly Flo got up from the chair and made her way into the hall. She didn't want her granddaughter answering the door at night, well not in this neighbourhood anyway. Angela was left alone with her mother for the first time since Joanna's arrival and she wasn't comfortable.

"Angela whatever are you doing with such people?"

"Such people? Mother she's my blood!"

"I'm not disputing that fact but you can't seriously like it here?"

"Actually I'm having the time of my life, so for once will you let me do what I want. Now I don't want to talk about it anymore, I just want to go out and have a nice evening alright?"

Joanna didn't answer her daughter but inside she was fuming. Perhaps with Angela out of the flat she would get more sense out of the old woman. As Flo made her way to the door she remembered to look through the spy hole and the sight on the other side of the door made her start laughing. Standing beside each other and decked out in all their finery and wearing matching tie pins, Herbie and Jimmy resembled Hale and Pace as the two Ron's. Immediately she felt guilty at the thought, at least they'd tried to make an impression for Angela. Opening the door she beckoned them inside.

"My don't you two scrub up well! Don't just stand there like a couple of pricks come through and meet her, oh and her mother!'"

Herbie Spires turned to his friend and raised his eyebrows as if silently saying 'what the mother as well!' As the three entered the sitting room the sight made Joanna feel as if she'd been transported onto the set of some old gangster movie. Herbie walked straight over to Angela and taking her hand kissed it gently.

"Pleasure to meet you darlin', you're the spit of your old man."

"Thank you Mr?"

"Spires but call me Herbie and this here's Jimmy."

"Thank you Herbie and pleased to make your acquaintance Jimmy."

"Likewise darlin'."

Jimmy was still standing in the open doorway as Angela gestured that she was ready to leave. As she passed him with her head held high he had to agree with Flo, she certainly carried herself just like Marty. As Angela walked into the hall, Flo gave both the men a look which told them not to forget why they were here. It wasn't necessary; they hadn't forgotten how could they? It was just that their reasons for being here were totally different to Flo's. Standing on the step until the three had left the building, Flo finally closed the flat door. She walked slowly back inside and for a minute had forgotten all about Joanna. It wasn't until she was in the kitchen and placing the kettle on the stove that she caught a glimpse of her leaning against the door frame.

"So are you going to tell me exactly what's going on or do I have to wait for Angela to get back?. Believe me, either way I will find out."

Flo McCann pointed to the chair and told Joanna to sit. Making the brew she didn't utter a single word which annoyed Joanna all the more. Finally she placed two cups down onto the table and took a seat herself.

"You're not goin' to like what I'm about to say, I don't like it much myself. All I ask is that you let me finish before you but in, which of course I know you will do."

Joanna Canning Brown was silent which told the woman to continue. It was eight fifteen when Flo McCann began to reveal all to her guest. Starting with the day of Marty's funeral, she relived every single thing that had happened

since and deciding not to hold anything back she even included Kitty McManus's little revelation. By the time she reached the part where Angela had decided to reclaim her father's business, the look on Joanna's face was such that Flo thought she was about to pass out.
"You alright girl?"
Joanna nodded her head but her expression said otherwise. Standing up Flo made her way over to the seventies style freestanding kitchen cabinet. Removing two cheap, not to mention odd glasses, she poured large brandies into each and handed one to the woman sitting on the opposite side of the table. Flo downed hers in one while Joanna took the tiniest sip and began to cough until she thought her heart was going to make an appearance.
"Get it down you! Ain't no fuckin' good takin' tiny sips. Neck it!"
Joanna did as she was told and the coughing seemed twice as bad. Flo waited until the woman had composed herself and when Joanna finally wiped the tears of choking from her eyes the onslaught began.
"Mrs McCann what do you intend to do about this little problem?"
"Ain't nothin' fuckin' little about it darlin' and it ain't just my problem, she's your daughter. The two lumps who picked her up tonight were Marty's oldest friends and I've asked them to

show her, well let's just say the not so fuckin' nice side of their world."
"Is she in any danger?"
Joanna's words cut Flo more than anything had since Marty's death and she stared daggers at the jumped up cow sitting opposite.
"Fuckin' danger! Whatever do you take me for? That's my boy's daughter out there and already I'd fuckin' die for her, so don't come here….."
It was now Joanna's turn to interrupt.
"Sorry that didn't come out as it was intended. Please forgive me?"
Flo didn't decline or accept the apology, instead she continued with what she'd been saying before being interrupted."
"If Herbie and Jimmy carry this off, then we've nothin' to worry about. If they don't, then I really haven't got the foggiest what to do next. Got any ideas?"
Joanna again turned white but she didn't wait for Flo to pour more drinks. Collecting the glasses she walked to the cabinet and refilled them both, only this time her measures were double that of her hosts. Necking the brandy she waited for the onset of coughing to start, it didn't. Flo looked the woman up and down and knew that Marty hadn't made a bad choice. She was tall and elegant and Flo could see that just like her granddaughter, Joanna must have been a real beauty when Marty had first met her.

"Tell me somethin'?"

Joanna Canning Brown placed her glass back on the table and stared into the woman's eyes.

"Did you ever regret your decision? I mean not choosin' to stay with my boy?"

"Every single day of my life for the last twenty five years but you can't live in the past and I've tried to move on. God knows no one's tried more than me but no man ever really stood a chance."

"Why?"

"Because, no one could ever measure up to your son. I may have been young but I loved him totally and utterly."

Flo McCann could see genuine tenderness when Joanna talked about Marty and she appreciated her honesty. Reaching over to the cabinet, she pulled the brandy bottle to the edge and carefully lifted it onto the table.

"I think you'd better call me Flo if we're goin' to sort that girl of ours out and I think we'd better have a few more of these as well."

As Flo McCann poured from the bottle, Joanna smiled as the glasses filled up. The smile would stay on her face until after midnight, when the remainder of the brandy had at last disappeared. Flo made up a bed on the sofa in the front room and after inquiring if her new guest needed anything, she slowly and more than a bit tipsy trundled along the hall to her room.

CHAPTER SIXTEEN

The Jag left the dismal streets and buildings of Bethnal Green and headed towards its more deserving destination of the West End. Jimmy sat up front with Herbie, leaving Angela alone on the large back seat and with neither man attempting to strike up a conversation; it gave her a feeling of awkwardness. She knew there were only two options open to her. One being to sit back and be the little lady, which she imagined they were hoping for. The other was to make a stand and be the daughter her father would have wanted. She chose the latter. Summoning up all the nerve she could muster, Angela took in a deep breath.
"So boys, where are we going?"
In unison Herbie and Jimmy glanced at each other out of the corner of their eyes but it was Herbie who gave the reply.
"Where would you like to go Angie?"
"It's Angela and naturally I would like to go to one of my father's clubs."
Herbie rolled his eyes upwards, it was a habit he'd had for years and one which Angela found annoying.
"Stop the car!"
"What?"
"You heard me, stop this fucking car

immediately!"

Neither man could believe the expletive that had just left the mouth of this angelic looking young woman. Doing as he'd been told, Herbie indicated and gently pulled the Jag into the curb. Jimmy swung his body round to face her and after releasing his seat belt Herbie did the same. "Gentlemen I may have been born with a silver spoon in my mouth and that's something I and not you have to live with but do not presume for one minute it makes me naive. Do you honestly think I wasn't aware of what you were up to? That I didn't know you two were in cahoots with my grandmother and that this whole thing was a set up?"

"Listen Angie."

"Herbie its Angela and don't let me have to tell you again. I may not have my father's name but it's his blood I have running through my veins. I may know very little about the lives you lead but I have a good imagination. I'm quick to learn and if it's the last thing I do I will reclaim my birthright! with or without, you or my grandmothers help. Now if you don't mind I think we should get going and I'd like to start at the Chamber club."

Inwardly both men smiled but didn't say a word. Admittedly they had gone along with Flo McCann's wishes but now everything was turning out exactly as they had hoped it would. Pulling the Jag out onto the road they drove to Angela's preferred destination. The city was alive and now appeared far more beautiful than it had in the cold light of day. Angela watched people stepping out for a night on the town, she noticed the neon lights that lit up almost every building and thought to herself this was at long last where she belonged. When the car reached Chambers, the traffic cones placed in front of the club were swiftly removed by the doormen. The street was once again buzzing and Angela thought the situation was weird almost déjà` vu but then this wasn't déjà' vu in the slightest, it was as real now as it had been three nights ago. Herbie held open the door for her and she felt like a super star as the passersby stared at the beautiful woman emerging. The unlikely trio walked up the steps to the main doors and before entering, Angela couldn't resist having her revenge at the doorman, who only a few nights ago had denied her entry into her own club. Placing her hand out as if imitating a gun she pointed it at the man and fired. Bringing her finger tip back to her lips, she blew out the nonexistent smoking barrel and then laughed out loud. The action unnerved the doorman. He knew that he'd seen her face before and that it wasn't that long ago but he couldn't for the life of him remember where from.

"Evening Mr Spire, Mr Forbes."
"Alright Drew, this is Marty's daughter."
To the doorman the introduction felt like an instant dismissal as he suddenly remembered where he'd seen the woman before.
"I'm so sorry Miss; please forgive me ignorance the other night I......."
Angela held up her hand and then laughed again.
"Don't worry about it Drew. Nice to see you are taking your job seriously and looking after my father's interests."
Not waiting for a reply, she followed her escorts inside. The Chamber, part club and part casino was a large imposing building which was flanked on either side by two city Banks and elegantly furnished with fine antiques. Jimmy thought she was bound to be impressed and was somewhat disappointed at her lack of enthusiasm but then he wasn't aware that it wasn't so very different from the surroundings Angela had lived with all her life. She'd found that life style pretentious and her views of the club were on an equal par. Herbie and Jimmy Forbes were acknowledged by all of the staff and in return they introduced Angela as Marty's daughter. Each time Herbie would begin by calling her Angie and she would correct him with the words Angela Canning Brown. It happened so many times that she began to think

he was doing it on purpose; of course nothing could be further from the truth. Herbie found her name too long a mouthful to keep repeating and anyway he thought Angie was a more fitting name for Marty McCann's girl. Both men knew that before the night was out Johnny Vale would be informed as to who had been in the club, they also knew that after tonight's little jaunt there would be no going back. It was now up to Angela to want what they did, if she changed her mind then this would all have been for nothing.

The Chamber catered to a more up market clientele, the type who had plenty of spare income to dispose of. Roulette and black jack tables filled the room and except for the odd celebrity and Earl the numbers were made up of mostly Americans and Japanese. Angela soon became bored with the stuffy atmosphere and asked to be taken to Morgan's. Having already experienced the club she knew it would be more to her liking. Herbie and Jimmy hadn't been to Morgan's for quite some time and they both hated the place with a vengeance. The birds were too young by far and the music was not only loud but as Jimmy always put it in his refined manner 'was shit and they wouldn't know a good tune if it came up and bit them on the arse. Give me Sinatra anytime.' Fifteen minutes after they first arrived the three left

through The Chambers main door and after a short drive, entered Morgan's. Podium dancers gyrated to the latest hits while men of all ages eyed up every part of their scantily clad bodies. Once again Angela was introduced to all and sundry and soon lost track of anyone's name. When the news that Marty's daughter was in the place reached the ears of the manager, he quickly came over to introduce himself. Herbie and Jimmy were taking no chances and when they saw Sammy Richmond approach, stood either side but slightly in front of Angela. The over protective gesture made her feel warm inside and she once more thought of her father. Sammy Richmond had been in charge of the club since the first day Marty had opened and he'd been a loyal employee, that was until the man had died, then he'd instantly become loyal to Johnny Vale. Extending his hand he wore a smile that was slimy and Angela thought he resembled a fat Cheshire cat, she'd always hated cats and this man made her skin crawl. As well as taking an instant dislike to him, Angela could see he was two faced. He was too familiar by far and from somewhere a voice in her head told her not to show her hand. Angela smiled as if greeting an old friend.
"Pleased to meet you Miss McCann"
'Her names Angie and......'
Pushing forwards she gently nudged through

the two men trying to protect her and reached out to shake Sammy's hand.
"For god's sake Herbie! How many more times, its Angela do I have to tell you. Pleased to meet you Sammy and its Miss Canning Brown."
Her friendly manner may have seemed hypocritical to most but remembering what pops had always told her about wearing a poker face so that no one knew what you were thinking, especially to someone who may do you harm, she was calm, relaxed and very charming. For a second Sammy Richmond seemed confused.
"Canning Brown? I thought you were Marty's daughter?"
"I am and it's a long story."
Sammy now grabbed her hand and shook it until she thought her arm would fall off.
"No need to explain, I'm just glad you're here. You do intend to take over right?"
Outwardly Angela smiled but inwardly she wanted to punch the man straight in the mouth. After looking from Herbie to Jimmy she stared directly into Sammy's snake like eyes.
"Without any shadow of a doubt Sammy. In due course I shall be meeting all of the staff individually. Once I've crossed the T's and dotted the I's with the solicitor I shall also want a full inventory of the clubs stock and until further notice I will be the only one signing any cheques. I take it if your so called boss hasn't been told

about my presence by now, then he pretty soon will be?"

"Miss Canning Brown some of the shits working here would sell their own granny's for a quid, so in answer to your question, yes he probably already knows."

Angela nodded and took a few seconds to work out exactly what else she should say. Knowing that it was acceptable to take guidance from Herbie and Jimmy but anything else had to be her decision, made her double check everything in her mind.

"Thank you for your honesty Sammy and when you next see Mr Vale I'd like you to repeat these words.' You know it's going to happen Mr Vale but sadly you will not know when. One thing is for sure, I want you to be in no doubt whatsoever that I will be reclaiming what is rightfully mine."

Turning to face Herbie, who now wore a gob smacked expression she smiled.

"I'd like to go now."

Together the trio turned and walked away, without a goodbye to the manager. Angela would bet her life on it that as soon as they had left he would be on the phone to his boss; in fact that was exactly what she was hoping for.

Outside in the cold night air, Herbie breathed a sigh of relief.

'Well you certainly told him girl!'

"Don't seem so shocked, I can stand up for myself you know. Now I need to talk to you both. Is there a place we can go where the walls don't have ears and its quiet?"

Jimmy who'd been steadfastly silent for most of the night suddenly piped up.

"Jerry Harris has a late night drinking den over in Stepney. He's a trustworthy sort and hates Johnny almost as much as we do."

Angela smiled. "Then Jerry Harris's it is."

The drive back to the east end didn't take long but everyone in the car was too hyped up with what had happened in the club to make idle chit chat. By the time they reached their destination Angela's watch showed ten past eleven. The large three storey building stood gloomily on the corner of Newark Street. The ground floor served as a public house during daylight hours and up until eleven each night. The revenue generated wouldn't have supported a place half the size but then 'The Travellers Rest' was no ordinary place. As soon as last orders were called it's ground floor became deserted. Doors were quickly locked and lights switched off. The place was fully licensed, stock was accounted for and all of the books were up-to-date. If the police or the revenue ever came calling then all was as it should be. That said if any unsuspecting stranger had dared to tread the steps that led down to the cellar, they would

have found a totally different scene. Below was a den of thieves and gangsters all drinking cut price alcohol and eating food supplied by the regulars who frequented the place after hours. The late club as it was known was a well kept secret among the criminal fraternity, a secret that they would go to any lengths to protect. The large bare brick walled room was dimly lit and had intimate tables lining the outer walls. The cellar wasn't classy in the least, quite the opposite but then the type of people who frequented this place were hardened drinkers who didn't give a toss what the décor was like. Jerry Harris had run The Travellers Rest for the last eight years and since his afterhours den had opened, he'd been coining it in. Tonight was no exception and when the trio walked down the side steps and entered the tiny foyer, the place was in full swing. As soon as Jerry set eyes on the two suited men with their matching tie pins, he smiled from ear to ear. Ignoring Angela as one of the bits of fluff that normally hung on the Scouser's arm, he limped past her and embraced Jimmy Forbes.
"Jimmy you old cunt! How's it hangin'?"
Jimmy Forbes draped an arm over the man's shoulder and led him out of Angela's earshot. Seconds later a shabbily dressed barman showed her and Herbie through the back to a private room that was kept for only the most important

visitors. The room was small, dimly lit and in the centre stood a round table and four chairs that had seen better days. As with the main room this area wasn't dressed for the scenery. If the walls had been able to speak the information they could have revealed would send most of London's underworld away for a very long time with no chance of parole. No do not pass go or collect two hundred pounds, just night after night of cell doors banging.

As Angela sat down the door burst open and Jerry Harris came running in or at least limping as fast as he could. Jimmy followed closely behind carrying three glasses and a bottle of scotch.

"Please forgive me Miss McCann; I didn't know who you were."

Angela smiled at the funny little man whose unruly red dyed hair stuck out in all directions. "There's no reason why you should know who I am and the names Canning Brown."

"Oh I'm sorry it's just when Jimmy said you were Marty McCann's daughter."

"Well Mr Harris you've got that right at least, now if you don't mind we have some very important business to discuss?"

Jerry backed out of the room bowing and scraping as he left and when the door finally closed, all three in the room burst out laughing. Angela turned to Herbie with a quizzical

expression on her face.
"Why did he act as if I were royalty, when I don't even know him?"
"Angie its......"
"Angela!"
"Angela it's a long story but to put it bluntly Jerry once had a run in with your dad, the result was the limp that you now see. The man was a first class athlete and by all accounts had a promising career as a footballer. That was until he met your old man. What happened wasn't pleasant but over the years your dad and Jerry somehow became friends."
"Nice I must say!"
Herbie didn't like her high and mighty tone.
"No its not but it's the way we, you will have to live if you want to survive in our world. Do you still want to be in this kind of world A N G E L A?"
Almost spelling out her name she was aware that Herbie was more than a touch annoyed with her. Needing to take back the upper hand that she thought he had stolen with his last sentence, Angela thought for a second as the two men sat on the edges of their seats.
"More than anything."
Both men let out a sigh of relief when she answered.
"Good then let's get down to the matter in hand, Johnny fucking Vale!"

With the odd contribution here and there from Jimmy Forbes, Herbie told Angela all that had happened since the day of Marty's death. Agreeing that nothing should be left out they even told her about big Bernie and their revenge on Seth Larkman. Angela listened and didn't once interrupt, speaking only when she knew Herbie had finished.

"So has either of you seen this Johnny Vale, since that little incident?"

Little incident made Herbie want to laugh, had she not heard that they'd battered the man's brains in. If she had taken in the enormity of what he'd said then Herbie realised she must be one merciless bitch and a harder bastard than her father had ever been. Without question Angela had heard every single word and some of it had made her feel slightly queasy. The one thing they didn't know was that no way on earth would she ever admit that fact to anyone, least of all the two men sitting in front of her. After all weren't they the ones who were praying she'd put their lives back on track.

"What I mean is does he have any idea that it was you two?"

"Not as far as we know and we have a pair of eyes and ears on the premises during opening hours."

"Who is that?"

Jimmy continued and explained all he could

about their informant without revealing the name before moving on to the job Johnny had planned and the bombshell Kitty McManus had dropped on poor Flo's doorstep. The two men were shocked when Angela again spoke but didn't mention the possible killer of her father. Instead her only interest lay in the proposed heist that was due to take place in a few days time. Herbie immediately became angry and stood up at the same time as slamming his fist into the table and raising his voice.

"Fuck me girl! Ain't you interested in the least as to who topped your old man?"

Angela remained calm and collective through his short outburst. Motioning for Herbie to take his seat, she didn't speak until she was sure he had calmed down.

"How dare you even suggest such a thing? Nothing would give me greater pleasure than to bring my father's killer to book but right now this firm needs cash to get it back on its feet. My father's murderer will be around for a while to come, unlike this job if we don't act now. I have some money that was left to me but I don't think my father would want me to use it for this. Until everything has been sorted out with the solicitors we have a cash flow problem. We need to sort that out and at the same time put Vale in his place."

Suddenly Herbie Spires felt a little foolish for his

outburst but still looked to the woman for justification regarding her choice of priorities.
"Do you have any ideas then?"'
"I'm not sure yet Herbie, I need a few hours to think things over. I suggest we all meet up at Nan's tomorrow at say, ten?"
Jimmy nodded his head 'Fine by me.'
Herbie Spires did the same but didn't outwardly speak. Angela decided to call it a night and Herbie, now tired from all the emotions he'd gone through, was in agreement. Jimmy wanted to stay on and catch up with recent events from Jerry, besides he didn't feel up to facing the Spanish inquisition from Marlene if he went home now. Kissing Jimmy lightly on the cheek Angela bade him goodnight, the three made their way out of the back room and into the bar. Jimmy Forbes remained inside while Angela and Herbie walked to the waiting Jag. Sitting quietly in the back as the luxury car smoothly passed down the many streets that led back to Bethnal Green, she said another quiet thank you to no one in particular and thought how the many gangster films she'd spent hours watching, had helped her though this night.

CHAPTER SEVENTEEN

Jerry Harris was sitting at a small table tucked away in a corner of the main room when Jimmy emerged from the meeting. He watched as his pal from way back, said his farewells to Herbie and Marty's daughter and waited for the man to make his way over. As Jimmy approached Jerry politely stood up and greeted his guest with a warm smile.
"Jimmy I was heartfelt sorry to hear about Marty. Terrible business, the man was a fuckin' legend!"
Jimmy Forbes frowned at Jerry's words and for a second thought he was taking the piss. Feeling the anger begin to rise he was placated just in time by Jerry's next sentence.
"I know we had our problems but that was all sorted long ago. I was well out of order back then and even though I wouldn't admit it to anyone else, I got what I deserved. Did you know Marty called in here a few times over the last couple of years?"
Jimmy wasn't in the mood for reminiscing tonight, there was too much at stake to make small talk.
"No Jerry I didn't, anyway what's the word out on the street?"
Moving his chair in and huddling over the table

so it was impossible for anyone else to hear, Jerry spoke in a whisper.

"Since Seth Larkman got done, Johnny's surrounded himself with bodies and I don't mean light weights either. He's been asking after you and Herbie. Seems you've both done a disappearin' act as far as the firm goes. Tell me somethin' Jimmy, you didn't do Seth did you?"

As much as the two had been friends for years, Jimmy wasn't about to admit to anything. In the world in which they chose to live, you'd die denying everything even if the person accusing you had been present at the event.

"Fuck me Jerry whatever do you take me for. Me and Herbie's just about ready for the knackers' yard, never mind anythin' else. Mind you, it's good to know people still think we're capable."

"No one thinks Jimmy, we all know but we'll say no more about it. I heard through the jungle drums about poor old Bernie, fuckin' tragic. How is the big lump?"

Jimmy suddenly felt a pang of guilt; he hadn't called in at the hospital or even phoned to see how the big man was doing. He made a mental note to rectify the situation in the morning.

"It was touch and go for a while but they think he's goin' to pull through thank fuck. So Johnny's got a small army of his own set up has he?"

"Not so fuckin' small by all accounts, possible turf war on the horizon then?"
"Jerry my old friend, that's entirely up to Johnny. I will tell you something for nothing; I don't expect him to relinquish his newly acquired little empire without a fight."
Sensing it was going to be a long night, Jerry Harris waved to the barman who quickly brought over two glasses and a bottle of Malt. With all fresh information exhausted the friends finally got round to discussing old times, old faces and anything they could think of that didn't involve the horror that they both knew the future held. When daylight had begun to appear and the malt had all but disappeared, Jimmy Forbes called a cab and made his way home. Due at Flo McCann's flat in only a few hours, he knew that if he didn't get even a little sleep then he'd be no good to neither man nor beast and least of all to Angela. Deep inside he'd realised even if she hadn't, that before too long Angela Canning Brown or McCann or whatever she wanted to call herself, would come to rely on him and Herbie totally.
While Jerry and Jimmy reminisced, Johnny Vale had immediately made his way, complete with several bodyguards over to Morgan's. Just as Angela had suspected earlier, the trio had not even closed the trendy glass doors behind them before Sammy Richmond was on the blower to

his new boss. Hopeful of scoring a few brownie points, he'd excitedly informed Johnny as to who had just been in and what was said. It was past midnight by the time Johnny and his henchmen arrived and the club had begun to wind down. Only a handful of punters remained but there would be no after hours service tonight. Sammy Richmond received the nod from the doorman via the high tech headphones that everyone was forced to wear and looked up to see his boss and four large men begin to descend the staircase. Sammy was scared, it was a feeling he couldn't explain but one he felt every time he was in Johnny Vales company. Not wanting to keep the boss waiting, he swiftly walked to the bottom stair ready to greet Johnny as he arrived.
"Mr Vale good to see you and I'd just like to say how smart you're looking."
Johnny Vale pushed the man aside.
"Cut the crap cunt, in the office now!"
Sammy Richmond only ever looked out for himself and had thought grassing on Marty's daughter would place him a little higher up in the pecking order. Seeing the look on his bosses face suddenly made him think differently, in fact he knew by the churning in his guts that getting involved with this little lot had been a bad idea.
"I was about to close up Mr Vale."
"Now!"

Meekly obeying the order he'd been given, Sammy Richmond followed behind his boss and the henchmen with his head bowed low. The office had wall to wall CC TV which covered every angle of the club and all the screens now showed the place was empty. The arrival of Johnny, his crew and the infamous reputation that followed them saw the last stragglers make a quick exit. Taking a seat against the far wall which was partially in the shadows, Johnny pointed to the chair that had been set out in the middle of the room. Sammy Richmond started to sweat profusely, he knew that he was in deep shit but couldn't for the life of him think why. As soon as his rear end touched the vinyl of the seat his arms were grabbed from behind and Sammy cried out in fear, though as yet no pain had been inflicted. From the shadows he heard his boss's voice.
"So tell me what happened?"
Sammy started to shake but racking his brains as hard as he could still didn't bring forth any new information.
"I already told you what happened boss!"
"Well maybe it was a little bit of a short version, maybe you're fuckin' holdin' out on me. I hope for your sake you ain't, 'cause I really, really ain't in the fuckin' mood for games."
"Honest boss I told you everythin' that happened, every single fuckin' word honest!"

Johnny Vale wasn't listening, he'd only let the little worm stay on because he did a good job as manager. Suddenly his patience ran out and from the darkness he clicked his fingers in the direction of one of his henchmen. Without a word the man swiftly removed a cattle prod from the inside of his jacket and proceeded to place it on Sammy's chest. A piercing array of screams rang out in the room but there was no one to come to his rescue. Seconds later and the prod was placed between Sammy's legs. Another of the bodyguards walked across the room and came to the assistance of the first. Grabbing a handful of their victim's hair, he jerked Sammy's head backwards making his eyes bulge as he desperately struggled to look down at his threatened groin. Just as the prod made contact, the man holding him let go. "Please boss! Please! I've told you all I know!" Again the sound of clicking fingers could be heard and another round of torture was inflicted. The whole of Sammy Richmond's body shook as the volts surged through his scrotum and up into his abdomen. Long threads of white snot hung from his nostrils for a second before falling onto his lips. Mixed with the large amount of saliva that was quickly emerging from his open mouth, Sammy's face soon became covered in his own bodily fluid. It felt like things were happening in slow motion, the second scream came only a second after the cattle prod had been administered but lasted for much longer. Now totally unable to control himself, his bladder released itself when the prod was moved onto his stomach and the searing pain again racked his pitiful body. Walking out of the shadows, Johnny Vale accepted he'd been told the truth earlier and knew he'd had a wasted journey. He decided to leave, there was nothing more to be gained by staying around this gibbering waster of a man. Without a second glance his four accomplices followed suit, leaving Sammy Richmond crippled in agony.

In Stepney Jimmy Forbes opened his front door and quietly stepped inside. He didn't want to wake Marlene at such an ungodly hour and began to tip toe up the stairs. The door to the living room creaked open and Jimmy flew round instinctively. About to hurl his body at whoever the intruder was, he stopped himself just in time when he saw his Caribbean beauty slip out of the room.

"Hi babe, whatever are you doin' still up?"
"Jimmy what a fuckin' night I've had! Lanky Lorraine's kicked off again and I've got small Sue sittin' in there with two black eyes. Poor cow was only just able to cover up the bruises from the last lot. Jimmy you've got to do something about her, she's a real nasty piece of

work."

Jimmy Forbes rubbed his chin with the palm of his hand; this was all he needed. It was one of his own unwritten rules that any girl working the streets didn't step foot over his threshold but to get rid of small Susan now, would mean having to deal with the situation and he was too tired to even think about it.

"I will babe but if I don't get some kip I think I'll fuckin' keel over. Give the soppy mare a blanket and tell her to get her head down."

Marlene nodded and watched her man slowly climb the stairs, by the time she had settled down their surprise guest and made it upstairs herself, Jimmy was fast asleep. At seven the next morning and feeling like he'd had no sleep at all, Jimmy was being roughly shaken awake by his girlfriend. Moaning and rolling over he tried to ignore her but Marlene wasn't easily put off.

"Jim you've got to get up. Small Susan is still down stairs and I ain't dealing with her again, she's your problem and you'll have to fuckin' sort it."

True the girls were his responsibility and beside he'd been with Marlene long enough to realise when she was pissed off and today would be a real hum dinger if he didn't do something fast. Most of the time Marlene was a pleasure to be around but if you pushed her far enough she could really get narky and what with everything else that was going on it was something Jimmy would rather not have to deal with. Reluctantly and with a hangover like he hadn't had in years, Jimmy Forbes pulled himself up and out of the warm comfortable bed. Of all days, lanky Lorraine couldn't have chosen a worse one to upset her boss. Storming into the living room he dragged the spare duvet off of a snoring Susan's body. Instantly she scrambling up and tried to cover herself with a cushion as Jimmy gave her a look of disgust.

"Leave it out you tart. You ain't got nothin' I and half the smoke ain't seen before. Get dressed and meet me outside in ten."

Walking from the house Jimmy unlocked the door to his Mercedes and climbed inside. He hated driving and it was only ever something he did as a last resort. Normally if Herbie didn't collect him then a cab would be called. He prayed that he didn't get a pull from Old Bill; with the amount of scotch he'd sunk last night he was sure to fail any attempt at a breathalyser. He drummed his fingers on the dashboard but just as her time was up and Jimmy was about to forcibly pull her from the house, a sheepish looking Susan emerged and joined her boss in his posh car.

"I'm sorry about all this Jimmy but I didn't know what else to do. That bitch is making my life a misery and the constant battering she's dishing out, well it's costing you and me dearly. I didn't earn a penny last night."

Her voice was beginning to grate and he glared so harshly at her that Susan Marsh realised it was time to shut up. They drove over to Kings Cross in silence until turning off into a back street.

"So where's the lanky bitch live then?"

His passenger pointed to a row of Georgian houses that had long since been converted into tiny one bedroom flats.

"Blue door flat 6. Can I stay here Jimmy? If I go in there she'll fuckin' kill me."

Leaning across her he pushed open the car door and gave the petite woman a shove.

"No you fuckin' can't! Over her dead body we'll sort this bastard out once and for all."

Climbing the steps that led up to the front door, Jimmy held his hand on the intercom buzzer until a deep agitated voice was heard on the other end.

"Bastards whoever you are, you've just fucking woke me up."

As Jimmy spoke and lanky Lorraine realised who it was, she didn't have the nerve to reply.

"Lorraine if you don't open this fuckin' door I'm goin' to break it down and you're a dead woman, man or whatever you fuckin' call yourself."

Grantly Soames had arrived in London ten years

earlier. Born to aging parents, who when he'd reached his teens didn't understand his sexuality, he'd longed to leave Devon and make his own way in the world. Boarding the first available coach, Grantly had arrived in London two days after his eighteenth birthday. Standing over six feet tall in his stocking feet, he had a way of belittling people with just the flicker of an eyelid. His outrageous campness had made employment almost impossible for him to find. The only place he finally had any luck was the seedy bars of Soho. One thing Grantley Soames wasn't shy of was hard work and after many months of abuse and hard toil, he'd finally raised enough cash for the transsexual operation he'd dreamed of for most of his life. Several courses of hormone drugs had completed the change and he now sported a superb pair of breasts with matching vagina. So pleased was she with her new body, that after six months living and breathing womanhood, she wanted employment where she would be able to show off her newly acquired assets. A mutual friend had reluctantly introduced Lorraine to the boss and Jimmy Forbes agreed to take on the transsexual, who now went by the name of Lorraine. Totally on face value, it had been something he'd regretted ever since but was too money orientated to get rid of her. Lanky Lorraine as she soon became known was a prima

donna who wanted all the best paying punters for herself and stopped at nothing to get what she wanted. She was also one of Jimmy's best earners and that in truth was why he'd let her get away with so much for so long. Slowly the heavy blue door opened enough for her large oval eyes to be seen. Jimmy didn't wait to be invited in, instead he slammed the door open as hard as he could. Lorraine Soames screamed out in agony and when Jimmy closely followed by Susan entered, she stood in the hall with her hand dripping in blood and covering her mouth. Small Susan ran to the aid of her friend and inspected the damage. As she pulled Lorraine's hand away, they all saw the two front teeth fall out and clink onto the tiled floor of the hall.
"Jimmy! How could you? She won't be able to earn now!"
Jimmy made his way over and yanked Lorraine's head back. Forcing her mouth open he looked inside and the bleeding gums made him smile.
"Well she was never much to look at anyway and perhaps this will be a vast fuckin' improvement on her blow jobs, god knows she could do with some help."
He was irate with the pair of them and couldn't believe the cheek of the smallest girl who only a few hours earlier, had been holed up at his place scared out of her wits.

"You are the biggest couple of two faced fuckin' mares I've ever had the displeasure of meetin'." Turning to small Susan, he leaned in close until she could smell the stale scotch on his breath. "It was you who wanted the whore sorted out. You fuckin' lot make me sick, well I'll tell you somethin' for nothin' don't fuckin' come runnin' to me when you have another bust up."
Jimmy started to walk out of the door but stopped at the last minute. Turning round to face both women and wearing his most menacing glare he spoke.
"Make sure you're both out earning tonight or there'll be trouble."
Neither of the women answered but he knew they took his every word as law. Emerging into the early morning air and with the now bright London sunshine shining down, he was about to drive over to Mrs M's when he glanced down and noticed several spots of blood. Tutting to himself loudly, he was more than a little pissed off as he got into the car and made his way home to change. He was going to be late and above all else he would have Marlene on his back wanting to know what had happened. Lately everything in his life, no matter how small, always turned out to be complicated. It had never been like this when Marty was alive, god he missed the man, now more than ever.

CHAPTER EIGHTEEN

After dropping Angela home, Herbie at last walked through the door. He was tired, hungry but more than anything desperate for his bed. The hall light was still on which was unusual. His wife always switched everything off before she turned in and as it was well after one he knew she would have gone to bed long ago. Suddenly the lounge door flew open and he was greeted by a stony faced Marge Spires. Dressed in her trademark ostrich trimmed negligee she had topped of her night wear by adding a Chihuahua under each arm. With her hair in curlers and thick anti wrinkle cream smeared all over her face she really was a sight. Instantly Herbie could tell that she wasn't in the best of moods and right at this moment he could do without anymore agro.
"Hello love, you're up late?"
Marge stormed over to where Herbie stood hanging up his jacket. Even through the thick cream he could see his wife's cheeks were red with anger.
"Up late! Your Joanie's been on the bleedin' phone all night. Me and the babe's aint had a minute's peace. I'd just settled down to watch East Enders when the phone rang and she didn't stop bleedin' rabbitin' on for over two hours!"

"Why what's wrong? No one's hurt are they?"
"Only me!"
"You! What's wrong with you?"
Marge Spires stamped her feet in an almost childlike manner and watching her was really starting to grate on Herbie's nerves. If he hadn't of been so tired he would have picked up his keys and walked straight out again.
"Well I'm the one that's had to listen to your sister goin' on and on all bloody night. I tell you Herb it's done me head in."
"For fucks sake Marge you can be one nasty cow at times. You know our Joanie's had it tough, unlike you. The fuckin' trouble with you is that you're spoilt and only think of yourself. Can't you find it in you to show a bit of compassion or is it only them scrawny little rats that matter to you?"
Herbie regretted his words as soon as they'd left his mouth. Marge wasn't that bad and the rats as he called them were her life. He knew things would have been very different for the woman if she'd had kids but that was life and there wasn't anything he could do about it. They both had everything that money could buy but still, sometimes it just wasn't enough. Money would never be able to give them the one thing they had both wanted all of their lives. Pools of tears had begun to form in Marge's eyes and Herbie immediately took her into his arms, slightly

squashing one of the dogs as he did so. It yelped and Marge instantly pulled away from her husband, giving him a look of daggers as she did so.
"Dwid daddy hurt my bwaby ahhhhh give mummy a kwiss."
Herbie sighed deeply and turning began to climb the stairs.
"Don't you want to know what she wanted?"
"Look I'm fuckin' knackered now can you just get to the point. On second thoughts Marge can't this just wait till the mornin'?"
"It's Danny!"
"What's up with him?"
"Nothin' but he's coming out tomorrow and your Joanie says she aint havin' him home not for all the bleedin' tea in china!"
Herbie shook his head. Continuing up the stairs he spoke to his wife and his tone was harsh, an indication to Marge not to push him any further.
"We can finish this conversation in the mornin'. Goodnight!"
Entering the kitchen after an unusually good night's sleep, Herbie seemed to have had so many broken nights since Marty's death; he was met with a sullen faced Marge. His wife didn't let things go easily and squashing the dog last night had caused her to be full of hell six hours later.
"I suppose you're off out again today?"

Marge didn't look at her husband and continued to fry eggs with her back to him.

"What do you want me to do, sit at home all day so you can fuckin' give me ear ache?"

"There's no need to speak to me like that!"

Turning to the three small dogs at her feet she ignored her husband.

"Has dwaddy got up in a bad mood my bwabies? Never mind we'll just ignore him."

Bending down Marge proceeded to feed the dogs small morsels of crispy bacon and Herbie grimaced at the sight.

"So what's happenin' with Danny?"

"He comes out today and as far as your Joanie is concerned he aint got nowhere to live."

"Then he'll have to come here."

"What!!!!!"

"Don't go getting' all uptight Marge! Look he's a good boy, just a bit daft at times and he loves you like a second mum. Let's give him a roof for a while, at least until he finds his feet."

Herbie knew how to push his wife's buttons and the mention of her being a mother figure would seal the deal.

"Well just for a while and he hadn't better lay about the house all day, you know how particular I am."

Instantly everything was settled and within the hour Herbie Spires had made his way over to north London and was now sitting outside

Pentonville prison. It was eight fifty and Herbie only had two hours to sort his nephew out before he had to be at Flo McCann's. First thing this morning he had phoned Angela to ask if the meet could be put back an hour. Herbie had liked the fact that she'd agreed to his request without asking questions. Fifteen minutes later and the main gate at last slid open and Danny Spires emerged. When he saw his uncles Jag a wide grin covered his face. Opening the car door he got inside.

"Hello uncle H thanks for comin' to get me."
"You're goin' to have to stay with me and Marge for a while. Your old mums still pissed off with you and she won't have you back at the flat, for the time being at least."

Danny Spires loved his uncle but he wasn't so keen on his aunt. Marge had always been polite but a little standoffish or as his mother was fond of saying 'A right stuck up cow'.

"Fine by me uncle H, never did like that gaff anyway."

When Danny was still a baby Joanie had managed to get a flat above one of the shops on Brick Lane. Now known as London's curry capital, Danny had come to loath the place. It was spot the white man as far as he was concerned and he hated the smell of curry that you never seemed to be able to get away from. Even though Danny Spires was mixed race he

never saw himself as coloured. When he'd started one of his many rants about his clothes stinking from all the smells coming from the takeaways his mother had reminded him he was being racial. Her words often rubbed him up the wrong way and caused arguments but he would never listen to her. As far as Danny was concerned he was white and woe betide anyone who tried to tell him different. It had been five years since Herbie had been in his nephews company and he now seemed like a stranger. Danny Spires wasn't a bad kid. He also wasn't thick, not by any standards but he was gullible and always out to make a fast buck. That was the reason he had just completed five years at her majesties for armed robbery. It seemed that whatever Danny turned his hand to, crime wise at least; he always ended up getting caught. The last lot of bother had seen him given an eight stretch and it had broken his mother's heart. With time off for good behaviour he was once more a free man but the odds for how long it would last were short.
"Right then what do you want to do first?"
"Well Unc I fancy a big old fry up and then off somewhere to get laid."
Herbie couldn't help but laugh. A fry up was about as much as Danny was going to get but he had to admire the boy's nerve.
Joanie Spires had raised her son alone. Jerome

Kingston had long been off the scene, in fact he'd disappeared the day Joanie had told him she was pregnant. Even in the eighties it was frowned upon for a white woman to have a black man's child and Joanie Spires was no exception. She'd ignored the comments and cruel jibes and done the best she could, with Herbie's added help, to raise her boy. Danny had been fine till he reached his teens and then like so many before him had gotten in with a bad crowd. Herbie had tried to warn him but all too soon it was court appearances and young offender's institutes. This last stretch had been Danny's fourth and the sentences were becoming lengthier. Herbie had decided that there was no way his nephew was going to stay out of trouble so he might as well join the firm. At least that way his uncle had a chance of keeping an eye on the boy. They had driven half way along Caledonian road when Herbie pulled the Jag over outside Terry's greasy spoon café.
"This do you?"
Danny looked the cafe over and could see from the state of the place and the patrons sitting inside that he was in for a real gut buster. The Scouser had first introduced Herbie to Terry's a couple of years ago and now whenever he was in the area Herbie Spires liked to treat himself to a full English with all the trimmings. Marge was dead set against this type of food but what she

didn't know wouldn't hurt her and besides Herbie was sick to death of steamed sea bass and lentils. They both ordered the full Monty and two mugs of tea and when they were half way through Herbie suddenly placed his knife and fork on the table and looked at Danny.
"What?"
"I've been talkin' it over with the Scouser and we're both in agreement that you should come and work for us."
"That's nice of you uncle H but I'd rather....."
"I aint askin' son I'm fuckin' tellin' you. My Joanie can't take much more of your shenanigans and if you are goin' to work on the wrong side of the law, then you at least need to learn how to do it fuckin' properly."
Danny knew when he was beaten and when his uncle was being serious. When Herbie Spires laid down the law you didn't argue and this was one of those times.
"You start today and for a few weeks will be like my fuckin' shadow. You won't open your mouth unless spoken to, got it?"
Suddenly Danny didn't feel so cocky and could only nod his head in agreement.
"Good! Now eat your grub before it gets cold. You'll need to line your stomach for later when you're presented with Marge's cooking."
Both men laughed out loud but Danny's was more out of nervousness than humour.

Reaching Flo McCann's building Herbie pulled into the kerb, switched off the engine and turned to face his nephew.
"Now listen carefully Danny. This is a very important meeting so behave. The Scouser will be there along with Marty's mum and his daughter."
"Daughter?"
"I'll explain everythin' to you later but for now just sit and listen and keep your fuckin' trap shut ok?"
"Is she a bit of alright?"
"Who?"
Danny Spires rolled his eyes upwards.
"Marty's daughter of course?"
Getting out of the car Herbie let out a loud laugh.
"She's well out of your fuckin' league Danny boy."
His remark somewhat offended Danny but he was now more than a little intrigued.

CHAPTER NINETEEN

Angela had woken early, she'd spent a restless night thinking about how she would deal with Flo and the tirade of moaning that she knew she would face as soon as her cards were laid on the table. The kitchen was empty and she lethargically walked over to the sink and filled the kettle. Placing the old fashioned whistler onto the hob, Angela took a seat at the small table and immediately her thoughts were lost in the events of last night. Staring blankly at the wall she was jolted back to reality as the kettle began to whistle. Jumping up from the table not wanting to wake her mother and grandmother, she turned towards the door way and laid eyes on both women, who stood quietly watching her. Neither moved a muscle which unnerved her but Angela knew she had to be strong. To give in at the first hurdle would prove to everyone that Flo McCann was right. Walking over and switching the gas off, she didn't utter a word and with her back facing the door she could feel the tension as her grandmother spoke. "So then love, have you made your mind up yet?"
Angela was annoyed that her grandmother would bring the subject up so early, not to mention the fact that her mother was in the

room.

"Nan!"

Flo McCann, decked out in a baby pink fleece dressing gown gave a shallow laugh.

"Don't worry about your mum my lovely, I told her everything last night and I might add she agrees whole heartedly with me."

"I suppose you would both like tea?"

Flo walked over to the unit and stood so close to her granddaughter that Angela could feel the hairs on her arm rise as their bodies touched.

"Don't ignore my question; have you made up your mind?"

Still Angela didn't reply, instead she carried on with the task in hand. When the pot was warmed and filled and the cups removed from the cupboard, she placed them all onto the table and looked up at her mother and grandmother.

"Right sit down the pair of you and listen to what I have to say."

Like naughty children, the two older women obeyed her command and their obedience played right into the hands of Angela Canning Brown.

"Nan I know what you had in mind for me last night and your little plan failed miserably."

Flo McCann was about to protest when Angela raised her hand, stopping the old lady before she had begun.

"Please let me finish. Nothing has changed and I

still have every intention of claiming what's rightfully mine."
"Oh Angela!"
Slamming the cup so hard onto the saucer, that it almost smashed, brought about a look of disbelief from the older women.
"Don't oh Angela me! Mother I want you to return to Canterbury and leave me alone to do what I came here for. As for you Mrs McCann, you are either with me or against me but whatever you decide it won't change a thing."
Angela got up from the table and without another word made her way into the bathroom, eager to get ready to greet her guests. Back in the kitchen the mood was sombre. Flo was fuming and Joanna was in a state of panic at the revelations she had just begun to grasp.
"Whatever are we going to do Mrs McCann? The stupid girl hasn't got a clue what she's getting mixed up in but then again, she's never been one to listen to reason."
"For fucks sake Joanna get a grip. Now here's what I think we should do. Firstly I want you to do as she asked and go back home. If you stay it will only get her back up, then there's no hope. Don't look so worried I'll keep you posted daily as to what's happening but for now I think it's best if you go and pack."
Joanna Canning Brown made no attempt to argue, for the first time in her life she didn't

have a clue as to what was going on. With no alternative, she would have to place all of her faith in the grey haired old lady. The fact that she was Marty's mum, coupled with the fact that Joanna didn't know where else to turn, helped make up her mind to do as she'd been asked. Within the hour Angela was made up and ready to greet her accomplices. Her mother was in a cab and on her way to the station and finally she could breathe a sigh of relief. The farewell hadn't been tearful. Angela was past all that and Joanna was trying to show a brave front, even if she did cry for virtually the entire journey home. Even though he'd had to return to Stepney and change, Jimmy Forbes was still the first to arrive at Mrs M's. Trying to parallel park the Mercedes was a nightmare and it ended up standing three feet away from the curb. Getting out of the car, he surveyed his attempt and rolled his eyes in frustration at the sight in front of him. Pressing the key fob to lock the car, he made his way inside. By now Jimmy couldn't give a toss, it was only ten thirty but he'd already had a gutful today. He'd wanted everything to be fresh and good this morning but after the episode with lanky Lorraine, he was beginning to feel it was a bad omen.

Angela stood at the door eager to welcome the first of her guests and as Jimmy walked into the hall, Herbie drew up outside. He was still laughing at the sight outside when he rang the door bell. Jimmy answered and when he saw his friend's expression, he was even more pissed off.

"Struggled to find a parkin' space did we?"

"Don't start Herb; I've had a hell of a day already."

Herbie Spires placed his arm around the Scouser's shoulder as they walked back in together. Danny followed closely behind but Jimmy only nodded in his direction.

"Sorry mate but I'd have given a million to have seen you sweating your guts out. I assume it took you several attempts?"

"You aint wrong there! I don't even know why I've got a fuckin' car, it's pure fuckin' torture every time I go out in it.'"

As they entered the kitchen Flo McCann gave them both a look of disgust but for the time being had decided to keep her thoughts to herself. Angela was the only one seated at the table and gestured for them to join her. She wasn't pleased when she spotted the stranger standing behind Herbie but she decided to wait until she knew who he was before making a comment.

"Right lads, now we're all here shall we get started?"

Herbie being the first to take a seat smiled at the young woman. It was a smile full of warmth but at the same time said 'right let's see what you're made of'. Angela recognised it straight away and immediately her guard went up.

"Nan! You are welcome to stay but only if you remain silent. I'm well aware of your views on the situation but nothing's going to change. We're all here to discuss business and nothing more, so what do you say?"

Flo McCann's chest could visibly be seen to rise and it wasn't with pride. Knowing that there was nothing she could do to change the situation, didn't make her feel any better in the least.

"I think it's a bit fuckin' cheeky seein's as it's my house, that I have to sit here and can't say anythin'. All I'm doin' is watchin' you commit fuckin' suicide. If I can't talk you out of this stupid idea, then its best I know nothin' of what you're all up to."

Grabbing her trusty Mac from the back of the door, Flo stormed from the flat and made her way as far as possible from the four idiots inside. Deciding to head for the market, she was hopeful that there at least, she'd find one of her pals to talk to. Obviously she'd repeat nothing of what was going on back at her own home but anything to take her mind off it would be a happy release. Flo McCann didn't care if the only person she bumped into was Edna Burrows, for once the woman's inane ranting would make for light relief.

Back in the flat and with her grandmother safely out of earshot, Angela once again took charge. Looking at and aiming her question at both men, she inquired as to who the person on the inside was. Jimmy Forbes turned to his pal, leaving the reply strictly up to him. Knowing Herbie was more than a little fond of Kathy Jones, he hadn't wanted to get into the finer points and it now left Herbie Spires feeling cornered.

"Angela it's true we have someone on the inside but whether they'd want to get involved is another matter!"

Angela knew it was time to cut the crap, either she made her presence felt or she gave up and went back to Canterbury.

"Anyone who does right by my father will be well rewarded. Now get on the telephone and see if the person in question is interested!"

Like a lamb Herbie reluctantly did as he was asked and made his way into the sitting room to phone Kathy Jones. With the bookies still closed to the public and Kathy being told to stay at home until called, the phone rang and rang. Fishing inside his jacket pocket, Herbie pulled out a small leather note book. Quickly scanning the entries, he found her home number. Dialling again, he waited for a reply. Kathy sat on the old sofa, coffee in hand and engrossed in another rubbishy teen magazine. The telephone bursting into life gave her a shock and she snatched up the receiver before it had chance to ring a third time. The television flashed in front of her with some chat show or other but she couldn't be bothered with it and had turned the volume to mute. Nervously she spoke into the handset.

"Hello?"

"Kathy its Herbie, is everythin' alright?"

"Yeh! Sure Mr Spires. Since the spot of bother at work, I've been given some time off."

"Without pay I bet? That tight bastard Vale wouldn't give you the drippin's off his arse!"

"I can manage for a while and to be honest it's good to be away from the place. I ain't been sleeping properly but then again it could be worse. Anyway what can I do for you?"

Herbie let out a loud sigh. The last thing he wanted was to cause the young woman any hassle. Having to put up with Johnny Vale day in and day out was enough of a burden for anyone to have to deal with.

"Kath I need to see you. It's nothing for you to worry about but something's come up. Any chance I can pop round to your place later?"

Kathy Jones didn't have to give the question a second thought. With all his heart, Marty had loved the man on the other end of the phone and if it was good enough for him then it was good enough for her. After giving out her address

and directions, Kathy Jones replaced the handset in its cradle and wondered what all the cloak and dagger stuff could be about. Staring at the silent screen, she was deep in thought when Johnny Vale called a few minutes, later. Telling her to start back at the bookies the following morning, she put all thoughts of the previous conversation to the back of her mind. After all, in a few hours time she'd find out for herself. As Herbie Spires came back into the kitchen and all eyes were on him but before Angela could ask, the Scouser spoke.
"Well?"
"I honestly don't know Jim. I'm going over to hers later today."
"Her? No one told me it was a woman!"
Herbie couldn't see the logic and her haughty bossy tone was beginning to get right up his nose.
"So? What fuckin' difference does it make?"
Angela stood up and walked over to the sink. She stared out at the dull grey skyline for several minutes before answering.
"You both told me last night what a dangerous game we're playing. Now you are bringing in someone who may well have children and a family, is that correct?"
Herbie could only nod his head.
"Well I'm sorry but I can't be party to that. You'll have to call her back and tell her it's off."

Finally Herbie Spires blew his top and his voice echoed off every wall and cupboard in the small kitchen. His anger was so strong that even Jimmy Forbes flinched at the venom in his words.

"Now listen and listen good you jumped up stupid little bitch. You come to the smoke; involve us all in your little fuckin' game and then when the heat gets too much you want to fuckin' bail out. Well I'm sorry to tell you but it's too late lady, you started this now you are goin' to see it through to the end OK!"

Angela gave a smug grin, one that both men had seen her father wear a thousand times and not in dissimilar circumstances to the one they were in at this very moment.

"For god's sake Herbie sit down! As usual you've got it all wrong. Hell will freeze over before I give up on getting the business back. I just don't want to cause anyone, especially a woman, more hurt than is necessary."

"Well that's alright then. Kathy Jones loved every inch of your dad and I know fuckin' hand on heart that she'd have died for him. If she comes through for us, then it will be worth the involvement, trust me."

Angela filled the kettle for the second time that morning and after lighting the gas, rejoined the men at the table.

"I do trust you, both of you. I don't suppose I

have a lot of choice in the matter but I know what you both meant to my father and that's good enough for me. What time do we meet this Katie?"

"Its Kathy and you don't. If she wants to get involved then I will set up a meet, until then I'll handle this alone!"

Jimmy interrupted just as Angela was about to read Herbie the riot act and she was glad that he intervened.

"Herb that's all well and good but we're fast runnin' out of time. I suggest that after you've had a chat, you bring Kathy over to the Cock and Comfort."

As hard as she tried Angela couldn't hold back her laughter. Through fits of giggles and with tears streaming down her eyes, she spluttered out her next sentence.

"The cock and what?"

Herbie Spires also wanted to laugh and his efforts at hiding it were somewhat more successful than Angela's. Jimmy Forbes didn't notice his friend's reaction, only those of the woman sitting opposite him and he wasn't one bit amused at her rudeness.

"Actually it's the Groom and Butler now but no matter how hard the brewery tries to change the image, it'll always be known as the Cock and Comfort and frequented by gays. Angela, as strange as it might seem, it's difficult not to be

noticed in the east end. If we have a meet in one of the locals word will get back to Vale in minutes, a gay pub is the best chance we have. Of course we could have used Mrs M's flat but I didn't think you'd want her to know all the details?"
Still snickering she nodded her understanding. "One more thing, if this take over's really goin' to happen then we need extra bodies. With just the three of us, well Herbie and me, then we won't stand a cat in hells chance. Now you've obviously noticed dozy bollocks sittin' here."
The Scouser's referral to him in such a derogatory manner got Danny's back up instantly. He was about to voice an opinion when he remembered his uncles words. For the first time Angela studied the young man and she had to admit to herself that he was rather good looking.
"He's Herbie's nephew and we've decided to bring him on board."
Angela smiled but only nodded her head in Danny's direction.
"Now as I was about to say, you need as much muscle as you can lay your hands on and although he might appear a bit daft he knows how to fuckin' handle himself."
Suddenly things were serious and the foolery stopped immediately. Angela looked from Herbie to Jimmy and for the first time they saw

fear in her eyes. The look was soon replaced by a hardened glare and it was Jimmy she focused her attention on.

"Then I suggest you do something about it. You both know I'm new to the game and I thought you were here to help me? If we need more bodies then get them!"

Herbie didn't want any bad feeling within their happy little band but although he could see her point, he was also a little resentful of her accusation that they didn't want to help her.

"Angela that's unfair on both of us. If Jimmy here had gone out and hired extra hands, you'd have been the first to complain that he was taking over."

Like her Father, apologies didn't come easily to Angela but she knew that maybe she'd over stepped the mark this time.

"Ok I'm sorry but if you're nervous about all this, can you imagine what I'm going through? If I get snappy from time to time, believe me it isn't personal. Money isn't an issue and I'd be grateful if you could sort things out for me Jimmy. Now if that's it, I suggest we all get on with what we have to do and I'll expect to hear from you both later today."

Her final sentence told them in no uncertain terms that the meeting was well and truly over and they got up to leave. Ever the dutiful host, Angela escorted the men to the front door and couldn't resist one last pep talk.

"Remember boys when this is all over, we'll have a good laugh at Johnny Vales expense."

They all smiled but their efforts were weak to say the least. As the three walked away Angela spent a second or two studying the rear of Danny Spires and she could feel a fluttering sensation in the pit of her stomach. Chastising herself she walked back into the flat and closed the door. Outside Jimmy got into the front of Herbie Spires car.

"What about your motor Jim?"

"Oh fuck it I'll pick it up later. After the time it took to park the bastard thing I aint o spend another twenty minutes trying to get it out."

All three men laughed as Herbie drove off in the direction of Bermondsey. Danny sat silently in the back and as yet the Scouser still hadn't spoken directly to him. He was starting to feel like a spare part but knew better than to say anything. Inside the flat, Angela walked into the kitchen and sitting at the table, held her head in her hands. Everything they'd discussed raced through her mind and she started to think that perhaps her Nan had been right. Slamming her hands on the table, she was angry with herself for even allowing the thought to enter her head and dismissed it instantly. She would see this through to the bitter end if only for the sake of her father's memory.

CHAPTER TWENTY

As Herbie Spires and Jimmy Forbes crossed the Thames and entered Bermondsey, Jimmy began to noticeably get uptight. He hated being out of his manor, come to that he hated being anywhere outside of the East End. Coupled with the fact that he loathed Mickey Colletta, it didn't make for a very happy man. Herbie could see but would have known without looking, that his pal was feeling uncomfortable. Herbie felt great, Mickey was a big shot over the water and even though little business was done between them, the two men had known each other for over thirty years.
"Jim I wish you'd fuckin' calm down. Every single time we have to come here, you get more wound up than a dodgy watch."
"I know mate but the man's a cunt!"
"Maybe he is but right at this minute, 'that cunt' as you so elegantly put it, is a necessity. OK?"
"OK!"
Pulling up outside the small restaurant Jimmy shook his head. The high street was always heaving with traffic but no one dared to park outside the Colletta Trattoria. Michael Colletta had been born to a third generation Italian immigrant. The original family had arrived from Sicily back in nineteen ten and the love of

anything from the old country was plain to see, even if the man had never set foot on Italian soil himself. His accent was pure London but he liked to put in the odd Italian phrase now and again. Somehow it made him feel more important and deep down he had a secret desire to be like the real Cosa Nostra. The father of three sons, Mickey much to the anger of his wife had made sure that the boys came into the business as soon as they were old enough. Mickey's attempts at acting the Don caused his family terrible embarrassment on a daily basis but they had all learnt early on, you never challenged the head of the house, not if you wanted to remain in good physical health. The building was adorned by a traditional red and white stripped awning which hung above a massive picture window. As Herbie and Jimmy reached the main door it was swiftly opened for them by a big man dressed head to toe in black and who permanently stood around the entrance. Several diners were tucking into ravioli and spaghetti and the smells made Herbie's mouth water. Spotting his guests, Mickey quickly came over.
"Herbie! Good to see you Pal."
Embracing Herbie, Mickey proceeded to kiss both cheeks of his guest. As he turned his attention towards Jimmy, the Scouser pushed out his hand as if to say 'I'll shake but I'm not

kissin' you.' Mickey Colletta laughed out loud and after turning his back on the man, placed his arm around Herbie's shoulder and led him to a quiet private corner. Jimmy Forbes was well pissed off at the rudeness but followed silently behind with Danny. A large carafe of Chianti was brought to the table and each of the men's glasses was filled to capacity. Neither Herbie nor Jimmy liked red wine but didn't want to offend their guest by asking for a beer. Throughout the meeting they tactfully sipped at the drink, trying not to wince as the bitter taste consumed their taste buds.

"So Herbie my friend what brings you over today?"

"I suppose you've got wind about Marty's girl turning up?"

"The grape vine mentioned something but I try not to listen to gossip. So tell me what any of this has got to do with me?"

Herbie nervously took a large mouthful of wine as he stalled for time. Desperately he struggled to come up with the right words for what he wanted to say.

"Everyone in the smoke knows there was never any love lost between Johnny Vale and me or even Jimmy here come to that. Now that the girls on the scene, she wants what's rightfully hers and who can blame her? You are one of the few people we know who's not afraid to go up against Vale but please don't think that's what we've come here for. Nothin' could be further from the truth. It's just that we knew, you more than anyone, would understand the birthright thing."

"I do my friend, I do but I still don't see where I figure in all of this?"

Again Herbie swigged at the wine and suddenly he began to feel it's warm calming effect.

"There's no way Johnny Vale's goin' to give up the firm without a fight and we're prepared for that, well mentally at least. Trouble is both my crew and Jimmy's have diminished to almost zero. Even if we were fully staffed, there isn't one among them who we could really trust. At least not when it comes down to taking on the so called big boss. We thought that you could perhaps help us out with a few good bodies."

It was now Mickey's turn to sit and think and the few moments he took had both men on the edge of their seats. Not in the market for a turf war, Mickey was aware how delicate the situation was but the importance of family would outweigh anything else as far as he was concerned. If it had been his boys, well then he'd have wanted exactly the same. Out of respect for Marty he felt it was his duty to help. Jimmy was more worried than Herbie; he knew that if they were turned down now, then it was all over. No other firm in the whole of the smoke would touch them. Mickey Colletta snapped his fingers and a telephone was brought over to the table. After dialling and a few seconds wait he began to speak.

"Mario! Get over here and bring George and Franco with you, oh and tell Geno it's time for his initiation into the family business."

Pressing the cancel button he turned to the men sitting at the table.

"I never liked that fuckin' wide boy Vale but Marty I had much time for. The boys will be here shortly and then we'll get this fuckin' show on the road my friends."

Herbie Spires winked as Jimmy looked over and both wore grins like never before. The three men continued to drink the wine, which for no apparent reason had converted Herbie instantly from whisky to the finer art of the grape. Even Jimmy gradually started to relax, that was until the front door swung open and four men walked in.

"Herbie, Jimmy, let me introduce you both to the boys. Mario and George here can sort out any trouble you care to put their way. Franco has more brains than most of us put together and then there's the good looking one Geno, he's my baby. He's more interested in fuckin' than fightin' but he needs to learn about business sometime and I thought one good turn deserves another, hey?"

Handsome was an understatement when it came to Geno Colletta. Tall and with raven black hair he was every woman's dream and he knew it. Danny had been standing silently at the back of his uncle and when he spotted Geno, took an instant dislike to him. He had tried to act as if he felt nothing when he'd met Angela but now this Italian hunk had turned up he was going to have competition before he had even made a play for her. The thought that she would probably be attracted to this Geno bloke gutted him. Danny could be described as sort of cute but he couldn't compete, not when it came down to looks at least. Contrary to his father's beliefs, at twenty four Geno Colletta was far from being wet behind the ears. Having just finished a four year course on business studies at Newcastle University, he had more up top than Mickey had in his little finger. His father didn't see his intellect, only the very hard earned cash that University had cost him. Geno didn't answer back but nodded in the direction of the men at the table and at the same time he eyed up Danny in a non to friendly manner. On his return from university, he'd decided to say nothing and toe the line, at least until he saw an opportunity to change things. In the five months since he'd been home, that opportunity as yet hadn't arisen but he was confident that when it did, he would be out of the Colletta's clutches forever. Herbie

Spires got up from the table. In turn he shook each of the men's hands and as he reached Geno Colletta, he instantly knew that Angela would be more than a little taken with the lad. Another bottle of Chianti was ordered and the restaurant closed to the public. All the men took seats around the table and the second meeting of the day began. After everything had been discussed and agreed regarding amounts and shares they all passed their mobile phone numbers over to Jimmy Forbes. He punched each one into his own phone and told them to be on standby as they could be called at any time of the night or day. When Herbie, Danny and the Scouser were back inside the Jag, and not until the car was five minutes down the road, did Herbie offer up his hand in a high five. Slapping his pal's palm Jimmy Forbes laughed.
"We're on our way Herbie me old friend, were' on our way."
"Too fuckin' right Jim and not before time I can tell you."
"Well I didn't reckon a lot to 'em. That young one seemed like a right fuckin' prick!"
Herbie Spires turned to face the back seat.
"I don't give a fuck what you think Danny so keep your trap shut!"
Herbie and Jimmy looked at each other and smiled. They both knew that it was just a case of young stags locking horns.

Dropping the Scouser back at his car, the friends agreed that if everything went to plan they'd meet up in a couple of hours. Herbie then drove over to Bethnal Green and Kathy Jones's tiny council flat. Her directions had been clear and he found the large block easily. Parking the Jag, he handed a twenty over to a group of youths standing on the pavement, with the promise of the same if all wheels and paintwork remained intact on his return. Even though Herbie Spires was a known face in the area, it didn't cut any mustard with the kids who frequently vandalised the estate. Feeling it was money well spent; Herbie and Danny climbed the stairwell to Kathy's home and grimaced at the stench of urine as they entered the stairwell. Watching everything from her fourth storey window, Kathy stood with the door wide open as they approached.
"Hello Mr Spires! Please come in. I've sent the kids over to the neighbours so we won't be disturbed."
Herbie gave his friendliest smile but deep down he hated having to involve her.
"Thanks Kath, this shouldn't take too long, oh and by the way this is my nephew Danny."
"Pleased to meet you Danny!"
After his reprimand in the car a while earlier Danny Spires didn't speak and only stared at the ground so he didn't have to make eye contact.

Sitting on one of the hard chairs in the poor but spotless front room and after declining her offer of tea, Herbie Spires wasted no time in getting down to the business in hand.
"Marty's daughter has turned up and......."
"Marty's what?"
"Yeh I know how shocked you must be but it's true. Angie is twenty five and hell bent on getting' back what's rightfully hers and before you ask, yes Johnny is also aware of her. She needs your help Kath but only if you're prepared to offer it. If you decide you don't want to get involved, then it won't reflect on you in any way shape or form."
Throughout his speech Herbie had focused on a single flower on the now dated wallpaper. Now finished, he looked up at his host to see Kathy Jones grinning from ear to ear.
"Anyway I can help Mr Spires I will and I really mean that. If I have to suffer another day of Johnny I swear I'll go bleedin' mad."
"It's good of you to offer Kath but to cross him could be very dangerous. We're all prepared to take that chance but you've got a family. Are you really tellin' me you're prepared to risk all that?"
"As I said before, I had a good teacher in Marty. Please don't worry about me I'll be careful."
Herbie didn't reply he couldn't because to be truthful it would have put the whole operation

at risk but inside he felt terrible.

"Right then, the little lady in question would like to meet you. Will the kids be alright for a couple of hours?"

After pulling on her coat, Kathy Jones reapplied her lipstick in the over mantle mirror.

"No problem! I thought this might take a little while so I already arranged it. Shall we go?"

"Give us a minute Kath. I just have to give Jimmy a call and then we're all set."

Removing his mobile Herbie used the speed dial to reach his friend.

"Jimmy we'll be on our way in a few minutes so can you go and collect Angela?"

"Already done, we're waiting at the cock as I speak."

"Fuck me Jim you don't half presume a lot. How'd you know Kathy would want to be a part of all this?"

" Because I know how she felt about Marty and if that wasn't enough to persuade her then I knew you'd move fuckin' mountains to get her here. Got to go, Miss Bossy Boots is on her way back from the bog!"

Herbie Spires stared into the receiver and couldn't believe the cheek of his mate but then he was never really surprised at anything the Scouser said or did. Holding open the front door for Kathy Jones, the three descended the smelly landing and when they reached the car,

Herbie handed over the final score as agreed. "They are all little bastard's round here Mr Spires. Fancy having to pay for your own bleedin' car! Still I suppose if it keeps it in one piece it's worth it."

Danny held open the car's rear door and once Kathy was seated he joined his uncle up front. Kathy was excited at the prospect of meeting Marty's daughter and couldn't contain herself on the drive over to White Chapel. She constantly moved around in the seat and when she couldn't hold back any longer leant forward so that her head was between the two front seats.

"What's she like Mr Spires?"

Herbie looked into the rear view mirror and grinned. Remembering his own euphoria when he'd received the letter from Marty's solicitor, he understood how Kathy was feeling.

"Who Angie? Well she's nothing like you're imagining."

In a voice that would have been welcomed at any private school Herbie started to describe his new boss.

"For a start her names Angela Canning Brown and she's terribly posh but fair dues to her she's nice with it. Before you ask, yes she's the spit of her old man, right down to his unruly mane of black curly hair."

Kathy Jones didn't ask anything else, she was

beginning to feel inferior and she hadn't even met the woman. From time to time Herbie glanced at her through the mirror. True she'd been looking tired recently and the loss of Marty had hit her hard but she now seemed a bundle of nerves. Kathy didn't see him studying her and continued to twist her hands in a wringing fashion.
"You alright girl?"
"I'm fine, why?"
"You seem uptight to me and it ain't the normal Kath I'm used to."
"I just wish I could manage to get some sleep. Every time I close my eyes all I can see is Seth's head on the desk with his brains fallin' out."
Herbie Spires suddenly felt responsible for the state Kathy was in, for a start she would be fine if it wasn't for what he and the Scouser had done. Mentally he made a note, when all this was sorted he was going see she was alright and he didn't just mean financially. At last the Cock and Comfort came into sight and Herbie apologised about the venue as he parked the car.
"No sweat Mr Spires, I suppose it's the safest place around?"
"Exactly Kath. It's a whole different set of people altogether, who have no connection to the likes of us or any other firm. Besides, even if they know who we are, they're all too bothered about who they're goin' to pull, to worry about

grassing us up. Did you know Johnny hates queers with a vengeance? He wouldn't give one the time of day let alone set foot in a place like this."

As the Jag came to a halt, Kathy Jones laughed out loud and suddenly realised that she was seeing her companion in a totally different light. The place was dark, noisy and smelled of sex but once again Jimmy Forbes had pulled a few strings. Crystal the landlady came over to welcome her guests, she'd been a friend of Jimmy's for years and had ran the cock and Comfort for nearly as many. It was Crystal, herself a transsexual, who had first introduced Jimmy Forbes to lanky Lorraine but unlike Lorraine, Crystal was absolutely stunning. Guiding Kathy and Herbie through the maze of gyrating bodies, she opened a door on the back wall and pointed for them to enter.

"You not comin' Crystal?"

"Not at the moment love but I will later with any luck."

Kathy giggled but Crystal instantly saw the look of horror on Danny's face.

"Just kidding. No I've had my orders love. Jimmy don't want to be disturbed and what Jimmy wants he usually gets."

Crystal closed the door behind them and they turned to see a long corridor. The bare glossed walls gave the impression of a tunnel with just one door at the far end. Kathy's court shoes clicked loudly as they walked along and she desperately but unsuccessfully tried to silence them. Not bothering to knock Herbie entered first and a sheepish Kathy followed close behind. Danny, just as he'd been told, seemed almost invisible as he closed the door and took a seat in the corner. Jimmy and Angela were already seated round a small table and with the only light source coming from a single forty watt bulb; it was hard for Kathy to see the woman clearly. As they neared the table she almost let out a gasp. The girl was not only beautiful but it was like staring at a mirror image of Marty. Angela saw the look of surprise on the woman's face and immediately stood up to offer her hand, just as Herbie butted in and began the introductions.

"Kathy I'd like you to meet Angie."

"Angela! if you don't mind. Pleased to make your acquaintance Kathy. I know this must all come as rather a shock to you but I'm afraid there's not much I can do about that. Please do take a seat."

Kathy Jones did as she was asked but not once did she take her gaze from Angela Canning Brown's face.

"I don't know how much, if any, information you have on Johnny Vale's forthcoming plans but anything you can tell us, will I'm sure be of great help. Of course it goes without saying that you will be well rewarded."

Something about the way in which Angela spoke made Kathy feel uncomfortable. Maybe it was the posh accent or maybe just the fact that she was her father's daughter.

"I know he has a man on the inside, a security guard named Brian Moore. From the snippets of information I've overheard, I think the rest of the guards are being paid handsomely to turn their backs for a while or not be on shift at all. It's something like that anyway. I know the name of the place he's planning to do over though?"

"That's fine Kathy, we've already got that. Have you heard anything recently?"

"No nothin', just seen some new faces that's all."

"Well thanks for coming and keep your ear to the ground. If anything comes up that you feel might be of interest then give Herbie a call."

"That might be a bit difficult as Johnny laid me off."

Sliding a plain manila envelope across the table, Angela smiled.

"I'm sorry to hear that but I'm sure this will help. Call it a bonus for your trouble."

Kathy Jones looked in Herbie's direction and the man nodded as if to say 'Take it!' She was a proud person but with things as tight at home as they were, Kathy was too poor to have any principles. Picking up the envelope she quickly

slipped it into her bag and stood up.
"Well if that's all I'd best be going."
"Hang on a minute Kath and I'll run you back."
"Don't bother yourself Mr Spires, I'm sure I can get a taxi."
She made her way to the door and glanced back before she left. The three were so deep in conversation that they hadn't even heard her last sentence. Kathy was annoyed not to mention feeling used and as she caressed her handbag and could feel the envelope through the thin fabric, she also felt cheap. The door to the room slowly closed and the latch made a clicking sound. Herbie looked up from the table and was disappointed that Kath had gone so soon. He was all set to give her a lift home but obviously she was in a hurry to get back to the kids and besides he had more pressing things here to deal with.
"So Angela was she any help?"
"Somewhat but we need to move fast if we are going to pull this off. Danny bring your chair over, there's no point in you being here if you're not involved."
Danny Spires was sitting at the table in seconds and now the three men were all ears and hung on her every word waiting to hear what the next step would be.
"We know Johnny Vale goes in four days time, so we'll go in three. Jimmy I want you to gather

up a couple of men from your new little army and pay this Brian Moore a visit. Find out every last detail and if he's scared of Johnny, then make him fear us even more. Whatever Vale's paying we're offering more and tell him there will be no repercussions. Herbie I want you to sort out a getaway car, come to think of it we're going to need at least two and some sort of delivery van. Oh and then there are drivers, they need to have good reputations and preferably not be linked to London. We also need somewhere to store our ill-gotten gains, apart from that I think we're about done. We'll meet up again tomorrow night to finalise the details, I'll give you both a call."
"Wo! Hold on a minute Angie!"
"Herbie how many more times do I have....."
It was now Jimmy's turn to get angry and his words came out in a loud barrage which took even his old friend by surprise.
"Cut the crap, this if far more fuckin' important than your fuckin' name darlin'. The things you've asked for are fuckin' major and you want them sorted in twenty four fuckin' hours? I don't know if you're just playin' at this but I'm telling you it can't be fuckin' done!"
Angela stood up and after pushing her shoulders back and lifting her head high she looked down her nose at the three men sitting at the table.

"Don't ever call me darling again, do you hear? There is no such word as can't, it's not in my vocabulary. It can and will be done and what's more you three are the ones to do it. We're in this now and we have a time schedule. Gentlemen we have no choice in the matter, as you all know what will happen if we fail and that I might add isn't an option. Now let's not have any more whining, just fucking get on with it!"

With that Angela walked from the room and out of the Cock and Comfort. Herbie, Jimmy and Danny sat in shocked silence unable to believe they'd just received a mouthful from a jumped up posh little bitch who knew nothing of the game they were in. Suddenly realising that she was out there alone and could be in danger, the three ran out of the pub. After a few minutes of running up and down the street like lunatics and when Jimmy Forbes was doubled over and panting for air they had to admit defeat. Angela, like the invisible woman, had disappeared.

CHAPTER TWENTY ONE

Flo McCann woke late the following day but she still didn't think that Angela would be up yet. She was a lazy little mare when it came to sleep just like her father before her. Marty was as bad at her age and never rose until ten at the earliest. Flo decided to get the breakfast started, the smell of bacon and eggs wafting through the flat was sure to rouse her granddaughter. When the last of the fried bread had been cooked and with still no sign of Angela, Flo mad her way to the spare room. Gently tapping on the door she waited for a response but when none came she quietly entered the bedroom. Although she could see that the bed had been slept in, she still felt anxious that her granddaughter was missing. With as yet no information as to what had gone on last night, the sight of an empty bed was unnerving. Going by the last few days, nine in the morning was still too early for Angela to be up and about. Flo thought to herself that there was little point in worrying, especially as she had no idea where the girl could be. Back in the kitchen she took her seat at the table and attempted to eat at least one of the meals she'd cooked. After two forced forkfuls and with a slight feeling of nausea, she had to admit defeat and pushed the plate away. Placing the dirty dishes into soak, Flo stared out of the window and mulled over the past few days events. After Marty had died she'd accepted that there wasn't much left to live for and then out of the blue, a beautiful headstrong young woman had turned up on her doorstep and changed Flo's life. Everything again had meaning and she was frightened that once more it could all be cruelly taken away from her. Maybe Herbie would know where Angela was, after all he was the one supposed to be looking out for her and Flo was sure that he wouldn't let any harm come to Marty's child. Deciding to give it until ten o'clock and if she hadn't heard anything by then she'd phone him, she went into the bathroom for her daily strip wash.

Angela had arrived in Knightsbridge a little after nine am. After realising that most of the shops didn't open until ten she walked around browsing in the windows. It was a gorgeous day and she was glad to be alive, if still a tad fearful of what the future held. Spying a trendy pavement café that was open for the early morning workers, she decided to have breakfast. Unaware as to the feast that had been waiting for her back at the flat and which now sat in the dustbin, she ordered some French pastries and fresh coffee. By the time she'd finished her last mouthful of food and ordered a second cup, most of the stores were now open for business. Starting in the smartest boutique she could find,

Angela was immediately put off by the snooty attitude of the salesgirl. Several places later she had lost the spring in her step and was quickly becoming disheartened. Everything was so trendy and didn't match up to the mental picture she had in her mind of what stylish and chic should look like. As she crossed the road and was seriously thinking about aborting her mission, she happened to glance down a narrow ally that led off of Bond Street. Something about the small rather tired looking shop caught her attention and she could feel herself being drawn along the pavement and into Pitchford Court. The window display was stuffy and dated but something pulled her inside anyway. As the old fashioned bell above the door signalled her entrance, she was instantly greeted by a surprisingly small but smartly dressed man.
"Good morning Miss, how may I help?"
"I'm looking for an outfit. I've been in almost every shop on the street but I can't seem to find what I'm looking for."
"Oh dear, why don't you take a seat and we'll have a chat about what it is you really want."
The old fashioned tub chairs were comfortable and as the man got out his pen and paper and began to take notes, things seemed to brighten and she started to feel hopeful again.
"Right from the information you've given me and please feel free to correct me at any time,

what you require is a smart suit that makes you look professional and in charge but without being too fussy?"

Angela smiled, she liked this man and for once she'd found someone who understood her.

"That's exactly what I want."

Getting up from his seat, the man was about to disappear into a doorway at the back of the shop when he turned towards her.

"It will take me a few minutes to gather up some stock. Can I offer you some refreshment? Tea, coffee or maybe you'd like something cold?"

"Tea would be lovely thanks."

Assuming they were alone, Angela was surprised when a woman entered the shop from behind a curtained door. The woman was even smaller in stature than her husband but that was where the similarity ended. Where the man was friendly and extrovert his wife was the complete opposite and Angela thought her quietness actually boarded on rudeness. She didn't say a word but gave Angela a really warm smile as she passed over the china cup and saucer. Having carried out her mission she once more retreated to her sanctuary that was hidden behind a fabric curtain. With the shop looking as it did, Angela wondered how they survived in the cut throat world of fashion but however they managed it, she was just happy that she'd found them. Even if they weren't able to give

her what she wanted, she was glad that they were at least trying to help her. Finishing her drink, Angela wondered what was taking the man so long. She had begun to imagine that she was all alone in the place when the curtain was at last flung aside and the shop keeper appeared laden down with armfuls of clothes.
"Here we are! I'm sure there's something amongst these that you will find suitable." Artistically he started to hang the garments up around the room and with each one Angela was truly amazed at the quality, fabric and workmanship.
"These are fantastic, what label are they? No don't tell me let me guess, Dior, Channel?"
"No no, they're just styles that my wife runs up in her spare time. She's much too shy to have them on show for the customers, even if I'm always telling her she's as good as any of the big names."
"I couldn't agree more Mr?"
"Parker, Noel Parker."
"Well Mr Parker would you mind if I tried a few on?"
Pointing towards a tiny changing room the man's smile couldn't have been any broader.
"Be my guest."
Thirty minutes later and Angela had tried on and purchased most of the stock that had been shown to her. The fabrics were exquisite and the

fit couldn't have been any better if they had been made for her. Thanking the man and with assurances that she'd be back for more in the very near future, she left the shop wearing one of Mrs Parker's creations. The streets were buzzing with city folk and day trippers and Angela received several admiring glances. Stopping off at a designer store, she purchased two pairs of expensive Italian court shoes with matching handbags. The style spoke volumes about the person who wore them, wealthy and powerful and just what Angela Canning Brown wanted people to think. Relieved that the shopping was over she had one more call to make before returning to Bethnal Green. Lyle Lyle and Levrington were one of the largest estate agents in London. The company's portfolio covered some of the most prestigious properties in the city, not to mention a clientele that could fill their own private who's who. Entering the contemporary office, she pushed her shoulders back and held her head high. Just by her dress and accessories the agent instantly had pound signs in front of his eyes. Before any of the others spotted her and his commission went out of the window, Lawrence De'ath made a beeline towards Angela and thrust a hand out directly in front of her.

"Good morning Miss, Lawrence De'ath at your service. May I be of any assistance?"

"That depends on whether you have what I'm looking for Mr Death."
"De'ath! It's De'ath Miss!"
Angela wanted to laugh. She had come across the same name back at school in Canterbury. The young girl in question had been teased mercilessly; it seemed no one wanted to be called Death.
"Exactly what is it that you're looking for Miss?"
Angela took a seat on the expensive leather chesterfield and seductively crossed her legs.
"I want an apartment in the city, although I suppose at a push it could be slightly outside. If that is the case, then nearer to the east end would be better. It has to be large, well furnished and lastly but most importantly I want occupancy by the end of the day."
"There's no way that....."
"Oh and I would just like to add that money is no object."
Her final comments were like music to his ears. If it was possible to be more slimy and smarmy towards her than when she'd first entered the office then he succeeded.
"Then Miss?"
"Canning Brown."
"Lovely name, I'm sure we can accommodate you Miss Canning Brown. I have several properties in mind but there is one in particular I think would suit you down to the ground."

Before she knew what was happening, Angela was inside Lawrence De'ath's Porsche and speeding through the city's streets. Pulling up outside a magnificent red brick building baring the name of Longthorpe Mansions, Lawrence De'ath was opening her door before she even realised he'd gotten out of the car. The converted Victorian building was slightly out of the city but only by a short distance and just as she'd been told the place was magnificent. Overlooking a quiet park at the front, the rent was not overly expensive by London standards but then at eight hundred pounds a week it wasn't cheap either. Situated on the third floor with three large bedrooms and a formal drawing room with dining area leading off, the place was just what she wanted. Handing over a large bundle of cash that more than covered the six months rent in advance, gave her all the credibility that she needed without being checked out. Passing her a large bunch of keys Lawrence asked Angela to sign a form before giving her a brief rundown of the do's and don'ts. With the formalities over he said his goodbyes and left her alone in the sprawling apartment. Wandering from room to room, she checked out the cupboards and closets and after making a quick list of the things she'd need, once again stepped out for her second shopping trip of the day. By the time she'd purchased

sheets, crockery and towels and arranged delivery for the following day, it was almost four in the afternoon. Returning to her new home to collect her shopping, Angela glanced at her watch and realised she was in deep trouble. Flo would be out of her mind with worry and had probably called in the whole of the east end to form a search party. Taking a seat on the sumptuous window seat that overlooked a private garden, she tentatively dialled her grandmother's number. Abruptly and after only one ring, the phone was snatched up and an anxious Flo McCann with Herbie and the Scouser hovering by her side, answered.
"Yeh?"
"Nan it me, I'm sorry if……."
"Fuckin' sorry! You selfish little bitch. We've been out of our minds with bleedin' worry and all you can say is sorry!!!"
Angela felt bad that she had put the old woman through such anguish but at the same time she was angry, no more than that, she was incensed at the way she was being spoken to. Purely on impulse and without thinking, she slammed down the receiver. A few minutes later and she stood outside in the cool air at last beginning to calm down. With a heavy heart, Angela reluctantly hailed a cab back to Bethnal Green. As the taxi pulled up outside, the curtains from Flo's sitting room window twitched and made

her smile. Even though she knew she was just about to face the Spanish inquisition it was nice that someone cared. Laden down with a massive bouquet that she'd picked up on route, Angela pushed the main entrance open and after climbing the stairs was greeted by a stern faced Herbie waiting on the landing.

"Angie what the fuck do you think you're playing at? We've all been goin' fuckin' mental up here imagining all sorts."

Ignoring the man partly due to his tone and partly because he'd once again called her Angie, she made her way inside. After hanging her bag on one of the hooks in the hall, she entered the kitchen where Flo and Jimmy Forbes sat at the table drinking tea.

"Oh so you've fuckin' deemed to come home then?"

"Nan don't start I'm not in the mood alright?"

Flo McCann got up from her chair and walked round to where her granddaughter now stood. Swiftly and without notification, the palm of her hand made contact with Angela's cheek. The slap was delivered with such force that her face was stinging before she'd had time to realise what was happening.

"No it's not fuckin' alright you cheeky little mare. Did you stop for one minute to think of the worry you put me through? Lord knows it ain't but a short time since I buried your dad and you let me fuckin' sit here thinkin' it had happened all over again."

Angela, still holding her reddened cheek, now understood what all the commotion was about. They actually thought she'd been kidnapped or even killed. Suddenly and as if from nowhere, she realised that it was exactly what could have happened and that realisation made her start to shake. Not once had she ever really felt afraid and yet here were three of the closest people to her and they all thought that maybe she was dead.

"Nan I'm so sorry. I'm stupid I know but I just didn't think."

Looking from Herbie to Jimmy, she silently mouthed the word sorry but instead of the forgiveness she was used to, they turned their gaze away.

"Look I made a mistake alright! I'm not dead, I haven't been abducted and I won't do it again. I'm new to all of this and its going to take me some time to learn the rules, now are you all going to punish me forever or can we move on?"

Flo walked back to her granddaughter and standing on her toes placed a kiss on her forehead.

"We'll say no more about it then but don't take liberties do you hear? I suppose you've got things to discuss and you don't want a fuckin' old codger like me pokin' me nose in, so I'm off to bingo. Mind, I wouldn't have been able to go half an hour ago, there's no fuckin' way I could have concentrated on me numbers with you still missin'."

"Nan!"

"Alright I'm going but you two lumps of lard make sure you keep an eye on her and don't give me that fuckin' look Herbie Spires! If you'd done your job proper last night, then we wouldn't be havin' this fuckin' conversation." She didn't wait for a reply; instead she walked from the flat pleased that her beautiful girl was safe, at least for the time being. The room was silent but Angela was eager to find out what the boys had been up to. Waving her hand, she asked Herbie to explain what had happened in the hours prior to her so called disappearance.

"We tried to tail that Brian Moore but it seems he's off sick today, I fuckin' hope he makes a quick recovery for all our sakes. Anyway we were able to sort out the crew and the cars and van are all on standby."

Herbie Spires was as pleased as punch with what he and the Scouser had achieved and assumed Angela would feel the same. He couldn't have been more off the mark and found that out when she spoke with a voice loud enough to raise the dead.

"Fucking sick! You idiot, it's no good sorting out men and cars if we haven't got a job to go to.

Did you not bother to find out where the man lived? That would have been the first thing I would do and no doubt my father would have done."

In a show of togetherness Herbie and the Scouser stood up at the same time and it was a battle of wills as to who got to speak first. Jimmy Forbes won.

"Don't you dare speak to either of us like that you cheeky cow! We worked with your old man for years and he never once talked fuckin' down to us like that. Lady you got to realise that you ain't goin' to get anywhere with that fuckin' kind of attitude. We did our best today and your old man would have seen that but then he was from the East End and not some jumped up upper class bitch who thinks she can just walk in here and be the lady boss at the drop of a hat."

Even Herbie's earlier reprimands hadn't been so stern. Angela felt like a child and even though she wanted to burst into tears, accepted that maybe she deserved his harshness and to feel the way she did. Pops had been her main stay in life but she would never have spoken to him in the despicable manner with which she now spoke to Herbie and Jimmy.

"Look it's not that I'm ungrateful and no doubt my father would have been a tad more tactful but look where that got him. You both know what and who we are dealing with here! We don't have time for mistakes or to wait for some tosser to roust himself out of his sick bed. Do whatever you have to but find him and do it fast. I've rented somewhere else to live and I want an urgent meeting with everyone there tomorrow at eleven, here's the address."

Angela passed a small neatly written card to both Herbie and Jimmy and as they read the address, were taken back that she was actually leaving the manor.

"Does Mrs M know you're going?"

"No not yet but leave Nan to me, she's got to understand that now more than ever I need my own space and in any case I don't want her connected to this in any way shape or form. If there isn't anything else can we call it a day? I'm totally exhausted."

Jimmy stood up and followed by Herbie walked over to where Angela stood leaning against the sink.

"If that's what you want Princess?"

"It is and by the way where's that boy?"

"You mean Danny? I gave him some time off. The poor fucker's only been out of nick for a couple of days and what with all this and havin' to put up with Marge's cooking, I thought he deserved a bit of a break."

All three laughed out loud and then both men kissed her on the forehead before saying goodnight. Angela experienced a real rush of emotion that was new to her. Holding back until they'd left and the door was firmly shut, she made her way to the bedroom just as a single tear fell onto her cheek. Sighing heavily, she brushed it away in sheer frustration.

CHAPTER TWENTY TWO

Brian Moore stood at the grimy basin in the tiny bathroom of his flat and examined his yellow tongue in the mirror. He knew he wasn't ill; it was stress pure and simple that was making him feel so unwell. The stories about Johnny Vale had circulated on the estate for years but since he'd had a rise in fame, everyone said he was more dangerous than ever. Unluckily for him, Brian hadn't been privy to this snippet of gossip until after he'd agreed to Johnny's proposition. Working at Jensen's for over twenty years, Brian Moore was a model employee and one of the most trusted members of the security team. Never having been married and living with his disabled mother, he had been totally devastated when she had died suddenly. The only thing that had seen him through was the tiny tablets prescribed by his doctor for depression. When he was contacted by the local council soon after his mother's death and informed that he had the chance of a right to buy his little home, he'd quickly bucked up his ideas and the thought of being a property owner went straight to his head. Walking round the small two bedroom flat, which still had the original cold steel window frames and was decorated in seventies bold wallpaper, he now began to imagine all the potential the place had. A new kitchen could be fitted, he could install central heating, in fact the list was endless and Brian was lost in a dream of how his home was going to look. His own little palace and it was all there, just waiting to be transformed. Excitedly he'd walked into a mortgage broker the following day, full of enthusiasm and ready to sign on the dotted line. Within a few short minutes he was told that he didn't earn enough at Jensen's to cover the repayments and unfortunately they wouldn't be able to offer him any assistance. Anger consumed every part of his body. Hadn't he always toed the line? Worked hard to provide for him and mum? This was the first time in his life that Brian Moore had a chance to make something of himself and the opportunity had been snatched away even before his old mum was cold in her grave. His depression instantly returned and it took all of his will power, just to carry out any kind of day to day functioning. Approached by one of Johnny's men, Brian had at first refused to have anything to do with the robbery but after being told in no uncertain terms that he didn't have any choice in the matter, he quickly warmed to the idea. Over the past few weeks as he'd thought more and more about buying his house and the refusal of help he'd received after applying for a mortgage, the robbery somehow now didn't seem so bad. It was his chance to carry out his dream and have a few quid over to spruce the place up and maybe even have a little left for a holiday. Deciding not to look a gift horse in the mouth, he accepted the deal and had gradually become more and more excited. That was until yesterday. As normal he'd woke at four am and started to get ready for his six o'clock shift. Suddenly he was doubled up in pain and began to wretch uncontrollably. Managing to make it into the bathroom, Brian held onto the sides of the toilet for dear life. The pan soon became filled with a brown watery liquid and when he had nothing more inside him and exhaustion took hold, he sat on the cold bare floor gasping. Tiny beads of sweat formed on his brow and his legs felt like jelly, they were so bad that as he tried to stand up he had to quickly hold onto the sink for support. When thirty minutes later things hadn't improved, he'd called in sick for the first time in twenty years. Today had started much the same but Brian knew he had to force himself to appear normal, the last thing he needed was to raise suspicion with only a couple of days to go. Dressing in the company's navy issue uniform he pulled on his anorak and was about to leave for his shift when the doorbell chimed. He frowned trying to think who could be calling this early but answered the door all the same. Turning the Yale latch he didn't have time to look outside before he was propelled backwards onto the floor by the force of the door being slammed open. Brian had never in his life seen the two men who now towered above him and assumed they were from Johnny Vale's firm. Jimmy Forbes had been instructed by Angela to visit the man along with one or two of the other crew. She didn't understand and Jimmy wasn't in the mood to explain, that in their line of work you carried out jobs like this only with someone you knew. Ignoring her command the two had visited Brian Moore together. Jimmy loved Herbie and more than anything he trusted the man completely, especially when it came to anything of a delicate nature, which this visit was. Staggering to his feet, Brian's eyes were wide and stared up at the men like those of a startled animal.

"Whhhhat's, what's the matter? I'm doin' everythin' Mr Vale asked."

Jimmy moved forward so that his face was almost level with Brian's.

"We ain't here from Vale pal. We're your worst fuckin' nightmare!"

Before the man had time to reply, Herbie used his full strength and kicked hard between Brian's legs. As his toecap made contact with Brian's genitals, a blood curdling scream escaped from the man's mouth. Not giving their victim time to regain his strength, Herbie kicked

out once more. The impact wasn't so severe due to the fact that Brian Moore had tried to cover himself with his hands but he still felt a searing pain.
"Please!!!!!!! Tell me what you want? Anything and I'll do it, just don't hurt me."
Jimmy grinned; this was turning out to be easier than he'd anticipated. Hauling Brian up off the floor, Jimmy almost threw him into the living room where he landed in a heap on the tired old sofa. The two looked down on Brian in a menacing fashion and Herbie noticed that a disgusting smell had started to fill the room. Leaning in closer to see where it was coming from, Herbie Spires began to heave
"I think he's shit himself Jim. You dirty bastard!"
Jimmy Forbes grabbed the man's cheeks between his finger and thumb and after nipping hard and making Brian pull a distorted face he spoke in almost a whisper.
"Are you scared of Johnny Vale?"
Brian Moore didn't answer but tried with difficulty to move his head up and down.
"Well you want to be doubly fuckin' scared of us. Now listen 'cause I ain't goin' to say this twice. The little caper you've got planned with Vale will still go ahead, only difference is it's a day earlier and you'll be dealing with us. You're still goin' to get the same cut, maybe a bit more if you don't cause us any agro but if you breathe a

word to anyone! Well let's just say you won't have to worry about your knackers again 'cause where you'll be goin' you won't fuckin' need 'em. Understood?"
Again Brian desperately tried to nod his head. At this precise moment in time he didn't care about the money or buying his house. The only thing on his mind was surviving this nightmare. Jimmy Forbes grabbed hold of the man's hair and after moving his face towards Brian's until they were almost touching, he spoke.
"I want you to carry on as normal, as far as you're concerned there's no real difference understood?"
"Yeh, yes!"
Herbie removed a small pad and a pen from his inside pocket. Placing a handkerchief over his mouth with one hand to lessen the stink, he held the pen in his other and was now ready to write. He nodded to the frightened man on the sofa to give them all the information they would need. Now slightly recovered, Brian realised that it didn't matter two hoots to him who was behind the job. If these men wanted information, then information they would have. He began to talk nine to the dozen and Herbie had difficulty in keeping up. It was almost as if this no one, this misfit of society, was actually enjoying having their undivided attention. For all of his life it had been as though Brian Moore was invisible.

At school he was bullied and girls were something he only dreamed about. Standing over six feet tall was the only attribute Brian possessed. Gaining weight had always been a problem and he was still as skinny as a rake. His uniform hung on him and having horrendous acne that had afflicted him for years, he wasn't a pretty sight. To a woman of partial sight, these cosmetic problems wouldn't have mattered, but Brian Moore's personality would. He was mean and he was sneaky. Never one to accept blame, at school he was always snitching on others to save his own skin. Even his own mother had detested the man and for the latter years of her life, completely ignored him. Now after so long, there were people who wanted to know Brian Moore and even after the pain had been dished out, he was enjoying all the attention. More than that, Brian was actually getting off on it. After explaining in great detail the plan and security procedures that the firm had to carry out, the men finally left. Brian still had an hour before his shift started so switching on his computer he hesitantly typed in a question. It didn't take long to find what he was looking for and he was soon on his way to work and well aware that now more than ever, he had to look normal. Brian didn't have a clue who his early morning visitors had been but he didn't ever want to feel pain like that again. He was too scared of the

men to go running to Johnny Vale and meekly accepted that he would allow things to go ahead and worry about any consequences later. If they stood by their word, then he could be out of London long before Johnny got wind of what had happened. Brian Moore would be sad to leave his old life and his dream of buying the flat but he would have enough cash to start afresh somewhere else in the world. He was confident that he could get through a police interview and if luck was on his side, would be seen as a victim. The internet was a wonderful device and after his earlier research had narrowed his new home down to two countries. It would either be Canada or Australia as neither had an extradition agreement with the UK. Brian Moore was no fool and knew it would be better living somewhere strange than to stay here and suffer the wrath of Johnny Vale. When Vale found out he'd been double crossed and that Brian had gone along with the treachery, well for now he didn't even want to think about that. Outside in the early morning air, Herbie Spires and Jimmy Forbes removed their mobiles and began to dial the new crew members.
"Fancy a cuppa somewhere?"
"I think we fuckin' deserve one Herb!"
"So do I Jimmy my boy, so do I."
The previous night Flo McCann arrived home late after her stint at bingo. Edna Burrows and a

couple of others had been lucky and the few quid they'd won had been crying out to be spent. Fortunately a pub was situated right next door to the Mecca, so none of the old girls had far to walk. Intending to only have the one, Flo was still knocking them back at last orders. The woman had managed to stagger home by midnight and not wanting to wake her granddaughter, she had gone straight to bed. The next morning saw Flo wake with a thumping head and she tried to think why last night, it had seemed such a good idea to get plastered. Making her way to the bathroom, she reprimanded herself for being such a silly old fool. After a quick wash she walked into the kitchen but couldn't for the life of her stomach any food. Instead she swallowed two aspirin accompanied by a half pint of water. Making herself a strong cup of coffee Flo sat down at the table and held her head. If Angela wanted something to eat, well she'd just have to get it herself.

An hour later, she was finally starting to feel like she was back in the land of the living but there still wasn't any sign of her houseguest. Tapping gently on Angela's door brought no reply, so she walked in. This time the bed hadn't been slept in and a feeling of panic immediately came over Flo as she mouthed 'for pity's sake not fuckin' again.' About to telephone Herbie Spires, Flo replaced the receiver when she saw the white envelope on the mantle. She didn't rush to open it but was glad that at least this time; the stupid girl had the sense to let her know where she was. Taking the letter into the kitchen, Flo refilled her cup with coffee and then began to tear open the note. What she read next made her spill the hot liquid all over the place.

'Dear Nan

Just so you don't worry, I'm letting you know that I've rented a flat nearer to the city. It's in a good neighbourhood and when everything's sorted out I'd like you to come and see it. The next few days are going to be awfully busy, so I apologise in advance if I'm not able to contact you. Please don't be upset with me, it's just something I have to do and I don't want you involved in any of this. I know you'll understand.

All my love

Angela'

P.S. In case of emergencies my new mobile number is 076161873970.

Flo couldn't believe that after yesterday and all the panic she'd put everyone through, she would risk it all again. The lying little mare must have already had the flat when she came home and she'd stood there and not said a word. Flo McCann was livid, well she was truly on her own now, and Flo prayed as hard as she could

that Marty was looking out for his girl.
Angela Canning Brown had spent the first night in her own place and she liked the feeling. The sun shone through the voile window dressing and the brand new Egyptian cotton sheets were cool against her skin. She turned on the radio and for a few minutes enjoyed the mellow tune that she hadn't heard before but still found very relaxing. Angela thought of all the years spent back at 'Journeys End Defiant' and couldn't remember one single day, when she'd felt such a feeling of belonging as she did right now. Sighing to herself she realised that if it wasn't for her father, she'd still be there, still doing mind numbing charity work and still engaged to the oh so boring Edward. Turning her gaze up towards the ceiling she mouthed the words 'Thanks Dad.' Glancing at the bedside clock Angela saw it was nine twenty and realised, that first morning in her new flat or not, she had to get up and make herself presentable before the firm of men arrived. Dressing in an expensive waffle gown, another of yesterdays purchases, she made her way into the contemporary kitchen and peered into the sparsely filled fridge. Groceries hadn't been high on her list of priorities but she had managed to pick up a few essentials and they would do until she had time to get to the shops. Preparing scrambled eggs and tea, she switched on a second radio as she

ate. Again the music was easy listening and by the time she'd finished she was feeling full, happy and ready to take on the world. A swift shower was followed by a time consuming session of applying her makeup. When the new boys arrived, she wanted to make just the right impression. Choosing another of the suits she'd purchased yesterday, Angela checked her reflection from every angle in the bedroom mirror. Satisfied with what she saw, she peered at the clock. Even though it seemed like it had taken forever to get ready, it was still only ten thirty. Without knowing what she was doing she began to pace the floor and with each step became more and more on edge. When her mobile started to sing, Angela almost jumped out of her skin. For a second she didn't pick it up but when she realised that the only people she'd given the number to was Herbie, Jimmy and Flo, she flipped open the receiver.
"Angela?"
"High Nan, how are you?"
"So you can be fuckin' arsed to answer your phone then?"
This was all she needed today. The men were due any minute and she had an irate senior citizen reading her the riot act down the telephone.
"Nan please don't be angry, I thought you would understand! Look I need some space, you know

I've got a lot to deal with at the moment."
"You've got a lot to fuckin' deal with! what about me?. You swan into my life after twenty five years and no sooner are we startin' to get to know each other and you fuckin' swan right out again!"
Angela walked towards the front window and pulled back the voile curtain with one of her immaculately painted nails. Luckily there was no sign of any cars at the moment.
"It's not a case of swanning in and out as you put it. You are well aware of what I'm getting into and I need to keep you out of it as much as I can. For god's sake! You're the one who's always going on about how dangerous this Johnny Vale is!"
Flo McCann raised her voice to such a scream, that Angela had to pull the phone away from her ear.
"Keep me out of it! You daft mare! I've dealt with more Johnny Vale's in my lifetime than you've had fuckin' hot dinners. At least if you're here, we can all keep an eye on you."
"Nan they are keeping an eye on me, so you don't have to worry."
Angela was all set to except more verbal abuse from the woman and was slightly taken back when all she heard was a gasp.
"Nan, Nan are you alright?"
"'Course I am, are you telling me that those two

lumps of lard knew about this?"
"Well only since last night but I can't see what that's got to do with anything."
"No my dear you wouldn't."
As quickly as the phone had burst into life only a few minutes earlier, it was now silent. Angela repeated her grandmother's name over and over again but there was no reply. How the call had ended made her feel anxious about the old woman but it would be impossible to try and sort the situation out at this moment in time. The people who were about to visit her apartment were professionals and she couldn't get out of the meeting now, even if she'd wanted to. Well not without losing face and Angela understood that everything in this kind of life was about reputation and face. Flo McCann had slammed her telephone down so hard that for a minute she thought it was broken. Now for the second time in as many days Herbie Spires and Jimmy Forbes had let her down big time. How quickly everyone forgot that less than a month ago she was treated like royalty. As Marty's mum, if she asked for something then it would have been done without question. Flo made her way into the kitchen and slumped down on one of the chairs. Never again would she be revered and the thought hurt her more than she could ever have imagined. For the first time in all her life Flo McCann was alone, not only alone but

also aware of her age and right now she was feeling every single year. She started to cry, softly at first then huge raking sobs that shook the whole of her tiny frame. The outburst ended with her calling out for her son.
"Oh Marty! Whatever's happenin'?"

CHAPTER TWENTY THREE

It was now eleven and Angela was more nervous than ever. About to phone Herbie and give him a mouthful because no one had turned up, she stopped when the intercom started to bleep. No one could get into the main building without someone pressing the entry button to one of the flats. The place had state of the art security so she wasn't unduly worried. Staring into the video monitor she was intrigued as to what her new employees looked like. Two men peered back at her and she felt unnerved by their scowling lived in faces. It had been agreed by Jimmy that whoever called at the flat from now until told differently, would have to give a pass word. This would be the only means of entry and would be changed on a regular basis. If the lady boss didn't hear the magic word, then you wouldn't get in. Angela composed herself and stood up straight, even though she couldn't be seen. Pressing the button she spoke into the microphone.
"Yes can I help you?"
"Bluebell Wood."
Angela giggled at the deep intimidating voice. When she'd first suggested Bluebell wood, Jimmy had said it was pathetic and something a pansy would choose. Angela had stood her

ground, saying that it was special to her and though not explaining why, said it was apt for this chapter in her life. Now hearing it come out of the microphone, she had to admit that it was a rather feminine name. To hear it escape from the mouth of someone built like a gorilla seemed comical, actually quite hilarious. When the large man looked up into the lens with a puzzled expression on his face, she immediately realised that while she was chuckling away, her finger had still been pressed on the speaker button. He'd heard her laughter which had embarrassed him and Angela was now mortified that she had made him feel that way. Not wanting to make the situation worse, she immediately pressed the entry button and the front doors clicked open. Franco Posello and George Sands took the elevator to the third floor and gently tapped on the door but Angela was still reluctant to answer, even though the password had been given. Staring through the spy hole, she saw just how big and powerful the two men were and it unnerved her. Dressed in dark suits and shirts with pastel coloured ties, they appeared the epitome of every normal person's perception of a gangster. Accepting that as she'd allowed them to come up, she had no choice but to open the door, she took in a deep breath. About to turn the handle, Angela gained a moment's reprieve when the intercom once more burst into life.

Deciding it would do no harm to make the men at the door wait a little longer; she made her way along the hall and again glanced at the monitor. This time the faces were instantly recognisable and she pressed the entry button without hesitation, before returning to the front door. The men stood patiently waiting, in fact Angela silently thought to herself that very little would faze them. Straightening her jacket and pushing her hair back from her face, she finally opened up to be met by the coldest most expressionless faces she had ever seen. At the same time as they crossed the threshold, Herbie, Jimmy and Danny made their exit from the lift. Jimmy Forbes walked into the flat and headed straight for the drawing room where he warmly greeted George and Franco but Herbie with Danny standing behind him, held back.
"Are you coming through or are you just going to stand in the hall all day?"
"Angie I mean Angela why didn't you ask for the pass word?"
"Because, I could see you in this silly."
She poked a manicured finger towards the monitor, gave a gentle tut and began to walk off.
"What if someone had a gun to my back and was using me to get inside this place to you?"
His words made her stop dead in her tracks. It hadn't been something she'd even given a thought to but now he had mentioned it, she felt

like a total amateur.

"Herbie I'm sorry! Every single day, no change that to every single hour. I'm finding out just how naive I am and how much I have to learn. It scares me more than a bit I can tell you. Do you ever get used to looking over your shoulder?"

"Simple answer? No Princess! If that day ever comes, then sweetheart you'll be a dead woman walking. Don't look so worried, nothings goin' to happen to you while we're around and by the time we're not, you'll be well and truly on your way so stop frettin'."

Brushing past her to join the Scouser, he looked into the neat screen that was hidden in the wall and saw Mario and Geno before they even pressed the buzzer.

"Princess I think the last of your guests have just arrived."

The only word Herbie heard before entering the room made him smile.

"Password?"

Geno Colletta smiled into the lens and stated the password.

"Bluebell wood."

Angela held her breath, even through the distorted image that the monitor portrayed; he had to be the most drop dead gorgeous man she had ever laid eyes on. Grateful for being on the third floor, as it gave her some time to compose herself, she fanned her cheeks with the palm of her hand. When they at last knocked on the door she opened it but didn't look Geno in the face. Concentrating instead on staring directly into Mario's eyes, she smiled.

"Please do come in, we're all here now so we can get things underway."

The men didn't strike up a conversation but Geno Colletta's eyes didn't leave Angela's body for one second. As she led the way along the hall, he scrutinized her from head to toe. Danny who was loitering in the hall had clocked the way Geno looked at the woman. He didn't like it one bit and as he went to join his uncle he stared daggers at the new arrival. His disapproval didn't go unnoticed by Herbie. When they had all taken a seat and accepted refreshments, Angela, Herbie and Jimmy excused themselves for a moment and went into the kitchen. Without going into every little detail the two brought her up to speed, regarding the meet with Brian Moore. After thinking about all that they had said and only when she was happy with the plan did the three rejoin their company in the stylish drawing room. When Angela could see that Herbie and Jimmy were sitting comfortably, she stood up and began.

"Welcome everyone. My name is Angela Canning Brown and I'm Marty McCann's daughter. I'm here to reclaim what's mine and to begin a new era in the McCann dynasty. I expect you've all heard of and possibly had dealings with Johnny Vale and that name alone might leave you feeling a touch on edge."

The new men looked at each other and smiled.

"The man is a liar and a cheat, not to mention the fact that he would stab you in the back as soon as look at you. That's probably what he did to my father but sadly we will never know the true facts. Now what we have planned could turn out to be very nasty and if you want to leave that's fine but if you agree to stay then it must be for the duration. Anyone want out?"

The room was silent but no one got up to leave, making Angela feel secure in Herbie's choice of men.

"Good, now I'll pass you over to my trusted friend and let him explain all the details. Mr Spires?"

Herbie got up from the sumptuous chair and was slightly embarrassed at her method of address. None the less, he carried out the meeting as professionally as he knew how. Explaining the heist and the reasons behind it, he continued to allocate individual tasks for each of the men to carry out.

"Any questions?"

Franco Posello raised his hand and all eyes were immediately staring in his direction. Not bothered in the least at his instant fame he continued to ask what cut they were all to receive in this. Jimmy had been expecting the question and took over before Herbie had time to respond.

"The money, as you are all aware is needed to put this firm back on its feet. We have little working capital at the moment. As you all know, our kind of business can't run successfully without a good pile of reddies always at hand. Miss McCann has a good inheritance from Marty but Herbie and me don't see why she should use that, when fuckin' Vale has hold of her clubs and businesses."

There was a muffled sound of agreement from every male in the room and Herbie realised instantly, that to these men it was about much more than money. Asking for quiet so that he could continue, Jimmy Forbes held up his hand.

"Mario, Franco, George and me will be on the inside and well tooled up. Herbie and Geno will stay outside the perimeter to keep watch etc. Now as you're all well aware, carryin' guns always has the chance of turnin' fuckin nasty! That said we're not taking liberties and expecting your help for nothing. Believe me when I say, that I'm not sure exactly how much we're talkin' about here. This job has come to us second hand courtesy of Johnny Vale, although he doesn't know that yet."

The room was filled with suppressed snickers and the mood was instantly lightened.

"We're expecting somewhere in the region of half a mill but that could change either way once the dust's settled and we've done the final count. We've agreed with Mr Colletta on a fifty percent split for your much appreciated help. Your boss will receive twenty five percent of that and the rest will be split four ways between you guys. After this job is over a wage structure will be put in place until everything else is settled and the clubs and businesses are back in the hands of the McCann family. Mr Colletta has agreed that until that time you will remain working for us."

Franco walked over to Jimmy and held out his hand, when the men shook on the deal it was sealed and as was tradition, there could be no going back by either party.

Angela had sat in silence throughout the talks and was now annoyed that she hadn't been consulted earlier. Surely it should be down to her regarding how much they would be handing over. Half a million pounds was truly a lot of money and to just give fifty percent of it away without even discussing it, made her feel as though she was nothing more than a trophy boss and that the men had taken over. Herbie could see by her expression that something wasn't right and nodded in the direction of the kitchen. As Angela made her way out of the room, the

new men were celebrating with a tumbler of the finest malt whisky that she had to offer. Too engrossed and excited about the deal, her departure wasn't even noticed. This alone, not to mention the money had Angela in a furious state of mind by the time Jimmy joined them in the next room.
"Just where the fuck do you two get off, making decisions like that without even consulting me?"
"Angie it......"
"For fucks sake it's Angela!!!!"
"Alright Angela! It wasn't a case of not consultin' you. Jimmy had to think on his feet and as far as them lots fuckin' concerned, they don't even know that you weren't in on it."
"Maybe so but half Herbie? That's a bit rich don't you think?"
"Princess these people are goin' to be riskin' their liberty tomorrow, not to mention possibly their fuckin' lives. Do you think they'd seriously consider it for a measly few grand? Maybe they would, I don't know but I for one certainly wouldn't even ask them to be part of this for less."
Angela sighed heavily. It seemed that everything she did and said was wrong, everything was way over her head and she was either looking like a spoilt child or a complete novice.
"No I suppose not but I just think that if they feel

you and Jimmy are in charge, then where does that leave me?"
Herbie Spires walked over and placed a hand warmly on each of her shoulders.
"Point taken and I promise, soon it will be made crystal but can we just get the job over with?"
Angela didn't speak but nodded her head in a defeated sort of way that left Herbie feeling guilty. With his arm draped around her shoulder, they joined the rest of the firm but Herbie didn't feel good. Perhaps she did have a point, when all was said and done after this little lot was over, she would be the new boss and the Scouser's behaviour tonight hadn't done much for her reputation. Knowing that most of the men in the room came from strong Italian families and were probably looking at her in the same way they looked at their mothers or baby sisters, they had to be put straight and pretty quickly. He had to rectify the situation and he had to do it now. Without her realising what he was about to say, Herbie Spires coughed loudly.
"Gentlemen if I could have your attention for a moment. As Angela said earlier, she is Marty's daughter and when this firms back on track, make no mistake she will be the one in charge. From now on if you have anything to ask please speak to her, as no decisions will be made without her say so."
Everyone instantly turned their gaze to Angela

and for a second she was embarrassed. Suddenly and from nowhere an inner strength filled every part of her body and she gave a smile that told anyone who laid eyes on her, that she was Marty McCann's daughter and not someone to be messed with.

"Thank you Herbie. Right if there's no further business I suggest we call it a day. Everyone knows what their positions are and what to do, so good luck to you all. Let's show Vale that a McCann's back in charge."

Everyone stood up in unison and after shaking hands with Herbie and the Scouser, lined up to say their farewells to the boss. In true Italian style they kissed Angela on each cheek, whilst tightly holding her delicate hand in theirs. It wasn't until Geno Colletta's turn, that Angela noticed a big difference in his goodbye. The kisses lingered for just a few seconds longer and the whole time, he didn't just hold her hand, he caressed it in a way that made the hairs on the back of her neck stand up on end.

Geno gazed deeply into Angela's eyes and for a few moments she seemed to fall into something she could only describe as a kind of hypnotic trance. It wasn't like anything she'd ever experienced before but at the same time she welcomed it with open arms. The trance was only broken when Geno's eyes left hers. The mutual attraction hadn't gone unnoticed by

Herbie, who gave the Scouser a look that said 'Watch him, the last thing we need is for her to go falling in love and let everything slip away.' When Geno Colletta looked at Angela all he saw was pound signs and power but to anyone else it was merely lustful interest. George and Franco were the first to leave but only seconds before Mario Pizzaro and Geno. The large room now seemed even bigger and Angela realised that she liked having people around her. Maybe that had been a lot of her problem back in Canterbury, rattling around in a massive house with just Pops, her mother and grandmother for company. Thankfully Herbie and Jimmy did the farewells and when they returned to the drawing room, Angela was excited to find out all there was to know about her guests. She wanted personal details on each of them and none more so than Geno Colletta.

"What's so fascinating about him princess?" Realising that she'd asked just a few too many questions about the man and that Herbie had picked up on her interest, left her feeling a little embarrassed and she quickly changed the subject.

"Oh forget I asked. Now what am I doing tomorrow?"

Herbie smiled to himself. After the incident earlier in the kitchen, he'd known this problem would arise.

"You're not doin' anythin', unless you see sittin' here and waitin' for the call to say everythin's as sweet as a nut, as doing somethin'."
Angela's smile was quickly replaced with a scowl and Jimmy whispered under his breath 'here we fuckin' go again.
"You expect me to do nothing! This is my firm as I reminded you less than an hour ago and you expect me to let everyone else do the work?"
Herbie Spires was tired and he was getting very fed up with having to justify himself and his actions every five minutes.
"Stroll on! I don't fuckin' need this princess. Look let me explain it simply and then maybe we can all get on with the job in hand. If a swarm of bees is out looking for food they don't take the fuckin' queen along for the ride and expect her to help out, now do they? The workers are expendable but if the queen got hurt, then the whole fuckin' swarm would be done for. Now do you understand?"
"Of course I understand and don't talk to me as if I were a child."
"Then stop fuckin' acting like one!"
Jimmy, never one to have any patience was becoming agitated.
"Look! Can you two draw a line under it? I need to get off and sort out some hardware from the bubble."
Angela looked confused.

"The bubble?"

"Yeh Phil the Greek, you know bubble and squeak?"

Angela still looked confused and Jimmy could only sigh in exasperation.

"Sweetheart I aint got time to go into the where's or the why for's regardin' cockney slang, it'll have to wait till another time."

"Well I'm not very happy about using guns either!"

Jimmy now puffed out his cheeks; she was starting to get right up his nose.

"Look! Let me quickly explain. Can you imagine doin' an armed robbery without arms? There would be confusion and we don't want that now do we? Everybody needs to know who's boss and them there guns, well let's just say they are like a giant badge that says 'Hey look at me I'm in fuckin' charge'."

Herbie and Jimmy both heartily laughed.

"Now can we just leave it at that? You ready Herb?"

As the two men reached the front door Angela ran along the hallway and as Herbie turned to face her, she wrapped her arms around his neck and buried her face in his chest.

"I'm sorry Herb but I am trying honestly I am. I promise I'll get the hang of all this and you'll be proud of me."

"I already am sweetheart. Now just relax and

when it's all over I'll give you a call, OK?"
"OK."
Angela closed the door behind her two godfathers as she like to refer to them and switched on the television. She had a feeling that the next twenty four hours were going to be the longest in history. Outside Herbie and Jimmy Forbes headed in the direction of the Jag.
"Drop me back home will you Herb so I can pick the Merc up."
"Where you meetin' the bubble?"
"Fuckin Eppin' forest of all places. Where's that nephew of yours?"
Herbie glanced up and down the road.
"Fuck knows! I aint hangin' about he'll have to find his own way home, the dozy twat."
No one had noticed when Danny Spires quietly slipped out of the flat with the other men. He had a bad feeling about Geno Colletta and decided to follow the Italian. Luckily for him they had arrived on foot so Danny was able to tail the men relatively easily. When they headed up west and arrived in Wardour Street the group dispersed and Geno continued alone. Danny kept to the shadows and when he saw Geno enter The Admiral Duncan pub on Old Compton street, he let out a gasp and murmured under his breath 'you dirty fuckin' queer'.

CHAPTER TWENTY FOUR

It was now early afternoon and Jimmy Forbes had agreed to meet Phil Papadakis at the Jubilee pond in Epping Forest. From Stepney the journey should have only taken about forty minutes but as usual the traffic had come to an almost standstill. Jimmy had dealt with the bubble on several occasions and had always found him fair. That said he still had a short fuse and if Jimmy was late the man wouldn't, couldn't due to his cargo, hang around. Turning left towards North Chingford Jimmy Forbes tried to gain some time only to see the speed camera flash.
"Fuck it! That's all I need."
This would push him to nine points on his licence, another three and he would be using Herbie or public transport permanently. Finally he reached his destination. The pond was huge but apart from two anglers over on the far bank the place appeared to be deserted. Stopping the car he glanced all round and thinking he'd missed the boat was about to drive off when Phil emerged from behind a large clump of bushes. Beckoning to the Scouser, Jimmy started up the engine and drove over to where the man and his small son were standing.
"Fuck me mate, it's all a bit fuckin' cloak and

dagger aint it?"

Phil Papadakis was a big man both in height and girth. His accent was cockney but some of his words still bore the twang of his homeland. He always seemed to be sweating and appeared to Jimmy as if he could do with a good wash.

"Jimmy my friend how the devil are you?"

Good Phil, very good in fact."

"I'm pleased to hear it. Let me introduce you to my boy. Arsenios, come and say hello. He's my fifth youngest you know and will be eleven next week."

The boy walked towards Jimmy and eyed him up and down.

"Hello Mr. Fuck me dad he's a big cunt!"

Phil Papadakis shook his head.

"Hey you cheeky little fucker! No manners, takes after his mother. Sorry Jimmy."

"What'd you say his name is Arse what?"

Phil's chest swelled with pride.

"It's Arsenios, means virile."

"How many kids you got now Phil?"

"Ten Jimmy and it's a drain I can tell you. I'm thinkin' about havin' the snip but my wife is still as horny as ever. The only trouble is..."

Phil lent in towards Jimmy so that his son couldn't hear him.

"Her fanny is so big now! It's not the same you know?"

Jimmy Forbes burst out laughing and soon Phil

joined in while a bemused Arsenios watched them both.

"Now then, down to business. Follow me."

Phil Papadakis walked over to his car followed by Jimmy and Arsenios who proceeded to open up the boot and reveal a small arsenal of weapons.

"Fuck me Phil you could have your own little war with this lot!"

"So what is it that you want today?"

"I need two shotguns, pump action, two handguns and plenty of ammo if you've got it."

"No problem I have all these. Arsenios show our guest the guns."

Jimmy leant into the boot and after pointing his finger at one or two before moving on he at last settled on the one he wanted.

"Ok, pump action Weatherby. Easy to use, lightweight at six and a half pounds. Twelve gauge, twenty eight inch barrel with dissipating vented top rib. Very nice gun, this model has an improved cylinder."

Arsenios handed Jimmy the weapon and he put it to his shoulder.

"Fuck me Phil, he's a proper little gun encyclopaedia aint he? It's nice, do you have two?"

"No problem."

Arsenios then walked to the back door of the car and took out a sports bag. He laid the bag on

the ground by Jimmy's feet.
"Help yourself."
Jimmy Forbs bent down and took a shine to the first gun he removed.
"I like this!"
Again Arsenios spurted out a description of the weapon.
"Beretta ninety two FS series. Semi-automatic, operates on a short recoil, fifteen round steel magazine. Its drop free when the magazine button is depressed, even when empty. Chrome lined barrels. Once again a very nice choice, you know your guns mister."
"No I don't but I know what I like. I'll take it, do you have two?"
"No problem."
"Funny, I thought you'd say that."
Phil laughed out loud and nodding his head signalled for the boy to put the rest away.
"Anythin' else I can help you with today Jimmy? How about a nice little flame thrower."
Jimmy laughed. Not today thanks Phil I aint really got a use for one. So how much is this little lot goin' to cost me?"
The boy quickly removed a calculator from his pocket and without any prompting from his father began to tap away on the keys.
"For you it's a very reasonable seven grand."
"Seven grand! That's a bit steep aint it?"
Instantly Phil Papadakis became serious and any

trace of a smile disappeared from his face. "Jimmy my guns are clean, no come back and you aint exactly goin' to use them for pigeon shootin' now are you? Besides I have a big family to feed."
Both men laughed and after shaking hands, Jimmy Forbes paid his dues and was soon heading back to the east end to modify the newly acquired guns.

DAY OF THE ROBBERY

George Sands was a perfectionist and just to make sure everything was as it should be, he'd paid the planned destination a visit in advance. The site resembled a graveyard at two that morning and dressed in black from head to foot, he had quietly crept around the perimeter. By the time the crew set off, George had confirmed that all of Brian's location details were correct and that nothing appeared untoward. By five thirty am, everything and everyone was in place. Herbie sat in the blue modified Mondeo that would act as one of the getaway cars. The second, a high performance Astra, had Geno Colletta behind its wheel. Mario, George and Jimmy accompanied by Franco were situated inside a black Transit Van, with the inscription of Handley's Jewel merchants emblazed in gold on both of its side panels. They wore navy blue security guard uniforms and each held a helmet on their laps. Everyone sat in silence waiting for Brian Moore to make his daily appearance and he didn't disappoint. At exactly five fifty five he turned into the top of the road. Well aware that the job was going down today, he looked around him nervously but didn't notice anything out of the ordinary. Herbie had parked far enough away so as not to be seen. Knowing how scared the little weasel had been when they'd visited him at home, he had an idea that if Brian spotted either him or the Scouser, he just might do a runner and they'd have to call the whole thing off. The road in question was all but derelict and the only remaining houses were boarded up and inhabited by squatters and junkies. None of the residents would be the least bit interested in what was going on and far too scared to go to the police even if they were. Jenson's prided itself on being one of the oldest holding companies in London, dealing mostly in jewels and fine art for companies that didn't wish to carry too much expensive stock on their premises. The precious items would be stored at Jenson's until required and then would either be delivered by the security vans or collected in person. Handley's Jewel Merchants were regular visitors to Jenson's and somehow Brian Moore had obtained information, that for reasons unknown, they wouldn't be calling on the fourteenth and fifteenth of the month.

Johnny Vale was all prepared to go on the later and still very much in the dark as to what Angela Canning Brown, Herbie Spires and Jimmy Forbes, were up to. At six thirty the black van pulled up to the main gate and after winding down the window, Franco Posello pressed the entry button. Brian Moore on duty in the guard box looked into the monitor. As soon as he saw the van he removed the security tape and raised the barrier for the van to enter, once safely inside he replaced the original tape with a blank. Every piece of security equipment on the premises was time coded but as the swap had only taken a few seconds, he was confident of the excuse that the tape had jammed so he'd had to change it. The original had its thin tape pulled out and Brian ran his fingers along the beginning, wiping all traces of the van and its occupants. Franco drove the hundred yards to the main entrance and after they had all put on their helmets and lowered the facial visors Jimmy opened the rear doors and gave George and Mario a helping hand out. The site was made up of a massive warehouse with a single small office building to the front. The only other entrance was via a large double door at the rear, which was heavily alarmed. The sight of the men would normally be common practice and through the lens of a camera everything appeared as it should be. Not having to hide or

sneak inside, made things a little easier although everyone was still highly pumped. With the van parked in its usual place thanks to Brian's information, the four walked as bold as brass into the building carrying a large black holdall. As if it was a daily ritual to them, the four men turned left into the main reception area and the only office on site. Jimmy and Mario pulled out the sawn off pump action shotguns and simultaneously fired shots into the ceiling. Due to the early hour, there was only a skeleton staff on duty, which made the job far easier.
"Hands in the fuckin' air all of you. Fuckin' now!!!!"
The three workers, who as luck would have it, all turned out to be women, did as they were told. The youngest, a girl who looked fresh out of school, began to cry and Jimmy once more took control.
"Stop fuckin' whining bitch, if you all do as we say, then no one gets hurt. Now into the centre of the room, come on fuckin' move it!!!"
Serena Blackthorn had only been with the company a couple of months and was yet to receive training in the event of a possible heist. She sobbed uncontrollably much to the men's annoyance and Jimmy saw that out of everyone, she could be the most troublesome. He nodded in the girl's direction and Mario instantly understood his look.

"If I have to fuckin' tell you again to stop blabbing, it'll be the last time! Now lay face down and don't move or look up, got it!"
The older women surrounded her and after hushed whispers, her crying subsided. Jimmy stayed with the women, gun pointing directly at them while, Franco, George and Mario made their way to the single door situated on the other side of the room. As Mario was about to disappear, Jimmy called out.
"You've got ten minutes, not a second more, now get fuckin' moving!!!!"
Disappearing through the doorway, the men entered a long hallway. Anyone else would have been expected to turn right, into the area kept for storing all the gold, antiques and fine art. The newly formed McCann crew had other ideas. It was supposed to be top secret that the holiday payroll for the Ford garage at Dagenham and weekly paryroll for Gatwick airport would be on the premises for three to four days. This wasn't the type of business that Jensen's usually carried out but after a dry run three months earlier, the managing directors had thought it too good an opportunity to pass up. The commission for holding the payrolls was huge and would raise the annual profits by a vast amount. In fact the information was so top secret, that a robbery was the last thing Jenson's was expecting. The room was secured only by a

reinforced padlock but it was nothing George couldn't sort out in a few seconds. Entering, the men saw two large wheeled cages measuring about three feet square. Franco grabbed one and Mario the other, while George held open the first of the doors. So far it had only taken three minutes and they knew that time was on their side. George pushed open the door that led into the office and Mario and Franco, followed behind wheeling their bounty.
"Fuck me boys that was quick!"
"Piece of piss Mr Goldfinger."
Everyone had fictitious names and had rehearsed and rehearsed them, so that no slip ups would be made. The crates were wheeled out to the van and the packages thrown inside. When the vehicle had been reversed and pointed towards the barrier, Franco gave two large hoots on the horn. This was Jimmy's signal; he now knew he had only five minutes at the most. At the gate Mario jumped from the van and made his way into the guardhouse. Brian Moore was expecting this moment but by no means looking forward to it. Without a word Mario punched the guard hard in the face and the man fell to the floor. Not wanting to take any chances he then pulled the security tape out and placed it into his overalls before smashing the recorder onto the floor. Pressing the gate release button, Mario Pizzaro was out of the building and back inside

the van two minutes later. Again the vans horn was sounded and Jimmy knew it was time to leave. He had one final word of warning for the staff before he went.

"Right if any of you press the alarm within the next five minutes, you'll fuckin' pay for it. We know all about you and where you fuckin' live. If you want to see tomorrow, fuckin' do as you're told. Understood?"

All of the women through tears and sobs vigorously nodded their heads. As soon as the barrier went up and the van was off the premises Brian Moore pressed the alarm. He was still slightly nervy about the whole operation but had much to his appreciation, been well groomed by Johnny Vale as to what to expect from the Old Bill. The force took several minutes to respond even though there had been a direct link to the station and in that time Brian thought long and hard about his future. He decided that he would go with the original plan and deny any involvement but just to be on the safe side he'd add a little sweetener to his story. The fear of Johnny Vale's wrath had kept him awake for the last couple of nights and he didn't see it would do any harm to inform the police about the man who'd been hassling him. As a model employee he'd deny all involvement but would offer the information that certain people had been trying to lean on him and none more so than Vale. His explanation for not coming forward earlier would be due to sheer terror but now that the robbery had gone ahead, he thought it was his civic duty to provide any information he could. Brian saw a chance to nail two birds with one stone and hopefully get Vale off his back, if only long enough to disappear. After all he didn't have a clue who the real culprits were. Going over his story several times until he thought it sounded plausible, he left the security hut and walked over to the office. Glancing at his reflection in the glass door, he saw that the only mark on his face was a swelling around his eye. Brian knew the injury wasn't nearly bad enough to convince the office girls, let alone the police. Before entering the building, he smacked the side of his head hard against the corner of the wall. The pain was excruciating and he knew just by the impact that this injury would now be more than convincing. Holding his head he staggered into the reception to be faced with three wailing women. The moment they saw him the noise stopped and their maternal instincts came to the fore. The youngest girl ran sobbing into Brian's arms, while the older women pulled up a chair for him to sit on. By the time the police arrived the scene was set and Brian had been deemed the hero. At his interview, he repeated word perfect the script that he had rehearsed and miraculously he was believed.

A short distance from Jenson's saw Herbie and Geno's cars parked down a small side street. This place was even more deserted than the last, with house after house boarded up. As the hands on the clock ticked by Herbie started to get edgy. It had been less than fifteen minutes since he'd seen Brian Moore arrive and had moved his car into the side street but it felt like hours. Robbery had been his line of work for most of his life but in the last few years, this sort of business was carried out by the younger crew members. Herbie and Jimmy, along with Marty, had dealt with all the planning but that was as far as it had gone. Now, suddenly less than a month since his trusted friends death and here he was bang in the middle of a hold up. As the black van turned into the street, he heard himself release a sigh of relief but instantly brought himself to book. You were never out of the woods until you had plenty of distance between yourself and the job and right at this moment they were far too close for comfort. Without a word the vans ignition was turned off and it glided silently towards the curb. Stopping directly behind Geno's car the men disembarked and after opening the rear doors began to unload the bags. Jimmy didn't know what the haul would bring but he had enough experience to tell by the weight of the bags that it was big, much bigger than they'd been told. After they divided the money between the two cars, Jimmy joined Geno in the Astra along with George and Mario. Herbie climbed back in the Mondeo and both vehicles pulled away, driving almost to the top of the street. They waited there for Franco, who had been left in charge of destroying the evidence. He had earlier drilled and plugged a small hole in the vans petrol tank. Franco crawled under the van and wiggled the plug free. A trickle of petrol began to flow from the tank and he quickly jumped back inside and drove along the road. Seconds later he stopped the van and ran back down the road. When the distance was deemed to be safe, Franco ignited the trail of fuel. Running as if his life depended on it, he jumped into the car and Herbie hit the accelerator before the back door was closed. The two cars had barely managed to move on when the van exploded and burst into flames. Luckily enough for them, the area was now so derelict and what with all the commotion going on just a few roads away, there wasn't anyone to bother about the noise. With their helmets now removed, the convoy resembled that of regular men on their way to work. The further they drove from Jenson's, the happier Herbie Spires became and he could actually feel himself begin to relax. Arriving in Docklands, they pulled into a disused warehouse where a white Transit van waited with its rear doors already open. Complete with ladders and the logo 'Johnson and sons Window Cleaners' dramatically emblazed in red on the side, it was the kind of vehicle that was often seen in the area due to the volume of office buildings. Each man hauled one of the large sacks of cash from the cars and loaded them into the van. Donning overalls and gloves they then set about cleaning the Astra and Mondeo, until not a trace of a human being remained. Herbie Spires and Jimmy Forbes climbed into the window cleaning van and left the others to get rid of the now offending vehicles. Geno Colletta and Franco Posello walked away from the scene and both went their separate ways. George and Mario on the other hand, had one remaining task to carry out. Still in their overalls and gloves and now once again wearing the helmets, they climbed into the vehicles and drove them out of the lock up. At the water's edge, jemmy bars were wedged against the accelerators and the handbrakes released. The cars moved forward until they disappeared over the edge and a loud splash was heard. Happy that it was a job well done, the two walked from the quay and down a small alleyway that led onto the main road. Once out of sight they removed the helmets and over clothing and placed them into plastic carrier bags. At the top of the alley, George turned

right and Mario left. They had been instructed to take public transport and to dump the carrier bags at the earliest opportunity but only into bins that were on the main thoroughfare and emptied regularly. The gloves were to stay on until they were almost home, then and only then could they too be discarded. Herbie and the Scouser drove back to Stepney and the small warehouse that Jimmy kept secret from all but a few. Jumping out, he undid the padlock and pulled the roller shutter high enough for the van to pass through. Inside and with the shutter once more firmly touching concrete, the men opened up the vans rear doors and surveyed their cargo.
"Fuck me Jim I can't get over how quick and easy it was!"
"Well Herb me old mukka, that's what you fuckin' get for thinkin' you're invincible. If Jensen's hadn't been so cock sure that a robbery wouldn't happen and had taken a little more care with the security then they'd have been safe. Besides any company that hires cock suckers like Brian Moore, deserve to get done over."
"I couldn't agree more, now how much do you think we bagged?"
Jimmy Forbes ran a hand through his hair as he peered inside.
"I wouldn't like to hazard a guess but I'll tell you

one thing."

"What?"

"It's a fuckin' lot."

"You daft cunt I can see that with me own eyes. Shall we have a count up or give her majesty a call?"

"We'd better call, don't want another tantrum after such a good day now do we? Anyway this lots goin' to take hours to sort out."

Herbie walked outside to get a better signal on his mobile. Tapping in the number he waited for Angela to pick up but the phone just kept ringing. Herbie could feel a dark cloud descend above him and he didn't like it. Running back into the lockup, he relayed the fact that she wasn't answering.

"Right we'd best get over there and fuckin' sharpish!"

"Hang on there's still work to be done here. We need to unload all the bags into those sacks. Knowin' our luck of late, if we leave the dosh where it is some wanker will break in and nick the fuckin' van."

After locking the van and securing the unit, both men got into Herbie's waiting Jag and set off for Angela's new apartment.

Angela Canning Brown had enjoyed the nicest sleep she'd had since arriving in London. After a long hot shower she'd placed her unruly hair in a towelling turban and sat down to breakfast.

About to bite into the delicious looking croissant, she was annoyed when the intercom went off in the hall. Aware that the job had been carried out successfully from all that she'd managed to hear on the radio, Angela assumed it was either Herbie or Jimmy arriving to give her the low down. The man staring into the screen had been the last person she was expecting to see and after her heart skipped a beat, she opened the front door. Quickly rubbing her hair with the towel, she peered into the hall mirror. Though not how she would have chosen to appear, she at least felt clean and presentable. Once inside and without a word she took him by the hand and led him straight into the bedroom. The following thirty minutes passed in a blur as Angela experienced the best sex of her life. She wouldn't allow herself to count her short and rare encounters with Edward, that had been embarrassing and totally unsatisfying. It could never be like this with Edward and she hoped that if it was all a dream, then it was one from which she would never wake. The sitting room telephone had rang and rang but she wasn't able to hear it during her deep throws of passion. Now lying curled up next to her lover, Angela was happier than she had thought possible. Silently she nuzzled into his chest, not wanting to spoil the intimacy that had just passed between them. When the intercom again burst into life, he sighed and told her not to answer.

"I have to, it may be important."

Angela's face was flushed and her hair was wild and unkempt as she left the bedroom and headed for the hall. Bleary eyed she looked to see who her visitor was and instantly became filled with panic. She pressed the entry button and ran as fast as she could back into the bedroom.

"It's them! You'll have to hide. If they find us in this state, I'm sure they'll kill you. For some reason they treat me like a child and its starting to get on my nerves. Now the hall cloakrooms right by the front door. As soon as I let them in and take them through to the sitting room, you shoot off."

Angela lent over the bed and couldn't resist planting a lingering kiss upon his lips.

"I'll phone you."

"Yes yes!!! Now get a move on or you won't get a chance to phone anyone."

Opening the cloakroom door, she almost pushed him in as Herbie's fist banged heavily on her flat door.

"Alright alright I'm coming!"

As she opened the front door the sight that greeted her gave Angela a fright. Both men had deathly white faces and Herbie's eyes were filled with dread.

"Whatever's the matter? Has something gone wrong?"
Jimmy Forbes barged passed his pal and sharply took hold of Angela by the shoulders.
"Whatever's the matter? You stupid little idiot! Me and Herb here's been imagining all sorts. Why didn't you answer your soddin' phone?"
"I must have been in the shower, why didn't you leave a message?"
Jimmy turned to Herbie for an explanation but he just shrugged.
"I got so wound up when there was no reply, I didn't think."
Angela placed an arm around each of the men's shoulders and gently led them into the sitting room.
"Look no harms been done, how about we have a nice cuppa and you can tell me all about how the job went."
Like two small boys they did as she asked, happy in the relief that she was unharmed. As soon as they left the hall, the cloakroom door gently opened and Angela's lover slipped out of the flat. Several seconds later, he'd managed to exit the building and as far as he knew, had done so without being seen. Danny Spires hadn't taken part in the heist. He had an appointment with his probation officer and Herbie had told him in no uncertain terms that he was going whether he liked it or not. Danny was also

instructed by his uncle that once the appointment was over he should get back to Angela's flat and from a distance keep an eye on the place. When Herbie had gotten no response from her phone he had tried to call his nephew but as usual Danny got everything wrong and had left his mobile at home. Angela's lover left the building just after Herbie Spires and Jimmy Forbes arrived and it didn't go unnoticed.

CHAPTER TWENTY FIVE

Before she'd been laid off, Kathy Jones always arrived early for work and now that she'd been called back, things weren't any different. When Marty McCann had been in charge, she'd loved her job but these days her good time keeping was only down to fear, pure and simple fear. It didn't pay to upset the boss and never knowing what mood he was going to arrive in didn't ease the situation. The last few days hadn't been as bad, though Kathy felt that was partly due to the large amount of cash she'd received from Marty's daughter. Her feeling of being cheap had quickly passed and by the time the taxi had pulled up outside her block of flats, half of her windfall had already been spent, in her mind at least. Closing the door behind her, she'd walked towards the front room to see Spider and Katie, snuggled up to Nadia and all watching television. The sight brought tears to her eyes and it wasn't the fact that her babies were safe. No it was the sight of poor Nadia, still just a baby herself and who would soon have a mouth to feed, long before the girl had even began to live. Kathy quietly made her way into the bedroom, certain that she hadn't been heard coming in. Taking off her coat and placing it neatly on the small chair under the window, she opened up the envelope and spread its contents onto the bed. Stifling a loud gasp, she realised that every note was a fifty and as she began to count, was amazed at the sum which was quickly mounting up. Five minutes later and with her task completed, Kathy surveyed every single piece of paper. A grand total of ten thousand pounds and it was more money than she had ever had in her life. Fleetingly she had a slight feeling of guilt at her earlier opinions of Angela Canning Brown but they were soon forgotten as she continued to dream about what she would spend all the cash on. Kathy Jones had grown up in the school of hard knocks and she wasn't stupid enough to go splashing cash around that would make her a target to all and sundry, not to mention the suspicions of her hated boss. No Kathy tucked the brown paper envelope behind the wardrobe and joined her family on the sofa. When Nadia said her goodnights and kissed the kids on the cheek, they each willingly reciprocated which was something Kathy thought she'd never see from Spider. Understanding that her children actually liked their babysitter, made Kathy realise that perhaps the girl underneath all the bravado was a kind sort. She decided that when everything had calmed down, a few new baby clothes, maybe even a buggy, wouldn't go a miss. Of course the holiday had to come first but

then with ten grand, they could have a whole load of holidays whenever they wanted.
Now at work and sitting behind the counter, Kathy Jones wished she could just be rid of her nightmare employer then everything in the world would be sweet. Lately a habit had begun to form and it wasn't something she was proud of. Whenever things were quiet and she was alone, Kathy had started to imagine ways of getting rid of Johnny Vale and some of her thoughts she wasn't proud of. About to start another of her daydreams, she was startled back to reality by the shop door being flung wide open. Her boss not so much walked but flew into the bookies with Al Kingston in hot pursuit.
"Switch the telly on Kath! Fuckin' now you dozy bitch!!! I've got to see the news."
"I can't Mr Vale. They aren't set up for any channels other than the racin'!"
"For fucks sake do I have to do every fuckin' thing round here myself?"
Like a madman Johnny Vale ran through to his office and the intrigue was too much for Kathy to bear. Following close behind she couldn't contain herself and had to ask the question, even though she already knew the answer.
"Whatever's the matter Mr Vale?"
Johnny gave her a look of amazement and Kathy thought that at this moment more than any, he truly was insane.

"What's the matter? You daft cow! Those fuckin' cunts have pinched my job and they think I'm goin' to let 'em get away with it!"
"Who you talkin' about Mr Vale?"
Pacing the floor backwards and forwards, Johnny didn't hear another word she said. Lost in a fantasy of his own retribution, he couldn't wait to get started.
"Al! Round up the lads and tell 'em to come tooled up."
Al Kingston did as he was told and went out into the shop front to use the telephone. He could see the Boss was wild and when the boss said jump you said how high?, especially when the man in question was Johnny Vale. Kathy Jones stood in the office and desperately tried to stifle a laugh. The boys had gone and done it, actually done it, the cheeky buggers.
"What the fuck are you standing there for with that gormless look on your boat? If you can't help, then fuck off home."
"You want me to lock up Mr Vale?"
Johnny marched up to her and Kathy closed her eyes in anticipation at what she thought was about to happen. When nothing did she opened her eyes to see her boss's face staring back, if he'd have been any closer, well it didn't bare thinking about.
'You sure you don't know anything about all this?"

"Me?"

Johnny Vale took a step back and threw his head back as he laughed.

"Course you don't, who'd fuckin' confide in a stupid bitch like you. Get out and don't come back till I tell you. Perhaps another few days without pay will teach you not to be so fuckin' gormless!"

Kathy collected her coat and walked straight from the bookies without looking back. It was a fantastic feeling, not to have to worry about money. The only down side was that she couldn't tell anyone, Kathy smiled to herself, she could live with that. She'd only got a few hundred yards when three police cars screeched to a halt outside the bookies. Ducking into a door way, she couldn't resist hanging around for a while, just to see what happened. A couple of minutes later Johnny Vale accompanied by Al Kingston, was led out to the patrol cars. Both were handcuffed and where Al went quietly, Johnny cursed loud enough for the whole world to hear.

"You bastards will pay for this. I ain't done nothin' and when you find that out, I'll fuckin' sue the Met for every penny it's got."

Kathy fished deep into her handbag and removing her mobile, dialled Herbie Spires number.

In Angela's plush sitting room the two men were

enjoying a celebratory glass of champagne, when Herbie's mobile burst into life. Placing his glass much to Angela's distaste onto her highly polished coffee table, he flipped open his phone.
"Yeh?"
The conversation was followed by a series of 'You're joking! When? How?' Closing his mobile Herbie wore a grin than stretched a mile wide and Jimmy realised something major had gone down but for the life of him, couldn't work out what.
"So what's fuckin' happened now?'
"You're never goin' to believe this but Old Bills only picked up Vale for the robbery."
Not waiting to hear more, Angela punched the air and ran around the room shouting 'Yes! Yes! Yes!' Jimmy Forbes refilled all the glasses and was about to pass one to Herbie, when he noticed the man's happy expression had instantly disappeared.
"Herb?"
"Yeh?"
"Who's pissed on your matches?"
"No one but I was just thinkin', it's not goin' to be long before he's back out on the street again. I mean we know he didn't do it and they won't be able to hold him for long, so there's no point in celebratin'."
"Trust you to be Mr fuckin' doom and gloom. We're here enjoying the moment and you have

to reduce all of us to a state of depression."

"It's not intentional Jim but I'm just tryin' to be realistic."

Angela felt as if her bubble had been burst but she didn't want either of the men to see her disappointment.

"Hey you two, why the long faces? We're no worse off than we were five minutes ago. We all knew, know that Vale won't let this go without a fight and we'll be ready for him when that happens. Now come on this bottle of Champers won't drink itself."

Herbie tried to manage a smile but at its best was a weak attempt.

"Come on for goodness sake. Where are the men, who only a few hours ago carried out a daring robbery? Where are the two people, I look up to most in this world and who are hell bent on putting me at the head of this firm no matter what? How about we go and count some money?"

The two men got up and Herbie once again placed his glass onto the coffee table. Angela instantly picked it up before it had a chance to ring the wood. Without thinking she took hold of Jimmy's glass that was still half full and which he was enjoying. Walking through to the kitchen, Angela placed her hands onto the work surface and looked up towards the ceiling. Heavily sighing she whispered 'Help me dad, please!'

Johnny Vale and his minder Al had been in custody for a little over three hours by the time Johnny's brief arrived. Having declined the services of the duty solicitor, the interviews had been held up much to the annoyance of the two C.I.D officers not to mention Johnny himself. By the time Richard Lewis was shown into the interview room for a quick debriefing, Johnny Vale was pacing the floor in an agitated manner. Brought from his cell as soon as his solicitor had arrived, Johnny didn't expect to be kept waiting, not even for five minutes.

"Where the fuck have you been? I don't keep your firm on a massive fuckin' retainer for you to turn up here hours after I've been arrested."

"I'm sorry Mr Vale but I've been in court this morning and I only received the message when I returned to the office."

Walking up to his solicitor and only stopping when their noses were almost touching, Johnny could see nothing but fear in the man's eyes.

"You had better get me out of here or there'll be hell to pay!"

Richard Lewis took a step back, desperately trying to put some distance between himself and the animal he had been sent here to defend. Taking a seat at the table, the solicitor snapped open his brief case and removed a note pad and pen.

"I'm going to do my very best Mr Vale. Now let's get a few things down on paper before we are called through, shall we?"

Richard Lewis asked question after question about where Johnny had been that morning, what time he got up, was he alone, what time he had arrived at the bookies. In fact so many questions that Johnny was now fuming.

"Fuck me you'll want to know what bleedin' colour pants I've got on next."

"And if they ask you that Mr Vale, then you will tell them."

Johnny couldn't believe what he'd just heard and was about to give his brief a mouthful when Richard Lewis carried on talking.

"This is a very serious charge as you well know. You say you didn't do it, so let's hope they don't have any evidence against you or you will be looking at a stint on remand. Be under no illusion that even if they have no evidence it won't stop them applying for an extension to keep you here for hours and hours. Now if we have a plausible explanation for every question they ask, then there will be no grounds to detain you any longer than is necessary."

Johnny once more began to pace the room, taking in all that had been said to him as he did so.

"Fair enough. So how long do you think this little lots goin' to take?"

"We could hopefully get you home for your evening meal."

"Fuckin' what? That's hours away!"

"It's the best I can do and in any case it's still better than spending the night in custody."

"Those bastards had better watch their fuckin' backs when I get out of here!"

Closing his case and setting it down on the floor, Richard Lewis didn't quite understand what his client had just said.

"Are you telling me that you know who the culprits are Mr Vale? If indeed that is the case, then all your problems are over."

"Don't be a prick Lewis 'course I don't know and even if I did, Old Bill would be the last people I'd speak to. Anyway don't be so fuckin' nosey! You represent me and that's all you need to concern yourself with."

The next moment two constables came into the room and informed the solicitor that it was time to start the interviews. The four men walked the short distance along a corridor until they reached a door with interview room number six written in bold letters. The solicitor entered, followed by Johnny and just one of the officers. The other stood guard outside. Already seated at the table were Steve Myers and Tom Walton, two of the plain clothes division who were present at the original arrests earlier that same day and who had also tried to question Johnny on the day of Marty's funeral.

"Mr Vale, Mr Lewis, do take a seat. I'm sure we can have this little misunderstanding sorted out pretty quickly."

Johnny's heckles were instantly up, he could see that Steve Myers was deliberately trying to goad him and he couldn't hold back.

"Pretty quickly! I've sat in that dirty fuckin' hovel; you call a cell, for most of the fuckin' day. Now how longs this goin' to take?"

"The wheels of justice run a little slow I'm afraid Mr Vale, even where you are concerned!"

Johnny instantly knew when he was having the piss taken out of him and this copper was really trying it on. All Richard Lewis's good intentions flew out the window as Johnny began a tirade of abuse aimed directly at the two detective's sitting opposite him. What should have been a reasonably simple exercise turned into an epic and the more he was questioned the more agitated Johnny became. Finally when the senior detective in the case had reached the end of his tether, he switched off the tape and ignoring Johnny Vale, spoke directly to his solicitor.

"Mr Lewis! Do I have to remind you that we are quite within our rights to apply for an extension? I'm really starting to get pissed off now and if your client isn't more forthcoming with his answers then he could be detained for

another thirty six hours."
Johnny was about to erupt when he was stopped by Richard Lewis.
"Might I have a few moments alone with my client detective?"
After twenty minutes the interview reconvened and on the advice of his solicitor Johnny Vale was now calmer and willing to answer the questions. At five that evening the steps of Bethnal Green police station saw Richard Lewis and Johnny Vale descend them. As soon as they were clear of the place, Johnny flagged down a mini cab and as he climbed inside, informed his brief to get Al Kingston out as soon as possible. Richard Lewis was left standing on the pavement and having to find his own way home. The solicitor was tired and fed up to the back teeth, Mr Kingston would just have to wait a while.

While Johnny and Al were still safely incarcerated at the local police station, Angela, Herbie and the Scouser had driven to the lock up, but decided to parked a few roads away. Herbie had insisted on checking everything out before the other two were allowed anywhere near. Walking down the alleyway, Herbie's eyes darted in every direction. When he was happy that the coast was clear, he opened up the roller shutter and made his way inside. Scanning the open space he was confident nothing had been touched since earlier and flipping open his phone he dialled his friends number. A few minutes later Angela entered followed by Jimmy, who swiftly pulled down the roller. After flicking on the lights, the three made their way over to where the spoils of the robbery lay hidden under a tarpaulin. The bags on their own didn't look very impressive and the men could see Angela's disappointment. Jimmy laughed out loud as he dragged a large table that stood against the far wall, over to the back of the van.

"Don't look so pissed off, there's a fortune in them bags darlin'."

Three stacking chairs were placed around the table and half of the first bag was emptied out onto it. Angela Canning Brown stared open mouthed and slowly shook her head from side to side.

"We can't count all this in one sitting!"

"You're probably right princess but we can make a damn good start. Right let's get stuck in."

Jimmy placed a large bundle of notes in front of the chairs and everyone took their seats and began to count. By six o'clock they were all flagging and Angela's finger tips were tender to the touch.

"I don't know about you two but I think I've had enough for one night. What's the total so far Herbie?"

The two men both grinned but wouldn't answer her question.
"Guess?"
"No come on, I'm too tired for this. How much?"
Jimmy Forbes was so pleased, that he fidgeted around on the hard plastic seat.
"Come on play the game! If you get it wrong we'll tell you how's that?"
"God you two are like children sometimes! Oh I don't know, five hundred thousand?"
"Nope."
"Well! How much then?"
"Well considering we're not even a quarter the way through, we've just reached one and a half fuckin' Million."
Angela Canning Brown rested her elbow on the table and held her forehead in her hand.
"I knew there would be a lot but not this much. We don't even know how much, I mean at best we're only guessing."
"Yeh princess but what a fuckin' lovely guess eh? Come on you're knackered, let's get you home."
Jimmy Forbes was reluctant to leave the loot but accepted there was no way they could move it tonight. Removing a couple of oil stained planks from the floor revealed a large mechanics pit.
"Not perfect but I suppose it'll do. Come on you two give us a hand!"
Herbie and Angela placed the counted cash into a holdall and the uncounted was returned to the

sack. Everything was thrown into the pit and covered with oily dust sheets then the planks were replaced. If anyone broke in, Jimmy could only hope that they wouldn't explore in too much detail and find the cash. Minutes later and the roller was once again securely locked and the trio were on their way. After driving Angela back to her apartment and seeing her safely inside, Herbie dropped the Scouser off at his Stepney terrace. Crossing the water and heading back to his home in Bermondsey, Herbie was agitated. This had been too easy, far far too easy. From the outside the house was warmly lit and when Herbie placed his key in the lock he was greeted by the Chihuahua's yapping and barking. It was nothing new and he smiled as he made his way into the dining room.

"Hi love." Marge called out from the kitchen. "Sit down it'll be ready in a couple of minutes." Danny was already seated and Herbie Spires could tell by his nephew demeanour that he was nervous. He just hoped that the boy hadn't done something stupid again. Ruffling Danny's hair as if he was still a child Herbie took a seat at the head of the table.

"Spit it out then!"

"What?"

"Come on Danny, I've known you all your bloody life now somethin's troublin' you."

Danny had spent all day worrying over what he

had seen but he'd finally reached the decision that he had to tell his uncle and then it would be up to him what he did about it.

"You know when we had that meet at Angela's and that Geno bloke was there? Well after we left I followed him. I don't know why but there was just somethin' about him I didn't like. Anyway he ended up in Soho and I watched as he went into the Admiral Duncan."

Herbie shook his head and smiled at his nephew as he did so.

"It takes all sorts son and if Geno likes a bit of pork sword who are we to judge?"

You don't understand, it don't end there."

Danny proceeded to tell Herbie all about Geno's return visit to the flat.

"So uncle H, unless the new lady boss is happy that he swings both ways and I very much fuckin' doubt that. We've got a bit of a problem."

Herbie Spires puffed out his checks and ran a hand through his receding gray hair.

"Let me sleep on it Danny and I'll have a word with the Scouser tomorrow. In the grand scale of things it's not that important, I think there's goin' to be bigger problems on the horizon than where Geno Colletta likes to dip his wick. Now not a word to anyone till I've decided what to do! Ah here she is and what delicious delicacies have you prepared for us this evening Marge?"

To Danny it had seemed that his uncle had

dismissed his news but nothing was further from the truth. Herbie was well aware of the sexual habits of both gay and heterosexual youngsters. He knew she was open to infection and HIV didn't bear thinking about, still Angela was an adult and had to make her own decisions. The only problem was she probably didn't even know about the Italians sexual preferences. Herbie tried to put the news to the back of his mind. For the next few days at least, he had far more pressing matters to worry about. The whole night was restless and sleep evaded both Herbie Spires and Jimmy Forbes. Jimmy could think of nothing but money and whenever he closed his eyes, pound signs would appear in front of them. He laid in the darkness smiling until the dawn chorus began. For Herbie it was a different story, his thoughts were filled with Johnny Vale's possible retaliation and Danny's new information. Dark and disturbing images invaded his mind all night of what was possibly, no almost certainly, to come.

CHAPTER TWENTY SIX

The next day and after several intense hours of flicking through the bank notes Angela Herbie and Jimmy had finished the final count. The bundles of cash were stacked neatly in large piles and neither of the men dared ask Angela, who this time was in charge of the calculator, what the total had amounted to.
"Well boys aren't you just dying to know what we made."
Herbie Spires had been on a downer ever since they'd arrived at the lock up but with Angela and Jimmy engrossed in the count, neither had taken much notice of his long face.
"Come on Herbie! Whatever's the matter with you?'
Standing up from the table and straightening his back, Herbie walked slowly round the lockup. Stopping at the large steel stencil that had been used on the van, he began to run the palm of his hand along the neat lettering of 'Johnson and Sons'.
"I'm sorry but I'm finding it hard to be excited when that bastards still walking the streets.'
Jimmy Forbes left the table. Walking over to his friend he placed a hand on the man's shoulder.
"Come on old mate, there's no point in thinking about what might never happen."

Herbie Spires immediately shrugged his friends hand away and staring directly at Angela his words made her shiver.

"What might fuckin' happen? I think we're all kiddin' ourselves if we think anythin' else. Jim we've both been in this game long enough to know that this lots not over, it's only the beginnin'."

Jimmy was in agreement, he'd never thought any different but to bring it up now and in front of the girl was out of order.

"Herb we both know what road we're goin' down but what point is there in frightening her! In any case, we don't even know if he's out yet!"

Herbie's eyes moved towards Angela as he shook his head.

"I aint tryin' to frighten anyone, I just don't think she realises what an evil bastard Vale is and don't be a prick Jim, if he ain't out now, then he soon will be."

"Will you two stop talking as if I'm not here?" Jimmy Forbes looked from Herbie to Angela. "Listen sweetheart, I don't mean to sound disrespectful but I have to agree with Herbie, I still don't think you're fully aware of what we could be up against."

"Well then for god's sake tell me Jimmy. How the hell can I be head of a firm, when all the time you and him are wrapping me up in cotton wool and treating me like a baby? Do you think that's what Dad would have wanted for me? Well do you?"

Herbie thought back to his friend and knew instantly that she was right. Marty was a strong person and he would have expected any child of his to be the same.

"She's right Jim, things need to change and if she can't handle it, I'm afraid that's her problem. We're both not far short of joining her Dad so sooner or later she's goin' to have to stand on her own two feet and its probably better done now than later."

Angela didn't wait for the two men to enter into further discussions. Walking over to where they stood, she leant against the van and stared at them both.

"Well thank fuck for that, now can we sort out about moving some of this money."

Herbie walked outside and made his way to the car. He returned five minutes later carrying three large sized holdalls. Danny's words of last night were still playing heavily on his mind but as yet he hadn't had chance to speak to Jimmy about it. He studied her face as she began to speak.

"We will take what we can tonight and move the rest out over the next few days. I know it's risky but there's nowhere safe enough to store it all, not without raising suspicion. It's funny really I didn't think having so much money could be such a problem."

Herbie had to agree but it was a good feeling all the same. He began to count out Mickey Colletta's share and couldn't help but ask a question as he did so.

"What are you proposin' we do with the rest after everyone's been paid?"

Angela grinned. Since the robbery she had thought long and hard about this and knew that sooner or later one of them would ask the question.

"Once the clubs are back in my hands and all the paperwork from the solicitors has been returned I intend to slowly filter it through the business and make it all legitimate. I know we will have to pay tax on it but that's life I'm afraid. That said, I think we should hold some back for new cars, maybe invest in a few antiques, jewellery etc and before we know it everything will be as clean as a whistle."

The three began to fill the bags with as much money as possible and ten minutes later Angela and Herbie stood outside, while Jimmy Forbes locked the shutter. Walking the short distance back to the car, Angela soon found out how heavy a bag full of money could be. Like her father before her she wouldn't admit defeat and struggled every step of the way. Herbie and Jimmy had noticed her difficulty as soon as

she'd lifted the bag off of the table but didn't comment. The bags were loaded into the boot of the Jag but only two would fit so the third was pushed onto the back seat, pinning Angela to one side. Cautiously Herbie Spires drove back to Angela's apartment not wanting to get a pull by the traffic cops. When all three people complete with the holdalls, were safely inside, they all in unison let out a sigh.
"So princess where do you want it?"
Angela though for a moment and scanned the hallway as she did so. Storage wasn't a problem in this place but at the same time she wanted somewhere that a person wouldn't come across it accidentally. She didn't want anyone else, including her new lover, to know that she had any cash on the premises, let alone hundreds of thousands of pounds.
"You can't see it Herbie but that cupboard runs under the staircase which leads to the next floor. I have a few boxes and suitcases in it but if we pull them out and stuff these to the back, I think it will all look innocent enough. Mind you, I hope I don't have to have the whole stash here!"
"No worry on that score princess, either me or Jim here will arrange a safe house tomorrow, alright?"
"Ok. Herbie, how much do we need to give to Mickey Colletta?"
"We've already discussed that Princess. It's fifty

percent why?"

"That's an awful lot of money. Look he doesn't know how much we really got; can't we just say it was less?"

"Darlin' in our line of work you don't do those sort of things. A deal is a deal and besides I know his boys weren't with us at the count but they aint fuckin' daft, they saw how big the bags were."

"I suppose so. Geno is coming round tonight to collect the money; I'll just have to tell him we still have to sort out the exact amount. Now would you both like some tea?"

"I don't think so, I've left Marge on her own a lot lately and I need to do some serious sucking up."

"What about you Jimmy?"

"No thanks; I'm in pretty much the same boat as him. Anyway you must have things you need to get on with. How's Mrs M taking all this?"

Angela felt a stab of guilt. With everything that had been going on over the last couple of days, she hadn't given her grandmother a second thought.

"To be honest I haven't heard from her. Maybe I'll pop over in a while and see how she's doing."

After the men had left, Angela was about to make herself a drink when she thought better of it. Images of Flo ran through her mind and she realised that the old woman could be dead for all she knew. Visions of her grandmother lying on

the floor in that tiny flat filled her mind and all because her own flesh and blood hadn't been bothered to see if she was alright. Picking up her handbag, she locked the flat and was soon hailing a cab to Bethnal Green. Climbing the stairs, Angela slipped the key which Flo had given her into the lock. She called out before she'd even closed the door.
"Nan! Nan are you in?"
A voice from the kitchen boomed back at her, making Angela smile.
"Course I'm fuckin' in, I do live here you know!"
Walking into the room she found her grandmother sitting at the table enjoying a cup of tea but she wasn't alone, staring at the unexpected guest Angela inwardly groaned.
"Pops whatever are you doing here?"
Her grandfather stood up and wrapped his arms around her just like he'd done when she was a child.
"Well that's a nice greeting, I must say."
Angela held the man as if her life depended on it. She hadn't realised how much she'd missed him and now that he was here, she didn't want him to ever leave. Realising that was an impossibility, she let go and didn't voice her feelings.
"I'm sorry. It was just such a shock to see you sitting here that's all."
Flo McCann reached over and grabbed another

mug from the cupboard. She had a knack of being able to reach everything in the small kitchen without leaving her seat and the sight always made Angela want to laugh.

"So now you've bothered to see if your old gran's alive or dead, I suppose you want a cuppa?"

Winking in the direction of Pops, Angela smiled and said 'That would be lovely.' The unlikely threesome made small talk for a while but when Angela couldn't contain herself any longer she asked the question that Flo had been dreading. It wasn't really the question so much as what she would say to his reply. For Angela to take over Marty's business was a definite no no where her grandmother was concerned but Flo didn't want to think about the girl going back to Canterbury either.

"Pops it's not that I'm not pleased to see you, nothing could be further from the truth but why are you here?"

Julian took hold of his granddaughters hand and stared deep into the beautiful face that he'd adored since the day she'd been born.

"Well, after your mother came home and gave us some cock and bull story about you needing to find your roots, I knew there could be trouble on the horizon. I've been aware for years what kind of circles your father mixed in and I know how headstrong you can be. No disrespect meant

regarding your son Mrs McCann."
"None fuckin' taken. My boy was no angel; in fact he could be a real nasty bastard when he needed to be."
Julian Canning Brown, for all his years on the bench and for all the low life's he'd had to deal with, found it appalling that a woman of Flo McCann's age could speak about her dead child in such a way and with such foul language to boot. His host could see the disgust on her guests face and it brought a grin to her lips.
"Bit too fuckin' blunt for you Judge am I?"
Julian didn't know how to reply to the question. To say he'd never heard such language from a woman of her age would be a lie but to hear it from Angela's grandmother was a little shocking to say the least.
"No I, well I....."
"It's alright Judge don't get your knickers in a twist. We're from different worlds and under different circumstances, our paths wouldn't ever cross. Well unless I came up in front of you in court that is."
Flo started to laugh at her own words until tears ran down her cheeks.
"I wish you could see both of your faces, they are a fuckin' picture. Don't look so shocked either. It's no secret I've been known to do a little liftin' in me time, mind that was when Marty was a boy and times were hard. Anyways I don't

suppose me etiquette is really an issue here, our main priority is this head strong little cow and that's all that matters."

Angela's head started to spin and she now wished she'd stayed at home.

"Can we get back to my question please? Pops why are you here?"

"To take you home darling, this silliness has gone on long enough. Now your mother may have given up easily but I damn well won't."

The reply was finally out and Flo waited with baited breath to see what Angela would say.

"Pops as I told mother, I love you all but this is something I have to do. Now you can try as hard as you like but I won't change my mind. If I came back now without seeing things through, can you imagine that I would ever truly be happy?"

Staring into her eyes Julian could see a strength that had never been there before. He wasn't sure if it was something he liked but he was still proud, that from somewhere she'd at last found her fight.

"But this is all a million miles away from what you are used to and how can you be happy living in such cramped conditions? Once again no disrespect intended."

Flo didn't answer but nodded her head in acceptance of his words. She had no delusions of grandeur and accepted that Angela had been brought up in splendour. To the likes of Julian Canning Brown this place must resemble squalor but at least it was her squalor and she was proud of it.

"I need to......"

"Don't interrupt Angela I haven't finished yet. What do you mean when you say it's something you have to do?"

"Pops that isn't a subject I wish to discuss. As you said earlier, you know the kind of life my father lived, so I assume you can guess what I mean. If you can't, then just let the matter drop."

Julian had imagined the task of bringing his granddaughter home would be easy, he now saw firsthand what his own daughter had come up against.

"Angela darling! I'm begging you please, if not for me then think of your mother and grandmother."

Slamming her hand down hard onto the table, a habit she had picked up recently and one which her grandfather took an instant dislike to, she stared coldly into his eyes.

"Think about mother! Think about grandmother! I've been thinking of those two for the whole of my life. Pops I'm not a child anymore and for the last time will everyone stop treating me like one. I'm here for a reason and when, no change that to if, I decide to come back to Canterbury it will be my decision and no one else's. I'm fed up to my back teeth of being told 'don't do this Angela, or do that. From now on I make my own choices and this one's not even up for discussion."

Julian could see he'd lost the argument. The girl standing before him was someone different to his dear sweet Angela. This girl was a stranger and he knew that she was lost to him and the rest of the Canning Browns forever.

"Can I at least take you both out for dinner before I leave?"

Angela smiled. 'That would be lovely Pops."

"Right I'll go and book a smart restaurant in town then......"

Flo started to panic; she wasn't any good in them fancy places. For a start she didn't know which knife and fork to use and having to hold her tongue and mind her language for a few hours would kill her.

"Hang on a minute Judge. I'm sure you've been to them lardy da places a hundred times before. How about I take you out for a real east end slap up meal?"

"Well I must say Mrs McCann that would make a pleasant change. Where do you have in mind?"

"Ever had pie and mash?"

Angela burst out laughing and her elderly grandparents, both for different reasons, couldn't understand what was so funny.

Just the idea of Pops walking into a pie and mash shop was hilarious. He was so sheltered was he to the common way of life, he didn't have a clue what he was letting himself in for. Even though Angela had been expecting a guest to help keep her bed warm that night and it was something she'd looked forward to all day, this was a sight she wouldn't miss for the world. Slipping into the hall, she delved into her handbag and removed her phone. A shiver ran down her spine as she dialled his number.
"Hi, yeh I've missed you too. Listen about tonight I won't be able to see you until later, something's come up. Is ten too late? Good I'll see you then. Ok bye."
The mental image of their bodies entwined deep in a passionate embrace, made her cheeks redden and she suddenly felt clammy and hot. After freshening up in the bathroom, she made her way back to the kitchen eager for the evening to begin. Soon Angela, along with her grandfather and Nan left the flat for their east end night out. About to hail a cab, Julian was halted when he felt Flo's hand on his arm.
"It's only a ten minute walk Judge and we're doing things my way tonight, right?"
Julian Canning Brown bowed low and swept his hand down towards the ground.
"As you wish Madam!"
"Oh get out of here you daft fucker."

Angela burst out laughing and they had only gone a hundred yards, somehow she thought tonight would be etched in her memory forever. Linking arms with both her grandparents, the three filled the whole width of the pavement as they strolled along. Looking from Flo to Pops, she realised that this was the happiest she'd been in her entire life. It wasn't that she didn't love her mother and other grandmother but simply that the people she now walked along with, seemed to be enjoying life without putting on an act. It was still early evening but the street was abuzz with people. Shopkeepers were drawing down the safety bars to their shops and market workers were closing up stalls for the day. Everyone nodded to Flo as she passed by and Julian thought to himself how much the woman must be liked. Looking back on his own life, he realised that he had no true friends and was probably liked by very few. Always the first to condemn the likes of the McCann's and their families, he was now seeing their way of life in a different light. Not the way that they lived on the wrong side of the law but the fact that they seemed close to so many people and liked by them too. He knew that if right at this very moment Flo McCann was to fall over, then a hundred people would come running to her aid, whereas he on the other hand would have no one. Even back in Canterbury people would

probably pass by and not give him a second glance. This realisation didn't make Julian Canning Brown feel very good about himself. In all honesty, he felt downright sad that for all his family's social climbing, they lagged far behind the likes of the McCann's. A few minutes later and after a short walk, Flo led them towards a rather dingy looking shop front.
"Here we are then, the best fuckin' pie shop in the whole of London town!"
On entering Julian was immediately struck by the dark green and cream ceramic tiles that covered the walls. It reminded him of the numerous public toilets that he had frequented years earlier. It was long before his marriage and wasn't a chapter in his life he'd been proud of. If it ever came to light, well that wasn't something he cared to dwell on but the similarities made him smile all the same.
"Pops are you alright?"
"I'm fine darling why?"
'Because you're smiling. What's funny?'
"It's nothing darling, just one of those silly things that one sometimes finds amusing."
Flo had left her dinner guests and was standing at the counter talking to Alfie the owner. They spoke in whispers and Angela just made out the words 'so make sure it's the best you've ever served'. Suddenly she was overcome by a feeling of pride. This old woman, who by nature

just happened to be her paternal grandmother, was worried what they might think of her. She was bothered that everything had to be nice and right at this moment Angela wouldn't change the woman for anyone else on earth. Seated at the best wooden booth Alfie Granger could offer, the three enjoyed a cup of tea. The place wasn't licensed but somehow alcohol wouldn't have made any difference. It surprised her but Flo McCann was actually enjoying the Judges company. Whether it was the surroundings or the fact that the rest of his family were absent she didn't know but he seemed relaxed and happy to be here. That sight told Flo that their way of life really wasn't so bad, not if a judge of her majesties was content to live it. If Marty could see them now he would have the shock of his life and inwardly Flo smiled at the thought. After they had all been served their meals and the Judge had ordered a second helping of green liquor, although Angela doubted very much if he knew what it was, they slowly strolled home. As soon as it was agreed that the Judge would sleep in Angela's room Flo brought out the brandy. They toasted the future, though both of Angela's grandparents didn't even want to contemplate what that might bring. By ten o'clock Flo McCann and her guest were tucked up in their beds and snoring softly. For Angela it was a different story, hopefully her night was only just beginning.

CHAPTER TWENTY SEVEN

Kathy Jones hadn't heard a word from her boss, in fact no one had heard from Johnny, not even Al Kingston. Al due to his cooperation had been let go much earlier than his boss, causing Johnny's solicitor a wasted journey, when he'd returned to the police station and tried to secure the man's release. Al hadn't been able to help with police enquires but all the same he'd been polite and responsive, something his boss didn't have the first idea of how to be. Over at the bookies, Johnny sat alone behind his desk. He was aware how quiet the place was, the monitors weren't blaring out results and the muffled sound of chatter that normally filled the place, was noticeably absent. The lost revenue didn't bother him. Money was the last thing on his mind at the moment and he was glad of the peace, which gave him time to think. Palms flat out and with eyes so wide he looked insane, Johnny was planning his revenge. He now accepted that regarding Marty's clubs and other business interest including the bookies, he had lost out due to the will. What really angered him was the fact that he'd been done over by that little bitch and her two sidekicks. It hadn't take Johnny long to work out who was behind it all, putting all the pieces together wasn't rocket science. Deciding that he wouldn't seek out all the members of the newly formed little crew, he would concentrate his thoughts on the three key people, who as far as he was concerned, had wrecked his future. The bitch that'd started all this trouble would be easy because without her bodyguards she had no one to look out for her. No, Angela Canning Brown would be last on the list but he would make her pay far more than she could ever imagine. An hour later and Johnny Vale had the blueprint of his plan stored deep within his mind. Walking over to the filing cabinet, he removed a crystal tumbler and a bottle of scotch. Pouring himself a large measure, he grinned widely at the thought of what was to occur over the next couple of days. Normally one of Johnny's heavies would be sent out to do this sort of dirty work but not this time, this time he wanted to carry it out himself. With the absence of his driver, he picked up the keys that hung on the hook beside the door. There were a few hours to kill before he could begin his mission, so he decided to drive home and grab forty winks. Walking towards the front door of the shop he suddenly stopped in his tracks, seconds later he was back in the office picking up the scotch. A few drinks always helped him sleep and he was so wound up over the past few days' events, that he knew without the bottle he would be wide awake for hours.

Angela raced back to her apartment and hoped he hadn't already arrived. She quickly showered and changed. Just as she'd carried out a final inspection of her appearance she heard the intercom buzz.
"It's open, come on up."
Angela watched the screen as Geno entered the building, he truly was a looker. They were about the same age and she had fancied Geno since the first time she had set eyes on him. She studied him from head to toe meticulously taking in every detail. His black Armani jacket, that slightly hid his crisp white shirt. His well fitting designer jeans, that hugged his muscular thighs and buttocks, even down to his shiny handmade Italian shoes. His build and looks were the finishing touch to what said to Angela 'Come and get me'. As Geno entered the flat no words were spoken. Walking over to her she accepted his gift of a single red rose and he tenderly placed his arm around her slim waist. Pulling her to him he firmly but gently kissed her neck pausing to take in the aroma of her hair, skin and expensive perfume. Geno flicked her long flowing hair from her neck and again kissed her silky skin sending a shiver down Angela's spine. Still holding her waist he moved slightly away from her and took a long lingering look.
"You are absolutely gorgeous."

Angela smiled sexily.

"Thank you."

She did look good it was all part of the plan. Unbeknown to each other, like a mating ritual they had both taken great care to show off their bodies in the sexiest way possible.

"Wine?"

Passing him the glass she caressed his finger for a second longer than was necessary and then took a seat beside him on the sofa. Studying his face she saw that his skin was as clear and as soft as her own. Geno now took in all of her beauty and he couldn't help but notice she was aroused. The red silk dress she had chosen hugged her every curve and Angela's nipples were hard and their form pressed against the fabric. Her pupils were enlarged and as she ran her tongue over her top lip it appeared to swell and glisten. Taking the glass from her hand he placed it onto the table and then kissed her passionately. Angela responded by kissing him hard on the mouth and Geno knew she was now ready to begin. Standing up he gently took hold of her wrists and pulled her to her feet. Expertly and with one swift action he had removed her dress. All but for a pair of red stiletto's Angela now stood naked before him and she truly had the body of a goddess. Eagerly she pulled at his jeans and seconds later he had kicked off his shoes as she continued to undress him. Angela wasn't surprised to find he wore no underwear but she was a little taken back by the size of his manhood. Edward hadn't been small by any measure but Geno, with his Adonis like body, was on another level. Angela couldn't wait any longer and pushing him onto the soft fabric of the sofa, she straddled him. Geno slipped in easily and the two were soon entwined with each other, their bodies moving as one. The passion was intense; Geno really was a fantastic lover. After climaxing together they stopped only to once more savour the wine before he entered her for a second time. It was mind blowing for Angela and this time surpassed the last. Geno took her in so many ways and she couldn't believe it could be so good. If this was a taster then she wanted more and he was only too pleased to oblige. Their passion would carry on late into the night and continue until early morning.

As Angela experienced excitement like never before, Johnny Vale's was about to feel his own. Checking his equipment for the second time, he decided to run the filleting knife along the sharpening block once more for good measure. Satisfied that his tool was now up to the job and after placing a revolver into the back of his trousers he knew it was time to get started. Gently closing the front door to the prestigious apartment complex, that he'd been proud to call home since the day Marty had died, he slipped out into the night. Public transport was out of the question and hailing a cab was too risky, so Johnny decided that the only option left to him was to walk. It was several miles to his destination and the whole time he thought of nothing but the robbery and what should have been his. The pavements were busy and the journey took far longer than he'd anticipated. By the time he reached Kings Cross, the insanity of earlier had returned with a vengeance. The Cross was alive with people and Jimmy's girls were out in force, just as Johnny knew they would be. Pulling the hood of his coat up over his head he took several minutes to pick out the first of his victims. For most of the girls trade had been slow and when business was slow, Jimmy was never happy. His happiness was paramount to them all, for they all lived with the delusion that he truly loved them. The thought of returning to their seedy little bedsits empty handed was a constant worry and as the night drew on, they could visibly be seen to get more and more uptight. Due to her size, Small Susan was an easy target for any man and when the opportunity to bag her first punter of the evening arose, she jumped at the chance. As Johnny Vale approached and slowed his pace as he passed, she called out in a loud voice. "Want to do some business darlin'?"

Johnny wasn't aware that any of the brasses knew him but he wasn't about to take any chances. Lowering his voice, the only word he spoke was a husky 'Yeh.' He pointed to a nearby alleyway and continued to walk, knowing that she would undoubtedly follow. Susan was used to plying her trade in any place asked of her and the particular alleyway in question had seen the bare skin of her arse rubbed up against its walls many times before. Following her trick along the street, they both disappeared as he lead her more than the usual distance, until they were out of sight of anyone passing by. Assuming that the man was shy, Susan took charge but as she moved her hand down to his trousers and began to release his penis, she felt something cold against her cheek. Placing his hand across her mouth, Johnny didn't give her chance to cry out. The blade glinted for a second in the moonlight, as he ran its tip from her eyebrow down to her chin. The cold metal was razor sharp and sliced cleanly through Susan's flesh so fast, that at first she felt no pain. By the time pain came and she realized what had happened, Johnny Vale was disappearing out of the alley and onto the main road. Clawing her way along the brick wall which was her only guidance, it quickly became more and more difficult. The blood fell thick and fast and where she'd desperately tried to

wipe the crimson liquid away, it had only proved to make matters worse. Her one good eye was soon sticky and blurred and vision was now almost none existent. Susan's screams were high pitched and loud but it didn't help her, not one stranger on the road offered any assistance. On seeing the state she was in, a couple of brasses and who were also girls of Jimmy Forbes, ran over. Silvia and Justine had both plied their trade on behalf of the man for the last couple of years. Silvia Hunt was one of the oldest girls on his books and had seen so many terrible things during her time at the Cross, that nothing much shocked her. That was until she saw the state of the poor woman lying on the pavement. Justine Smith leant in close to have a good look at Susan and instantly vomited up the burger she had consumed just a few minutes earlier. Placing a hand across her mouth she retched uncontrollably and had to rest against the nearest wall. After taking in a few gulps of air, she composed herself and told Silvia that she couldn't stay around.
"That's right Justine you just fuck off! Nice to know who we can rely on in a crisis."
Justine Smith ignored the remark. Who the hell did Silvia think they were, sisters of mercy? A decent place to stay and putting food on the table was the only things she was interested in. As far as the other girls were concerned, Justine

didn't give a toss and wasn't bothered who knew. Making herself scarce, she walked quickly along the road glad to be away from the agro and blissfully unaware that within the hour, she too would fall victim to Johnny Vale's second act of revenge.

No one wanted to be drawn into a police investigation least of all the brasses and after using her jacket to stem the blood loss Silvia hailed a passing mini cab and ordered the driver to take Susan to the nearest hospital. The driver who had himself just carried out a spot of business with another of Jimmy's girls, was about to drive off when he saw the twenty Silvia dangled in front of his eyes. Johnny Vale didn't witness any of this. Deciding not to hang around, he'd headed for the nearest pub he could find. The Crossways was a tired looking place and filled with mostly pensioners who'd been regulars for more years than they cared to remember. With a dominos tournament in its final stages, the oldies were too engrossed to even notice the stranger in the corner. Ordering a scotch, Johnny then took refuge until any excitement had died down and was surprised when nothing happened. No ambulance was called and none of the other girls came in and relayed what had just gone down. Jimmy had always taught the girls that if a situation arose, you didn't make a fuss and Silvia on realising

they weren't about to get any help, had carried out her boss's teachings to the letter. When he was confident that the coast was clear and that no alarm had been raised, Johnny Vale left the warmth of the bar and began to seek out his next victim. Still feeling nauseous, Justine Smith only began to calm down when she reached one of the numerous quiet back streets. She hated the job and a crazy punter was just one of the daily hazards a brass came up against. Even so it wasn't something you ever got used to but the fact that it had been small Susan and not herself, brought overwhelming relief. She decided to give it another hour and if things hadn't livened up, then she'd call it a night. Slowly walking along, she soon became aware of footsteps approaching her from behind. Turning to face her next possible trick, Justine smiled when she saw his face. It had only been the once but she could remember seeing her boss with the man a few months ago.
"Hello there! Aint you a friend of Jimmy's?" Johnny had hoped this wouldn't happen but as it had then he had no option but to cover his tracks and there was only one way out. Smiling as he moved in close to Justine, he pulled out the blade before she could tell what it was. Skilfully he thrust the whole of its length into her stomach and pulled upwards just for good measure. Mesmerised by her fluttering eyes, he

stayed in the same position for a few seconds. As he pulled the blade away from her tight fitting top, most of Justine Smiths intestines followed. Stepping back as the warm entrails hit the pavement with a splash; he saw that his clothes now had blood on them. This annoyed Johnny and he kicked out in anger at the body lying at his feet. Rather than go back home to change he decided to chance not being seen and continue with the job he'd set out to do. The streets were dimly lit and the patches on his clothes and shoes were dark but not recognisable as blood. Making his way back to the original crime scene, it would now be Sylvia Hunt's turn to suffer at his hands. As she pleaded for her life, he gave a sickly grin before plunging the knife deep into her chest. Horrendous screams rang out and Johnny continued to stab her over and again until she was silent. Within an hour the number of victims now tallied three and Johnny was on the lookout for more. Jimmy Forbs would normally have had ten girls on the street that night but due to Lanky Lorraine's earlier accident the number had been slightly reduced. Walking further along he soon heard the ambulance and police cars that had at long last begun to fill the area. Weighing up the situation and the growing risk of being caught, Johnny decided to quit while he was ahead. The cross was busy with people so he wasn't worried

about being singled out and though it went against the grain he opted to ride the night bus home. Determined to get some sleep before he carried out plan two, he was more than happy he'd achieved all that was possible, at least for tonight.
Jimmy Forbes had just finished, as far as he was concerned, a night of lust with Marlene and rolling over he felt exhausted but fulfilled, unlike his girlfriend. A few years ago he could have kept going several times a night every night but over the last few years that had gradually dwindled to the now once in seven days that Marlene was supposed to be grateful for.
"Alright babe?"
"Jimmy you were fantastic as usual."
Luckily for him and indeed for her, in the dimly lit room he was unable to see Marlene roll her eyes towards the ceiling. Gently beginning to drift off to sleep, Jimmy was annoyed when the phone started to ring.
"You get it Mar and whoever it is, tell 'em to fuck off."
Reaching over her meal ticket, Marlene picked up the receiver and was about to relay his words when she stopped.
"Jim! Jimmy there's something very wrong, here you'd better take this."
Sitting bolt upright Jimmy Forbes snatched the

phone from her hand and was about to begin ranting and raving when he too stopped. Expecting it to be another bust up between small Sue and lanky Lorraine he was shocked to hear the voice of an Irish woman on the other end. Explaining that she was a sister at St Joseph's hospital, she went on to ask if he would come down and visit a young woman that had been admitted to the emergency department. Unable to give any name, the sister explained to Jimmy that due to her injury and the emotional state she was in, it had been necessary to sedate her. Luckily enough before drifting off, she had asked them to call her friend. Not mentioning Jimmy's name, she had pointed to her handbag but fell asleep before she could tell them anymore. Looking inside her bag, the Sister found an address book and the fact that his number was the only one inside, had made her think it was worth a chance giving him a call. Without waiting to hear more Jimmy Forbes replaced the receiver and was dressed and in his car a few minutes later. It crossed his mind to phone Herbie but he thought better of it and decided to wait until he knew the extent of the damage. There was no point in worrying his old pal unnecessarily. Arriving at the hospital, he ran past the admissions desk and straight into the emergency department. The young admin assistant tried to stop him but it was useless.

Spotting the Sister who was now accompanied by two uniformed officers, he explained that he was the man she had telephoned.

"Thank you for coming down. Now we've managed to stitch up the young woman's wound but I'm sorry to say that the surgeon couldn't save her eye."

Jimmy's eyes were wide open with shock and images of a disfigured Angela invaded his mind.

"If you'd like to follow me I'll take you through."

The young constables, eager to show their authority, began to ask a barrage of questions but the ward sister soon put a halt to the inquiry.

"Not now gentlemen if you don't mind, there will be plenty of time for questions later."

Her authoritarian voice and large build stopped the two young men in their tracks and she led Jimmy towards the curtained cubicle. Drawing back the curtain, Jimmy was surprised to see small Susan lying on the bed in a deep sleep.

"I'm afraid she's still heavily sedated but if you'd like to spend some time with her then that's fine. You do you know this woman Sir?"

Jimmy Forbes shook his head.

"I'm so sorry it looks as if we may have called you by mistake. It's just that we thought by the woman's ramblings and the phone number she was able to give us you would know her?"

With cold eyes and no offer of his name, Jimmy Forbes stared into the ward sister's face.

"I aint never seen her before in my life!"
Jimmy fled the hospital almost as quickly as he'd entered but used the side stairs instead of the main entrance. Old Bill had a way of holding you up for hours and he didn't have time for their questions tonight. Outside he leant against the wall and lit up a Marlboro. He hadn't had a fag in months but he was now glad that he still carried the half empty pack around with him. About to take his first drag, he annoyingly threw the cigarette to the ground when his mobile phone began to ring. Eyeing the display, Jimmy recognised the number as home and thought that poor Marlene must be going out of her mind. He decided to play things down so as not to scare her.
"Hi babe false alarm. There's nothing to worry about I'm just....."
Cut off mid sentence he couldn't believe what she was saying and had to sit down on the pavement to take it all in.
"Jimmy there's worse to come! Nicky Sampson, you know that Indian pimp from down the cross? Well he's just been round and told me Silvia and Justine have also been attacked."
Jimmy Forbes clenched his fists at her words but said nothing as she continued to speak.
"They're dead Jimmy, some bastards......."
He didn't wait to hear more and with a feeling of nausea snapped his mobile shut. Jimmy Forbes

arrived home at five am the following morning and poured himself a large scotch. In just a few hours a third of his work force had been wiped out and he was in a state of shock. Jimmy couldn't believe that two of his girls were dead and both in the same night. He'd had problems in the past with punters cutting up rough but never anything like this. Jimmy realised that the Old Bill would be on his doorstep pretty soon and that was the last thing that any of them needed. Why Oh why had that stupid cow written his phone number down? Waiting until six thirty he finally picked up the phone and called Herbie Spires. Everything would have to be put on hold as the manor would soon be teaming with the boys in blue. It wasn't common practice for any fuss to be made over a hurt Tom but with so many in one night, the pigs were going to take this seriously for a few days at least.

CHAPTER TWENTY EIGHT

In their opulent bedroom, Herbie Spires and his wife lay back to back both in a deep comfortable sleep. Herb was snoring and due to his constant teeth grinding, it had taken Marge over an hour to finally drift off. Going to bed at her routine eleven pm, the last thing she'd expected was to be joined by her husband. He always sat up well into the early hours watching television and that was only when he could be bothered to spend an evening in her company. Hearing him take a shower and then smelling the overpowering aftershave that he favoured much to her distaste, she knew it would be a bad night. After a whole evening of hints and compliments, Marge had reluctantly sacrificed herself to the thing she hated most in life and finally given in to her monthly carnal duty. Like a statue, she had laid rigid as he pounded up and down, almost crushing her with his weight. A large grunt signalled that Herbie had finished and when he at last rolled over, she felt nothing but pure relief. Her marital duties would always be a chore but also taken seriously, providing she could live in the splendour that she'd become accustomed to. Even if the mere thought of his body on top of hers repulsed her, she knew which side her bread was buttered. Nothing in life was free and letting her husband have his way, was a small price to pay, even though she sometimes felt no better than the whores who walked the streets of the city. The act of sex sickened her and nothing he tried had ever in the whole of their married life been able to arouse any kind of passion. Herbie had spent hundreds of pounds on romantic weekend's away, sexy lingerie, even resorting to blue movies but they were all futile attempts to change his wife's opinion of what should and shouldn't happen in the bedroom. Realising that this was it, as far as any kind of loving would ever go, Herbie Spires accepted his lot and made the most of the meagre sex that was allocated to him once a month. Unbeknown to his wife, Herbie did on the odd occasion seek relief from one of Jimmy's girls but it was few and far between and not enough to make him feel guilty. In the early years when every waking moment of Marge Spires life had been filled with the idea of babies, she'd let him fill her with his seed almost nightly. Now with her body clock at a standstill and all chances of a Herbie junior out of the window, she considered it a job of duty, for a man who'd asked nothing of her other than to be loved. The Spires rose every day at seven thirty sharp, a ritual they'd settled into soon after taking their vows. When the telephone burst into life an hour early, they both jumped

out of their skins at the annoying noise. It was a total taboo in the house, to be woken earlier than Marge's regimental time dictated. Marge was slender and fit and much quicker on the draw than her husband. Although Herbie knew the call would be for him and had tried to reach the telephone, he failed miserably. Snatching up the reproduction ivory and brass candlestick phone, which Herbie hated with a vengeance, she shouted into the mouth piece.
"Yes?"
"Marge its Jimmy, I need to speak to Herbie now!"
"Do you know what the time is?"
"Yes I do thank you very much, now just put Herbie on!"
"Well I never! Don't ever phone my home and…."
Herbie Spires grabbed the receiver from his wife's hand and regretted the act as soon as it was done. To deprive Marge of anything that she didn't give willingly, no matter how small, always resulted in a week of sulking and being ignored. Something as trivial as eating the last biscuit in the packet was enough to set her off. Turning his back towards her, he began to whisper but when he heard her roll over and sigh heavily, knew he would be in for the silent treatment for a lot longer than a week. Herbie Spires didn't care. After getting his leg over, he

could go a month without speaking to his wife and as things stood at the moment with Angela now on the scene, he wouldn't really notice. Thank god she couldn't tell what he'd been thinking a few hours ago. If she'd found out that while he lay on top of her his mind had been filled with thoughts of Kathy Jones, then sex would be off the menu permanently. For a second Herbie was off on a plane far far away as he thought about last night and the realisation hit him that it wasn't love making. It was a cold and lonely deed that he could have carried out alone. Laying beside him in a huffy mood, made him finally see her as she really was, a self obsessed nasty greedy ice bitch and he was fed up to his back teeth of living like this. The agitated tone of his best pal's voice brought him back down to earth.
"Herb! Herb you there?"
"Yeh mate course I am. What's happened Jim?"
"What's happened? Some bastards done my girls over that's what."
"What do you mean done your girls over?"
"Just get over here and fast. I need your help mate, I ain't got a fuckin' clue where to start."
Herbie climbed out of bed and made his way to the bathroom. Quickly cleaning his teeth, he dressed in the same clothes as he'd worn yesterday and without a single word to his wife walked out of the bedroom. Almost at the foot

of the stairs he turned round. Instinctively he could feel her eyes boring into the back of his head from the landing above.

"And where do you think you are going?"

"Marge I haven't got time for an argument, the Scouser's in trouble and I need to get over there fast."

"But I have an appointment at the beauty parlour this morning and I hoped you'd stay home with the babies! And what about Danny? I don't want him staying in bed all day!"

Collecting the car keys from a small dish that was always kept on the hall table, he didn't look up as he spoke.

"For fucks sake grow up. They are not babies but fuckin' dogs, if you can call 'em that. Personally they look like fuckin' rats to me. As for my nephew, he's a guest in my house! If he wants to stay in his pit for a fuckin' month then that's fine by me."

"You are a nasty man Herbie Spires!"

Herbie wasn't listening as he slammed the front door behind him. Glancing round at the front lawn and trees that were basking in the early morning sunshine, he was relieved to be out in the fresh air, no matter what lay ahead at Jimmy's. Due to the early hour the traffic was light and Herbie cruised along at a comfortable fifty miles an hour. He wasn't worried about getting a pull due to the fact that it was common knowledge the Old Bill weren't early risers. If they were unlucky enough to pull the short straw, then their time would be spent in the local cafes having a fry up, until after eight at least. Reaching the Stepney terrace in record time, Herbie jumped from the Jag without locking it up. Marlene was already at the door and by the expression on her face; he could see there was big trouble in store.

"Thank god you're here; he's in a right two and eight."

Ignoring her totally, Herbie made his way inside to find Jimmy pacing the floor in front of the fireplace. Looking rough and unshaven, he could see his pal had had little if no sleep.

"Right what's happened?"

As if Herbie was invisible, Jimmy stared straight through him. With bloodshot eyes and pale skin, he now looked all of his age and the sight scared Herbie. Jimmy Forbes shook his head but offered no words of explanation. Instead he sat down heavily in one of the armchairs, where only a few days earlier the two had sat and shared tea and a laugh.

"Come on mate, I'm here now. Whatever it is, it can't be that bad can it?"

"Can't be that fuckin' bad! I ain't got one girl left on the street."

"I don't understand mate, you ain't makin' any sense!"

Leaning forwards Jimmy held his head in his hands and began to relay the past nights events. "Susan's cut up real bad and will probably never fuckin' work again. Justine and Silvia are both layin' on slabs in the morgue. Herbie they all gave me aggro from time to time but at the end of the day they were good girls and didn't fuckin' deserve that."
"There's some real perv's out there and you're as aware as anyone that this kind of thing happens from time to time mate."
"Fuckin' hell Herb what you on? Course the odd girl gets hurt goes with the territory but not three in one night and not to this degree. None of the others are prepared to go back out and can you fuckin' blame 'em? There's only one person to blame for this and we both know who that is."
It was now Herbie Spires turn to stay silent, he didn't want to even consider that Johnny Vale would resort to anything like this. It wasn't turf war or a gangland shooting, no this was sick and depraved and if he was capable of it then what else could he do.
"You heard from Angie?"
"No, I thought I'd wait for you before going over. When I went down the hospital I was all prepared to see her in the bed and when it was one of my girls I breathed a sigh of relief I can tell you. Even so, small Susan looked so vulnerable that I couldn't help but feel

responsible."
"They know the score when they take the job on Jim, you aint to blame!"
"Ain't I? Without greedy bastards like me and the fuckin' dirty cunts who cruise the streets there wouldn't be any work for 'em. So you tell me mate, who is to blame?"
Herbie didn't have an answer and quickly changed the subject.
"How about you have a wash and get changed, then we'll head over to see the princess?"
Slowly and with the effort of a man far older than his years, Jimmy pulled himself from the chair and walked towards the door. Placing his hand on the door knob he looked directly into his friends eyes.
"It ain't something I'm looking forward to but I suppose we've got no choice but to tell her, for her own safety at least. I'm just prayin' that this little lot won't make her pack up and head back to Canterbury. Either way, I can't let this go Herb. I'm goin' to have that cunt if it's the last thing I do."
"I know mate, I know."
Jimmy opened the living room door to find Marlene on the other side. Luckily he was too angry and tired to reprimand her for listening in; instead he called back over his shoulder to Herbie.
"Give me a few minutes to sort myself out and

we'll get on our way."

Angela had risen early and gone over to Flo's flat to say a final farewell to Pops. It was a short visit but she couldn't let him return home without giving him a hug and a kiss. Feeling better regarding his unannounced visit she hailed a cab and after dropping him at the station, headed back to her apartment. Last night after an enjoyable meal, they had all returned from the pie and mash shop and a lengthy discussion had ensued. The result was a reluctant Julian Canning Brown agreeing to return to Canterbury providing Flo kept him updated regularly. The Judge had achieved exactly zero just like his daughter before him and he wasn't looking forward to the reaction he would receive from Elizabeth and Joanna. It was strange but as he boarded the train, Julian knew that he would miss the old woman with the foul mouth. He laughed heartily at the absurdity of the idea.

Oblivious to all that had occurred the previous night, Angela couldn't wait to get home and speak to the boys about what to do next regarding the takeover. Now more than ever, she was determined to see things through and her grandfather turning up unexpectedly, had only strengthened her resolve. Finding Herbie and Jimmy waiting on the doorstep as the cab pulled up unnerved her and she paid the driver

but didn't wait for her change.
"Hi!"
The men only nodded as she approached and she could instantly tell by their faces, that whatever was troubling them wasn't good. Desperate to hear what was wrong, she struggled to hold her tongue until they were all inside and away from prying ears. Angela placed a pot of fresh coffee on the stove as they all took seats at the granite breakfast bar. She didn't ask any questions and as difficult as it was, waited patiently until Jimmy was ready to relay his nightmare of the previous night. As with Herbie, he described all that had occurred in great detail and even though she showed no emotion, another trait inherited from Marty, inside she felt sick. At last the story of Johnny Vale's violent expedition came to a close and everyone sat in silence. Herbie had no more to add than what he'd said earlier and Jimmy was totally knackered and too empty to carry on. Angela on the other hand was deep in thought as she focused her eyes on the central vase in front of her. From a small child, she'd found that if she blocked out everything and concentrated on one single object, she was able to think far better. After finishing their coffee Angela suddenly began to speak.
"Right, as far as I can see, we have two options."
Herbie's ears pricked up but Jimmy couldn't

even be bothered to look up.
"And they are?"
"One, we invite Johnny to join the firm and…."
"No fuckin' way José! You are havin' a fuckin' laugh if you think…..."
"Herbie calm down. Now hear me out please and don't interrupt."
At that precise moment Angela could hear Pops voice and knew that she may be a McCann by her father's blood but she also had a lot of the Canning Browns running through her.
"The second option is to wipe him out once and for all!"
Herbie Spires, who'd just taken a mouthful of coffee, began to choke and Angela had to slap hard on his back several times with the palm of her hand.
"Alright?"
With eyes filled with water, Herbie nodded and his words came out in almost a whisper.
"Fuckin' wipe him out! You mean actually top him?"
"That's exactly what I mean."
He looked across the breakfast bar to Jimmy, who still wasn't prepared or able to comment. The man was lost in some dark guilt filled place, that he wouldn't allow anyone else to enter. Herbie knew that the Scouser would bounce back but until then he was on his own.
"Angie, Angela! You can't just go and wipe out

someone who's a known face. Well not without a good reason anyway."
"So you don't think we have a good reason? Just look at him!"
Herbie once more stared at his friend and knew she was right.
"Look, if you don't want a turf war then there's a certain protocol you have to follow."
Angela looked confused. She couldn't understand how getting rid of their troublesome rival, would possibly cause anyone else bother. Herbie could see the confusion in her eyes and by the way she wrinkled her brow, just like her old dad had done whenever there was a heated discussion.
"Let me explain. In the smoke everyone has their own turf, as you well know."
"Yes and?"
"If a firms boss, well for arguments sake let's say disappears. The lucrative manor he ran would now be up for grabs. It becomes a free for all, ranging from the other firm bosses, right down to the little scroat's on the street who fancy their chances."
"Don't be so ridiculous Herbie, now you're making it sound as if no one ever dies."
He was now having to try very hard to control his temper and kept reminding himself that she was new to all this and still had a lot to learn.
"Of course they die but if you want someone

topped, you have to seek permission. Not everyone follows the rules but that's when you open up a can of worms and invite trouble. Believe me, the vultures would land and Marty's business would be picked over like a carcass before you've even had chance to get your arse in his chair."

"But the business was mine anyway; it's Johnny Vale who's trying to steal my birthright."

"Darlin' the other firms won't see it like that. He was your old man's number one and with that title comes respect and rules that have to be followed."

"Rules are there to be broken."

"And so are bones and believe me that's a road we don't want to go down!"

"So how do we get permission? No forget I said that, just get it Herbie!"

"Personally princess, I think we should wait a while and see what happens. Johnny's let us know he's not happy, that's if it was him?"

"You daft cunt! 'Course it was him."

Both Angela and Herbie's heads turned at the same time. The man, who sat with them at the table but had been lost for a while, was now well and truly back.

"Jim! Nice that you've joined us again."

Ignoring Herbie's sarcastic comment, Jimmy Forbes concentrated his eyes directly on Angela and she was compelled to look away. Every vicious violent act that the man had been part of over the years, was now apparent as his eyes burned with desire for revenge. Averting her gaze and concentrating on the granite work surface, Angela continued to talk.

"I'm not suggesting that we do it right now and if it makes you happy Herbie, then we'll give it a few days. As for your concern regarding who the culprit might or might not be is irrelevant. We have to get rid of Vale one way or another and at least like this, he's out of our hair for good. I know you want payback now Jimmy but I'm a strong believer in the saying 'revenge is a dish best served cold' and anyway, I expect it may take a few days to sort everything out."

At that precise moment after hearing her words, Herbie knew she was her father's daughter. Marty could be the kindest man in the world but he could also be the most brutal. Sitting here listening to her talk cold bloodedly about killing someone, made him see that she had the strength to run the firm with or without them. Silently Herbie Spires prayed that Johnny Vale had made his point and would just slip away without any fuss but deep down he knew his prayer was futile.

CHAPTER TWENTY NINE

Marge Spires, due to Herbie's early departure had been forced to eat breakfast alone. Sitting at the mock Italian marble table, she tenderly looked down at the three little faces staring up at her. Cutting up the remainder of her toast, she patiently and in turn, fed each one of her babies. Thinking back to when Herbie had left this morning, Marge became more and more annoyed at the situation he had put her in. She only ever left the dogs alone if either he was home, or the cleaner Janet Matheson would agree to stay on a couple of hours to mind them. With Janet off in Basildon visiting her sick mother that only left Herbie and Marge had planned to work on him. The awful sex she'd had to put up with last night had been the beginning of her plan to soften him up and now he'd had to go and spoil it all. Well he wasn't going to get away with it; no Marge was going to take great pleasure in making sure he suffered. Kissing the tip of her index finger she gently touched the nose of each of her Chihuahua's, before getting up and clearing the table of crockery. Making her way up the stairs to get ready for her trip to the beauty parlour, she could hear the patter of tiny feet, as her beloved dogs followed close behind. Herbie would go mad if he could see them, it was always an unwritten rule that they weren't allowed any further than the bottom of the stairs. Marge smiled to herself, what he didn't know wouldn't hurt him and there was a lot Herbie Spires didn't know about his wife. She stopped outside Danny's room but there was no sound of him stirring so she made her way to her room. After taking a shower in the adjoining en suite, she entered the bedroom and gently lifted the tiny dogs onto the satin quilt that covered the bed. "Don't mummy's princesses look cute?" Walking to the kidney shaped dressing table that was laden full of expensive perfume, most of which were still in the boxes and piled on top of one another, she began to apply her makeup. All the time she continued to chat away to the dogs but the three small faces ignored her words, oblivious to what she was saying. Tinky, the eldest and laziest of the three had made a puddle in the middle of the bed. Gem was furtively gnawing on the bolster cushion, that had been custom made to match the rest of the soft furnishings and Lizzy the youngest member of the family, had made her way under the quilt to have a snooze. Marge saw the damage that they'd caused but chose to ignore it. Herbie was too deep in her bad books to complain and Marge was quietly pleased with that fact. Over an hour later and dressed from head to toe in the

latest Gucci fashion, she was almost ready to leave. Reluctant to put the dogs into the custom made kennel, which had cost over two grand and had yet to be used. She knew to leave the little monkeys alone in the house was more than her life was worth. Their earlier naughtiness could be forgiven but the damage three sets of teeth, albeit very small teeth could cause, didn't bare thinking about. Picking up Tinky and Gem she placed one dog under each arm and walked outside. Opening the mesh and hardwood kennel door, she grimaced at the thought of her babies being forced outside but luckily the weather was warm which was a small consolation. Lizzy had just started to yap at being left alone and the sound pulled at Marge's heartstrings as she returned to the kitchen to collect her. The sad look in those tiny brown eyes made her want to sob and she decided that her husband's suffering would be the worst she'd dished out since they'd been married. As quickly as she could, she closed the kennel door and tried unsuccessfully to ignore the triple yapping as she re entered the house. Without looking she called back over her shoulder.
"Don't cry babies, mummy won't be long. It's all daddies fault but mummy will get him back, don't you worry."
Without her babies scampering round her feet, she already felt as though she'd lost a limb and

grabbing her handbag, ran out of the front door. The beauty parlour was only a short drive away and Marge had worked out that if she went straight there, by the time she'd had her hair and nails done, she could be back in about two hours. The electric gates swung open and her gold convertible swept out of the drive. Herbie Spires had reprimanded his wife on numerous occasions about not bothering to close the garage and gates behind her. This morning was no exception and she would realise before the day was out, just how dearly that act of laziness would cost her. With the radio blaring and her thoughts engrossed in leaving her babies, Marge Spires didn't see Johnny Vale's car. Even on a normal day she wouldn't have noticed, due primarily to the fact that she didn't know the man and that his Mercedes was nothing out of the ordinary in this neck of the woods. Marge was so wrapped up in herself that she never really bothered about anyone else, not unless it affected her in some way. Johnny on the other hand had made it his business to find out all there was to know about both Jimmy Forbes and Herbie Spires. After stepping into Marty's shoes, he'd viewed the information as a kind of insurance policy and now the policy was maturing. Snatching a couple of hours sleep after his hectic night of cutting up Jimmy's girls, he'd headed to Bermondsey at five in the morning. Witnessing Herbie rush to the aid of his pal, he was confident that the second part of his master plan would easily fall into place. It wasn't on the agenda to do anything to Marge Spires and when she had sped off two hours after her husband, Johnny had seen it as an opportunity. Over the years he'd heard the constant moaning to Marty and he had a good idea of the poor excuse for married bliss that Herbie Spires had to endure. For all of that, Johnny was still aware that the man cared for his wife and would be gutted if anything happened to her. From various snippets of conversations, Johnny had come to the conclusion that there was a way of getting to Marge, which was far worse than any physical pain he could inflict on her.

Pulling into the secluded drive, he glanced up at the mock Tudor over the top house. It was big by any standards but to Johnny that was all it had going for it, to him it shouted of nothing more than 'council estate boy done good.' After switching off the engine and getting out he made his way through the side gate. Expecting to have to break a window, he was pleasantly surprised when the sound of yapping began outside. A quick glance to his left, told him this would be a lot easier and quicker than he had at first thought. Opening the kennel door far enough to scoop up one of the dogs but not far enough to let the others escape, he lifted out Lizzie. She whimpered at the stranger holding her and Johnny sneered back at her. He could see that Marge Spires' choice of dog was even worse than her choice in houses. Gripping her under his arm as her mistress had done only a short while earlier; he opened a small but razor Sharpe knife. Seconds later a high pitched squeal could be heard, as he sliced across Lizzy's neck. Job done, Johnny threw the tiny body over his shoulder and onto the patio. The same fate was in store for Gem but when he held up Tinky she lunged forward and snapped at his nose. The nip brought water to Johnny's eyes. Wiping his face with a gloved hand, he saw a small amount of blood. By now Tinky had seen her sisters lying on the patio and she yapped for all her worth. Holding her up in one hand, he used his fist to punch the little dog on the side of her head. The impact was so hard on the frail creature that her neck immediately snapped. Grabbing her by the scruff of the neck, Johnny impaled her tiny body on the railing of the ornamental wall. About to leave he had second thoughts when he saw the small top window in the utility had been left open. Reaching down he released the large casement and then climbed inside. Silently he moved through the house, all the time laughing to himself at Herbie's choice of decor. When Johnny got to the top of the stairs

he had intended to leave a disgusting calling card on Herbie's bed but when he opened the first door he came to and found Danny Spires sleeping, it was an added bonus, one Johnny Vale couldn't have wished for in his wildest dreams. Quietly he moved across the room and swiftly straddled Danny. With Johnny's full weight bearing down on the man and with his arms pinned to his sides underneath the sheets he had no chance of escape. As Danny woke up he felt trapped by the covers and with his eyes now open and the cold steel blade digging into his neck, could only stare at his assailant.
Johnny Vale removed a cable tie from his pocket. Placing the knife beside him he proceeded to make the tie into a noose.
"Right cunt! When I say, you are goin' to lift your arms and place both hands in this. If you try and be fuckin' clever then I'll stick this blade right through you. Understood?"
"Yeh ok, take it easy!"
Danny could only guess as to who his assailant was but it didn't stop the fear that had begun to take over.
"Right! Now get out of that bed and walk down to my motor. No funny business or I'll slit your fuckin' throat. Do you understand?"
Danny, dressed only in his boxers, did everything that was asked of him and a couple of minutes later the boot of Johnny Vale's car

was opened and Danny climbed inside. After placing tape over his victims mouth Johnny Vale slammed the boot shut. Without a second thought and leaving the front door wide open, Johnny got into his car and drove away. Guilt and remorse were alien emotions to him; the only thing he did regret was not being able to see that stupid bitch's face when she returned home. Marge Spires made good time after informing her stylist she had a deadline to meet and that she couldn't possibly be late. Simone Leonard had been the top stylist at Fredrick's for five years and for the last three of them, had cared for Mrs Spires crowning glory. The woman was so open and boastful, that there wasn't much Simone didn't know about her client. Even details of Marge's bedroom antics, or lack of them, were common knowledge in the salon. Many a laugh had been shared by the girls in the staff room, over what the woman thought was normal sexual practices but to all the stylist was anything but. Generously tipping Simone and after making her following weeks appointment, she was helped on with the small box jacket that had cost more than her stylist earned in a month. With not a hair out of place, Marge walked from the shop into the blazing sunshine. Deciding not to drop the roof of her convertible, on account of not wanting to spoil her hair, Marge set off for home. The roads were quiet and the convertible pulled into the drive less than two hours after it had first left. After closing the front gates Marge was momentarily stopped when she saw that the front door was wide open. Thinking that it was most likely down to that stupid boy Danny she entered the hall and called out.

"Lizzy, Tinky, Gem, mummy's home! For your sake Danny Spires I hope you are out of that bed and have a good reason for the house being left wide open!"

It took a second for her to remember she'd left her babies outside. Excitedly she ran to the back door and headed out to the kennel. Tinky's tiny impaled body was the first to be seen and the screams coming from the doorstep of the house were such that most of the neighbours couldn't help but hear. Marge turned to see Lizzy and Gem lying motionless on the patio. The continuous howling rang out for several minutes as Marge's heart was broken into a million pieces. Stan Howard the pool man, who wasn't due to call until the following day but had a last minute cancellation, found the horrendous scene. Having Herbie's mobile number in case of any problems with the newly installed pool, he dialled as quickly as he could.

Angela, Jimmy and Herbie were still deep in discussion regarding their next plan of action. Herbie was still trying as hard as he could to

convince them to delay any revenge and just wait and see if anything else happened. He was fighting a losing battle, as with every reason he came up with not to retaliate, they came back at him with a dozen more as to why Johnny Vale should be wiped off the face of the earth for good. When his mobile burst into life he was glad of the distraction and got up to take the call in private. Walking into the sitting room, he glanced at the display but didn't recognise the number that was showing.
"Yeh?"
"Mr Spires? It's Stan."
"Who?"
"Stan the pool man! Oh Mr Spires you need to come home as soon as possible, something terrible has happened."
In the back ground, Herbie could just make out a wailing sound that reminded him of the time he'd ran over a dog on White Chapel high street. The high pitched noise made his blood run cold but he didn't wait for Stan to explain. Snapping shut the phone, he ran back into the kitchen.
"This will have to wait, something's very wrong at home."
Almost at the front door, he was suddenly aware that he wasn't alone and turned to see Angela and Jimmy by his side.
"Whatever it is, we're in it together. Want me to drive?"

"Thanks Jim but I need to get home now, not in three hours time."

No one spoke in the car until after they crossed the water and had entered Bermondsey. Angela wasn't scared but she was unnerved at what they were going to find. For now she thought it best to let Jimmy do the talking and sunk back in the Jags luxury seats.

"So did this Stan geezer give you any fuckin' ideas?"

Herbie swung the Jag into the ornate drive way as he spoke.

"No but we're about to find out."

With the front door still wide open, Herbie Spires ran inside with Angela and Jimmy following close behind. Walking from room to room, Herbie didn't think of going outside but as he neared the kitchen area, the wailing became louder and louder. For all the violence Herbie Spires and Jimmy Forbes had witnessed and often taken part in over the years, the sight on the patio, had even them feeling gutted. Marge sat on the cold stone slabs clutching Tinky in her arms. Gem and Lizzy's tiny blood stained bodies lay motionless in her lap. Stan Howard stood very still just staring down at the woman, whose mind had now left this world. Herbie immediately ran to his wife's side but she pushed him away. Trying to pick up one of the pups, he instantly replaced it as she let out a

hideous scream.
"Marge, Marge love where's Danny?"
There was no answer and immediately Herbie spires raced into the house. Seconds later he reappeared but was still none the wiser.
Turning to the Scouser his face was ashen.
"The beds empty and I'm prayin' to god that he went out before all this happened."
Jimmy walked over to Stan and forcing a fifty into his palm, led him to the side gate.
"Forget what you saw mate.'
"How can I forget, it's a sight that'll stay with me forever.'
"Maybe it will but it's in your best interest to forget it. Tell yourself that you never even called here today, understood?'
Stan Howard nodded and with his head hung low, walked from the garden and the scene that would be his nightmare for many years to come. The sight of Herbie desperately trying to consol his wife was almost too much for Angela to bear and after Jimmy had got rid of the pool man, she walked over to where he was standing next to the now empty kennel.
"Jimmy we have to do something and do it now. That psycho can't be allowed to get away with this; I mean who knows what he's planning next?"
"Do you think I don't know that?"
He saw the hurt in her eyes at his harsh tone and

wished he'd chosen his words more carefully. "I'm sorry but it's a bit hard to take, seeing your best mate in a heap on the floor like that."
"I know and it might seem a bit callous but this situation is the least of my worries. It's now about much more than a few, though very much loved dogs. If he can get to you as he did and then come after Herbie, then what's on the cards for my family? When I came here to claim what was mine, I didn't envisage dragging my family into it. I wouldn't put it past that crazy bastard to go to Canterbury and wipe out the whole of the Canning Browns and what about Nan?"
"Don't you think I ain't thought of that as well?"
"Then do something about it. Ignore what Herbie wanted earlier, whoever it is you have to see, see them now. That maniac has to be stopped!"
Her words shocked Jimmy but he was also glad that she was thinking like her father. Over on the patio, Herbie was oblivious to Jimmy's departure as the man slipped out of the side gate and drove off in Herbie's Jag. Marge was inconsolable and this time her rejection of him placing an arm around her was for a very different reason. Herbie could accept his wife's refusals on the sex side but this was pitiful. The one time he should have been able to comfort her, only left him feeling useless and totally inadequate. In the space of a couple of hours

Herbie's life had been torn apart, now the only thing he could hope for was that his nephew was safe.

CHAPTER THIRTY

Already in Bermondsey, Jimmy Forbes didn't have far to travel to his destination. On his recent visit to the restaurant with Herbie, he'd been wound up like a top at having to be in the same room as Mickey Colletta. This time as anger raged through his veins, he looked forward to seeing one of the only people who could help them. Walking into the trattoria at twelve o'clock, Jimmy thought that it possibly wasn't the best time to call. The place was filled with business men on their lunch and the staff were racing about in all directions, trying to cope with the demand. Catching a glimpse of Mickey at the far end of the restaurant, he headed down the main aisle of tables. As expected he didn't get within twenty feet of the man before three heavies blocked his path.
"I know I ain't got an appointment but I need to see Mr Colletta now!"
The minor commotion was brought to Mickey Colletta's attention and he nodded his head. A silent signal was the only indication the men needed and the three bodyguards immediately stepped aside, allowing Jimmy to pass.
"Hello there Scouser and to what do I owe the pleasure?"
Mickey's greeting would normally have pissed

Jimmy off big time but he had too much on his mind, to let the man ruffle his feathers. Leaning forward, Jimmy whispered in Mickey's ear that he need to talk in private. Without having to reveal more, Mickey clicked his fingers and seconds later the three men were once again by his side. Jimmy Forbes was taken through a back door that led to a winding staircase. Shown into a small room on the first floor, he was offered a seat. Ten minutes later, Mickey casually walked into the room and joined his uninvited but by now very nervous guest.
"Now Jim, what's so important that you couldn't make an appointment? I'm a very busy man!"
Jimmy Forbes could tell by his voice, that he wasn't happy with people turning up unexpected. The tone also told him, that the reason for him being here had better be good. Jimmy knew or at least hoped he had no problems on that score.
"I'm sorry to bother you Mr Colletta but we have a major problem on our hands. Johnny Vale's gone nuts and Angela doesn't really have a clue what she's up against."
"Angela?"
"Yeh, you know, Marty's daughter!"
"Oh! The little girlie finding life at the top a bit difficult is she?"
"Well she ain't actually managed to get to the top yet, on account of Vale's interruptions."

"I think you'd better tell me more Jimmy, this sounds interesting to say the least."
Again nodding to one of the minders who stood at the door, Mickey motioned for drinks to be brought up. He had a feeling that today's lunch was going to be a long affair. After Jimmy relayed all that had happened in the last twenty four hours and the bottle of wine had been drunk he now looked into the face of his host. Jimmy tried to make out the man's thoughts but it was useless. Mickey Colletta hadn't got where he was by being easily read and that fact annoyed Jimmy.
"So?"
"So what?"
"Look Mickey; I've come here desperate for your help."
"So you have Jimmy but tell me, what's in this for me?"
"What's in it for you? Marty's girls in trouble and you want fuckin' payment? We've just done a job which was profitable for all of us so aint there any loyalty?"
Instantly Jimmy could see the man stiffen and knew that he'd stepped way over the mark. Mickey Colletta stood up, he had taken exception to Jimmy's comment. In the blink of an eye two of the heavies were by his side and Jimmy was scared.
"Careful with your words Scouser! Remember it

was you who came to me!"
"I know that and I apologise but Mickey, if it was one of yours wouldn't you want to know that they could rely on Angela in a crisis? You and Marty went way back that's why I'm here."
Mickey Colletta's face softened as he sat back down at the table.
"I still laugh when I remember some of the things we got up to. He was a good man Jimmy but I've already helped you with some extra bodies so how do you think I can assist you this time? Oh and by the way, I aint seen my share from the heist yet?"
"Sorry about that but with all the fuckin' aggro we've been 'aving I aint had time to sort it."
"Well fuckin' make time!"
"I will and once again I apologise. Gettin' back to why I'm here, I know Johnny's a serious player, was even before Marty died but there's no reasoning with a nutter like him. We want you and the other firm's permission to make him disappear."
Mickey Colletta's eyes opened wide, he couldn't quite take in what was being said to him.
"You make it sound like we're some kind of mafia Don's."
"Aint that exactly what you are? If we don't get the go ahead and Johnny gets topped anyway, then the rest of the firms will be on that girl like flies round a honey cart. They'll pick all of her

business's to the bone until every one of 'em has a share and that poor little mare is left with nothin'. We aint got time for politeness Mr Colletta this needs sortin' now!"

"Hold on a minute, do you realise what you're fuckin' askin'? For a start you making us sound like somethin' from the Godfather won't help matters. I think you've been watching too many films pal."

"Mickey we all know the score and if anyone can clear it with the others, it's you. Everyone's aware Johnny's a bit of a wide boy but what he's done in the last twenty four ain't normal. If you refuse this request then there's no telling what he might do next. I don't need to warn you that if he succeeds your family could be the next under threat."

Mickey Colletta stood up but unlike before he calmly straightened his jacket.

"Johnny fuckin' Vale don't frighten me Jimmy. He's a nobody so don't try and threaten me with that."

Jimmy realised that he was digging himself into a hole so deep; he'd need a twenty foot ladder just to see over the top. Holding both hands out and palms up towards his host, he tried once more to plead their case.

"Nothing could be further from my mind Mickey. It's just that if Johnny's got ideas above his station, then what's stopping him coming after a slice of your action and maybe even all the other firms. Besides if he finds out who was behind supplying the bodies for the job, well he might take it personal like. I mean a rational man wouldn't even contemplate it but then again, Johnny Vale ain't exactly all the ticket at the minute, now is he?"

At last Jimmy thought he was making headway and for a second began to relax. Mickey hadn't made any comments on his last sentence and Jimmy could see he was deep in thought. When he at last began to talk, Jimmy knew this was his last chance and listened intently to what the man had to say.

"I can see where you're coming from and maybe you have got a point. No one wants to rock the boat, especially when everyone's been getting along so nicely. Johnny's a loose cannon and before long if it ain't you, then it will be someone else who wants rid. It won't be so long till my boys take over and I don't want them having to deal with a cunt like Vale. We're on the verge of going legit you know? Having said that my brain box of a boy ain't got any guts, I tell the missus he must be the fuckin' milkman's 'cause he ain't no boy of mine. You know, sometimes I think my Geno's from another planet."

All the family stuff was starting to get up Jimmy's nose, he needed an answer and he was pissed off that he just had to sit and take

whatever this man wanted to ramble on about.
"Anyway Jimmy I can see your problem. Leave it with me and I'll see what I can do but I warn you, if you do get the green light then it's up to you. No one will be prepared to get their hands dirty. Understand?"
"Loud and clear Mr Colletta."
As Jimmy got up from the table and was about to leave the room, a chill ran up his spine at Mickey's next sentence.
"There's just one more thing Jimmy. Before I give my blessing and regardless of what the others have to say, I want to meet this girlie. Just to make sure I ain't agreeing to relieve the world of one fucking nutter, only to replace it with a soppy cow that'll let any low life run rings round her."
"Understood and thanks for this."
"Don't thank me, no one's said yes yet."
Stepping out of the restaurant, Jimmy breathed a sigh of relief. He'd never really dealt with any of the big boys in the past that had always been left to Marty. Right at this moment, he realised just how small fry him and Herbie were. They both liked to think they were the bee's knees but if it hadn't been for their dearly departed friend, they never would have amounted to anything more than Jimmy the ponce and Herbie the fence. Driving back to Herbie's place, albeit a short distance, gave Jimmy time to reflect on the

meet that had just passed. Angela was a fast learner but he didn't think she was up to associating with the likes of Mickey Colletta. In the short time she'd been in their lives, he'd become close to her, closer than he could have ever thought possible. Now through his own actions, he'd dumped her in at the deep end and there was nothing he could do about it. Swinging into the drive that had cost Herbie several grand to install, he wasn't looking forward to what lay ahead. The front door was still wide open from when they'd all first arrived. Walking in, he closed it behind him and headed through the house towards the kitchen. Passing the sitting room he saw Angela on the sofa with her arm around Herbie. There was no sound as he entered the room but Angela saw him out of the corner of her eye. Gently easing her arm away from Herbie, she walked out and the Scouser followed her. Closing the door behind him, Jimmy turned to face her.
"How's he doing?"'
"It ain't him as much as Marge. We had to have the doctor out but she went mad when he tried to sedate her. He suggested taking her into hospital because of her mental state and poor Herbie had no choice but to agree."
'What a fuckin' mess!"
"I know but we'll get it sorted, one way or another. How did you get on?"

Jimmy walked into the kitchen and poured himself a scotch from the bottle on the table. Angela had earlier used the same bottle for Herbie, giving him a large measure in the hope of calming him down. Luckily for her, it had seemed to do the trick.
"I hate that cunt Colletta."
"That's as maybe Jim but did you make any headway?"
"Kind of."
"Kind of! What's that supposed to mean. Don't think me pushy or anything Jim but I have a whole family to worry about and you come back with 'kind of!' I need to know that they're safe."
Jimmy Forbes tried to embrace her, tried to make things better but Angela wasn't having any of it. Roughly she pushed him away and her face wore a cold dark expression that Jimmy had seen so many times before over the years.
"Angela I know it's not what you wanted to hear but things take time. Doing business the right way is what makes our kind of world go round. You have to learn patience or that hot head of yours will get you into real shit."
"Ok! ok. Well do you think I should phone home and warn them?"
"Fuck me girl are you mad, tell a judge that he might be on a fuckin' hit list!"
"He's retired you idiot."
"That's really goin' to make a difference, I must

say."

"Oh, so I'm supposed to just sit back and hope they are alright, am I?"

"You ain't got a lot of fuckin' choice in the matter, not if you don't want Old Bill coming down hard on all of us."

Angela took a swig of the scotch before leaving Jimmy standing alone in the kitchen. She returned to the sitting room and a defeated looking Herbie. As she entered, he looked up with a face that was etched with all the troubles of the world. Sitting down on the sofa, she once again placed a comforting arm around his shoulder.

"Come on Herbie, I'm sure your wife will be alright in time."

Sorrowfully he shook his head.

"She won't, I know she won't, those dogs were her life. Things were bad enough in this house before but now, god only knows."

As he realised the meaning of his words, Herbie Spires picked up the crystal tumbler that still held a good measure of scotch and hurled it at the wall.

"Listen to me, that poor cows gone off her trolley and all I care about is me. Then there's Danny, I mean where the fuck has he got to? If he's got into even more bother, that's goin' to tip my Joanie over the edge for sure. Angela all this badness has to stop; trouble is I don't think I've got any fight left in me."

Resting her head on his shoulder to shield her face, Angela quietly began to cry.

Down the road from the Spires home, Mickey had been on the telephone for most of the afternoon. By six o'clock that evening, he'd made contact with the seven largest crime bosses in the city. Lifting the restaurant telephone for the last time that day, he dialled Jimmy Forbes's mobile. The Scouser was still sitting in the kitchen; he couldn't face joining Herbie and Angela in the other room as he didn't have a clue what to say. Over the years the two had faced more than their fair share of scrapes together, even doing a stint at her majesty's pleasure. This latest lot of aggro was different though and when it came down to emotional stuff, Jimmy hadn't a clue where to start. When his phone began to ring, the noise brought a moments relief. Lifting the flap, the menu showed the caller's number and the words 'Italian prick', making Jimmy smile.

"Yeh?"

"Jimmy its Mickey. I've got some news and I'm goin' to send the boy over to deliver it in person. Where are you?"

Jimmy explained that he was still in Bermondsey and gave out Herbie's address. Normally this was strictly a no no but under the circumstances, he couldn't see any harm. As soon as Mickey

Colletta had finished talking, he summoned Geno into the restaurant. His son had been out the back in the kitchen, reluctantly learning how to make pizza bases.
"What?"
"Fuck me I spend thousands on a university education and you can't even address me with an ounce of respect. I don't know why I fuckin' bother with you; maybe you should stay out there in the kitchen. Then again the chef reckons you're no fuckin' good at cooking either."
"Don't start Dad."
Mickey Colletta shook his head in exasperation. "Sit down a minute; I want you to run an errand for me. Now listen well, 'cause you are goin' to have to repeat what I'm telling you."
Thirty minutes later, Geno on his trusted Vespa pulled into Herbie's drive. He rang the doorbell and leaning against the wall, waited for a reply. Jimmy walked quickly into the hall and opening the sitting room door, poked his head round. "Stay where you are, it's nothing to worry about just a bit of information I've been waiting for." Angela gave him a look that said 'What are you up to' but Herbie was oblivious that any conversation was even taking place. Jimmy opened the front door and beckoned the messenger inside. Geno Colletta was about to repeat what his father had told him, when he was silenced by the Scouser, who placed his

index finger onto his lips. The two walked into the kitchen and Jimmy closed the door behind them, so as not to be heard.
"I think you've got some information for me Geno and I hope it's what I want to hear?"
Geno Colletta placed his crash helmet onto the table and nosily looked around the kitchen.
"Depends what it is you want but either way don't shoot the messenger."
Jimmy Forbes laughed but the sound was hollow and Geno picked up on it straight away.
"How's Angela?"
"She's fine why?"
"No reason, I just haven't seen her since the day of the job and I thought I'd ask that's all. Not private property is she?"
"She is as far as you're concerned sunshine. Let me and Herb worry about her, now what have you got for me?"
The conversation lasted a further five minutes and in that time Jimmy Forbes heard all he needed to know. Escorting Geno to the door, he couldn't resist a dig at the handsome young man.
"Your old man ain't got a lot of time for you has he?"
"No skin off my nose Jimmy, he's a cunt! The Colletta's aren't a family you'd choose to be born into I can tell you."
"Is it on account of you battin' for the other

side?"
Geno Colletta's eyes opened wide with fear. "Don't look so scared I aint about to go openin' me trap but if I know them, it aint goin' to be long before your old man finds out, now is it?" Ruffling the man's hair as you would a child, Jimmy had got his point over. He had years on Geno and the man had better not forget that fact. Aware that they now all knew he preferred men, Jimmy was confident that Geno would steer clear of Angela. Whatever the little tosser had been planning regarding her was now dead in the water thank god. Closing the front door Jimmy's smile was as broad as a Cheshire cats. As he took a seat with the others in the sitting room, Angela heard the vespa pull away and inquired as to who the visitor was.
"No one really, everything's fine princess. Oh! and by the way we've got forty eight hours to D-day."

CHAPTER THIRTY ONE

Since Johnny's rampage had begun and with Danny's disappearance the small McCann crew had tightened ranks. Angela, Herbie and Jimmy had decided for safety reasons to stay at Herbie's place. Franco was keeping watch in a car parked close to the property and the rest of the boys had been told to keep their heads low and ears to the ground. Any sighting or word regarding Vale leaving the bookies was to be reported back immediately. Flo McCann had been a concern to Angela but when Herbie had explained that she was looked upon in the east end at least, as a kind of matriarch and that no one would dare to lay a finger on her, then she started to feel a little better regarding her grandmothers safety. Angela and Jimmy Forbes had managed to snatch a few hours sleep in the sitting room arm chairs. Herbie had been plied with so much scotch, that he'd passed out on the sofa and it had at least given the others a break from constantly having to watch over him. Stretching her arms up towards the ceiling, Angela assumed she was the first to wake. Running her tongue over her teeth, she could feel the thick film that had built up over night. A disgusting taste in her mouth helped make up her mind to have a hot cuppa and get freshened up.

Opening the curtains just enough to let a shard of daylight into the room, she smiled at the sight of Jimmy with his head lolled to one side. Moving her gaze to the sofa, she froze when she saw it was empty. Not bothering to wake the Scouser, Angela fled the room terrified at what Herbie may have done. Her fears were unfounded as the mouth watering aroma of bacon filled the hallway. Peering into the kitchen, she could see the cause of her worry standing at the stove, complete with feminine apron and happily cooking away.
"Herbie! You gave me the fright of my life when I woke and you weren't there."
"Sorry Angie, Angela. Bacon butty?"
Nodding her head she took a seat at the table and poured a cup of fresh steaming coffee.
"What time is it?"
"A little after ten, I expect you had a bad night."
"Well an armchair wouldn't be my first preference of a place to sleep, mind you Jimmy still looks gone to the world."
"He'd sleep on a linen line Princess, old school is our Scouser!"
As if the conversation had summoned him, Jimmy Forbes walked into the room resembling a tramp. His stubble was more of a beard and Angela smiled at his appearance. Not speaking, he joined her at the table and poured himself a large mug of coffee. Angela knew how he felt,

she wasn't very good first thing in the morning either and by the look on Jimmy's face, she could tell he was the same. Allowing him to drink in peace, until he was sure the man was well awake, Herbie then began to talk.
"So mate, what you got to tell me?"
Jimmy frowned in Angela's direction, as if to say 'what have you been saying' and she read his face instantly.
"Don't go blaming me, I haven't said a word. I walked in here about two minutes before you did."
"She hasn't mentioned anything but don't take me for a twat Jim, I know something's going on."
"Look mate, we, no I thought, you've got enough on your plate without worrying about Vale and all that stuff. We can sort it out and you can take care of matters at home."
"Matters at home are already sorted. In case you've forgot, Marge was admitted to the local nut house yesterday. The only thing that is playin' on my mind is that there's still no sign of that little scrotum Danny."
Angela was taken aback at the coldness in his tone, when he spoke about his wife.
"Well what a thing to say! The nut house?"
"Look princess, as far as my marriage goes, it's been dead in the water for years. When Marge had the pups to fill a void, she got on with her life and I got on with mine. This little episode

has crucified her and me walkin' around on eggshells tryin' to mollycoddle her ain't goin' to change things."

"I know, but all the same!"

"Angie! This is an arsehole of a life and the sooner you accept that fact, the better it will be for all of us."

As if ignoring his words, she turned her attention to the Scouser, who with mug raised to his lips was trying to hide a smirk.

"And what did you mean last night about we've got forty eight hours to D day?"

Again he frowned at her but he also knew that now was probably the best time to have the discussion that could, no would, change her life forever. With Herbie seated and the two of them trying hard to bore into his thoughts, he began.

"I went to see Mickey Colletta yesterday. Seems like we've got the go ahead regarding Johnny."

"That's fantastic."

"Hold on a minute princess, have you really thought this through? No one will help us, it's our problem and we have to deal with it."

"I know that but as I said yesterday, we don't have a lot of choice in the matter."

Jimmy wasn't having second thoughts but he needed to know that she understood the implications and was still prepared to go through with it.

"Maybe not but who exactly did you have in

mind to carry out this little job."

For a moment Angela was stunned. Foolishly and a little selfishly she'd been convinced that after the business with Seth, the two men now sitting with her at the table would do it.

"I thought......."

"I know exactly what you thought but that's taking liberties. Me and Herb are getting a bit long in the tooth to start playing assassins. Anyway suppose somethin' went wrong. If you had a gun could you pull the trigger or are you always goin' to let other people do your dirty work?"

"I need air and some time to think."

As she walked out of the room, Herbie went to go after her but was stopped by Jimmy.

"Leave her mate; she needs to think this one through herself. We ain't always goin' to be there for her when the going gets tough, let's just wait and see shall we?"

Herbie Spires rejoined his pal at the table, where they sat in silence. Due to the coffee, Angela's mouth tasted even worse than earlier but she didn't care. Grabbing her coat, she opened the front door and headed out into the bright new morning. The streets of Bermondsey were still relatively quiet and she walked along for quite a while without seeing another human being. Angela hadn't noticed what direction she'd gone in but soon came across a small community

park. Pushing open the old cast iron gate, she made her way over to one of the benches and sat down. Placing her hands inside her coat pockets she felt the outline of her mobile phone. Removing it she stared at the blank screen and wished with all her heart she had someone to confide in. Scrolling down its menu, his name jumped out at her and she leant forward with the phone pressed tight to her ear willing and waiting for him to answer. They had only slept together a couple of times but right at this moment and with Danny still absent, he was the only one she could turn to.
"Hello?"
"Hi it's me, I need your help."
He didn't ask any questions, other than where she actually was and within ten minutes Angela saw him enter the park.
"Thanks for coming but I really shouldn't involve you. It's just that I needed someone, anyone, just to listen."
"Thanks a lot."
"Oh sorry I didn't mean it like that. It seems I'm no good at anything lately."
"I can think of a couple a things."
Angela blushed and playfully slapped his chest as he took a seat beside her.
"What's got you so worked up?"
Now she didn't know if this was such a good idea. If Herbie and the Scouser found out she

was confiding in an almost stranger, they'd go ballistic.

"Let's treat this as all hypothetical shall we?"

"Whatever you want."

Angela Canning Brown proceeded to tell him about a friend of hers and the problems she was having regarding a certain man. She explained that this man had probably killed her friend's father and that now her friend had the chance of revenge. The only problem was that this friend, could possibly end up having to do the job herself and she didn't know if it was something she was capable off.

"So what do you think?"

"What would you say if I told you I already knew about it?"

Angela was stunned and her mouth was slightly open with shock.

"I think you should put the fact that he may have killed your, sorry her father to one side. If this man is stopping her achievin' what she wants, then she has to give serious consideration to how badly she wants that thing. I suppose she could go away and forget all about it but somehow I don't think your friend could live with the thought of never having tried. No I think she should stand up for her convictions and do what she knows has to be done. Not much help am I?"

"It's ok, you only confirmed what I was already

thinking. Anyway I'll tell my friend what you said and hopefully everything will turn out alright."
Geno laughed.
"I take it that cunt the Scouser has told you all about my sexual preferences then?"
It was now Angela's turn to laugh.
"Geno it makes no difference to me. We had a bit of fun but it was no more than that. I have wondered why you came to me though."
Geno now felt embarrassed but he really had come to like the young woman and so felt he owed her an explanation.
"You won't like my reason."
"Try me."
"Well I saw you as a bit of a meal ticket. I know it won't be too far off the horizon before my old man finds out. When that happens I need to be as far away from the city as possible."
"And now with your share from the robbery you can do just that."
"Yeah I now have enough to go somewhere nice."
"When are you leaving?"
"In just under a week."
"Then I wish you all the luck in the world and I truly hope you find some happiness Geno. Be assured that if your father does find out how you live your life, it will not have come from my firm. Stay safe lovely man."

He kissed her tenderly on the cheek and then walked from the park. Angela stayed seated at the bench, until he disappeared round the corner and out of sight. She wasn't aware that Franco had been following her every move but even if she had known it wouldn't have made any difference. He may have seen her meet Geno but he didn't know what had passed between them. Herbie Spires and Jimmy Forbes were still in the kitchen when she returned. They heard her close the door and hang up her coat but neither called out. Walking into the silent room, she wasn't surprised to see them still there.

"I suppose you want to know where I've been."

"Not really, ain't that right Herb? We're not interested in where you've been, only what you've been thinkin' about. One way or another you need to make up your mind and quickly."

"Well gentlemen you'll both be pleased to hear that I have. I gave what you said a great deal of thought and I've decided to go ahead with our plan. I can't let that lunatic remain on the streets and if I want my father's business back, then I have no choice but to follow it through. If that means having to shoot the bastard myself, then so be it. Happy now?"

"Angie! It's never been about you havin' to top Johnny but we had to make sure you wouldn't crack up on us. Me and the Scouser's still got enough claret running through our veins to see

off that cunt, even if we are a bit rusty."
"Good, so when does it happen."
Jimmy Forbes cringed at her question. He'd delayed telling them both about Mickey's request and knew he couldn't hold off any longer.'
"Bit of a slight hiccup there princess."
Herbie slapped his forehead with his palm while turning his head from side to side.
"What have you done Jim?"
"Fuckin' hell!, there you go again. I ain't done nothin'. All the other firms gave their consent apart from Mickey Colletta. Said he wanted to meet Angela before he made up his mind but I can't see there being a problem. I'm just a bit worried she ain't up to conversing with someone like Mickey, well not yet anyway."
"You are talking as if I'm not in the room again."
"Sorry but we're on about a real hard cunt here, princess!"
"I can handle myself. I've seen enough gangster films to know what to say."
Herbie again slapped his forehead.
"Fuck me she thinks she'd Robert De Nero! Angela men like Mickey Colletta have been in the business for more years than I care to mention. He knows every trick and con going and if you walk in there acting all high and mighty. Let's just say he won't give his consent and along with Johnny Vale the three of us could

end up gettin' topped."

Angela walked over to where the two men sat. Standing between the parted chairs, she placed a hand firmly but warmly on each of their shoulders.

"Please just trust me!"

Jimmy Forbes removed her hand and holding onto it with both of his, he stared into her eyes. "We ain't got any choice; he wants us over at the restaurant by two this afternoon. Can me and Herb just run through a few things, questions he might ask you?"

"I'd rather you didn't Jimmy and I'm not trying to act all high and mighty. I need to be honest and not be concentrating on remembering all that you two have told me. After all if he's as sharp as you say, wouldn't he see through a rehearsal of answers?"

"Point taken"

Herbie got up from the table to clear away the breakfast things, he knew it was all going to be a disaster but hadn't the heart to tell her. Sitting around in the living room, they had been ready to go for over an hour. Herbie didn't take his eyes off the clock and Jimmy had helped himself to more than a generous amount of scotch. Angela surveyed them both and thought that out of the three, she appeared the least nervous. She wasn't foolish enough to believe she was brave; only the fact that she hadn't met the man

and didn't know what she was up against. As the minute hand hit one forty, Herbie Spires jumped out of the armchair.
"About time we were leaving. The traffic can be a bitch and the last thing we need is to be late."
Walking into the hall, Herbie collected the Jags keys from the table and went out of the front door. By the time Jimmy and Angela emerged, he was in the car with the engine running. Travelling in silence was becoming common place with the trio and the drive over to the restaurant was no exception. As they pulled up outside the Trattoria, Mickey Colletta's doorman removed the traffic cones from the road allowing them to park. Angela looked out at the building and her comment made the men cringe.
"It's a bit eighties, don't you think?"
"For fucks sake that's just what I meant, she ain't got a chance."
Herbie removed his seat belt while trying to calm his pal.
"Don't get uptight Jim or you'll make us all into fuckin' nervous wrecks. Now let's just go in all friendly like and hope for the best, Ok?"
"Ready Angie, Angela?"
"As I'll ever be."
Herbie entered first with Angela close behind him. Jimmy followed a few seconds later on account of pausing to acknowledge the heavy standing outside. The restaurant was empty

after the lunch time trade and Mickey could be seen at the far end now having his own intake of food. As the front door had opened, Mickey Colletta's three dining companions rose up from their seats. All wore menacing looks and only stepped aside, when their boss gave the order.
"It's ok fella's these are my guests."
Standing up Mickey walked over to Angela and Herbie began the introductions.
"Mickey, I'd like you to meet Angela."
Before he could finish, Angela cut him off and completed his sentence herself, thinking that it would throw more weight if she used her father's name.
"Angie McCann, Mr Colletta and I'm very pleased to meet you at last. Herbie and Jimmy have told me lots about you and all good I might add."
She sneaked a sideways glance at Herbie and winked. Mickey took hold of her hand and kissed it lightly enough, that his lips merely skimmed the surface. Leading her by the same hand, he guided Angela towards the table.
"And I'm pleased to meet you too, do take a seat, Miss McCann."
Turning to his three men, Mickey told them to go out front and take a cigarette break.
Frowning, they obeyed the order but in no way were they happy to leave the boss alone with members of another firm. Jimmy smiled to

himself but it swiftly disappeared when Angela instructed Herbie and him to do the same.
"Now just hang on a minute princess, I don't......"
"Never mind 'I don't', just do as I say."
Like little boys, Herbie Spires and Jimmy Forbes made way outside leaving Angela alone to face only god knew what.
"So Miss McCann, I understand you need my consent to carry out a hit"
Angela instantly knew she had to show a bold front. Any hint of a submissive personality and she would be doomed.
"Mr Colletta I don't need anyone's consent! Believe me when I say, that with or without you, Johnny Vale's disappearance will happen. That's not to say I wouldn't like your blessing. From the things I have heard, my father held you in great esteem and that in turn was reciprocated by your good self. I would like to think that after a time, you will see me in that same light and that the future will be kind and plentiful for all of us."
Mickey Colletta took an instant shine to the young woman, who had more front than Southend and wondered why his own sons, couldn't be more like her. From the moment Angela had stepped into the restaurant, she'd immediately recognised the ambience Mickey had tried hard to achieve. It also told her that he

loved all things Italian and she took a calculated gamble that also included anything to do with the mafia. The line Angela had just spun Mickey Colletta came straight out of one of the numerous movies she'd watched while holed up in her room back in Canterbury.

"You're a very bold and head strong young woman Miss McCann. Don't get me wrong, that's not a failing. Living as we do, you would fall at the first hurdle without it. I hear you've had some trouble over the last couple of days, Johnny Vale is insane and totally out of control."

"You're so right Mr Colletta but there's just one problem."

"And what might that be?"

Angela took her time in answering and deliberately savoured the wine; she guessed he had chosen especially for the meeting.

"Mmmm delicious. The problem is that since Johnny went off the rails, no one can get near him. From what I can gather, he spends all his time at the bookies and if you knew my father well, you'd remember that place is like a small fortress."

"I see your dilemma Miss, can I call you Angie?"

"Please do."

"I suspect you're going to ask me to help you further?"

"Indeed I am Mr Colletta, there's no way we can carry this off without someone of your standing.

I have something in mind, though whether you will be in agreement is another matter."
"I must say Angie; you have the face of an Angel but the cheek of the devil. Run it past me anyway."
Angel told Mickey that she wanted Johnny Vale dead but she didn't want to lay that responsibility onto either Herbie Spires or Jimmy Forbes. She offered Mickey Colletta a payment of five hundred thousand if he would make her problem go away, to which he readily agreed. Fifteen minutes later and Angela, much to the surprise of Herbie and Jimmy, emerged from the restaurant all smiles and ready to go. Waiting until they were back in the car, Jimmy couldn't contain himself any longer.
"Fuck me princess, looks like you might actually have pulled it off."
For once she allowed herself a small amount of vanity, if in reality she was shaking in her shoes.
"Not only have I pulled it off but he's agreed to do it for us."
"How?"
"Oh ye of little faith. I told you both I could do it but would you listen? Oh no, you had to go on and on about how I didn't stand a chance against Mickey Colletta."
Jimmy was already fed up with the sound of her voice. For a minute he thought he was back in Stepney with Marlene.

"Alright alright! Point made. Well done Angie, I can call you that can't I?"
They all laughed out loud and were now a bit more comfortable with the situation.
"Now can we go home and get some kip? I'm fuckin' knackered."
"I don't know some people just have no stamina! How about we go back to Herbie's, you two can have a nap and I'll cook us all a nice meal?"
Jimmy turned in his seat to where she sat smugly in the back.
"Cracking idea princess but I'll have to go over to Stepney later, these clothes are starting to smell a bit."
"Yeh I'd noticed."
"Cheeky cow!"
They all laughed out loud. Angela didn't know if it was just nervous laughter but no matter what, it still brought a little light relief at the end of a very tense day. Suddenly Angela realised that she was starting to enjoy her new found role as boss. Tomorrow would probably be a different story but right now she was happy and at least for tonight, she was going to make the most of it.

CHAPTER THIRTY TWO

When the restaurant door swung shut and he was sure Angela had gone, Mickey Colletta picked up the phone. He still knew the Bethnal Green number from his dealings with Marty and grinned as he dialled.

Johnny Vale was once more holed up in his office with only a bottle of scotch for company. After returning from his late night stint at brass cutting and again when he'd slain the three little rats, his only comfort had been alcohol. It was all that kept him calm these days and the only thing that helped him to sleep. He wouldn't allow entry into the bookies to anyone, not even his own heavy Al Kingston. Johnny's mind was in such an insane state of turmoil, that he couldn't see the writing on the wall, couldn't see that there would only be one outcome. As far as he was concerned it was only the beginning. Sitting in complete silence, palms flat out on the desk, Johnny stared into space. Images of his revenge attacks flashed before his eyes and he enjoyed them, enjoyed every last gruesome detail. Imagining Marge Spires face as she saw the little bodies on the patio, had him salivating excessively and he wiped small droplets of foam from the corners of his mouth. Danny was still confined in the boot of his Mercedes, he could be

dead by now for all Johnny knew but the man couldn't care less. The telephone had rung several times over the last couple of hours and each time he'd ignored its ring. This time however, something broke his trance and compelled him to answer.
"Yeh?"
"Johnny me old son, nice to know you're still in the land of the living!"
"Who the fuck is this?"
"Johnny its Mickey, Mickey Colletta."
Now recognising the voice, he sat bolt upright in his chair. Marty had dealt with the Colletta firm from time to time but Johnny was never really involved. The only time their paths had ever crossed was if Johnny was acting as body guard for his boss. It was unnatural how he'd hero worshiped the man, looked upon him as a kind of mentor and now here he was actually talking to Mickey Colletta in person.
"Mr Colletta! Good to hear from you."
Thinking of the conversation that had passed between him and the little McCann girl just a short while ago, Mickey smiled.
"The words spreading on the street regarding your little bit of bother with the McCann offspring and I just thought I'd call to see if you needed help in any way."
"That's very kind of you Mr Colletta but I think I can handle things. I've dished out a bit of a

payback on the fuckin' Scouser and that tosser Herbie Spires. As for the posh bitch, dealin' with her is goin' to be a piece of piss."

"Glad to hear it mate but to be honest, that wasn't the only reason I called. A bit of business has come up and as you know I would normally have been in touch with Marty. That's a fuckin' impossibility now, unless you have a direct line to him upstairs, so I thought I'd see if you wanted a piece of the action?"

"Tell me more!"

"Not a good idea on the blower Johnny, how about you come over to the restaurant tonight and we'll have a bite to eat and discuss business?"

"I'd really like that Mr Colletta, what time?"

"About eight alright?"

"Yeh, yeh eights fine."

"Good and from now on Johnny, call me Mickey ok?"

With that the line went dead and Johnny Vale sat in his chair with the receiver still glued to his ear. He couldn't believe what had just occurred and suddenly things were starting to look rosy, very rosy indeed.

Herbie and Jimmy were out for the count in the overstuffed armchairs that filled Herbie's sitting room. Even the delicious aromas that came from the kitchen weren't enough to rouse them. After several times of calling them both to dinner,

Angela wearing Herbie's apron, walked into the room.

"Are you two going to eat this meal or shall I throw it all in the bin."

Herbie rubbed at his eyes with the back of his hands as he struggled to sit upright.

"Sorry princess must have been more tired than I thought. Jimmy! Jim wake up."

Jimmy Forbes slowly opened his eyes and yawning, clicked his tongue against the roof of his mouth. The sight of the two men in front of her made Angela roll her eyes upwards. In a whisper that was only just audible she sighed to herself 'God help us'. Returning to the kitchen, she filled the table with serving dishes and sat down. Angela was put out that after working hard in a hot kitchen for a couple of hours, they couldn't even be bothered to eat what she had prepared. Deciding not to let the food go to waste, she was just about to serve herself when they finally walked in. Taking a seat Herbie was the first to tuck in but it was Jimmy's table manners that shocked Angela the most. Shovelling the food into his mouth was an understatement, it was as if he hadn't eaten in a week and she just stared as he continued to eat and eat and eat.

"Pay no attention to him Angela; he's always like this."

With a mouthful of food, Jimmy began to speak.

As he did so the table cloth received a fine mist of gravy and Angela tried not to let him see that she was bothered by his lack of table manners.
"Right then, what did you cook up with Mickey or are you goin' to keep us in the dark?"
"Of course not! I'm just grateful that he's agreed to help us."
Jimmy began to get agitated but he still continued to shovel food into his mouth, to the extent that when he spoke he spluttered and small tiny half chewed pieces came flying out.
"He's a cunt Angela and he don't do anythin' for nothin'."
"Maybe not but it didn't stop you running to him yesterday did it? And Jimmy can you stop talking with your mouthful, it's really putting me off my meal."
"What you on about?"
"Jim calm down, she don't know you well enough yet and you have got the fuckin' manners of a pig."
"So what Herbieeee! You gettin' as fuckin' posh as her or what?"
Angela was tired of his childish behaviour and stood up from the table.
"For goodness sake Jimmy grow up. It's not posh behaviour to have a little etiquette, now either you shut up or I'm leaving."
Jimmy Forbes beckoned with his hand for her to sit down but the atmosphere was still tense for a

while. He offered no apologies but when the situation had calmed and they had all eaten, Angela told them all about Mickey's plan. Both took on board all that she said and it surprised her that Jimmy didn't argue the point. Though in all honesty there really was nothing to argue about. After finishing his meal, Herbie Spires had left the table and gone into the hall. His telephone conversation was quiet and short and even though Angela didn't mean to eavesdrop she still heard him mention the name Kathy. Johnny Vale woke with a groggy head at around six that night and remembering his dinner appointment, rushed to get changed. As time was getting on, he didn't really think about the phone call from Mickey in any great detail. Always keeping a couple of spare outfits in the back cupboard he chose one of his favourite Paul Smith suits accompanied by a crisp white shirt. At last he admired himself in the mirror that hung on the back of the door. The outfit lacked something but he didn't have time to worry about that now. Slipping out the back he walked two streets to where his car was parked. A short while later, he pulled into the curb and walking across the road, plucked a rose from a bunch being sold by one of the many street traders. Handing the young man a fiver, he received a puzzled look.
"What?"

"They are nine ninety nine Sir."
"What for one fuckin' rose?"
"No Sir, the whole bunch."
"I don't want a fuckin' bunch, I just want this one.'"
The young lad who was no more than sixteen and who hadn't been doing the job for more than a week, came straight back at Johnny Vale.
"It's the bunch or nothin' I'm afraid."
"Who the fuck do you think you're talking to you little toe rag!"
In the next instant Johnny had thrown the remaining bunches from the large black bucket and proceeded to force the boys head into it. The trestle table collapsed with the force and buckets and flowers shot onto the street. The boy coughed and spluttered and Johnny sidestepped the splatter of water. A passer by stopped to watch the commotion but when he saw who was dishing out the punishment, continued on his way. Johnny would reprimand himself later that he was far too lenient but he finally let the lad up and he gasped for air. Bending down, Johnny picked up one of the roses and snapping it in two threw the stalk at the boy. Walking towards his car he placed the pale cream bloom into his lapel and admired himself in a window.
"Not bad, not fuckin' bad at all."
Now back in the car he turned on the radio and

pulled the Mercedes out onto the road in the direction of Southwark Bridge that would take him to Bermondsey. Momentarily he turned down the music and listened for any sound coming from the boot. Happy that there was none he once again cranked up the volume and continued on his way. The roads were busy even for this hour of the day and for the first time in ages; Johnny was lucid and thinking with a clear head. He recalled the telephone conversation of earlier that day and something, he couldn't quite work out what, but something wasn't right. Mickey Colletta had been his role model but the man hadn't given Johnny the time of day before now. Suddenly here he was offering a business deal and it stunk, stunk to high heavens. When Marty was around deals were always kept close to his chest. Johnny was always by his side but Marty rarely confided in anyone. He was supposed to be his right hand man but he didn't tell him anything, didn't trust him enough to let him know exactly what was going on. No there was definitely something fishy about all of this but Johnny decided the best way to find out was to act dumb. He accepted that there was a chance he was being paranoid and that Mickey Colletta now looked upon him as a boss but whatever it was, he wouldn't be taking any chances. Parking the Mercedes a couple of roads away from his

destination, Johnny walked the short distance to the restaurant. Mario Pizzaro stood outside and seeing Johnny approach, held open the door. Nodding his head in acknowledgment, Mario gave a sly grin which put Johnny instantly on his guard. Now an employee of the McCann firm, Mario still popped back to the restaurant when he had time off. It had been a part of his life for so long and his allegiance would always be to Mickey. Johnny Vale wasn't aware that Mario had been part of the robbery and Mario Pizzaro was conscious of his duties tonight. Doing as he'd been instructed, he now gave the man a warm smile making Johnny feel welcome.
"Evening Mr Vale."
"Mario, the boss in?"
"Yeh Mr Vale go ahead, he's somewhere down the back."
The place was abuzz with diners and Johnny thought it must bring in a nice little earner without having to do any dodgy deals. Every table was full and Dean Martins 'that's amore' softly filled the air, from the overhead speakers. Johnny hadn't eaten much in the last few days and the aromas coming out of the kitchen had his taste buds working overtime. If he'd thought Marty's club needed a makeover, it was an understatement compared with this place. The décor was what most Londoners would assume an Italian restaurant should look like but in

reality, couldn't be further from the truth. Red and white checked clothes adorned the tables and each was topped off with a candle in a well used bottle of Mateus. Bread baskets hung from the walls and the waiters all wore long white aprons double tied around their waists. At the far end of the restaurant, Mickey Colletta held court with a young brunette who knew the score but wasn't about to pass up the offer of a free meal. As Johnny approached, Mickey whispered a few words into the girl's ear and she stood up in a huffy manner. Aware of just who Mickey Colletta was, she didn't make a fuss but her eyes gave away her disappointment and Mickey slapped her behind as she passed. Standing up himself, Mickey walked towards his guest.

"Johnny! Glad you could make it me old son. Mario do the business."

Within seconds Johnny's arms were raised and he was being frisked. When Mario felt the pistol in the arch of Johnny's back he grabbed a napkin so as not to leave his prints on the piece before removing it. The gun was then placed inside the drawer of the serving dresser.

"Bit much aint it, taking away a man's protection?"

"Sorry Johnny but we can't take any chances and besides we're all friends here, aint we?"

Johnny Vale smiled but his eyes darted in all

directions waiting for someone to strike. When his host placed an arm around Johnny's shoulder, he nearly jumped out of his skin.
"Fuck me you're jumpy mate! Things startin' to get to you are they?"
"Not been to good lately Mickey but I'm goin' to sort those back stabbing bastards out once and for all. I've been really busy the last couple of days and it's good to have a break, thanks."
"You're welcome! We have to look out for each other in this fuckin' game and no mistake. Come through to the back room and we can talk in private."
Still not at ease Johnny Vale did as he was asked. The room was intimate with just one table and he imagined it was a private hire space or one used by Mickey to seduce the numerous young girls he was renowned for dating.
"Has there been any word on the street as to how they received my little gifts?"
"Nothin' Johnny. I only know what you mentioned on the phone and you didn't go into much detail."
Johnny Vale proceeded to fill in all the blanks. Staring into his guests face but not giving away his feelings, Mickey could see a mad man pure and simple. If he'd had any doubts before, they now vanished.
"I'll put some feelers out and see if anyone's heard from them. Take a seat and let me order

you some food."

The two men sat down at the table and Mickey clicked his fingers. Seconds later wine and a large bowl of pasta with a fantastic looking sauce appeared. As Mickey Colletta served them both from the same bowl, Johnny knew it was safe to eat and heartily tucked in. They continued to make small talk throughout the meal but once it was over Mickey had one burning question he wanted answered.

"Now then Johnny! What really happened to Marty McCann?"

Johnny Vale was so pleased with his new found business associate that he couldn't wait to spill the beans.

"When I first went to work for him, I thought he was the fuckin' dogs bollocks but when I saw all the drug money he turned away, well let's just say it started to piss me off a bit. He didn't have a problem with the Scouser and his brasses but when it came to smack or Charlie, he didn't want to know. Fuckin' hypocrite, double standards as far as I was concerned. Anyways it got me thinkin' and I knew if given the chance I could run things far better, trouble was I knew I would never get the chance. Finally I had enough and decided to get rid. I went for a short holiday to Spain but came back a day earlier than planned."

"'But when the Old Bill looked into Marty's

death you must have been the prime suspect?"
"'Course I was but you're forgetting one thing Mickey; we're still scum in the eyes of the law. Having Marty McCann no longer grace the streets of the smoke was like winning the lottery for a lot of 'em."
"So how come you didn't get back till a day after Marty's body was found?'
'That's where I'm clever see. My cousin, who's a bit of a gambler and heavy drinker, owed me big time. I offered to squash his debts if he did me a favour. I sent him off to Spain for a couple of week's holiday a week before I was due to fly out. We're similar in size and build, not to mention the fact that we really look alike. We spent some time together, topped up the old tans etc and then I flew back on his passport a day before I should have come home and he came back the next day on my passport. He wasn't goin' to complain at an extra day's holiday and he was more than grateful not to owe me anymore. Fuckin' blindin' plan even if I do say so myself."
Mickey Colletta smiled which Johnny took for admiration so he carried on talking.
"The night Marty went into the Thames we had a private meeting back at the bookies. Previously the Romanians' had contacted him about a drug deal and you know Marty's view on drugs was always negative. He said the Romanians weren't

to be trusted and he wanted things to stay the way they were. We had a few drinks and everything was ok between us. I'd already slipped a couple of roofie's into his scotch and once they took effect he was putty in me hands. The beauty with roofie's is that after a few hours they can't be detected. By the time his body was pulled out and they'd done the autopsy there was no trace and the cause of death was put as drownin'."

Johnny Vale laughed at his own cleverness.

"No one could argue 'cause he really had drowned. There was no struggle and it was common knowledge that he couldn't swim. I tell you Mickey he was like a sittin' fuckin' duck; I just drove old Marty to the Thames and pushed him in. Everythin' would have been sweet if that fuckin' bitch hadn't turned up."

"Not bad Johnny, not bad at all. Anyway I think we need to get down to business."

"So Mickey what's the deal."

"Well I'm toyin' with the idea of starting up a long firm. It ain't been done for a while and I think the times about right to hit some big companies hard. Ever done it before?"

"Na, Marty did one but that was long before I joined the firm. Good scam though ain't it?"

"Fuckin' blindin', if it's done right. Anyway, I've got a few people lined up who are a bit on the naive side to say the least. Their credit is more

than good and they are begging to do some business with a gangster, as they like to call me. Normally I'd have had their fuckin' bollocks cut off for that sort of disrespect but I can wait until they've served their purpose. I suppose you're wonderin' where you come into all of this?"
Johnny Vale nodded but didn't add anything.
"As you know I'm a very busy man. It would be difficult for me to be there all the time, what with everything else and I can't spare the time to oversee the day to day running. A long firm needs to be expertly executed and I need someone I can trust and that's when I thought of you. Electrical goods are where the money is, everyone's after a cheap mobile phone or laptop these days and there are plenty of companies falling over themselves to supply wholesalers. I've got my eye on a couple of warehouses to use as distribution centres, in fact one of them is perfect. Well I think so anyway. It's just off Roman Road, want to take a look at it tomorrow?"
Johnny Vale instantly knew the score but didn't let on. If tomorrow was goin' to be show time then he'd make sure he got in first.
"Sure, what time?"
"I've got a few appointments tomorrow, so what if we say about twelve. Perhaps if you're in agreement we could have a spot of lunch afterwards."

"Sounds good. So where is it?"
Silently from the shadows Mario swiftly moved across the floor and placed a cheese wire round Johnny's neck. With as much pressure as he could muster he pulled the wire though Johnny Vales throat. His head wasn't completely severed but almost and he made a gurgling sound as the life left his body. Mickey quickly wrapped a tablecloth around his victim to prevent the blood from causing too much mess and then felt inside Johnny's jacket pocket and retrieved the keys to the Mercedes. The sight of the body still sitting at the table with a red and white tablecloth over its head soaking up his life's blood was almost surreal but it didn't faze the men in the least.
"Nice work Mario! Now did you see where the cunt parked his car?"
"Don't know Mr Colletta he was on foot when he reached this place."
"Then take a couple of the others and walk the streets he must have parked it close by. When you find it bring it round the back."
Mickey Colletta's men did as they had been asked and within half an hour they found the Mercedes and were soon parked at the rear of the restaurant. Mickey had just said goodbye to a couple of regular diners when he spied Mario at the back of the restaurant. Smiling at his other guests as he passed, Mickey quickly made his

way over to where Mario stood.
"What is it?"
"I think you need to take a look for yourself."
Outside in the yard the boot lid of the car was raised to reveal the body of Danny Spires.
"What the fuck!"
The stench was overpowering as Danny's every orifice had opened up and released their contents. The tape was still partially fixed across his mouth but it was evident that the pressure of vomit had forced it to move on one side.
"The poor fucker, look likes he's choked to death. Any ideas who he is?"
All the men shook their heads.
"Dump it round the back of the bookies and leave the boot open. Take these keys and open up the back door to the place. Make sure you aint seen then get back here as quick as you can. Oh and use the phone at the bookies to inform the Old Bill about the stiff."
Back in the restaurant Mickey Colletta picked up the phone and began to get impatient when it rang several times.
"Hello."
"Hi Harry its Mickey Colletta. Got some pig food for you at me restaurant and it needs collectin' urgently."
"Boooootiful Mr Colletta. I'll be sendin' me boy as usual, should be with ya in a couple of hours."
Mickey replaced the receiver without a goodbye.

He was angry; this was supposed to be a simple process but was quickly turning out to be very complicated.

CHAPTER THIRTY THREE

Jimmy Forbes, after going home to collect fresh clothes, had returned to Herbie's for the night. He still wasn't a hundred percent about how his mate was truly feeling after what had happened. Thinking that if they spent more time together it would perhaps help in some way, he was back from Stepney within the hour. Angela had chosen to go home to her apartment. As fond as she was of Herbie Spires and Jimmy Forbes, having to spend another evening watching television with them was a bit more than she could take. They were both happy for her to go, safe in the knowledge that one of the boys would be following her every move. Opening the front door, it felt good to be home and she walked over to the telephone and dialled Flo's number. The phone rang a few times before being picked up and Angela began to wonder if it was a bingo night and her grandmother wasn't home. About to replace the receiver she was stopped when she heard the elderly woman's voice.
"Hello?"
"Hi Nan! Just thought I'd see if you were alright."
"Course I fuckin' am! Didn't think I'd hear from you again so soon though?"

"Don't be like that Nan. After tomorrow we can spend as much time together as you like."
Flo didn't comment on what her granddaughter had said or the implications her words could have. It wasn't her age or the fact that she wasn't listening, it was purely down to being afraid.
"I might not want to; I do have a life of my own you know."
Angela sighed, sometimes Flo McCann sounded like a broken record and it was beginning to get on her nerves.
"I know you do, now please let's not get into an argument. Have you heard from Pops?'
"I phoned him this morning, though I couldn't tell him much on account of I hardly ever see you.'
Angela pulled the phone away from her ear and began to laugh, the woman was intolerable.
"Nan I have to go now there's someone at the door; I'll give you a call again in a couple of days. Take care, love you."
She didn't wait for a reply and after replacing the handset walked into the kitchen and poured a glass of wine. Flo McCann was put out at the abrupt ending to the conversation, she had a few more reprimands to deliver and she didn't take kindly to being cut off. On the other hand she was more than happy with her granddaughters parting words. 'Love you Nan' made her heart

swell. Angela spent the next hour lounging in a hot soapy bath with a topped up glass of wine in her hand.

Everyone woke early the next morning. Angela hadn't needed the assistance of her alarm and even Jimmy Forbes was wide awake, well before Herbie brought in a steaming hot cup of tea. By nine o'clock Angela had paced the floor a dozen times and had started to imagine she was going out of her mind. The original plan was for the boys to collect her but she couldn't wait. Hailing a cab she arrived at Herbie's just after ten.

Jimmy was taking a shower and Herbie was cooking breakfast when she rang the bell. The sight that greeted her when the door was opened did bring more than a smile to her face. His apron of yesterday had been replaced with one bearing a figure of a woman, dressed scantily in black lace bra and suspenders. Herbie saw her smirk and quickly became embarrassed at her teasing expression.

"The other ones mucky and this was all I could find, alright!"

Walking passed him towards the kitchen she continued to snigger.

"I believe you but if anyone else saw it, well let's just say two men getting on in life and sharing a house?"'

"Don't be so bleedin' stupid."

The smell as she entered the kitchen, suddenly

made her feel nauseous. Usually she could eat as much as either of the men but today was different. Herbie Spires started to open more bacon and she stopped him immediately.
"Not for me thanks. If I eat a single thing I'll be throwing up all day."
"That's not good princess. You can't face seein' the lawyers on an empty stomach."
"Maybe just a piece of toast then and I'll have to force that down."
Jimmy Forbes walked in as she was about to take her second bite and nodding a good morning, sat down to the massive fry up Herbie had prepared. As with last night he began to eat with such speed, that food seemed to fly in all directions. The sight made Angela heave and she clasped her hand over her mouth as she ran in to the hallway. Climbing the stairs, she only just made it to the en suite in Herbie's bedroom in time. Nerves were starting to get the better of her and Angela was angry that coupled with the fact that she'd always had a weak stomach, she was now throwing up.
"Now look what you've done, do you have to eat like a fuckin' pig?"
"Herb shut the fuck up, you're sounding more and more like Marlene every day. If I want nonstop nagging, I can get that back in Stepney."
The bathroom which until now Angela had never used was just as she'd imagined.

The house was new but the room was still decorated out in an old Victorian theme. It was beautifully clean but nothing in it matched. The fitments must have been the cheapest Marge could find and although from a distance they appeared right, on close inspection were nothing more than that. Kneeling on the floor and positioning herself over the lavatory, for what to Angela seemed forever, she dry heaved over and over again. Finally when she realised that her stomach wasn't prepared to let go of anything, though there was very little to let go of, she stood up. The basin, even after Jimmy's ablutions, sparkled and Angela bowed her head and drank large mouthfuls of water. After drying her eyes and combing her hair, she slowly walked back down stairs and prayed Jimmy had finished his breakfast.

At eleven o'clock and just as they were thinking about leaving the house a police car turned into the drive. Herbie answered the door and the next voice Angela heard was her dear friend. "Oh my God!"

Along with Jimmy she rushed to the door to find Herbie Spires leaning heavily against the wooden frame for support. Gently they pulled him away and after Jimmy steered him towards the sitting room Angela learned about Danny's death from the two policemen. They informed her that a statement would be needed but under

the circumstances they would return later. Angela was stunned and couldn't believe what was happening. Obviously neither Herbie nor Jimmy were in the know, the only person who may be able to shed some light on all of this was Mickey Colletta. Snatching up the keys for Herbie's car from the hall table Angela set off for the restaurant. Unbeknown to Angela, Mickey Colletta had been expecting her but as she entered he smiled and feigned his surprise.
"Hello sweetheart, thought you'd be a bit too busy for payin' any social calls?"
"I know Mickey, today should have been a big event in my life. I was supposed to be at the solicitors now finalising all the paperwork but we've had some terrible news."
happened and Mickey's face was a picture of shock and horror.
"So where Johnny Vale is now I haven't a clue but I thought you were taking care of things for me?"
"I was sweetheart but he legged it before I had chance, the low life cunt! The Old Bill will be on his case now for sure. When the heats died down I'll get me boys to make a night time visit to the bookies and see what they can find out. You never know, he may have left a clue as to where Angela thanked the man and placed a kiss on his cheek before she left. Mickey wiped it away he was off to."

with the back of his hand. He would fill the little tarts head with stories of Johnny being seen at the airport. Over the next few years he let her and the other firms know that there had been sightings of Johnny on the Costa del Sol, not to mention one eyewitness seeing him in Turkey. Mickey Colletta would let the little girl claim her inheritance, let her build up all of her father's businesses and when enough time had passed he would walk right in under the guise of Johnny Vale and take it all away from her.
The funeral of Danny Spires was a grim affair. Marge had been brought from the secure unit and was now being pushed in a wheelchair by Jimmy. It took every bit of strength Herbie could muster as he supported his sister Joanie down the aisle. Due to Danny not being a known face, it was just the five of them and to Angela that made it even sadder than if the place had been filled to the rafters with mourners.
Nine months later and now heavily pregnant, the pregnancy was confirmed on the day of Danny's funeral; Angela knew she should start to take things a little easier. The trouble was that in her line of work if you took your eye off the ball for a second there was always someone ready to rip you off. There had been a pregnancy scare, when six months after Angela took control of her father's empire; Julian Canning Brown suffered a massive stroke. After

a check up at the hospital, on the insistence of Herbie, Angela was given the all clear. Her last contact with her grandfather had been on one of his away days to the east end. All her promises to him that she'd go to Canterbury for a visit had never materialised, at least not until the day of his funeral. Angela had been racked with guilt and for a while, the closeness she'd at last found with her mother, returned. Back in London, she'd promised faithfully that she wouldn't be a stranger but Joanna knew her daughter was only telling her what she wanted to hear. Angela's life had moved on and in her world, there was no room for an upper class mother and grandmother. Her pregnancy hadn't reached full term when she accepted that the Canning Browns were no longer a part of her life. From the moment she had informed them about the baby, they had apart from Pops, distanced themselves from her. Now he was gone things weren't about to change and as far as she was concerned she was happy for it to stay that way. Flo was always popping into one of the clubs to make sure her granddaughter was alright and as luck would have it was present on the day Angela's waters broke. Like a royal birth she was chauffer driven to the Portland hospital and at eight fifteen that same evening little Marty McCann came kicking and screaming into the world. Flo McCann's flat was an open house for

the following few days and everyone even Herbie Spires now felt brighter about the future.
5 YEARS LATER
Angela had effortlessly settled into the role of Boss. She still relied heavily on Herbie and Jimmy for advice but they now took more of a back seat role in the day to day running of the business. After hiring, with the Scouser's help, a new crew of twenty men, she was satisfied that her back was well covered. The betting shops were closed down and sold off with the exception of the one that Johnny Vale had resided in, for some reason Angela couldn't let that one go. The sales brought in enough cash for her to remodel the clubs, bringing them up to date and generating more profit. Little Marty had a private nanny but Flo was forever calling at Angela's apartment to make sure the hired help was doing as she was supposed to. Angela didn't mind and she was pleased that her little man had at least one great grandparent that took an interest. Angela much to the disgust of Herbie and Jimmy had begun to move, albeit slowly, into the drug world. Demand was high and the clubs were a perfect venue to move huge amounts of cocaine. It didn't take long before she found herself turning over hundreds of thousands of pounds. She knew it wasn't something her father would have agreed with but times changed and she couldn't take the

chance of stagnating. Violence was now the norm and her men would and did anything she asked of them. Angela McCann had changed her name by deed poll soon after little Marty was born and she now had a hardness about her. The realisation that she had to live with the blood of other human beings on her hands was tough but it wasn't enough to stop spurring her on. To Angie McCann, the only thing that mattered was succeeding with the McCann dynasty. She had to make sure, for little Marty's sake, that it would reign for many years to come. A couple of days earlier Angela had received a call from Herbie. He had informed her that the Scouser was sick. It was nothing life threatening but serious enough all the same.

"What can we do for him Herbie?"

"Well he's all but finished with his brasses so I was thinkin' you could give him some work. What about reopenin' the old bookies on Redman's Road?"

"Oh I don't know about that Herbie. I said after my father died and well you know, what with Danny and everything, well I said that one would remain forever closed."

"I know princess but don't you think it's about time you laid that old ghost to rest?"

Angela thought for a moment and as she watched Marty charging round the apartment chasing a fly, decided that her old friend was right.

"Meet me there about ten tomorrow and we'll have a look."

The shop was deathly quiet. Grubby white sheets hung from all the monitors that were now dated and would have to be replaced. As Angela entered the office, she instantly stopped dead in her tracks. A feeling, as if someone had just walked over her grave, was so strong that she actually began to tremble. Herbie, who had followed close behind, saw her paleness and placed an arm around her shoulder. Leading her towards the desk, he held her hand as she wobbled on her feet.

"Here princess, sit down. Are you alright? 'cause you sure as hell don't look it."

"Herbie I just had the weirdest thing happen, like someone walked straight through me. It wasn't horrible or anything, just strange. I've never experienced a feeling like it in my life before. Tell me something, why have you and Jimmy never talked to me properly about my father's death? I know there are all sorts of stories going around but what do you really think happened?"

"Princess, why are you rakin' over old coals? Even if you knew the truth, there ain't much that can be done about it now? I mean there's nothin' that's goin' to bring your old dad back, now is there?"

"I suppose not but sometimes I think, no I know, I can feel my father's presence."

"Don't start with all that fuckin' mumbo jumbo, it gives me the creeps."

The sight of a seventeen stone hard man, who was frightened of something that might not even exist, was somehow comical and brought a smile to Angela's face and made her laugh. It wasn't a hearty side splitting laugh but it made her feel slightly better.

"So what do you think, would Jimmy really be happy working in here?"

"He would love it. I know the old fucker thinks he's ready for the knackers' yard and this will give him a new lease of life. Thank you princess."

"Herbie! You and that old fucker as you so fondly call him, never have to thank me for anything. Without you I never would have succeeded. God when I look back at how wet I was behind the ears but neither of you gave up on me and for that I will be eternally grateful. Anyway I need to get back as its the nanny's half day so can I leave you to lock up?"

"'Course you can princess and I'll give you a call in a bit, no doubt you'll hear from the Scouser later today as well."

Seated in her car Angela was just about to turn over the engine when her mobile burst into life. The number was withheld and she would of normally have ignored it but today she was in a rush and not thinking straight.

"Hello."

"Hi Angie its Mickey Colletta here."

Angela frowned. It had been at least five years since she'd last seen the man and she couldn't for the life of her think why he would be calling now. True they were both in the same line of work but she had made sure that their paths didn't cross. There was something about him that she just didn't like. Oh he'd been helpful regarding Johnny Vale and she had over the years received the odd message from him about any sightings of Johnny but that was s far as it went.

"Hello Mr Colletta how nice to hear from you, how can I help?"

Mickey proceeded to inform her that he had up-to-date information on Johnny Vale and he needed to see her urgently. Angela glanced at her watch and knew she was tight for time.

"Will it take long Mickey?"

"Not long at all but it is imperative that you tell no one and come alone."

Angela smiled at all the cloak and dagger stuff and after she agreed to meet him and had written down the address, sped away in the direction of Roman Road. The directions Mickey had given took her to a warehouse. It was situated just off the main drag, in a small square on Hewlett road. The outer fence was broken and by the amount of overgrowth in the parking area, she could see that the place hadn't been used for more than a few years. Angela sat in her car for a while trying to work out why he had wanted to meet her there.

Earlier that same morning Mickey Colletta had arrived at the disused warehouse. Parking on Roman Road which was still quiet, he placed several coins into the meter. Walking along Hewlett Road, he thought how he could have been the last man in the world, as there wasn't another living soul in sight. Making his way round to the back of the building, he saw a frosted window that had only a small amount of glass left in it. Picking up a rock, Mickey tapped gently round the frames edges, releasing the few remaining shards. Reaching inside, he turned the handle but had to pull hard as the metal frame had rusted badly over the years. Not watching his diet for most of his adult life had made entering difficult but after pushing and shoving for a minute he was at last able to squeeze his body through the gap. Bringing along a torch had been a good idea as the place was in almost total darkness. He shone its bright beam from one side to the other causing several pigeons to flutter in the rafters and for a few seconds he stood completely still. The birds had unnerved him but they also confirmed that the place was empty so it didn't stop him continuing to explore the inside. A large old fashioned lathe stood alone in the centre area and by the few tools that were strewn on the floor, Mickey could see that the place had once been some kind of joinery factory. On the left hand side wall, a rickety metal staircase led up to a small office. It looked unstable but he wanted a vantage point to see all that was going on, without being seen himself. Taking his time Mickey climbed the stairs one at a time and finally reached the top. The office door withstood a lot of leaning on, before it at last gave way and the smell coming from inside was sickening. A tired looking desk was positioned at one end of the room and on top lay several decomposing pigeon carcasses. Mickey pulled out a handkerchief and used it to cover his nose as he walked the length of the room. Another small window looked directly down on to the parking area and he could see just about everything that was going on. It was desolate and quiet and Mickey knew it was the perfect place for what he had in mind. Back on the ground floor he released the rusted shutter door before leaving. Deep in thought Angela McCann was startled back to reality as she heard Mickey's car pull up beside her own. Getting out she greeted the man with a kiss but Mickey Colletta felt no emotion for the woman. She had

did a good job building up her firm but at the end of the day this was business pure and simple. Clasping his hands together Mickey checked to make sure that his leather gloves were smooth and tight fitting.
"Looking good girl!"
"Thank you Mr Colletta."
"Come on now, we've known each other long enough for you to call me Mickey. Your old dad would have a right fuckin' giggle if he could hear you."
Angela smiled and was instantly relaxed at the mention of her father's name. Once inside Mickey pulled down the shutter. Daylight now filled the space from the numerous holes in the roof and Angela wrinkled up her nose at the musty smell.
"So Mickey, what's all this about news of Johnny Vale?"
Mickey Colletta spun round on his heels and Angie McCann could see the pistol in his hand. The same gun, complete with fingerprints, that had been stored since the death of Johnny Vale. It had been a perfect plan of Mickey's and one which was now being put into action.
"Mickey whatever are you doing?"
"Look sweetheart this aint personal but did you really think I was goin' to let some little girlie muscle her way in and take over a lucrative business just because her old man had left it to

her. Don't get me wrong, I was fond of your old man and when he got snuffed out I was heartfelt and I don't mind admittin' that fact. I was about to see off Johnny Vale myself and expand me little empire when as luck would have it you turned up."

"But Johnny's still out there somewhere!"

Mickey Colletta laughed.

"That's what everyone thinks, what I wanted them to think. I've bided my time and now I need to collect."

"But..."

Angie McCann didn't get a chance to say anymore. The bullet hit her squarely between the eyes and she dropped to the ground. After everything she'd been through, Angela's life was snuffed out on a cold dirty warehouse floor and no one would ever be brought to justice for it. It was sad and unfair but then life was unfair. Before he left, Mickey Colletta dropped the gun and Johnny Vale's lighter, a short distance from the body. As slow as the Met were, even he had to admit that they couldn't miss these two pieces of evidence. After the dust had settled he would take over the clubs, drug trade and as many of the McCann businesses as he could and god help anyone who tried to stop him. This had been a long while coming, a long while in the planning but now it was finally here and he would soon be the biggest and most feared boss in the whole of London. Due to a tracker being fitted to her car, something the Scouser had seen fit to do without her knowledge; Angela's body was found before the day was out. Herbie Spires and Jimmy Forbes were inconsolable and had instructed all members of the firm to go out and find the culprit. Of course that wouldn't happen but when only a few days later Mickey Colletta started to muscle in on the drug deals Herbie soon had his suspicions.

The funeral of Angie McCann was carried out with military precision and every known face from the whole of the smoke attended without exception. Jimmy was put in charge of looking after Flo and Herbie concentrated on little Marty. The boy didn't have a clue what was going on but as Angela's coffin was carried in he began to cry for his mummy. When the service was over, people congregated outside in small groups. Mickey Colletta approached Herbie to offer his condolences and it took all of Herbie Spires' strength to hold his rage inside.

"This lot is proper tragic my friend!"

Herbie knew there was one small way he could seek out some kind of justice. As little Marty started to tug on his coat sleeve Herbie began to speak.

"You know what saddens me the most Mickey? This poor little sod 'cause he aint got no mother or father now. We did toy with the idea of tryin' to contact your Geno."

"Geno? My Geno but why?"

Herbie Spires now had a broad grin across his face.

"You really don't know do you? It was never confirmed but always rumoured within the firm that he was the father. Guess we'll never know now. Did he look like this as a boy?"

Mickey stared intently at the child and Herbie could visibly see the colour drain from his face. Herbie Spires scooped up Marty into his arms and without another word walked towards Jimmy and Flo McCann. He didn't need to look back to see the face of a man who had taken the life of this little boy's mother. The little boy who was his only grandchild and who he would never be allowed contact with. Poetic justice, in a sad kind of way and a devastating regret, that Mickey Colletta would have to live with for the rest of his life.

THE END

EPILOGUE

Angie McCann's will was watertight. She had left everything to her son Marty. Herbie Spires had been made his guardian and had power of attorney until the boy was twenty five. Mickey Colletta had hoped to buy the clubs at a knock down price but after Herbie's revelation at the funeral he paid full market value. It was very little in the way of making amends for what he'd done to his grandson but all the same it would mean that the boy had plenty of money. It went deeply against the grain as far as Herbie was concerned but after talking it over with Jimmy, they were both in agreement that it didn't really matter who the buyer was. After all, it was only business and at least it would bring closure on the matter. Within a year the deal was finalised and all the money was placed in trust. It would give the boy a life of luxury when he was older and one fact Herbie was proud of, it was now all legitimate money. Unlike his mother there would be nothing to taint little Marty's life. Herbie Spires was now officially retired. Kathy Jones along with Katie and Spider had moved into the Spires household. Raising the children as if they were his own brought him more pleasure than he could ever have imagined. Marty attended the local infant's school; Spider was at the polytechnic studying to be a motor mechanic and Katie was at junior school. No man could ever have been prouder than Herbie Spires, when the girl had called him dad. Kathy no longer had to work and cared for Herbie in a way he'd never experienced before. He repaid her kindness, by providing the kind of lifestyle she had only ever dreamed about. He tended the garden and actually enjoyed the peace and quiet that was until the kids came home from school. The expensive bespoke kennel had long since been demolished and replaced with a calming water fountain. Marge Spires never left the private hospital; her mind was such that she didn't even recognise her husband. Herbie gradually dwindled his visits, until they were nonexistent. His relationship with Kathy never progressed further than a platonic one but Herbie was content just to be with her. From time to time, he would venture into the east end to catch up on gossip and see his old friend but it wasn't a life he wanted anymore.

With the betting shop on Redman's road now gone forever, Jimmy was again forced to dabble with the odd Tom or two but it was nothing like before. He continued to reside in Stepney with Marlene but was yet to put a ring on her finger, Marlene still lived in hope. Bernie Preston only partially recovered from his injuries. He still lived with his old mum but they now had a specially adapted bungalow.

Saturday afternoons would see him collected by Jimmy and wheeled to the local betting shop for a flutter and then onto the pub for a beer but Bernie would only ever be able to drink his pint through a straw.

Journeys End Defiant was reluctantly sold to a property developer, much to Elizabeth Canning Browns unhappiness. The place was too large and too expensive to run for the women to continue living there. The sale raised enough capital, to purchase a small house on the Devon coast and the remaining Canning Brown women would be able to live out the rest of their lives, in the manner to which they'd become accustom. After Angela's death Joanna had cut all ties with the McCann's. She wanted no contact with her grandson; as far as she was concerned he didn't exist.

Mickey Colletta ended up a lonely old man. Not one of his children bothered with him and he wasn't allowed any kind of contact with little Marty. Over the years, he had without success, tried to locate his son but every time Mickey got remotely close, Geno would move. He was currently in Brazil and happily living with his partner Fabio. He would never be aware of Marty's existence but even if he had, returning to England wasn't an option.

Flo McCann was alive and well and approaching eighty. She still lived in the small council flat and was as proud as punch with the upbringing that her grandson was receiving. The boy was the apple of Flo's eye and most Sundays she would be collected by Herbie and taken over to Bermondsey to spend the day with Marty and the others.

The past few years hadn't been easy for any of them but like true East Enders they had soldiered on, it was in their blood and they knew no other way.

17064306R00280

Printed in Poland
by Amazon Fulfillment
Poland Sp. z o.o., Wrocław